A Tr

Glasgow-born Lynne McEwan is a former newspaper photographer turned crime author. She's covered stories including the Fall of the Berlin Wall and the first Gulf War in addition to many high profile murder cases. She currently lives in Lincoln and is in the final year of an MA in Crime Fiction at the University of East Anglia.

Also by Lynne McEwan

Detective Shona Oliver

In Dark Water
Dead Man Deep
The Girls in the Glen
The Gathering Storm
A Troubled Tide

A Troubled Tide

LYNNE McEWAN

CANELO CRIME

First published in the United Kingdom in 2025 by

Canelo Crime, an imprint of
Canelo Digital Publishing Limited,
20 Vauxhall Bridge Road,
London SW1V 2SA
United Kingdom

A Penguin Random House Company

The authorised representative in the EEA is Dorling Kindersley Verlag GmbH.
Arnulfstr. 124, 80636 Munich, Germany

Copyright © Lynne McEwan 2025

The moral right of Lynne McEwan to be identified as the creator of this work has been asserted in accordance with the Copyright, Designs and Patents Act, 1988.

All rights reserved. No part of this publication may be reproduced or transmitted in any form or by any means, electronic or mechanical, including photocopy, recording, or any information storage and retrieval system, without permission in writing from the publisher.

No part of this book may be used or reproduced in any manner for the purpose of training artificial intelligence technologies or systems. In accordance with Article 4(3) of the DSM Directive 2019/790, Canelo expressly reserves this work from the text and data mining exception.

A CIP catalogue record for this book is available from the British Library.

Print ISBN 978 1 83598 065 1
Ebook ISBN 978 1 83598 066 8

This book is a work of fiction. Names, characters, businesses, organizations, places and events are either the product of the author's imagination or are used fictitiously. Any resemblance to actual persons, living or dead, events or locales is entirely coincidental.

Cover design by Blacksheep

Cover images © Shutterstock

Printed and bound in Great Britain by Clays Ltd, Elcograf S.p.A.

Look for more great books at
www.canelo.co
www.dk.com

To all the young folk who continue to inspire me.

Keep going. You'll get there.

Chapter 1

Shona Oliver pulled on her white helmet. Beside her in the lifeboat, the experienced helm Tommy McCall, and newly qualified recruit, Sophie Gibb, followed suit. It was a glorious day to be out on the water. As a full-time detective inspector, and part-time RNLI volunteer, Shona hoped neither the Procurator Fiscal nor the coastguard would be in touch today.

'Quite a crowd,' Tommy said, as he expertly backed the D-class *Margaret Wilson* out from its cradle at the bottom of the slipway, then turned her bow into the estuary.

Shona nodded, her sharp, brown eyes already sweeping across the craft on the water and the participants on the shore for the RNLI Kirkness's inaugural triathlon event: the Solway Sprint – a 700-metre swim, followed by a twenty-kilometre cycle, then a three-kilometre trail run around Knockie Point – held in conjunction with a local club.

'Okay?' Shona called over the rising roar of the outboard engine to Sophie, who was kneeling next to her.

'I'm really worried I'll make a mistake,' Sophie replied nervously. Strands of bright auburn hair whipped around her pale face, teased from beneath her helmet by the wind. At twenty, she was only a few years older than Shona's daughter Becca, but growing up on a farm had given the young agricultural student a level-headed maturity beyond her age. She had a strength and physical confidence which Shona knew would stand her in good stead.

'Feels different when people are looking at you, doesn't it?' Shona said, mindful of the hundreds of spectators on the shoreline. 'You'll be fine. Anything you're not sure of, let me know.'

Shona's own first shift had been nearly twenty years before at Tower station, on the Thames, when she'd also been serving with the City of London Police. A private pleasure boat had lost power and needed a tow. A mundane job. Sometimes, mundane was good.

'And one other thing...' Tommy said, his weather-beaten face cracking into a broad grin. 'Nobody knows it's your first day.' He winked.

Sophie laughed, the tension broken.

Today, the firth was serene: running snug between the wooded, rolling hills, its glassy surface reflected slow-moving white castles of cloud. Swimming outdoors was never a risk-free activity, but the dangers of cold water, hidden objects, wind and weather could be mitigated with the careful planning and local knowledge of lifeboat skipper and boatyard owner Tommy McCall.

They made a tour of the course, Shona and Sophie leaning over the inflatable's hull to tug on the ropes anchoring the swim buoys. Shona waved to the three men in the sailing club's safety boat, which had also been drafted in for the day. After the previous month's torrential rain, there had been doubt about high water levels, but conditions were now perfect, with calm seas for the swim and dry roads for the bike ride. The stunning June weather was set to continue through the weekend.

'Good to go?' Shona asked Tommy, and the skipper gave a nod. It was approaching high tide and the resultant slack water in the estuary would provide a safe window of two hours for even the slowest competitor to complete their swim. Shona got on the radio and confirmed that the organisers could start the thirty-minute countdown to the race.

Back on shore, Shona removed her helmet and shook out her dark brown curls. There was something she wanted to do before the event began.

The race marshal noted her RNLI kit and let her through into the competitors' area. Over a hundred participants had signed up. Three groups — male and female adults, and a mixed youth class over a shorter course — would set off in successive waves. Shona searched for her fellow lifeboat volunteer and village postman, Callum, who was competing in his first race. But despite his six-foot-three-inch bulk, she was unable to pick him out among the uniformity of wetsuits, goggles and numbered swim caps. She knew he was 22. *Two wee ducks,* Tommy had quipped, *who'll likely overtake you.*

Finally, Shona spotted her other objective — the tall frame and blonde ponytail of her detective constable Kate Irving. Kate was standing with her friend and training partner, PC Hayley Cameron, who was tipped for triathlon success at national or even international level. Both officers were sipping drinks, checking their smartwatches and doing last-minute stretches.

Shona knew her colleagues at Dumfries CID called her 'Wee Shona' behind her back, even though growing up, she hadn't been aware of other girls being much bigger than her. Now, as she approached the group of female triathletes, she wondered if lassies these days were just built on a grander scale. Becca was a full six inches taller than her mother, but these wetsuited Amazons — with their powerful shoulders and long thighs — looked like they'd been chiselled from granite.

'Boss,' Kate acknowledged Shona's arrival.

'Morning, ma'am,' Hayley added. She had broad, freckled cheekbones and a wide infectious smile beneath her yellow swim hat inked with the number five. In contrast to Kate's plain attire, Hayley wore a high-end wetsuit adorned with sponsorship logos.

Shona held up her hands. 'Off duty today, so no need for formalities.'

'Still can't resist a uniform, though, can you?' Hayley grinned, indicating Shona's RNLI-badged immersion suit, complete with its yellow wellies.

'The water's only twelve degrees. I'd prefer to be wearing this rather than your get-up if I had to go in.'

'Hayley moves too fast to feel the cold,' Kate said, pulling on her swim hat – which bore the number nine – and casting an admiring, if slightly envious, sidelong look at her colleague.

'So do you,' Hayley said, giving her friend a playful push. 'And we'll try not to trouble the lifeboat. It's such a worthwhile cause. I hope your fundraising goes really well.'

'Thank you,' Shona replied, genuinely touched that Hayley wasn't so focused on her performance that she'd forgotten the other business of the day. 'I just wanted to wish you both good luck for the race.'

'Thanks, boss,' Kate said. 'Conditions are fine so we should see some impressive times. But we'll all be trailing in Hayley's wake.'

'Andy not here to witness your triumph?' Shona said, looking round for Hayley's partner, PC Andrew Purdy, also a serving officer working out of Loreburn police office in Dumfries.

'He's on duty at the agricultural show up the road, but he's with me in spirit.' Hayley raised her protein shake in a toast, before draining it and tossing the empty beaker into her kitbag.

Four other women from the triathlon club came to join them.

'Quick. Group picture with my girl gang!' Hayley handed Shona her phone.

Everyone bunched up, arms around each other, smiling. One camera-shy individual hung back but was eventually coaxed forward by the others and joined the group at the opposite end from Hayley.

Shona snapped some shots and returned the phone.

'Thanks, ma'am,' Hayley said.

'You know,' Shona began, 'I'd like to have a chat with you about joining CID. Is that something you'd be interested in?'

Hayley stared at her. 'It's my aim.'

'Glad to hear it.' Shona smiled, gratified by Hayley's enthusiasm. 'We'll speak soon.'

The other women crowded round. Shona took that as her cue to leave them to their race preparations and Hayley began scrolling through the images, as the others pronounced on the best photo to share. *Not that one, I look like a walrus*, Shona heard someone say among the laughter.

A short, stringy man in his sixties wearing a triathlon club polo shirt arrived and took their phones and valuables for safekeeping. Shona waved to Hayley and her friends, then mouthed a last *good luck* as she set off back to the lifeboat station.

She searched for Callum one last time in the packed transition area, bending to pick up a race tag, which in the strengthening breeze had fluttered down from the crossbar of a sleek black road bike. She called to the bike's owner, who was heading off towards the youth competitors' area, then quickened her step, tapped his arm and returned the number. He acknowledged her shyly, with a raised hand to express his thanks.

Giving up any hope of finding Callum in the crowd, Shona began navigating the families who were wrangling kids, icecreams and dogs. Outside the Royal Arms, her way was further slowed by locals and visitors alike, pints in hand and soaking up the sunshine. She saw her daughter Becca, who'd earned a break after recent exams, laughing with friends, and holding a drink of her own – a soft one Shona hoped, since she was only seventeen. Some of the patrons reached out and patted her appreciatively on the back as she passed, saying there were drinks behind the bar for the whole crew later, and cracking jokes about wearing wellies in this weather. Shona laughed, caught in a sudden upswell of emotion. It was just an ordinary summer's day, repeated in seaside towns and villages all over the country. The last few years had been tough, the twin pressures of work and family almost overwhelming. But recently, she'd found that while her burdens hadn't eased, she'd uncovered new sources of strength with which to face them and her natural optimism had returned. She smiled as she chided herself. *Just enjoy your day. It's simple. You're home. You're happy.*

'Did you see Callum?' Tommy asked as she joined the rest of the crew on the slipway. Sophie was talking excitedly with some of the spectators and appeared to have got over her nervous start.

Shona shook her head. 'It's like a seal colony up there. Couldn't pick him out.' She turned to Tommy's partner Freya, who'd arrived with mugs of tea. 'Thank you, I'm ready for this.' She took a grateful sip. 'How's things in the shop?'

'Busy,' Freya said in her Orcadian lilt. 'They've stocked up on all the favourites – mugs, toys, tea towels and baseball caps. The volunteers were here at dawn to get everything set up.'

Tommy cocked his head at the latest PA announcement and consulted his watch. 'Better get going.'

Shona drained her mug and handed it back to Freya. She and Sophie re-joined the lifeboat, and they motored out to their position beyond the swim course.

On the shore, all eyes turned to the male competitors, who readied themselves, wading out from the shallow beach by the sailing club until they stood in a line, waist deep. On a nearby pontoon, the club's commodore gave a long blast on the air horn.

The swimmers set off, yellow caps dipping and then resurfacing from the dark water of the estuary as their strokes settled quickly into a rhythm. Sophie had the binoculars and soon picked out Callum in a respectable position in the middle of the field.

On the beach, the women were lining up, splashing the cold seawater on themselves in preparation for the plunge forward. The estimated swim time was fifteen to thirty minutes. Kate had confided to Shona that Hayley was aiming to do it in under thirteen.

Soon, the hooter sounded amid renewed cheers from the shore. The women powered forward, arms arching and puncturing the water's surface like a close-packed shoal of leaping salmon.

The first of the male swimmers had already rounded the furthest buoy and were heading back to the beach. Tommy kept an eye seaward for any incoming vessel that might have missed the coastguard's notice of the event, while Shona monitored the radio traffic and kept watch shoreward at the cheering crowds. It wasn't unknown for a child or an over-enthusiastic spectator to take an unscheduled dip themselves in all the excitement.

The initial tight grouping of women had quickly thinned out. Shona took the binoculars from Sophie and saw that Hayley, in her number five cap, already had a strong lead, with Kate's number nine in the chasing pack not far behind. Shona handed back the binoculars with satisfaction. Anyone with that level of dedication and determination would be an asset, and Shona made up her mind to speak to Hayley on Monday about joining her team in CID.

Tommy caught the look. 'You got a horse of your own in this race?'

'Possibly two.' Shona grinned.

Minutes later, Shona glanced back from her watch on the shoreline. Hayley seemed to have slowed down as she approached the furthest buoy and the turn for home.

Simultaneously, Shona saw the raised arm of a swimmer and, further out, the spotter in the safety boat sit bolt upright.

'Something's wrong,' Shona said, her heart rate skipping up a notch as she looked at the figures amid the once smooth water, now churned by both flailing limbs and a breeze that was picking at the small wave tops.

'No, Callum's fine,' Sophie said, binoculars still trained on their lifeboat colleague, who was racing up the beach to grab his bike.

'Hold on,' Tommy said. Shona gripped the anchor point as the lifeboat swung towards the swimmer in trouble. The radio crackled, a message from the safety boat confirming what Shona had already seen, followed quickly by two long blasts on the air horn, the signal for all swimmers to exit the water.

There was little chance the tide would drag the distressed swimmer out to sea, but every moment counted – a second's delay could be the difference between life and death.

As they got closer, Shona saw one person was struggling to save another. Somehow, she knew who it was before the numbered caps confirmed it. Kate was desperately trying to float on her back while keeping Hayley's face clear of the water.

They reached them moments before the safety boat. Shona and Sophie leaned over, grabbing the two women as Tommy cut the engine. Shona's first assessment confirmed things were serious. Kate was moving; Hayley was unresponsive.

'Kate, are you hurt?'

'No,' she spluttered, desperately fighting to stay afloat. 'I'm okay… Please… Hayley. Just stopped… Choking.'

Shona and Sophie caught hold of Hayley, feeling beneath her arms for a grip.

'Ready?' Shona said to Sophie. Without waiting for an answer, she counted, 'One, two…' On 'three' they both hauled, landing the unconscious woman like a giant fish in the bottom of the lifeboat.

Kate, freed of her burden, began treading water.

'Get Kate checked at the first-aid point,' Shona ordered the three stunned-looking men in the safety boat as she felt Hayley's neck for a pulse. Tommy was already backing the lifeboat away.

Sophie was running through the RNLI's Big Sick, Little Sick – a rapid casualty-assessment criteria – but there was no doubt it was as bad as it could be.

Shona began CPR but with each chest compression, water came out of Hayley's mouth. There was no movement. No Pulse. Nothing. They rolled her on her side briefly to clear the airway, then resumed.

Adrenaline coursed through Shona's veins. Keep going, she told herself. All she could think about was Hayley's family, and the horror and devastation they'd experience if she couldn't save her.

Tommy opened the throttle. Sophie wordlessly took over the chest compressions as Shona clamped the manual resuscitator over Hayley's face, squeezing the bag and forcing air into Hayley's lungs as the lifeboat bucked in choppy sea.

They reached the slipway, but Shona still couldn't find a pulse. The window of recovery was closing. It had been nearly four minutes, Shona estimated, since Kate had raised the alarm.

Other crew members and two paramedics, Alex and Naomi, were racing forward to lift Hayley from the lifeboat. She was blue, cold to the touch, her eyes wide open as they laid her on the stretcher.

Some people had respectfully moved away. Others hadn't and the rest of the shore team herded the crowd back as best they could, but Shona still felt the weight of dozens of pairs of eyes on them.

Alex's knife sliced open the front of Hayley's wetsuit, and he rubbed her chest dry with a towel. There was a flash of pale skin quickly obscured by Naomi's green uniform, as she leaned in and attached the defibrillator pads.

'Clear,' she said, ordering everyone back.

Shona saw Hayley lurch, a grotesque parody of consciousness, then fall back on the stretcher, and she immediately reapplied the resuscitator mask. The medic felt under Hayley's chin, then shook his head and resumed chest compression. After two minutes that seemed to Shona like a lifetime, the process was repeated with the same result. Success rates declined rapidly after three or four attempts.

Shona was vaguely aware of other emergency vehicles as they arrived, but her world had narrowed to squeezing the ventilator and the rhythmic counting of Alex, the paramedic. Time seemed to stretch and twist. It felt like only a few seconds since they'd hauled Hayley from the water, but the muscles in Shona's hands were aching as if she'd been doing this for hours.

A second ambulance with its rear doors open was backing through the crowd to the slipway. After the fourth shock sequence, Alex and Naomi exchanged a glance that told Shona all she needed to know.

'We'll keep working on her all the way to the Royal,' Naomi assured Shona as she took the ventilator from her. Alex went with Hayley into the back of the emergency vehicle. As the doors began to close, he looked up and met Shona's eye. He shook his head, and Shona knew there was no more hope. Moments later, the ambulance sped along the road, through the now silent crowd, sirens blaring.

Shona was still on her knees on the slipway. She looked up to see Kate with a foil blanket around her shoulder and Hayley's partner, Andy, who she must have called as soon as she reached the first-aid point, sobbing in each other's arms. Callum was there, still in his cycling bib shorts, his blonde curls darkened and plastered flat by sweat and seawater, ushering them away from the crowd and towards the boathouse, his expression sombre.

Tommy came forward, put a hand under Shona's elbow and raised her to her feet. Wordlessly, he handed over her phone, which he'd brought from the lifeboat station.

Shona dialled her detective sergeant's number.

'Murdo, we've a sudden death. You and Ravi better get down here.'

Shona looked out at the estuary. The wind had died as suddenly as it had appeared, and the surface was calm once more. It had been a morning of such promise. But now Shona was flooded by a troubled tide of questions, chief among them: just how did a fit and healthy young woman, a police officer, drown at an organised event with the lifeboat standing by? It was her job to find the answer.

Chapter 2

The Solway Sprint was abandoned. At the lifeboat station, Shona compiled a list of potential witnesses and sent one of the uniformed response officers to collect and bag Hayley's things. She changed into jeans and T-shirt and was waiting near the boat hall door when DS Murdo O'Halloran arrived. The *Margaret Wilson* was inside, having been recovered to her cradle and towed from the shore by the launch tractor. She was a crime scene until forensics pronounced otherwise.

'Poor Hayley. Terrible thing to happen,' Murdo said. 'You all right, boss?'

Shona saw Murdo's practised eye take in her appearance – the damp, tangled hair and creased clothes a stark contrast to her usual smart business suits and straightened bob. At fifty-one, he was a decade older than her and had put every one of those years to good use cataloguing the misdemeanours, chargeable or otherwise, of the region's criminal fraternity. Cops in their fifties were assumed to be running down to retirement, and one look at his crumpled suit and overweight, former rugby-player's frame might convince you that he was no different. But Shona couldn't see Murdo ever turning in his badge. Dumfries was her patch, and despite witnessing Hayley's drowning, she'd be the senior investigating officer if the Procurator Fiscal decided further inquiries were necessary. She wanted to ensure no stone was left unturned, and Murdo was the man for stone-turning. It was the death of one of their own, even if it was likely accidental, and she wanted to be certain that nothing had been missed.

'I'm fine.' Shona smiled wearily, knowing he'd draw his own conclusions. 'So, priorities… Kate's upstairs, waiting to give her statement.' She indicated over her shoulder to the mezzanine crew room, then outlined the tragic events of the afternoon. 'A single scenes-of-crime-officer is coming from Glasgow to collect any material evidence – which in the circumstances is likely to be minimal – and clear the lifeboat to return to service.'

'I'll get uniform to do the preliminary statements from your list,' Murdo said, holding up his phone to show he'd received Shona's document. 'Ravi's on his way. He can talk to Kate. You're only up the road. Why don't you get off home and I'll bell you when we're done.'

There was sense, as well as compassion, in his suggestion. She'd set the wheels in motion, done all she could for now. It would be useful to check on things at High Pines, and she desperately wanted to confirm Becca was okay and hadn't witnessed too much of the afternoon's proceedings.

Shona nodded her assent, then added quietly, 'Hayley's partner, Andy Purdy, was here. He was in bits. Saw the paramedics working on her.'

'Jeezo, that's bad.' Murdo shook his head.

'I got one of the response officers to take him to the Royal.'

'I'll call his sergeant, Willie Logan. He'll keep an eye on him.' Murdo paused and licked his lower lip. 'Listen, d'you want me to inform Hayley's family? I've kenned them a while.'

Shona saw her other detective constable, Ravi Sarwar, approaching along the seafront road. His long, loping stride was relaxed but his expression was serious. His off-duty black jeans and brightly patterned open-neck shirt were on the smart side of casual; his sunglasses were perched on fashionably cut hair.

'I should really talk to Hayley's family myself,' Shona said. The public nature of her death meant there was a chance something would turn up on social media soon, if it hadn't already. Wetsuits lent anonymity, but Hayley's was distinctive. 'Are there parents? Brothers or sisters?'

'Oh, aye, there's family,' Murdo said, in a tone that made Shona think he'd encountered them professionally. 'Mother passed away years back, but the father, Clem, is still around, and there's three brothers and a sister.' Murdo sighed. 'Wee Hayley gone. I cannae believe it. I remember her as a probationer, always thought she'd go far. Maybe end up wi' us.'

'I thought the same, Murdo,' Shona replied, and the weight of Hayley's vanished future – CID success, international triathlon fame, perhaps even an Olympic medal – pressed down on her. Her hands, still aching from squeezing the resuscitator, gave an involuntary twitch, as if muscle memory alone might give Hayley one last shot at breathing again. 'If you know the family, perhaps it's best. Thank you.'

'Boss,' Ravi said as he reached them. 'How's Kate doing?'

Her two detective constables were like siblings. Ravi baited Kate, who fell for it every time. But Shona had seen the desire to outshine each other melt away when it really counted and knew this was one of those rare occasions.

'She's fine. She'll be pleased to see you,' Shona said, and was gratified by the relieved look, quickly supressed, that passed across Ravi's handsome face. 'Can you do Tommy's and Sophie's statements while you're there? I'll send you mine. We've not much to add. Kate's the key witness, though all she seems to know is that Hayley stopped swimming and appeared to choke.'

'Nae problem, boss,' Ravi replied. 'You can leave her with me. I'll make sure she gets home okay.'

–

Shona walked home through the crowd, now thinned to mostly locals who knew her variously as cop, lifeboat crew or landlady of High Pines. The boutique B&B business had become unsustainable once Shona's husband, Rob, had gone to prison for historic financial crimes, although he claimed he wasn't guilty. But there were some things he was undoubtedly guilty of – an affair among them – which Shona couldn't forgive. She looked up and saw her home, sitting like a lighthouse in the trees above Kirkness, its four storeys of firth-facing windows shining in the late afternoon sun. They'd reconfigured the ground-floor guest bedrooms into two self-catering units with their own small patio – or *sitooterie*, as it was locally known – but if it hadn't been for a recent injection of cash from her old schoolfriend-turned-Hollywood actor, James McGowan, the business would probably have gone under.

Friend was how she labelled James publicly, but it was too tepid a word for the deep connection they shared. On a prison visit to Rob, she'd confessed what had happened. He was angry but had dismissed it as purely retaliation for his own, recently uncovered but historic, affair with his PA. Shona loved James and believed he loved her. She was thankful to have him back in her life. But what, ultimately, did she want from the relationship? It was something she hadn't yet figured out.

Shona went in by the lower gate and climbed up through the steep terraced garden, filled with herbs and brightly flowering, salt-tolerant plants, none of which she knew the names of. She'd hoped to catch the guests, reassure them and answer any questions as best she could within the confines of her position as both landlady and detective inspector, but beyond the wetsuits hung over the garden chairs, both units were empty.

Another flight of stone steps took Shona around the side to the kitchen level, where she found Becca nursing a mug of tea. One look at her daughter's face told Shona she had indeed witnessed quite a lot of the afternoon's events. Becca flung herself into her mother's arms and hugged her fiercely, the tumbled mass of her long curls merging with Shona's own.

'Oh my God, Mum. It was horrible. Is it right she's one of Kate's friends?'

'She was. Murdo's going to inform the family, so you can't say anything yet.'

Becca pulled back and nodded. 'The guests were asking me about it. I told them I hadn't any more details, and if the event was rescheduled, they'd get priority booking and we'd email them as soon as we knew the date. Is that okay?' She examined her mother's face for approval.

Shona smiled and held her close again. 'That was exactly the right thing to say, darlin'. Well done.'

The speed with which her daughter had adapted to the responsibility of their altered circumstances continually surprised Shona. After her initial wariness, Becca had embraced James's presence in their lives and his purchase of a third of High Pines. His involvement with environmental causes had always been in his favour. But her daughter had said that it was the respectful way he treated Shona — something that her father, Rob, had fallen short in, by Becca's estimation — that had been the deciding factor.

Becca and James had worked together on a green business plan, and their garage already sported two new electric-vehicle charging points. At present they were used exclusively by their guests, as Shona refused to part with her ageing Audi, due to her 2500 square mile, mostly rural, policing patch. The force was switching over to electric vehicles but not all police offices had charging points yet, leading to some officers sitting conspicuously in their squad cars in supermarket carparks, topping up their batteries.

'Listen.' Shona held Becca at arm's length to show she was serious. 'I want you to have a break away from the business. Now your exams are done, will you think again about that festival your friends from the home-schooling group are going to tomorrow?'

The Secret Forest was an eco-conscious, week-long arts and music festival held at the old RAF Dumfries airbase. Although Becca was full of praise for its ethos and band line-up, and there was tent space available for her, she had so far refused to sign up for it.

'Aw, Mum.' Becca's shoulders slumped between her mother's hands, instantly knocking years off the maturity she'd just displayed in dealing with the guests and reducing her to the teenager she was. 'It's too complicated. There's no time to get cover for here, and you'll be at work, and...'

'Don't you trust me with the business?' Shona asked with mock severity. Ever since Rob had gone to prison, Shona had noticed that Becca was less and less willing to be parted from her mother, and the impending move to halls at Glasgow University in the autumn seemed to have intensified her fears. But Shona was determined to make the move a positive experience for her daughter. She wanted Becca to seize opportunities that her own background – growing up in her grandmother's care, on a rough council estate – hadn't offered, no matter how painful she'd find it to be parted from her only child, her only blood relative.

Before Becca could answer, the back door opened and someone shouted, 'Hello.' She took the chance to wriggle free from her mother's grasp and bolted for the stairs to her bedroom.

'Think about it!' Shona yelled after her daughter.

'Bad time?' Freya said, as she and Tommy appeared from the utility room.

Shona waved them to seats at the kitchen table and reached to switch the kettle on.

'No. I want Becca to head off with her friends tomorrow. If you'd asked me a year ago if I'd be the one persuading my daughter that going to a festival, with all its shenanigans, was a good idea, I'd have said you were mad.'

'Becca's a sensible lass,' Freya said.

'I know, that's just the point. I want her to have some fun. I feel like we've swapped roles. She'll be lecturing me on the length of my skirt afore long.'

'When d'you ever wear a skirt these days?' Freya said, giving Shona a sceptical look.

It was true she seemed to oscillate between smart trousers and jackets for work, jeans for cleaning the rental units, and immersion suits for the lifeboat – in contrast to Freya, who was always groomed and co-ordinated, even on a country walk.

'I've dresses. Somewhere...' Shona countered.

'Aye, well, I believe bustles went out of fashion some time ago.' Freya grinned.

'She's a right comic this one, isn't she?' Shona said to Tommy, who'd been silent since they'd arrived. When he didn't answer, Shona and Freya exchanged a look.

'I'm going to pop down and see if your guests are back,' Freya said, getting up. 'They were in the bar earlier and looked a bit glum.'

After her shop stint, Freya had headed over for her shift at the Royal Arms, juggling multiple tasks, like so many other volunteers, in order to make the day a success.

'Folk are already speculating about the lassie's death,' she said, quietly. 'All these wild stories. Everything from rip currents and cold-water shock to raw sewage and toxic algae.'

When Freya had gone, Shona placed a mug of tea in front of Tommy. 'So, what do you think?'

'Your lad, Ravi, asked me that. Thon lassie, fit and experienced, well equipped, in those water conditions...' Tommy shook his head. 'Heart attack, stroke, seizure of some kind. It's all I can think of. When's the post-mortem?'

'Tomorrow,' Shona said, careful that no hint of apprehension coloured her tone.

But Tommy gave her a shrewd look. 'You were there. What does your copper's sixth sense tell ye?'

'No such thing, Tommy.' She smiled. 'We get to see more sudden deaths than other folk, and maybe that makes us better guessers, but that's all it would be – a guess.' When he didn't reply, she continued, 'I haven't seen anything yet to say it wasn't an accident. Something no one could have predicted.'

But still there was this creeping sense of unease she couldn't shake. Hayley's death was especially shocking on this beautiful summer's day, but she'd been on enough shouts on the lifeboat to know things could go wrong whatever the conditions.

Perhaps it was because it had all happened on her doorstep that it had, quite literally, brought home to her once more the fragility of life in the most brutal way possible.

'Okay?' Shona said.

Tommy, who was staring into his mug of tea, nodded.

There was a lot riding on the outcome for everyone. Tommy's role in setting up the event was sure to come under scrutiny in any inquiry. And there were other, more practical, considerations.

The triathlon club was due to donate half the revenue from the event to Kirkness RNLI, and each adult participant had been encouraged to fundraise £50 via a JustGiving page. The goal of the event had been to bring them closer to the £100,000 target, the cost of a new D-class inshore lifeboat – the workhorse of the RNLI for over six decades.

The *Margaret Wilson* had given many years of service, but she wouldn't last forever. There was no government funding, so they relied entirely on public donations. In a coastal area like the Solway Firth, the RNLI was the fourth emergency service, there for everything from rescuing fishermen from burning vessels to recovering holidaymakers cut off by the tide, and even delivering the odd baby. For Tommy, as lifeboat helm, it was crucial that he had both his crew's and the public's confidence that he could be trusted to make life-or-death decisions. Shona meant to be thorough in her inquiries – she owed Hayley that much – but she'd need to tread carefully. People had long memories and she couldn't afford to get this wrong. A careless comment by officers interviewing a witness, or a badly worded press statement, would be all it took to fuel the rumours that Freya had told her were already circulating. Support and funds would drain away, Tommy might feel he had to resign from the lifeboat and Shona would hold herself responsible.

Freya reappeared with Becca in tow.

'No sign of your guests,' Freya said. 'And Becca and I have come to an agreement. She'll have a few days away and I'll do your room changeovers tomorrow.'

Freya did odd shifts at High Pines, especially when cooking was involved, but Shona knew she was busy at the Royal Arms.

'Freya that's so kind but—'

The resolute Orcadian held up her hand. 'Not up for debate. You'll be occupied with what happened this afternoon for the next few days or so. And if I need help, Tommy will do it.'

Tommy looked far from keen, but under the intensity of Freya's gaze, he gave a shrug of agreement.

'Better go and pack, young lady,' Freya said as Becca grinned at her mother, pulled out her phone and headed back upstairs in a stream of excited chatter.

Shona was as impressed by Freya's persuasive powers as she was grateful for the practical help, which she had to admit would make the new guests' arrival much easier. Her profuse thanks were interrupted by her buzzing phone, which she assumed had to be Murdo. However, it turned out to be the divisional press office, confirming the information to be released for this evening's news in response to enquiries that had flooded in.

'That's fine,' Shona said, when she listened to the statement. 'We're investigating the unexplained death of a twenty-eight-year-old woman at the event. Anyone with information should come forward. Right now, that's all I have to say.'

Chapter 3

Next morning, Shona sat in the parking area of High Pines, while Becca made yet another dash back upstairs for some forgotten item.

Hayley's post-mortem was scheduled for ten a.m. at Dumfries and Galloway Royal Infirmary, and Shona calculated she had just enough time to drop Becca at The Secret Forest first. She checked her phone for messages, but there was nothing new. It was too early to text James in Los Angeles, the eight-hour time difference making it after midnight where he was. They'd spoken the evening before, when he'd been on his way to the gym – part of his rehab for the near-fatal injuries sustained during the filming of the Robert Burns biopic in Dumfries. The movie had reunited them, but it had also come perilously close to parting them forever.

When she'd told him about Hayley's death, his concern had been all for her and Becca, and she'd appreciated that he didn't immediately talk about the potential effect of the accident on the business. Shona checked the news, then tapped her phone against the steering wheel in irritation. This morning's headline – *Triathlon Tragedy on Deadly Firth* – wasn't unexpected but neither was it welcome.

She was just about to get out of the car and yell her daughter's name, when Becca jumped, breathless, into the passenger seat.

'Forgot my sustainable loo roll for the composting toilets,' she said. 'Lucky we bulk order it.'

The loo roll had been one of James and Becca's innovations, along with energy-efficient appliances, low-voltage downlights, solar panels and eco-friendly paint.

'Composting loos aren't really selling it to me,' Shona said, sliding on her sunglasses. 'What are you looking forward to most?'

Becca considered, then screwed up her face like a child relishing a forbidden treat. 'I should say expanding my knowledge of carbon offset and developing-world reforestation projects, but really it's the wood-fired hot tubs.'

'That's more like it.' Shona smiled as they drew out of High Pines. 'And you'll be careful about your personal safety, won't you?'

'Mum, I'm not twelve years old.' Becca sighed.

Shona winced. It was an unfortunate reminder. Becca hadn't been much older than that when a brush with drugs at school had got her expelled. It had been one of the catalysts for their move north from London. Looking back, it had been a blessing in disguise, although Shona would never have thought it at the time.

Shona tactfully avoided any mention of the incident. Reminding teenagers of past mistakes was rarely productive, but she wasn't able to let the matter rest. 'Becca, promise me you won't take anything, and you'll keep in touch with your friends.'

'What? Don't you trust me?' Becca shot back, deliberately echoing their conversation of the previous day.

'It's not that...' Shona began. Their exchange stuttered on throughout the half-hour journey to RAF Dumfries, but however Shona phrased it, Becca avoided making any categorical promises. Was she planning to take drugs in order to fit in with friends, since *everybody does it*? Or was this just regular teenage assertion of independence? Shona reckoned Becca was too sensible to expose herself to such risks, but, in her professional experience, that was what most parents thought right up until they were proved wrong.

Shona arrived at the hospital mortuary and hurriedly changed into scrubs. She bundled her hair into the surgical cap and pushed through the double doors into the pathology suite.

'I'm so sorry, Sue.'

Professor Sue Kitchen was alone in the suite. With her arms folded, she was leaning her considerable height against a worktop containing various wicked-looking medical instruments.

'Traffic's a nightmare.' Shona felt particularly embarrassed, as she'd called her friend specifically and asked her to do the PM. It required the professor to give up a Sunday morning and travel from Glasgow, where she was a senior member of the teaching staff at the university. Professor Sue Kitchen's nickname was 'Slasher Sue', partly due to her champion fencing background but also to the speed at which she worked – and she was living up to that moniker now.

'I've done a preliminary examination,' Sue said, waving away Shona's apologies and striding to where Hayley's body lay covered with a sheet, on the dissection table. 'How, I'm asking myself, did this apparently healthy and athletic young woman die? Water in her lungs suggests she drowned. Is there any reason your victim might have concealed a medical condition? There's no mention of diabetes in her records.'

In the glare of the overlit pathology room, Shona felt like a particularly ill-prepared student caught in the headlights of Sue's grey-eyed stare. 'I suppose it is possible. Hayley was ambitious, driven to succeed. She might've concealed some health issue if it would harm her selection chances. Why?'

Sue gripped the corner of the sheet and Shona took a deep breath, steeling herself for the first sight of Hayley's body. There was discolouration across her chest from the resuscitation attempts which, added to the lividity from settling blood, gave the corpse the darkly marbled appearance of a tomb effigy. Her red-gold cropped hair was swept back from her forehead, and she looked surprisingly peaceful. Shona was relieved to find that without animation, the body appeared less like the Hayley she remembered, as if the overwhelming force of her personality outdid even her own imposing physicality.

Sue's voice brought her back to the business in hand. She pointed a gloved finger at a series of small marks on the hips and thighs.

'Evidence of intramuscular injections on the body.'

Shona blinked. Whatever she'd been expecting, it wasn't this. 'Drugs? It's not natural causes, then?'

Slasher Sue rocked her tight grey curls from side to side, weighing up her response.

'Did drugs play a part in her death? That's the key question. And if not medically prescribed, were they self-administered performance enhancers? People who dope cheat themselves, their teammates and the whole sporting community,' Sue said with feeling.

Shona was shocked, both by the implication and the vitriol Sue displayed. A pathologist of her experience must have encountered any number of difficult and distressing scenarios across her table, from murdered children to suicide by bus. But then the professor was a former national épée champion, now a fencing judge, and she'd also been a competitive rower and coached the university team – perhaps drug misuse in sport was a particularly personal topic for her.

'Do the marks definitely indicate she was doping?' Shona found it hard to accept that Hayley, a police officer and a promising athlete, could have chosen to behave in such a reckless manner.

'It's difficult to say,' Sue conceded. 'We're not talking about someone who's an addict in the conventional sense. There's no evidence of her injecting into veins, or between fingers or toes, but there are some sites on her abdomen. Heroin users call it "muscle popping". Unless she was diabetic or suffered from anaphylaxis, those marks are hard to explain.'

'And they couldn't be the result of injuries during training or the triathlon itself?'

'You know the course, what d'you think?' Sue challenged.

Shona had to admit the marks didn't seem like something sustained from bumping into objects, falling or bike-related injuries.

'There is something else.' Sue, who'd been circling the table, stopped and began to position Hayley's leg in preparation to turn the body over. Shona stepped forward to assist, but the manoeuvre was expertly completed without her help. Sue pointed to a small bruise on the back of Hayley's thigh.

Shona was considering if any of the injection sites could be attributed to the paramedics' attempts to resuscitate Hayley, when Sue appeared to read her thoughts.

'An injection mark on the back of her thigh is unlikely to have been administered by a medical professional. Partly because of its placement, but also this…'

Sue crossed to the worktop and her gloved hands unfolded Hayley's wetsuit, which had been carefully removed by Professor Kitchen's assistant, in order to preserve evidence, and currently sat on a large metal tray. Shona saw again how the paramedics had cut through the front of Hayley's wetsuit in their fruitless attempt to shock her back to life.

Sue switched on a magnifying examination light and Shona saw a tiny pinprick of brightness in the black neoprene.

'A puncture?' Shona said.

Sue nodded. 'It corresponds with the mark on the back of her thigh. It's an odd place for a self-administered injection – there are plenty more accessible muscle areas. I'd say the other injection marks are older, but this one has fresh bruising evident.'

'How long before death?'

'A maximum of a few hours. The other marks… up to fourteen days.'

'Do you have a cause of death?'

'At this stage I'm not going to speculate beyond respiratory failure due to drowning. I'll run toxicology tests.'

'What will you look for?'

'If she was doping, it's likely she'd use a cocktail of drugs,' Sue warned. 'Something like EPO – a favourite of professional cyclists – is very hard to detect beyond an elevated red blood cell count. After death, these drugs can be concentrated or dispelled. There will be a lack of stomach contents, due to her vomiting as a reaction to drowning. A full toxicology report won't be available immediately. It would be useful if I had sight of any biodata from her heart rate monitor so I can factor that in.'

'I can send you that, if you think it will help.'

'D'you remember that case in Cyprus where the victim's smartwatch showed to the second the time of death? Her husband, who claimed to have been unconscious and tied up by intruders, was grassed up by his Fitbit, which showed that he'd, in fact, been pacing the room for a good twenty minutes before he "escaped" and called the cops.'

Shona nodded.

'Well, that's the sort of data the Procurator Fiscal expects these days. Have the whole country tagged if they had their way. Though I doubt it would put either of us out of business.'

'True.' Shona's fingers circled her own wrist for a moment. She only wore her Fitbit when she went running, but one of the first things she'd done at the scene had been to make sure Hayley's top-spec Garmin watch was bagged and tagged, along with her Samsung phone, which had been held for safekeeping during the race by one of the club officials.

'I've already got a warrant. Vinny's made a start on Hayley's devices,' Shona said. Vincent Grieg was her forensic data specialist, nicknamed 'Vinny Visuals' for his CCTV wizardry. 'He mentioned that data can be misleading in drowning cases, due to water passing between the monitor and the skin, which can record as a false heartbeat, but I'll get him to send it across.'

Sue nodded, before returning Hayley's body to the supine position. She then gently re-covered it with the sheet.

'Ciara will be back shortly,' Sue said, referring to her regular mortuary assistant, 'and we'll proceed with organ removal. You're welcome to stay, but I can call you if I find anything amiss. I'm not expecting to. I doubt she was an alcoholic or a heavy smoker.'

'Thanks, Sue,' Shona said, still trying to process what she'd just learned about a colleague she'd thought she knew, if not well, then at least well enough. 'Would there have been any outward signs if she was doping?'

'As an amateur, even an elite amateur, she wouldn't have been subject to testing. It's well known that anabolic or androgenic substances such as testosterone can cause masculinisation in women – so, facial hair or voice deepening can occur. But others have side effects like anxiety, insomnia or raised blood pressure, which wouldn't be immediately noticeable.'

Shona nodded.

Sue reached out and put her strong hand on Shona's shoulder. 'Knowing the victim always makes it more difficult,' she said softly. 'But they're not there, you know. The body is merely an empty vessel, but reading the signs correctly can tell us a lot about not only their departure, but how they chose to live.'

Shona nodded, and Sue seemed satisfied that this rare display of bedside manner had been effective. She'd probably deployed the same tactic before on queasy students, but Shona still felt grateful for her friend's understanding.

'Could there be any other explanation for the puncture marks?' Shona said.

Sue spread her hands. 'Always possible,' she said in a manner that made Shona think it was decidedly impossible. 'It's a capital mistake to theorise before one has data.'

'Is that pathology 101?' Shona smiled.

'Nope: Sherlock Holmes.' Sue smiled back, then her face became serious. 'But this isn't fiction, and I appreciate you need to pursue any potential lines of inquiry as quickly as possible. I'm sorry, Shona, but unless Hayley was receiving treatment that's absent from her medical record, I don't think I'm wrong here. Toxicology may give us the answer, one way or another.'

Business out of the way, Slasher Sue moved on to pleasantries.

'So how bad was the traffic, then?'

'I'm sorry I was late, Sue. I was taking Becca to that festival at the old airbase. I expected the roads to be quiet on a Sunday morning, but I got caught in a tailback.'

Sue beamed. 'She's coming to us in September. Archaeology, isn't she?' The professor had long had her eye on Becca, who, with her height and broad shoulders, was a potential recruit for the fencing or rowing teams, or both. 'I'll make an athlete out of her yet.'

Judging by what Shona had seen and heard this morning, she wasn't so sure that was a good idea.

Chapter 4

Shona was still deep in thought as she climbed the stairs to the CID office at Cornwall Mount. Police officers were only human, but the idea that Hayley was doping felt like a personal betrayal. She knew it was irrational, a knee-jerk reaction to being proved wrong in her assessment of the young woman as a potential CID recruit. While it wasn't illegal for Hayley to have obtained certain performance-enhancing drugs for personal use, the importing and distribution of such substances was a criminal act, of which she must have had knowledge. There was also the possibility that other triathletes were taking similar substances, and therefore were also at risk. From the windows, she caught a glimpse of cars and camper vans – some with paddle and windsurfing boards on roof racks – heading for the Solway coast. At least the headlines hadn't provoked a mass exodus from the area. But until Hayley's cause of death was determined, Shona knew she'd be compulsively checking the lifeboat crew app on her phone, in case there were any similar call-outs to swimmers in distress for Kirkness or Kirkcudbright in Scotland, and Silloth, Workington and St Bees on the Cumbrian side of the border.

And what about Kate? Did she know what Hayley had been doing? She pondered whether speaking to Kate privately in advance might be a good idea, then rejected it, calculating that her detective constable's reaction in the public space of the briefing would be a more accurate indication of what she knew about her friend's potential drug use. It's harder to lie when everyone's looking at you for answers.

Murdo must have been watching out for her. When she came into the main office, he was not at his own desk, in the far corner, but standing a little way down the side corridor, waiting by the conference room.

'Everyone's ready,' he said. 'I've brought you a coffee.'

'Thanks, Murdo. I'll just be a minute.'

Shona went into her office, which was separated from the main area by half-glass panelling equipped with vertical blinds for privacy, although anything above a low conversation was audible outside. She placed her laptop bag on the desk, looped her jacket over the chair, then shook loose the hair sticking to the back of her neck. What she was about to say would upset a lot of folk, but it had to be done.

In the conference room, Shona nodded to the support staff and the assembled officers – Ravi, Kate and two Specials from uniform. She sat down and placed her notebook and phone in front of her.

'Right, folks,' Shona called the briefing to order. 'Thank you for coming in on a Sunday. I've talked to the fiscal, and we're currently treating Hayley's death as unexplained.' She let the implication sink in before continuing, 'Andy Purdy completed the formal identification at the hospital last night.'

There were murmurs of sympathy.

'Professor Kitchen's preliminary post-mortem findings have raised an additional line of inquiry.' Shona paused, making eye contact with everyone around the table. Their faces registered either apprehension or puzzlement, or a mixture of both. 'I'm sure I don't need to remind you all,' she continued, 'that matters discussed here are not to be shared with anyone – even other officers or colleagues outside the team.' A few nodded in response. Shona took a breath. 'The professor is considering whether the use of PEDs – performance-enhancing drugs – was a factor in Hayley's death, and we need to help her answer that question.'

There was a moment of shocked silence, then a flurry of muttered comments. Shona raised her hand and the buzz subsided. She noticed Kate had gone white. She seemed impervious to the looks of concern the others were giving her.

'Slasher Sue's saying Hayley's death was her own fault?' Kate blurted out, glaring at Shona.

'No, Kate,' Shona replied, her expression sympathetic but her voice firm. 'We need to keep an open mind at this stage, but there are marks consistent with intramuscular injection that are currently unexplained.'

'She wasn't a doper. She was a cop.' Kate's voice was loud in the stuffy confines of the room. People shifted in their seats. Ravi put his hand on Kate's arm, but she threw it off.

'*Professor* Kitchen,' Shona said, emphasising the pathologist's formal title, 'is running toxicology. In the meantime, our key priority is still tracing everyone at the event who might potentially have information that'll help us piece together exactly what happened. How are we doing, Murdo?'

Kate slumped back in her seat, eyes on the table.

Shona felt a surge of compassion but didn't regret her decision to reveal Sue's findings at the briefing. The shock of Kate's reaction was visceral, and it confirmed what she'd hoped: her DC didn't appear to have been complicit in any doping.

'We're checking with the list of registrations...' Murdo began. 'Some folk left the scene straight away. A few claimed they pulled out before the swim or didn't turn up at all. To be fair, the organisers have done a competent job.'

'But let's not take that list as gospel,' Shona finished. 'We need to cross-check and identify everyone there. The press office is putting out an appeal for information, later, so expect phones to start ringing. Public safety is paramount, and I'm sure you can all appreciate the community's concern, and rumours are circulating.' Shona thought of what Freya told her yesterday about the gossip in the bar. 'We need to calm those fears without revealing evidence that might later prove to be crucial, so no discussion of the professor's findings, please.'

Vinny Visuals sat at the far end of the table, fingers moving over his tablet. 'Vinny,' she called. When he didn't look up, she raised her eyebrows at his fellow analyst, Chloe, who was sat next to him, and who Shona had come to regard as his interpreter. She helpfully nudged him in the ribs.

Vinny stared at Shona for a moment, then launched straight into an answer to the question she hadn't yet asked. 'In terms of the Garmin, it would be easier if we could access it through the app on her phone, but we need the PIN.'

'Kate, can you ask Andy if he knows Hayley's PIN?' Shona said.

Kate kept her eyes on the table but nodded.

'What specific data do you want?' Vinny asked.

'At this stage of the investigation, I'm keeping an open mind, so whatever you've got.'

Vinny blinked at her, and Shona turned to Chloe.

'The Garmin's Bluetooth was switched off,' Chloe explained. 'The data was retained on the device and hadn't been uploaded to her stats, which she'd have accessed through the Garmin Connect app.'

'Is that unusual?' Shona asked Kate.

'No. For events...' Kate began in a shaky voice. 'It's better to upload to Strava or social media afterwards, along with selfies and pictures of medals, etc. As a serious competitor, you wouldn't just auto-upload all your stats. That's giving the competition too much information.'

'So, what data can we access with the PIN?' Shona directed her question back to Chloe.

'There's a calendar for the last seven days, which will immediately give us heart rate, training activities, GPS. So, in terms of placing her in locations and typical vital signs, we can give you a useful timeline. We can go back further, if you need to.'

'Good,' Shona replied. 'Prioritise the biodata and send it to Professor Kitchen as soon as you can.' She looked around the table but didn't invite questions. 'Thanks, everyone. Back to work.'

In Shona's office, Murdo puffed his cheeks then blew out a long breath.

'That's a turn-up for the books, no mistake. Is Slasher Sue sure?'

Remembering Murdo's attachment to Hayley, Shona went easy.

'No, but she's sure enough to flag it as a line of inquiry. How did your visit to the family go?'

'As I expected,' Murdo said, his face impassive. 'Family disowned her when she became a cop, but they still had to be told. Didnae see any tears.'

Shona realised this had been an additional reason why Murdo had volunteered. He wanted to protect her from a hostile or indifferent reception from the family of the woman she'd just tried her best to save.

'Thanks, Murdo. Can you ask Kate to come in? I need to check if there's anything she wants to say or add to her statement.'

Murdo nodded stoically. He went to Kate's desk, placed a hand on her shoulder as he leaned in to tell her, then returned to his own seat.

Shona's phone buzzed. She'd sent off a brief email to Detective Chief Superintendent Davies when she'd left the post-mortem and was expecting his call. 'Sir?'

Kate was looking through the glass panel in the office door, but Shona held up her hand, indicating she'd have to wait.

'My condolences for the loss of your colleague,' he began.

'Thank you, sir.' Shona's heart sank. He'd concluded what she'd feared. 'Colleague' meant there was a potential conflict of interest in her officers investigating Hayley's death. A Major Investigation Team from another division would be tasked. The case needed to be handled in a thorough but sensitive way, and now she'd lose any control over that. 'Does that mean you're referring Hayley's death to an MIT?'

There was a pause. In large rural divisions, it wasn't uncommon for officers to have prior knowledge of victims or witnesses, and it was taken for granted they were professional enough not to let this interfere with an investigation; in fact, it often gave them insights into the dynamics of the case. But Hayley was a police officer and that required extra caution.

Shona quickly calculated, from the background sounds, how long she'd have to make her argument for remaining SIO. It was Sunday morning, so if Davies was at home and had just stepped out from a family BBQ, she'd have to make it quick. Or was he in the office at Kilmarnock HQ? The silence made her think the latter. Davies was a by-the-book cop, five years from retirement. If a case required his attention, he'd be at his desk, which – Shona knew from previous visits – displayed no framed photos of the grandkids, or other personal items. Who'd blame him for wanting to maintain a cordon sanitaire around his home environment? With Hayley's death, Shona didn't have that option.

'I want you to continue,' he said, eventually. 'At least until we know what we're dealing with. These are challenging times for us, and the media will jump on any police and drugs connection. We need to keep a lid on this and you're best placed to do that.'

'Thank you, sir,' she said.

'And if there's even a whisper of foul play, call me. I want this dealt with quickly and quietly, Shona,' he said, and ended the call.

Nothing about their conversation had gone as Shona had expected, but for once she and her boss were in agreement. Bringing in an MIT from Glasgow would point a big neon arrow at the investigation, and possibly Tommy and the lifeboat too. She was relieved but unsettled by Davies's clear message. There'd been some unfavourable press lately over racism, sexism and homophobia within the force, and the treatment of female victims. Shona could keep the case, but if it exploded in a mass of negative headlines for Police Scotland, he would hold her responsible.

Shona was still reflecting on this when Kate came in, red-eyed, and shot a venomous look at her boss.

'How are you, Kate?' Shona began, indicating the chair opposite. 'I understand this must be distressing for you.'

Kate slumped heavily into her seat and looked as if she was about to question how Shona could possibly understand, then remembered she was speaking to her DI, the person who'd hauled her best friend from the sea.

'I'm okay. You know.' She shrugged, as any further explanation was unnecessary.

'I think you should consider taking some time away and seeing a counsellor,' Shona said, softly. Having witnessed Hayley's death was sufficient justification for Kate to step back.

'You're side-lining me?' she said, indignantly.

Shona had doubts about Kate's emotional fitness to work. Weighed against this were the undoubted insight and skills her DC could bring to the investigation, and the critical issues they were facing over holiday staffing. The truth was, Shona needed Kate on the case, but if she wasn't up to the job, Shona would have no choice but to sign her off.

'I'm giving you the opportunity to tell me how you are, and we'll decide together how to proceed.'

Kate drew in a deep breath and straightened up, looking Shona in the eye. 'I'm fine, really, boss. I owe it to Hayley to find out what happened. I'm confident I can be an asset to the investigation. It's what you'd want, if it was your friend, isn't it?' She gave her DI a defiant and knowing look.

Touché.

'Okay.' Shona nodded. Tommy often said people were rarely aware of their own strengths until they were tested. This would test Kate to the limit, but she was a competent and resourceful officer. 'I've no objection to you continuing for now. But you'll tell me if you find it too much emotionally?'

'It's because I'm emotionally engaged,' Kate replied, pointedly, 'that I'll do a good job.'

'Is there anything else you'd like to add to your statement, or tell me about Hayley?'

Kate considered for a moment, then shook her head.

Shona paused, mulling over the pros and cons of what she was about to suggest.

'I'm going to interview Andy Purdy tomorrow morning, and I want you to come with me. I can ask Ravi, if you'd prefer. Everyone would understand.'

Kate waved away the idea that anyone should take her place.

'And if we discover something you don't like?' Shona said.

'We won't,' Kate said. 'Because I was her best friend and I know there's nothing to find.'

Chapter 5

That evening Shona walked down to the shore in an attempt to escape – or at least find peace to process – the events of the day. At the RNLI station, she saw a light on upstairs in the crew room. She went through the side door. In the boat hall, the *Margaret Wilson* lay snug in her cradle, cleared and ready for the next shout.

Shona found Tommy alone, poring over marine charts.

'Sorry I wasn't around for training this morning,' she said, as he pushed a mug of tea across the table towards her.

'Aye, well, you had a good excuse.'

'Do you want to do the debrief now?'

There was a procedure after every shout, which ensured that as well as identifying any issues and learning lessons from the rescue, volunteer crew members got support if they needed it.

Her roles didn't usually collide quite so markedly. It was proving an unusual situation for all sorts of reasons. Her police statement reflected she'd been first on the scene after Kate, almost unheard of for a detective inspector.

'We can do,' Tommy said, rolling up the chart. 'How's the lassie's family?'

'Her partner's still in shock. She didn't have much contact with her father and siblings,' Shona said, glossing over Hayley's relatives and their history.

'D'you have a cause of death?'

'Drowning, as we expected. But there may be an additional medical factor we're still investigating,' Shona replied carefully, then paused. 'It was nothing you could have predicted.'

Tommy just pressed his lips together and nodded. The organisers of the triathlon were likely to face scrutiny over safety protocols. Rumour, gossip and public opinion were another matter, but she would do everything she could to find answers quickly, and minimise the fallout for Tommy, the station and the area.

'Sophie did well,' Shona said, sipping her tea. First shouts were always a milestone: knowing other people trusted you with their lives, that you'd earned that trust.

'Pity it was a fatality,' Tommy replied. 'But she's a canny lass that one. Might even make helm one day, unless you fancy it yourself?'

Shona never stopped marvelling at the quality of training she'd received, in everything from navigating to casualty care – training that could take an ordinary person with no maritime background all the way up to helm, a position in which they held themselves responsible for the lives of their crew and the casualties they rescued.

'Well, if I ever give up the day job and become a plain old B&B landlady, I might give it a go. Anyway, room for us both.'

'Aye, an embarrassment of riches for the station.' He grinned.

Shona glanced at the crew-room clock. Just after seven. 'Paperwork?'

Tommy gave her a shrewd look, picking up on her desire to be elsewhere. 'Right, I'll ask you how you're feeling, and direct you to support services and remind you the rest of the crew are here if you'd like to talk. Happy wi' that?'

Shona nodded.

'Anything else you want to say?'

Shona shook her head.

'Aye, right, off you go.'

'Thanks, Tommy.'

Shona was at the top of the stairs when he called her back.

'Becca away at yon festival?'

'Yeah, dropped her off this morning.'

'Whit about your guests?'

'All settled in for the night. Please thank Freya for me.'

'I'm off to the Royal Arms for a bite. Freya's just finished her shift. You can join us an' thank her in person.' Shona's body language must have signalled reluctance. 'I mean, if you'd rather have an evening tae yourself, that's okay.'

'It's not that, Tommy... It's just I'm having dinner with James,' she said, suddenly feeling coy in a way that both irritated and curiously pleased her.

'What? James is here?'

'No, he's in LA. We FaceTime.' When Tommy looked uncomprehending, she continued. 'Every Sunday, we cook together. His food always looks great, while mine's barely edible. We light candles, have a glass of wine, eat dinner. We chat, like you do. Time difference means it's brunch for him, dinner for me.'

Tommy frowned and Shona felt a stab of anxiety that she'd misread the moment. She was, after all, still a married woman, though she believed her relationship with Rob was unsalvageable. But here she was, a respected police officer in the community and lifeboat volunteer, cheerfully admitting to dating another man, albeit online. Sure, Tommy had made it clear in the past how far short Rob fell in his estimation, even before he was jailed, and by contrast how he'd willingly recruit James to his crew, if only Hollywood wasn't so far. But people were capable of holding conflicting views at the same time and what might be considered a form of adultery by some was a step too far for Tommy.

'I'd be happy if you didn't pass that around,' Shona said, hoping she sounded suitably contrite at having overshared.

After a moment, Tommy looked at her, incredulous. 'You eat your own cooking? I already know you're brave, but...' He broke into a wide grin.

'I'm really not that bad, Tommy,' she said, mock indignation covering her relief.

'I mean, can you no' slip a takeaway pizza ontae the plate when James isnae looking?'

'Believe me, I've considered it, but nothing gets past him. And it's really best you don't say anything. If the media got hold of the story...' She remembered the volume of attention James had to deal with, good and bad, from the press, as well as online. They'd kept the relationship low profile, although many of her friends and colleagues likely knew. She also didn't want to hurt or embarrass Rob, though Tommy might say it was more consideration than he deserved.

'Who am I gonna tell? Your ain cooking? Naebody would believe me.'

'Right, I'm not standing here all night while you insult my culinary efforts. Enjoy your evening.'

'Off you go, but dinnae be a stranger.'

Shona heard him laughing as she ran down the stairs, and she smiled with amusement and relief as she stepped out into the evening sunshine and headed home.

Chapter 6

The next morning, despite the early hour and the grim purpose of her impending visit to Hayley's partner, Andy Purdy, Shona was in a good mood. She'd made a risotto last night, in tandem with James, and although hers had been practically inedible, she'd had an enjoyable evening. They had agreed early in their transatlantic relationship to make the most of their time together, saying what was on their minds instead of letting it go unsaid. Shona found she could ramble on about the mundane things without James looking bored. He was always eager to hear the local news, even if it was only that the neighbour's new cat was leaving dead birds as presents outside their kitchen door, freaking Becca out.

Physical reminders of his previous visit remained at the house. He'd given Shona his cherished and well-thumbed copy of *The Collected Works of Robert Burns*, which had been his constant companion during filming. It sat on the lounge table – an unspoken promise that its owner would return to consult it once more.

The sun shone on the estuary as she pulled out of High Pines. Lately, she made more of an effort to appreciate how lucky she was. *Take a breath*, James would say, *and look out at that view for me*. He still carried a heart-shaped pebble from the shore and when she'd found a near-identical one, she'd slipped it into her own pocket. Now and again, she'd turn it in her hand, when the distance between them felt too great, imagining James did the same.

Shona pulled up behind Kate's Mini, which was parked in front of Hayley and Andy's boxy starter home on the outskirts of Dumfries. The place had the deadness of a dormitory estate in daytime. The houses were semi-detached brick two-storeys, with short drives and postage-stamp front gardens that mostly doubled as additional parking spaces. Hayley's was one of a handful with a separate garage to the side. Shona reckoned it would be full of triathlon kit, as the house was unlikely to boast much storage space.

Kate joined her on the pavement. There were dark circles under her eyes but otherwise she looked the same as usual, her blonde hair in a high ponytail and her pale grey suit smart and businesslike.

'Did Andy Purdy know Hayley's PIN?' Shona said, hiking her bag over her shoulder and locking the Audi.

'He did. I've passed it on to Vinny.'

'How was Andy when you spoke to him?'

'Devastated, as you'd expect.'

'And how are you this morning?'

Kate shrugged. 'Okay.'

'I still think you should talk to the force counsellors.'

'I will,' Kate assured her.

It took several knocks for Andy Purdy to answer.

The front room had a fusty smell and was dim, lit only by the flickering light of the soundless TV. Andy hurriedly bundled a duvet behind the sofa and squinted at the light as he opened the blinds. He was barefoot, unshaven, and wore grey tracksuit bottoms with a crumpled white T-shirt. On one side of his head, his cropped dark hair stood on end; Shona reckoned he'd probably been sleeping on the sofa since Hayley's death. From the hallway, she'd glimpsed a framed poster at the top of the stairs: the words *Sleep Eat Swim Ride Run Repeat* imposed over the stylised graphic of a woman. It can't have been easy to pass on the way to the bedroom, a reminder of Hayley and her ambitions in life.

'I want to thank you both for what you did,' Andy said shakily.

'It's fine, Andy,' Shona said softly. 'We were happy to help. I'm only sorry we weren't able to do more.'

'It's good she had friends with her at the end.'

From the corner of her eye, Shona saw Kate bow her head and bite her lip.

'Today,' Shona said, moving the conversation quickly on, 'we're really just here to see how you are and update you. Have you any questions?'

He shook his head.

'I know you spoke to Ravi at the hospital. Is there anything else you'd like to add?'

Shona didn't think Purdy was the brightest copper on the beat. She'd sometimes wondered how long his relationship with Hayley would last. He was a plod. Solid enough. And perhaps Shona was wrong – maybe a relationship where both partners weren't high-flyers stood a better chance. In any case, as a cop, he would understand the significance of her question as the precursor to a revelation. Perhaps he was still in shock, because nothing registered on his face. He shook his head again.

'Okay, Andy, there's something I'd like to discuss with you. Can Kate make you a cup of tea?'

'I'm fine, unless you want one, ma'am?'

She looked at Kate, who stayed in her seat, and Shona got the impression she didn't want to be in the kitchen when the PM results were raised.

'Professor Kitchen found some marks on Hayley that indicate intramuscular injections. Can you tell us anything about those?'

Andy looked blank. 'No. I can't.'

'The professor is questioning whether Hayley used performance-enhancing drugs. Do you know anything about that?'

He bristled, then shook his head vigorously. 'Impossible. How could she be using PEDs, and me not know. What have you found?'

'Will you submit to a drug test yourself?' Shona said, ignoring his question.

Kate stiffened and Andy stared at Shona, incredulous.

'It's purely routine,' Shona assured him. 'No different from the random testing policy all officers are subject to.'

Andy barked a short, mirthless laugh.

'Hayley can't have been doping.' He inched forward in his chair, his expression hardening. 'I've never seen any evidence. Kate? Have you?'

'No.'

'What about recreationally?' Shona pressed.

'Drugs? She was a police officer.'

In Shona's experience those two things weren't mutually exclusive. In her City Police beat days, almost the entire squad – with a few exceptions, including Shona – were using a mixture of energy drinks, amphetamines and cocaine to get through their shifts. Random testing was based on a senior officer's 'reasonable suspicion' of a controlled substance being used, but as long as no one was swinging from the light fittings or biting suspects, the need for boots on the ground took priority, and eyes were turned away from minor infractions.

'Well?' Shona said. 'To your knowledge was Hayley using recreational drugs? Pills? Injected substances?'

'Absolutely not. And if you want to test me, sure,' he challenged, 'though I don't see how it's relevant.'

It wasn't, especially. Andy was no athlete. She'd wanted to see if drugs, in any form, were something he and Hayley had shared, but there was no shiftiness, no sign he was recalibrating his answers to protect himself. If he was lying to her, he was doing it well.

'Happy for us to search?' Shona said.

'You want to search our home for drugs?' Andy replied, his voice rising.

He must have known she'd get a warrant because, after a moment, he threw up his hands in a gesture of submission.

'Aye. Suppose so. Nothing to hide. We were getting married. Did you know that?' He looked from Shona to Kate, who dipped her head in confirmation. 'Not sure what I'm going to do without her.'

Shona had thought that about Rob when he'd first gone to prison. *It seems impossible now, but you'll adapt*, she wanted to tell Andy, but it was too soon and their circumstances were too different. Her feelings about Rob would certainly have been less complicated if he had died, she thought guiltily. But then there would be no chance of a reconciliation between Becca and her father, and she didn't want her child to carry a wound like that for the rest of her life.

'Okay, Andy.' She'd hit him hard; it was time to go a little easier. 'I'm sorry if that was difficult. I want you to see we're being rigorous in finding out what happened to Hayley. D'you understand?' When he gave a slight nod, she continued, 'Can you think of any reason why Hayley would have injection marks?'

He shook his head. 'None.'

'Okay. Thank you. We'll leave you in peace now. The search team will come this afternoon. It's just routine. Is there somewhere you can go until then? Family or friends?'

He nodded.

'Okay. We'll wait while you pack a bag.'

'It's fine,' he said, getting up and slipping his bare feet into trainers. 'I can go now.'

Outside, he handed them his house keys. As he drove away, Kate rounded on Shona.

'Was that really necessary? He's in a right state. There must be some mistake. Slasher Sue has got it wrong.'

Shona thought of Sue's distaste for cheats. Had she jumped the gun in her analysis, seeing what she wanted to see? Could she have been wrong about Haley's use of PEDs?

No, the professor was much too professional for that, and Andy Purdy hadn't offered any alternative explanation for the injection marks, which had been Shona's key objective of the visit.

'Don't think me unfeeling, Kate. It was why I wanted you with me today.' Shona stepped closer, looking up into her DC's grief-stricken face. 'It may not seem like it now, but it'll be better for you both in the long run if you understand how diligent we've been. I don't want either of you to have questions over the investigation. It won't help you grieve or heal.'

Back in her car, Shona watched Kate's Mini pull away. If Hayley had indeed been using performance-enhancing drugs, was it likely that Purdy, or her triathlon teammates, didn't know about it? She was pretty sure Kate didn't. But as well as being a fellow cop, Kate was scrupulous by nature. Hayley was smart; she'd have known it.

After a further minute's deliberation, Shona took out her phone and called Murdo.

'Any updates for me?' she asked.

'Ravi and I are going over statements. We've a few triathlon club members to talk to yet.'

'Andy Purdy denied Hayley was self-doping.'

'You believe him?'

'Not sure.'

'He's a cop, he's mibbaes worried about being complicit in illegal activity.'

Murdo, it seemed, had quickly come to terms with the potential outcome of their investigations. Or perhaps he was simply more practised at separating the job from the personal.

'True,' Shona said. 'Andy seemed genuinely shocked but defensive, but maybe he's stalling until we find more evidence. He's agreed to a search. Can we get someone over this afternoon?'

'I can. Think we'll find anything?'

'If he knows, he'll have got rid of it already. If he doesn't, she'll have hidden it well.'

'Aye, probably.'

'Can you get Ravi to check on Andy's service record and background?'

'Nae problem.'

'Thanks, Murdo. I'm on my way back to the office. See you later.'

Shona sat with her eyes closed for a moment, letting the warm sunshine streaming through the windscreen soothe away the tightness around her forehead and jaw. She'd meant what she'd said to Kate about the benefits to Hayley's friends and family of a thorough investigation, but it had still felt like a demolition act on Hayley's memory.

She sighed and opened her eyes. She was about to head off when she saw a text from Becca, saying she had met some other students starting at Glasgow University in the autumn. Shona smiled and sent a thumbs-up reply, taking this unsolicited contact as Becca's apology for the lack of reassurance she'd offered her mother on the journey to the festival.

As she turned the key in the ignition, her phone rang, and the screen showed: *No caller ID*. Shona's first thought was that it was Becca or one of her friends on a borrowed phone, rather than the usual cold calls about insurance or replacement windows.

It was neither.

'This is Dave Hennessey from the National Crime Agency. Hope you don't mind me calling you unannounced.'

This wasn't unusual in itself. The NCA's remit made its officials part detectives, part customs officers, and the trafficking of drugs, people or counterfeit goods through her patch meant they'd sometimes worked together in the past.

'It would have been polite to contact my Super and to have sight of paperwork in advance, but I won't hold that against you,' Shona said, hoping it wasn't some complex job that would stretch her resources even further in the middle of peak holiday time. 'How can I help?'

'I'm part of the team investigating DCI Delfont's murder.'

Shona felt the sky momentarily darken, as if her former boss had reached out from beyond the grave, put his fingers around her throat and squeezed.

Delfont was a name she had been hoping never to hear again. More so, given what had happened only six months earlier, when Shona had been complicit in covering up the details of his murder.

'I see.' Shona fought to keep the apprehension from her voice.

'Can you tell me when you last had contact with DCI Delfont?'

'When I left the City of London Police.'

Why was he calling her? A rapid series of possibilities flitted through her mind. There had been a witness? Had Delfont left behind some kind of evidence that might implicate Shona?

'I just wanted to let you know we're treating Delfont's death as the work of organised crime. I'm really calling just to tick all the boxes.'

God, how she hated that phrase.

'As it's the death of a serving officer, we must be thorough,' he added.

She'd played the same card with Andy Purdy over Hayley's death and it stung to be on the receiving end.

'More thorough than with a member of the public.' It slipped out before she could stop herself. Suddenly, she could see why Andy had come across as defensive, although she still thought he knew more than he was saying. 'I'm sorry,' she added quickly. 'I know it must be a difficult case.'

'No offence taken, DI Oliver,' he said smoothly. 'You know what I mean. If it was up to me, we'd leave it. From the evidence I've seen, Delfont got what was coming to him – he was obviously corrupt.'

It was what she'd tried to tell her bosses all those years ago and look where it had got her. Drugged, assaulted, and forced from a job and a city she loved. Her attempts to expose Delfont had begun nearly a decade earlier, but the fallout still dogged her.

Shona and Thalia had been careful to maintain an appropriate level of contact since that fateful night in the Lake District six months earlier, when Shona had found her friend shocked but defiant about what she'd just done, and pulled Delfont's lifeless body from the water, three neat bullet holes in his skull.

In that moment, she'd agonised over what to do, but there'd really been no doubt in her mind. Thalia was a victim who'd been driven to cross a line, but now she could make a life free from their tormentor, the man who'd drugged and assaulted them both, and others.

They'd kept in touch at a level that wouldn't raise any suspicions, messaging once a month or so. *How are you? I'm fine. Busy at work, but not too stressed for once!* And an emoji or two. When Thalia texted that she'd had *trouble with the noisy neighbours but they've moved on*, Shona had known the 'noisy neighbours' were the Met detectives initially in charge of the case. Now the NCA were involved, which meant a widening of the investigation to organised crime groups.

'Do you expect to make arrests?' Shona asked. The possibility that Thalia's conscience had got the better of her and she'd turned herself in was a remote one, but even that scenario was fraught with danger for Shona.

'We hope so,' Hennessey replied evenly.

'Let me know if there's anything I can help you with.'

'Thank you, DI Oliver, I will.'

Chapter 7

Later that afternoon, Shona was in her office, reviewing her strategy document and preparing to email the fiscal's office, when Slasher Sue's number flashed up on her phone screen.

'Hello, ma dear,' the professor said in her jaunty, Edinburgh accent. 'I've some preliminary tox results for you.'

Shona got up and chapped on the glass separating her office from the main CID room. When everyone looked up, she pointed to Kate, Ravi and Murdo in turn and beckoned them in.

'Hang on, Sue, I'm putting you on speaker. I want the others to hear this.'

There was a brief pause while everyone found a chair and Shona returned behind her desk. 'Go ahead, Sue. What have you got?'

'Initial toxicology result shows traces of gamma-hydroxybutyrate in her blood. I thought you'd want to know.'

'GHB?' Shona said, looking at the equally puzzled expressions on the others' faces. 'As in the date-rape drug?'

'It can be used as a performance enhancer,' Sue explained. 'It increases growth hormone release and stimulates fat metabolism for weight loss, and it's also used to aid sleep. It's popular with bodybuilders.'

'And could it be a factor in her death?'

'As I mentioned, I'm expecting to find a cocktail of drugs – but yes, I think it's significant.'

'Hello, Professor,' Murdo said, then jumped right in: 'GHB works quickly, doesn't it?'

'The bulky muscles have good vascularity, and therefore the injected drug quickly reaches the systemic circulation, bypassing the first-pass metabolism.'

Murdo and Shona exchanged a look that showed they both interpreted that as a *yes*.

'Does the data from her Garmin throw any light on this?' Shona said.

'This is where it gets complicated,' Sue replied. 'Her resting heart rate averages 34 bpm and a maximum exertion of 185 bpm. GHB would cause her heart rate to slow, but the data shows an alarming arrhythmia, with heart rates from 44 to 200 bpm in a matter of seconds. It may be because she was an athlete and was swimming. Most research into the effects of GHB has been done on baboons, so it's not directly applicable.'

Kate stared at her notebook, gouging a repeated line in the page with her pencil. Shona felt a welling-up of frustration at Hayley's actions. She knew it was partly irrational anger that the promising constable had somehow hoodwinked her. But then she remembered that morning's phone call from the NCA and how she'd acted when faced with a difficult choice. She'd helped cover up a murder, albeit one she'd played no part in herself and couldn't have prevented. It had been her duty to set the wheels of justice in motion, but she'd chosen her friend over the law. And Hayley had chosen to cheat. *It's not the same*, she told herself, though she knew it was just a question of degrees. And Hayley had paid for her mistake with her life, while Shona was still living with what she'd done. Perhaps Shona had no right to condemn her.

She sighed. 'As a police officer, she'd have been briefed on the dangers of drug use. Why would she risk it?'

'Maybe that's why she did risk it,' Ravi said. 'Thought she knew better.'

Kate shot him a look of pure hatred.

'Okay, let's say Hayley was a regular user,' Shona said, ignoring Kate's flash of anger. 'What's the margin between a safe amount and a dose sufficient to impair consciousness?'

'Depends on the strength. And maladministration is always a possibility,' Sue replied. 'Its metabolisation by the liver before Hayley's death means it's impossible to be precise about the dosage. I don't have the full tox results, which might take between four and six weeks, but there's another scenario which I think you should consider.'

Shona frowned. 'Go on.'

'You'll remember the fresh injection site on the back of the thigh, and the corresponding puncture in the wetsuit?'

'I remember you thought it was odd.'

'What if the GHB was delivered via something like an EpiPen? Nottingham Police had twelve separate reports of GHB spiking in clubs in less than a month. Three women were hospitalised in Sheffield and there's been high numbers of universities reporting incidents in the past. Taking into account the drug's use in date-rape scenarios, and the puncture location, it's possible she was injected by a third party.'

'Someone killed her?' Kate blurted out. A series of emotions flashed across her face – shock, outrage, and just a hint of triumph that she'd been right and Hayley wasn't responsible for her own death. Shona thought Kate should have learned to mask such feelings by now. She'd better learn quick if she wanted to progress any further in her career.

Sue continued without any response to Kate's outburst. 'Given GHB works within five to fifteen minutes, it would be reasonable to say it was done after she arrived at Kirkness.'

The thought that someone was roaming around her village injecting people with drugs made Shona's blood run cold. This wasn't some inner-city nightclub. It was a community whose reputation and businesses depended so much on welcoming visitors that she found it unconceivable. But she knew she needed to think the unthinkable if she was to unravel what happened to Hayley.

'Ravi, did you find anything like an EpiPen at Andy and Hayley's house search this afternoon?'

'Nothing. No drugs or paraphernalia at all.'

'Sue...' Shona began. 'You think it could be murder?'

'It would be one of my working hypotheses.'

'Then it's mine, too.'

—

Shona told everyone they could have a fifteen-minute break, but that she wanted them back at four p.m. for a briefing. She sat at her desk, bullet-pointing the key information Sue had given her, working through their implications for the investigation.

It boiled down to one question: did Hayley misjudge the dose or effects, or did someone else inject her with — as Scots Law termed it — *a wicked intention to kill*?

If it was the work of a third party, she couldn't see how they could argue their actions would be anything other than fatal, given Hayley was about to plunge into the sea, even with safety boats in place.

Outside, in the main CID area, Murdo was booting up the interactive whiteboard. Ravi came into her office and set a takeaway coffee from the cafe down the road on her desk. She thanked him and took a sip. It was time.

She took in the dozen or so faces that looked at her in expectation. Some of the support staff were already away on holiday, but she was relieved to see she still had key players like Vinny and Chloe, a couple of experienced Specials, and Hannah Crawford, the round-faced, fifty-something data input operator and unofficial den mother. Murdo trusted her with any task that required tact, ingenuity or persistence.

Shona took a whiteboard marker and wrote Hayley's name at the top of the board. Then she outlined what Professor Kitchen had said. She added *cause of death*, followed by two radiating arrows labelled *self-admin substance* and *third-party action*.

'Murdo, can you give us an update on the triathlon competitors?'

He nodded to Hannah, who was pushing up the sleeves of her cardigan as if physically preparing for a hefty job.

'D'you want to take this?' Murdo said.

'We've traced ninety-two, and have eight outstanding.' Hannah consulted her tablet. 'It was a sold-out event. Apparently, it's common practice to sell on your entry if your plans change, or you get sick or injured.'

Shona looked at Kate. 'Is that strictly legal?'

Kate shrugged. 'T&Cs generally forbid it, but you can find places for things like the London Marathon or the Great North Run on eBay or runners' forums for inflated prices. Technically, if you can't make an event you should defer until next year. Selling your entry pisses off those who didn't get a place in the original ballot.'

'The eight outstanding are individuals not affiliated to any of the triathlon clubs,' Hannah said. 'Jimmy and Tom are going to chap a few doors for us.' She tilted her head to indicate the uniformed Specials. 'Find out who they sold their entry to, then interview them in case they saw something but didn't come forward.'

'Thank you, Hannah.' Shona smiled, knowing that was one job she wouldn't have to chase up. 'Murdo, Ravi, anything from the interviews with the triathlon club members?'

'Everyone at the club is shocked, bewildered,' Murdo said.

Ravi, sitting at the front, one ankle resting on the opposite knee, nodded in confirmation. 'We brought up the subject of PEDs in general terms. Everyone denied doping was an issue at amateur level and claimed they'd no idea where you'd source it from.'

'What about the background check on Andy Purdy?' Shona said, perching on the corner of a desk.

'Nothing unexpected,' Ravi replied. 'He met Hayley during their police basic training. He's local to the area. Only has a

Facebook account with three old posts about football on it, so not active on social media. Plays golf occasionally, goes clay pigeon shooting. Liked by his colleagues. No work issues. Is he a suspect?'

'Why would you think he had anything to do with it?' Kate rounded on Ravi. 'He worshipped Hayley. And he was on duty at the agricultural show until I called him.'

Shona remembered Andy and Kate in each other's arms as the paramedics attempted to resuscitate Hayley. He had got there quick, but he'd only been fifteen minutes up the road. It would be an easy alibi to check.

'Kate,' Shona said, getting up from her perch on the desk. Her tone was even but the warning was there. 'It's routine, you know that. But I agree, he has no obvious motive.'

Kate reddened, aware eyes were on her, even if most were sympathetic.

'Was anything at all recovered from Hayley's house this afternoon?' Shona went on.

'As I said, no drugs. I checked if it was worth calling a dog team in, but they're not trained for PEDs – they could do us opioids, ketamine or amphetamines, if they come up in Slasher Sue's tox screening, though.'

Shona nodded. It was the kind of creative thinking Ravi excelled at. Plus, he liked dogs, although his partner, Martin, was less keen on the responsibility and had so far vetoed the idea of a pooch of their own, much to Becca's disappointment. Dog-sitting their pup was high on her wish list.

'We bagged her laptop and found an older smartphone in a box in the garage,' Ravi continued. 'Andy didn't recognise it but admitted it could be a model previously owned by Hayley that she put into storage when she upgraded. Vinny's gonna work his magic on it, aren't you, pal?'

Vinny regarded Ravi for a moment, then gave a single cautious nod, as if any public admission that doing what was, after all, his job might land him in trouble later.

Shona crossed back to the whiteboard and raised the pen. 'Given there are other injection sites, we still need to eliminate the possibility that the injection was self-administered. The fiscal will kick the can right back to us if there's any doubt.' She tapped the nib on the *self-admin* label.

'If they were self-administered,' she continued, 'you'd need to know what to take and when. The internet is the likeliest place, so perhaps we'll find something on her computer.'

Shona saw Chloe nod and make a note on her tablet.

'And Ravi,' Shona added. 'Tomorrow, I want you and Kate to have a chat with Andy Purdy about this EpiPen theory. Did Hayley own one for any reason we might have overlooked? See what you make of his reaction. And find out from uniform if there've been other incidents locally.'

'Anything else?' Kate said. There was an edge of sulky sarcasm which to Shona indicated that Kate was still resisting the idea that Hayley was using PEDs. At other times this would have earned Kate a quiet word in Shona's office, but beyond a hard stare over her glasses, she opted to let it go. If anyone could harvest useful information from Andy, who might not even be aware he possessed it, Kate was the detective for the job.

Shona indicated the *third-party* label on the board, knowing this would provide more effective motivation to her DC. 'And you can't remember any incident before the race? Any encounter during which Hayley might have been spiked?'

Kate shook her head.

'Right, well, when you have a chat with Andy, see if Hayley mentioned being threatened by anyone.'

'She never said anything to me,' Kate replied, frowning.

Shona thought back to the moments before the race began, and the strong bond she'd observed between Hayley and her teammates – *my girl gang* – when they'd appeared like a platoon ready for battle, but none had mentioned anything significant in their statements.

'She may not have confided in you or Andy, believing you'd be compelled to act on it, but we need to check with him. Murdo and I will chase up the triathlon club chairman tomorrow. See if she mentioned anything to him.'

When Kate looked doubtful, Shona added, gently, 'She could have been protecting you, Kate. Perhaps she didn't want to put you in a difficult position, personally or professionally.'

Kate looked down, avoiding her gaze, and Shona decided it was time to draw the briefing to a close. Hannah was making notes of the actions she'd opened, and would update the system and the whiteboard after they'd finished.

'Right, thank you everyone. Keep going. We'll get there. Someone knows what happened to Hayley. Someone will talk.'

—

Rob's weekly call slot from Brixton Prison was Monday, seven p.m. Shona always made sure she was available, but it didn't stop her feeling resentful about the lack of flexibility when she was busy. She hurried home, dumping her laptop on the kitchen table just as her mobile rang.

After brief pleasantries, Rob asked if Becca was around, but their daughter was at the festival and, anyway, preferred to limit phone contact to once a month. They'd been close before Rob went to prison and he didn't seem to understand why Becca felt a sense of betrayal that his actions had led to this. Shona, who'd never known her own father, didn't want them to become estranged, but worried that pushing Becca into more contact at this stage would be counterproductive.

'An NCA cop called me,' Shona said. 'They're investigating Delfont's organised crime connections in conjunction with his murder.'

Rob was unaware of Shona and Thalia's role in Delfont's demise, and she intended to keep it that way.

'But that's brilliant!' Rob exclaimed. 'They're bound to find something that proves he targeted me to keep you quiet about his corruption.'

Shona almost responded, *If you hadn't been distracted by shagging your assistant, you might have noticed your banking team was money laundering*, but she bit it back. It was Shona's discovery of the affair, not Rob's imprisonment, that had dealt their marriage its fatal blow.

'Well, we'll see,' Shona said. 'I'll call your barrister if I hear anything more.'

'And I'm not happy with the financial projections from your friend James,' Rob said, sourly. 'What does an actor know about running a business like ours?'

'His £250K investment means we still have a business,' she retorted, knowing he was baiting her. Her relationship with James wasn't revenge for Rob's affair, but she could see why he'd think it was. She decided against mentioning that it was Rob's gambling that had almost bankrupted them.

'You should be grateful,' she said evenly, 'that you still have a share of a viable business thanks to Becca and myself, and countless others who've helped us, including James.' It would be years before Rob got parole and she didn't want to think that far ahead. And with James back in America, she didn't know where their relationship was going. High Pines was not just her business, it was her home, her community. Now it was tied to two men, either of whom could pull the plug on her life – her daughter's life, too.

Beeping on the line signalled that Rob's phone-card credit was running out.

'I miss you…' he began, and the line went dead.

Chapter 8

The next morning, Shona and Murdo met in the carpark at Cornwall Mount, then set off in his Astra to interview the chair of the triathlon club and discover if there was anything he could tell them in the light of Slasher Sue's revelations. The night before, partly in preparation for the interview and partly to empty her mind of the anger churned up by Rob's phone call, Shona had looked through the triathlon stats and league tables. She wanted to understand Hayley's world, what her motivations might be. As they drove through the heavy Tuesday morning traffic, she updated Murdo on what she'd found. Most of the top athletes were based in Glasgow, Edinburgh or the Highlands. Hayley was head and shoulders above anyone locally.

'You think one of her teammates could be involved?' Murdo said, pulling out to overtake a parked bus.

'I was thinking about the race timing last night. Access to the athletes' area was restricted by marshals from about thirty minutes before the race. They only let me in 'cos I was wearing my RNLI immersion suit. GHB acts within twenty minutes. It must have got into her system while she was in the transition area.'

'No CCTV there, I'm betting,' Murdo said as they turned up a driveway and Shona saw the sign for a private health club.

She shook her head. 'But plenty of people were recording on their phones and doing selfies. Let's ask the triathlon club to round up what the members shot.'

In addition to being chairman of the triathlon club, Gordon Anderson was the manager of the Elite Health Spa. Shona recognised him as the fit man in his sixties who'd taken charge of the competitors' phones at the race. He'd swapped his triathlon team polo shirt for a navy version embroidered with a silver leaping salmon, the spa's logo. He showed no sign of remembering her, but she supposed she looked a little different in her smart dark suit and smooth bob.

He led them into a comfortable lounge overlooking a swimming pool with two lanes marked off. A few people were in the water, swimming lengths.

Shona outlined why they were there. When she mentioned performance-enhancing drugs, his face paled beneath his suntan and he looked horrified.

'Of course I can ask for phone footage and pictures, but I want to make it clear: our club members are keen amateurs. The idea that they'd engage in illegal behaviour, do potential damage to themselves or risk their lives just to be crowned "king of the glens" is just unthinkable.'

But Shona, a runner herself, understood how obsession might take over. How, beyond competitiveness, self-worth and self-image can become bound up in being faster, fitter.

'You can test-screen the whole club if that will convince you,' he added, seeming genuinely shocked and puzzled.

'That won't be necessary, Mr Anderson.' She smiled. She'd have dearly loved to take him up on his offer but could think of no legal mechanism, or indeed budget, to achieve it.

'Can you tell me about Hayley's relationship with other members?'

'There's a group who all work shifts, so they arrange to train together. John Paul Burns, Gail Livingstone and Mari Watt.'

Shona saw Murdo jot down the names, all familiar to her from the local leader board.

'And did they all get on?'

'Aye. Mari's one of our biggest fundraisers.'

'So, the club is important to her?'

He gave her a puzzled look. 'Oh, aye. But it's important to loads of folk.'

'And Hayley never talked to you about being threatened?'
'Never.'
'And you never heard of anything that concerned you?'

Shona left the question deliberately open, knowing that at times like these it was the apparently unconnected incident, the nail sticking up in a sea of floorboards, that often snagged the memory.

But he just shook his head. 'Like what?'

'Someone asking questions that seemed odd? Members reporting an unfriendly encounter out on a training run? An aggrieved motorist?' Shona stopped and looked enquiringly at the chair, but it seemed he had nothing else to add.

She took out her wallet and handed him a card with her contact number on it.

'If something occurs to you, no matter how small, I'd appreciate you giving me a call. And please don't discuss anything we've talked about today with the media.'

He shook his head vigorously, as if the very idea of any conversation that involved doping would taint his club permanently. If Professor Kitchen turned out to be right, then it was something he'd have to deal with sooner rather than later.

'There was one thing. It's very likely nothing,' he warned, but it was as if his desire to be seen to fully co-operate, and thereby exonerate the reputation of his club, had overtaken him. 'Hayley and Mari did have... well, not exactly a falling-out,' he stressed. 'Mari wanted to organise a long-term fundraiser over the next year. Hayley joked – how did she know we'd all still be here in a year? Mari thought it went against the spirit of the club, you know, commitment and that. I thought it was an unconscious slip, that maybe Hayley was turning professional, and I think some of the others maybe guessed that too. It was all smoothed over, but you know...'

'When was this?'

'About two months back.'

'How did you feel about the prospect of Hayley moving on?'

'If she wanted to turn pro, I was all for it. Can you imagine what it would do for our membership if she made the World Championships? Not to mention our ability to get funding for community projects.'

It was the most animated Shona had seen him since they'd arrived, but then his expression clouded as he realised this particular dream would never happen.

It seemed Anderson had nothing to gain and everything to lose by Hayley's death; Shona discounted him from her list of potential suspects. They said their goodbyes and Shona left him staring out over the pool.

'Boss,' Murdo said as they went back down the steps to the gravelled carpark. He tilted his phone screen towards her, and she saw he'd pulled up a Facebook page.

Shona's eyes focused on a familiar face. The woman stood smiling at the far end of a line of wetsuited figures, Kate and Hayley among them.

'This is Mari Watt. Ye ken her?'

Shona checked the date and timestamp. It was the picture she'd taken with Hayley's phone. It must have been uploaded before the start of Saturday's race. She remembered how the woman had been coaxed into joining the group, and had made a wide loop to avoid standing next to Hayley.

Murdo tapped on her profile, his thumb resting on Mari's occupation.

'She's an oncology nurse?' Shona stared at Murdo. Mari Watt would have both the access and the knowledge to pull off something like this. 'We need to have a word with her.'

'Aye,' said Murdo. 'I was thinking that myself.'

—

That afternoon, back in the office, Murdo got everyone into the conference room. Shona updated them on what the triathlon chairman had said about the falling-out, which Shona had confirmed with the two other members of the shift workers' running group – Gail Livingstone and John Paul Burns – though Hayley hadn't confided in them about any threats.

'But Mari was Hayley's friend. And it wasn't really a falling-out.' Kate was indignant. 'She's a children's cancer nurse, for God's sake.'

'There are several recent cases I could refer you to, DC Irving, which would mitigate that assumption.' Shona could see the headline: *Angel of Death Strikes at Triathlon*. 'Mari Watt is a person of interest.' She turned to include her sergeant in the conversation. 'Murdo's already talked to the hospital.'

'Aye,' he confirmed. 'They're saying she's never been subject to disciplinary proceedings, but we've only got their word for that at the minute.'

'So, Kate, you know Mari Watt – all the background you can get, please,' Shona said. 'We'll interview her later this afternoon after her shift finishes. How did you get on this morning?' She switched her gaze between Ravi and Kate, who were sitting at opposite sides of the table.

Kate cleared her throat, but Ravi got in first. 'Andy could give us no reason for Hayley to own an EpiPen.'

Kate was leaning forward, elbows on the table, a look of suppressed excitement on her face. 'Andy said if it *was* murder,' she added quickly, 'there was someone who could be involved. A property developer, Jack Kennedy. He'd made threats against Hayley after she arrested him for breach of the peace.'

Shona raised her eyebrows at Murdo, who nodded. 'I know the name. St Aiden's Park development.'

Ravi shifted in his seat, his body language indicating to Shona that he was less than invested in this line of inquiry. 'There's a record of Kennedy's arrest, but no one else in uniform seems to know about these threats,' he said.

'But it might not be something you'd share with your colleagues,' Kate insisted.

Shona agreed. As a female officer, Hayley may have believed it would look weak if she couldn't handle the aggro, although it was possible she'd confide in her partner at home.

'What about Hayley's beat partner? Has anyone spoken to her?'

'PC Joanne Mitchell,' Ravi said. 'I gave her a call. She remembers the arrest but doesn't know anything about threats made afterwards.'

'Did Hayley ever mention anything about it to you?' Shona asked, but Kate shook her head.

'Kennedy went before the sheriff and was fined.' Ravi consulted his notebook. 'There was a scuffle outside a restaurant and the owner called us 'cos he was worried his window would get panned in. Kennedy's solicitor claimed his client was a respectable businessman. He apologised to the court. Drink was taken, as the saying goes.'

Most people would label this kind of behaviour high jinks, Shona thought. It might even have enhanced his reputation. She was aware that if Kennedy had been a business*woman*, then public opinion would have been more critical, her reputation severely damaged. A drunk man was just high spirits. A drunk woman showed a lack of restraint and judgement.

Ravi shook his head, ignoring Kate's scowl. 'He's a previously clean record. If he wasn't happy with Hayley's actions, why not make a complaint about her through official lines? I bet he has contacts. Injecting her with GHB seems a bit elaborate.'

'D'you think Andy's lying?' Kate hit back.

'I think Andy Purdy, in his grief, is looking for someone to blame for Hayley's death. Preferably someone who isn't Hayley.'

Kate jabbed her pen angrily at Ravi. 'We found nothing at the house. She wasn't doping.'

'Absence of evidence isn't evidence of absence,' Ravi shot back.

Shona, who'd begun to feel like a referee in a grudge-ridden tennis match, thought it wasn't the right time to remind Kate of the historic injection marks. Sue's toxicology results would put that to bed, one way or another.

Shona held up her hand. 'I agree Kennedy does not appear to have a strong enough motive.'

Ravi smirked victoriously at Kate, a move Shona was sure he'd deployed on his four older sisters growing up. It was a miracle he'd made it to adulthood. Shona frowned at him, and he took the hint, moderating his expression.

'He's not among the triathlon competitors, is he?' Shona directed her question to Hannah, who consulted her tablet, then shook her head. 'How many have we still to interview?'

'We've found five more,' Chloe said.

'And the other three?'

'Not yet.'

'Could be system glitches,' Vinny said. 'Or they could've given false details.'

Shona looked back pointedly at Chloe; it wasn't what she wanted to hear.

'We'll keep looking,' Chloe said.

'We do need to interview Jack Kennedy and establish his whereabouts. Even if it's just to eliminate him.'

It was Kate's turn to look smug.

'Ravi,' Shona said, 'get on to his office and see if he's around for a chat.'

With the lack of any drug finds at Hayley's home, it was becoming obvious to Shona that confirming, or excluding, self-administration was going to take longer than she'd hoped.

'Okay, leaving Mr Kennedy aside, is there anyone else who posed a potential threat to Hayley? Murdo, you said she was estranged from her family?'

'Aye. Her father Clem and her three brothers were at home on Saturday. When I gave them the news, Clem's words were: "She was dead to us when she joined the cops."'

'I don't know this family.' Shona frowned. 'Is there any criminal intelligence on them?' If there wasn't, it could mean they just hadn't done anything significant enough to catch her eye yet.

'The Camerons are mair like an old established family business.'

'And that business would be?'

'Anything that isnae nailed down. The grandfather could get you whatever you wanted, and his grandfather was reputed to be a successful whisky smuggler during prohibition.'

'Is it credible they could be involved in her death?'

'If she'd been run over or someone torched her house, mibbaes. But why now and why this method? I cannae mind there ever being a case where a police officer's been targeted like this.'

To be fair, Shona couldn't either. 'What's her family's link with drugs?'

'Rumours are they're small-time dealers. I've nothing tae back that up. Nane o' the main family members has ever been charged with anything. The mother was local, but Clem is fae Cumbria originally, but he's been here forty-odd years. I think there's an uncle in Carlisle jail that's a bit of a player. I can ask Dan tae give us what he can.'

DS Dan Ridley, from the English side of the border, had worked with Shona's team previously and was well liked. She thought him a talented and intuitive detective and, although he was a decade younger, they'd become friends. They shared an outlook that put people at the heart of policing. Shona also had a more personal reason to trust him. When she'd really needed his help, he'd come through for her: he was the only person, other than skipper Tommy McCall, who knew she'd been in Cumbria the night Delfont died.

'Are the family important to the investigation? Hayley didn't talk to them,' Kate said.

'Dumfries is a small town,' Murdo replied. 'Bound to bump into them sometime.'

Kate opened her mouth, then closed it again.

'What?' Shona said.

'When we were out a couple of weeks ago, Hayley saw her wee sister in the pub. Had an argument.'

'How much of an argument?'

'I didn't overhear what was said, but Hayley told me it was nothing.'

'And you didn't think to mention this before?' Shona said, severely.

Kate looked crestfallen and Shona regretted her sharpness.

'Look, it's fine,' Shona reassured her. 'It raises an important point. Hannah, set up a timeline for Hayley's death. Vinny, can you incorporate the Garmin data into that?' When Vinny nodded, she continued, 'Anything you find, folks, fill it in.'

Chapter 9

The triathlon chairman had been as good as his word. That afternoon, phone video and stills began flooding in, adding substantially to the workload of the already stretched civilian support team. The now-crowded office felt stuffy and overheated, a late-afternoon listlessness punctuated by the soft clacking of the vertical blinds stirring in the faint breeze from the open windows. They'd long since given up on the air conditioning. Shona had sent repeated emails and made calls to building services, and although someone turned up intermittently, it never improved.

Vinny and Chloe were accessing metadata for each video clip or image and logging it into chronological order, producing a fractured visual jigsaw of the day of the triathlon.

Shona abandoned her jacket over the back of her chair and prowled their workstations, stopping periodically to study wetsuit-clad figures giving thumbs ups to the camera, fetish-level videos of bikes, and influencer-style clips on the best trainers. She wasn't sure what she was looking for, but in the absence of CCTV, it was all they had. It felt pointless, a make-work exercise, but experience had taught her that in 95 per cent of cases, attention to detail proved the difference between success and failure. The other 5 per cent was generally luck, and they needed that in spades.

Shona returned to her office and took a gulp from her water bottle. She'd told Vinny to prioritise material from the twenty minutes before the race, especially any images of Hayley. Hannah was collating and cross-referencing statements from people in the transition area at that time, but that was practically every competitor, plus the support staff. Shona rolled the cool bottle against her forehead, searching her mind for any overlooked way to pin down the precise time when Hayley might have been injected. Kate couldn't remember any suspicious incident, but Shona wondered if asking her again might shake something loose.

Through her open office door, Shona saw Murdo shoot to his feet. She glanced at the wall clock. They were due at Mari Watt's house shortly, but they weren't late. Background checks hadn't turned up anything useful, but the sheriff had granted a search warrant and Shona was keen to get it executed early enough to minimise disruption to the woman's two young children, aged five and six.

Murdo crossed the office in a rush sufficient to free his shirt tails from the waistband of his suit trousers, but he made no attempt to tuck them back in.

'Boss.' He held up his phone, his face and tone grave. 'I've had a call. A seventeen-year-old girl has been found unresponsive at The Secret Forest. Suspected overdose.'

Shona was on her feet so fast that her chair went over.

She snatched up her phone and called Becca, but it went straight to voicemail. The panic in her chest was like a trapped bird, and she was finding it harder and harder to breathe. Her daughter had dutifully texted her once a day, so why wasn't she answering now? Shona had refrained from raising specific queries – *are you eating? Are you sleeping? How much have you had to drink?* – reasoning that it was a necessary first step on the road to independence for both of them. It hadn't stopped her worrying and now her fears were proving justified.

She dragged her chair upright, untangled her jacket. 'We need to get over there.'

Murdo's phone rang. He answered and held up his hand.

'We've got a name. Erin Dunlop. Address in Dumfries.'

Shona leaned against the side of her desk and let out a long breath. Thank God. It wasn't Becca. Almost immediately, the guilty flipside of relief flooded into the space left by her fading terror. It wasn't her daughter, but it was someone else's.

'Sorry, Murdo,' she said straightening up and rubbing her hands across her face.

'No, I'm sorry. I kenned Becca was at the festival. I shouldnae have made you feart like that. Didnae know we'd get a name quick and…'

It was obvious the same thought had crossed both their minds.

Shona bit her lip, moved by his concern. He'd always had a soft spot for Becca. He and his wife Joan had numerous godchildren, but no bairns of their own. Shona knew she could always rely on Murdo. Now, she realised, Becca could always rely on him too.

'Thank you, Murdo,' she said quietly.

'Aye, well…' he began gruffly. 'Nae bother. I'll round up the team.'

—

Erin Dunlop's body had been discovered in her tent that afternoon. Earlier, her friends had split into two groups to pursue different activities, and each had assumed she'd been with the others. When they'd realised she was missing, they'd returned to the campsite and made the horrifying discovery.

When Shona arrived at the old RAF Dumfries base with Kate and Murdo, they were taken to the camping area by festival security in an all-electric SUV driven by a young woman called Pippa, who had bright pink hair and a Home Counties accent. In the middle of a small loch, built to retain water for firefighting during World War Two, stood a huge wicker-and-straw sculpture.

'That's Glaistig,' Pippa said.

The figure was half-woman, half-goat, the lower part of its hybrid form partially hidden by a flowing green dress.

Murdo leaned forward from the rear seat. 'She's a spirit o' the hunt, vengeful to hunters who kill hinds instead o' stags, or helpful, watching over bairns who stray away from their mothers.'

'She wasn't very watchful on this occasion,' muttered Shona.

'We burn her at the end of the festival,' Pippa said, flatly.

Murdo and Kate went off to talk to the victim's friends, while Shona waited for the forensic pathologist in the wooded area dubbed *The Sleep Zone*.

As she waited, she tried Becca's number again – straight to voicemail – but felt only irritation rather than anxiety. There wasn't time for anything other than a brief word, which she felt, in the circumstances, would be reassuring for both of them. And Becca must have known that her mother would be worried. The campsite area had been taped off. News of the death had to be all around the festival by now. With the exception of the forensic wagon, the police vehicles had remained in the site carpark, but they were highly visible all the same.

The paramedics had pulled Erin from the small blue tent and attempted to resuscitate her. Her body lay covered by a sheet until scenes-of-crime-officers got there with their forensic tent. Shona slipped on gloves and pulled the cloth back, briefly studying the girl's face and hands. Clad in a T-shirt and cut-off jeans, she looked younger than her seventeen years. Shona patted the front pockets of the girl's shorts, but they were empty. Then she remembered they'd already established identity. Any personal possessions found by the paramedics would already have been bagged by uniform.

She let the sheet fall back and turned to pull back the tent flap. The smell of rotting fruit and vomit filled the enclosed space, and there were already flies buzzing. Half the floor was taken up by an airbed and sleeping bag; the other half was filled with a jumble of clothes, rucksack, a cardboard takeaway food box and a refillable drinks container. She gently examined the area with an outstretched finger. The girl's phone was missing

– Shona thought that suspicious – although an expensive-looking camera lay untouched. Nothing in the tent suggested violence. Shona sat back on her heels and let the flap fall shut. She knew from Becca's own lack of kit that the campsite had been pre-pitched, utilising reclaimed tents to reduce single-use purchases, and the organisers hadn't wasted any space. She guessed this was the maximum density the fire service would allow, but it was to her investigation's advantage. The proximity of other tents might yield some witnesses – even if they didn't realise at the time what they had heard or seen.

Shona was a little disappointed to find the attending pathologist wasn't Slasher Sue, even though she realised that as energetic as the professor was, she couldn't be everywhere. Instead, it was a new face, and when he introduced himself as Ivan Jones, Shona detected the hint of a South Wales accent. She peeled off her gloves and they shook hands. He was tall, with powerful shoulders and close-cropped sandy hair, and Shona wondered if he was also a rower. After all, physical strength was surely an asset in pathology – more so, perhaps, than in other areas of medicine – when it came to handling patients.

'She's been dead at least a couple of hours,' he said, straightening from his examination of the body. 'It's a warm day, so rigor will have progressed quickly. I can't be more accurate than that.'

'Any sign of violence?' Shona said.

'No indication of strangulation. Fully clothed. No obvious defence injuries on her hands. The marks on her face are from post-mortem changes, not bruises. I'm guessing she was found curled up on her side before the paramedics arrived.'

It confirmed what Shona had thought. 'Likely cause of death?'

'I'll need to do the full exam but the indication of emesis around the nose and mouth suggests choking. And given what Professor Kitchen is already working on, I think toxicology will be issuing you with a loyalty card at this rate,' he said pointedly.

He'd come to the same conclusion as Shona: Erin Dunlop's death was likely drug-related.

Shona thanked him and arranged a time for the post-mortem the following day.

'The professor sends her regards, by the way. Sorry she couldn't attend but she's in court tomorrow.' He paused. 'I hear you lot call her "Slasher Sue".' He grinned, displaying two rows of perfect white teeth. 'That's a tidy nickname, that is. I hope you'll go easy when it comes to mine.'

Shona smiled. It would likely be Ravi who'd coin a name that stuck. 'Not in my power, I'm afraid. But if you prioritise the toxicology, I'll put in a good word for you.'

—

Pippa drove Shona to a roped-off area of the chill-out zone, where witnesses had been gathered beneath sail-like sunshades. Shona passed chalkboards offering tarot reading, candle making and a Japanese fan workshop, and saw Murdo and Kate, heads bent over their tablets, taking statements from Erin Dunlop's friends. To Shona's surprise and irritation, Becca was perched on a straw bale off to one side, chewing her nails. She jumped up when she saw her mother approaching.

'I knew you'd be looking for me. I didn't want you to have to search,' Becca said, stopping a discreet distance away. Shona felt slightly disappointed that her daughter didn't come in for a hug.

'Why didn't you call me?' Shona demanded while speed-assessing her daughter's demeanour and appearance, and finding no sign of pallor, dilated pupils or drowsiness. Or indeed, contrition.

'My phone's locked up at the charge spot. I didn't get the chance to go back for it after Christie found Erin.'

It struck Shona that this also might be the location of Erin's missing phone. If nothing valuable had been taken, she could discount theft as a possible motive, and it pointed to her being alone when she died.

'And Murdo didn't tell you I was calling?' Shona was aware she sounded more like an aggrieved parent at school pick-up than the SIO on a sudden death.

'He called you.'

Shona pulled out her phone. She'd put it on silent when the pathologist had arrived so she could concentrate on his findings. There were three missed calls, a voicemail and a text – all from Murdo.

'It's okay, Mum. I get it,' Becca said, but still didn't step any closer.

'I'm sorry, darlin',' Shona said with genuine remorse, the final tide of irritation draining from her. 'Was she your friend?'

'Not really.' Becca glanced over her shoulder. Three girls sitting together on the far side of the circular enclosure were watching her. 'I know Christie, and Amy and Sophie. Erin had a place to do photography at City of Glasgow College. We're all in a Facebook page for students going from here.'

'When did you realise that she wasn't with you?'

Becca sat down heavily on the straw bale.

'It's not like a lot of festivals,' Becca began. 'Most stuff is on in the daytime to minimise power use. Some of us were at The Clearing – that's the main stage where the bands and the DJ sets are. Erin was there when we had pizza at lunch. The others went to check out the climbing wall and do yoga with goats. That's where we thought she was. We all came back to chill out at about four p.m. Mine's the red tent next to Erin's.'

'Did you see her take anything?' Shona said, lowering her voice.

'No. A few beers. That's all.'

It was like a shutter had come down. Shona couldn't tell if it was the truth but if she pressed her daughter in front of her friends, she'd get nothing more. The three girls were still watching the exchange, occasionally whispering to one another behind their hands in a way that took Shona straight back to the teenage playground.

'Do you want to come home?'

'Now?' Becca asked with something like panic.

'If you want.'

'I can't, Mum. What about my friends?'

'They might want to go home too. You've all had a terrible experience.'

'They don't. We want to be here for each other,' Becca retorted, glancing once more towards the other girls. 'Are we done?'

'Do they know I'm your mother?' Shona said.

'They might,' Becca replied evasively. 'Can I go?'

Shona watched her daughter walk over to her friends and sit down without looking back.

She had a vision of Becca as a child, aged four or five, running up and down the long hallway in their Camden flat. The dull thuds of her stockinged feet sounded on the polished wooden floor, and Shona's police hat kept falling over her eyes as her loud mee-maws mimicked a squad car siren. Was that the last time she'd been proud that her mum was a cop?

She felt a lump of something akin to grief come into her throat. Until that moment, Shona's concern had been that this experience would make Becca clingier. She was blindsided to find the opposite was apparently true.

Chapter 10

Shona left Murdo at the festival site, suggesting he look among Erin's possessions for a locker key that might lead them to her phone at the charge spot. She took Kate with her to inform Erin's mother.

No officer liked the death knock, and many considered it the worst part of the job. Shona couldn't change what she was about to tell her, but she deserved the respect of hearing it, face to face, from the senior investigating officer. If it lessened the pain of such dreadful news, even by the tiniest amount, then it would be worth it.

Sandra Dunlop's house was on a 1970s ex-council estate close to the river. In addition to Erin, there was Sandra's partner, Peter Anderson, registered as living there. The harled walls on the end terrace had recently been painted white; a hedge and lawn in the small front garden were both neatly clipped. When Shona opened the front gate, a figure came to the kitchen window and briefly lifted the net curtain, before dropping it back into place. There was a delay after Shona rang the bell. Both she and Kate had put on their suit jackets, despite the heat, and were wearing their police ID cards on lanyards. People reacted differently. Some rushed towards anticipated bad news, desperate to be proved wrong. Others hung back, extending the last seconds before the axe fell.

'Mrs Dunlop? I'm Detective Inspector Shona Oliver and this is DC Kate Irving. May we come in?'

'Oh, God. Tell me. Is it Peter?' Sandra Dunlop was small and slim, in a geometric print summer dress. Her smooth dark hair in a side-parting was a match for her daughter's.

'Peter is fine,' Shona said softly. 'May we come in?'

The woman's hand flew to her mouth.

'Oh my God, it is Erin, isn't it? Is she... Is she?'

Shona stepped quickly forward and took her arm, as Sandra slumped back against the flowered wallpaper of the hallway.

'I'm okay. I'm okay.'

She patently wasn't, and Shona knew she had about thirty seconds before the initial shock turned to full realisation and things got a lot worse.

'Kate.' Shona tilted her head to the kitchen and then, gripping Sandra by the elbow and encircling her waist with her other arm, guided her into the lounge and onto a sofa, sitting down next to her. 'I'm so sorry, Mrs Dunlop. We'll get you some tea. I'm going to talk you through what's happened and what happens next.'

The lounge looked out through open patio doors to a garden covered in artificial grass and children's play equipment. As far as Shona knew, Erin had been an only child, but perhaps she'd got that wrong.

'Are you on your own, Mrs Dunlop? Is there anyone else here? Where's Peter?'

'He's at work.' She saw Shona looking outside. 'I'm a childminder. The wee ones are away home. I thought you were Kirsty, back to pick up Jack's blanket, he...' Suddenly, she began taking great gulps of air. 'What's happened to Erin?'

Shona leaned forward and took the woman's trembling hand. 'I'm sorry to tell you she was found dead at The Secret Forest festival this afternoon. At this stage we don't believe she was the victim of violence, but she may have taken a substance that caused her to fall unconscious and choke.'

It was best to get it all out at once. When a young woman dies suddenly, murder and sexual violence are often the parents' immediate conclusions. Shona wanted to spare her those thoughts at least.

Kate brought tea, and Shona took the packet of tissues from her bag. The three women sat in the well-kept room with its pale grey walls, mustard-coloured sofa, toy boxes and framed black-and-white photographs, until the initial storm of grief had passed.

'When can I see her?' Sandra's sobs were easing.

It was generally the first question relatives asked in this situation. Shona had experienced this same scene too many times, and it never got any easier.

'This evening. Erin's father…'

'Peter's her stepdad,' Sandra said, wiping her eyes. 'Her father lives in Carlisle. His name's Ian. Ian Dunlop.'

'Would you like Kate to call Peter and ask him to come home? Our colleagues in Cumbria can tell Ian what's happened, if you'd like?'

'Aye. That would be good.' Sandra unlocked her phone and handed it to Kate so she could copy both numbers. 'Her father left about two years ago. Erin was very angry. I was trying to keep her in line, best I could.'

Kate left the room and Shona could hear her in the hall, making the calls.

'Erin's no' long back from living in Carlisle. Said she wanted to live wi' her dad. Mixing wi' a rough crowd there, she was. I wasnae happy. Think she got intae drugs when she was there. Then she fell out with him. I got her home. She got clean when she was here. If it's drugs, it'll be them fae Carlisle that's responsible.'

Shona thought about her own daughter's reaction to her father's absence. At first Becca had clung to him – visits, phone calls, letters – but then things had changed. It hadn't been Rob's choice to go to prison, just the result of his previous poor decisions, but Becca blamed him just the same.

'Recently, Erin seemed tae turn a corner,' Sandra said. 'Got interested in photography, was doing really well. All of them photos are hers.'

She pointed a still-shaking hand at the framed images on the wall and there was pride in her voice.

Shona saw the pictures were close-ups of seashells and pine cones, and a landscape shot taken on a beach she recognised as Port o' Warren, on the Solway Firth. 'They're beautiful,' she said.

There was a flicker of a smile from Sandra, but it was quickly eclipsed once more by grief. 'She talked to me an' I really listened. What did I miss? Why would she go back tae drugs? I just dinnae understand.'

Shona knew how that felt. How often did she watch her daughter from the corner of her eye, trying to solve the persistent maternal question of how Becca *really was*, beneath what she chose to reveal.

DS Dan Ridley could help them with the Carlisle link; she made a note to get Murdo to call him later.

Kate came back into the room. 'D'you want me to organise a search team for here?'

Shona frowned at her. 'This isn't a crime scene, so it won't be necessary.'

'But drugs—' Kate began.

'Not necessary,' Shona repeated. She knew what her DC was thinking: *You searched Hayley's house, so why not here?* But the two cases were poles apart, and if Kate had been thinking clearly, she'd have seen it.

Shona turned back to Sandra and gave her a reassuring smile. 'If she had a laptop or an iPad-type device it might help us find out who she's been in contact with. You'll get everything back. I promise we'll find out what happened to your daughter.'

'Her laptop's upstairs.' Sandra eyed Kate as if she didn't trust her not to ransack her dead daughter's room.

'Do you feel up to fetching it?' Shona said. 'Then we'll arrange for you to go to the hospital. Is Peter on his way, Kate?'

Kate, who'd loitered by the door and not retaken her seat, as if she couldn't wait to be out of the house, looked up distractedly from her phone screen. 'What? Yes. He's coming.'

Sandra got to her feet wearily. When Shona heard her reach the top of the stairs, she rounded on Kate. Her offhand manner was tactless and showed no concern for Sandra's emotional state. 'What is the matter with you?'

Kate stared at her boss. 'Nothing.'

'I think it's best you go outside and wait for Peter Anderson to arrive.'

'I don't know what he looks like.'

'Kate,' Shona said, trying to moderate the exasperation in her voice. 'If you can't recognise a distressed member of the public outside his own front door then you're in the wrong job.'

Kate flushed but said nothing.

Shona had been intending to ask Kate to remain with Sandra and act as family liaison officer, taking both her and Peter up to the hospital mortuary and keeping them informed throughout the investigation; she saw now that would be impossible.

Peter Anderson's car arrived a few minutes later. He sobbed when he first heard the news, trying to comfort Sandra even as he struggled to contain his own grief. Shona thought theirs was a close and loving partnership, but Erin had obviously been the centre of their lives. She stayed with the couple until the point she felt they needed some privacy. A car would come for them. Ravi would have to act as their family liaison officer until Shona could figure out what else could be done.

When Kate got into the Audi's passenger seat, Shona turned to her.

'You need to take some time off.' God knows, they couldn't afford to lose a DC now, with two investigations running.

'That's your solution to me raising questions about the investigation? You're grounding me?' Kate replied. 'I was being proactive, I thought you encouraged that. You've said it often enough.' Kate's voice was laden with sarcasm.

It was like dealing with Becca when she was fourteen. Why didn't Kate get it? She needed to grow up. *Do you want to think about what you've just said, young lady?* It was on the tip of her tongue, but she caught herself just in time. Instead, she said nothing, her furious expression enough to send scarlet flames up Kate's pale cheeks.

Kate's eyes widened as she realised that she'd crossed a line. 'I'm... I'm sorry... boss. I don't know what's wrong with me.'

Shona took a deep breath, aware her own reaction had been driven as much by Erin's death and her worries about Becca as it had by Kate's behaviour. Kate wasn't a teenager, but a grown woman who'd experienced a terrible loss.

'It's grief, Kate. Sometimes grief is the fuel that powers you. Sometimes it's what drags you down. I don't think you've processed what happened. And apart from tactlessly adding to the distress of a woman who's just lost her daughter, I think it may also be preventing you remembering things that could be important about Hayley's death.'

Shona half-expected Kate to react angrily, but instead she just nodded.

'I've gone over and over what happened before the race.' She shook her head. 'There's nothing. Someone murdered my best friend right before my eyes, and I missed it. What sort of police officer... What sort of detective does that make me?'

Shona knew both Kate and Hayley were ambitious, driven individuals; perhaps that had been the foundation of their friendship, more than the job or triathlons. Hayley's death had cut at the root of who Kate was, and Shona should have seen it.

'Don't put me on leave, boss. Because if I can't be part of this case, I may as well pack it in.'

If she'd been in Kate's position, she'd have said exactly the same thing. It was this, more than any apology Kate could have made, that swung the balance in her favour.

'What about the incident with Hayley's sister?'

'I was in the toilets, helping someone who'd been sick. I didn't see what happened.'

'Okay,' Shona said, starting the engine. Her idea that reinterviewing Kate herself might result in some forgotten crucial detail now seemed futile. Kate had gone over and over events in her mind, much as Shona would have done herself. There was nothing else to be found. 'Go home. Get some rest. We'll start again tomorrow.'

Shona had meant what she'd said to Erin's mother, the calm assurances she'd given that there would be resolution and justice. But she knew that wasn't always possible. So far, they'd very little to go on. No witnesses, no suspects. As she glanced back at the terrace house, with its neat garden and fresh paintwork, she wondered if she'd pass it in years to come – the flowers faded, paintwork peeling – and ask herself if she could have done more to find the people who'd sold Erin the drugs and casually snuffed out her life.

—

After the heat of the day, a cool dampness had rolled into Kirkness from the sea, sending all but a few hardy holidaymakers scurrying indoors. As Shona drove along the empty shore road, taking the left turn up the hill to High Pines, Murdo called her to confirm they'd recovered Erin's phone from the charging point and to remind her that he'd rescheduled the visit to the oncology nurse, and Hayley's fellow triathlete, Mari Watt's house for the following morning.

At High Pines, Shona found Freya folding sheets in the utility room. Even the dash from the car had chilled her, and the sudden warmth and scent of fresh linen were comforting.

'I heard about the trouble at yon festival,' Freya said.

'Becca knew the lassie. I asked her to come home, but she won't.'

Freya looked Shona over with a practised eye. 'Sit doon and I'll make you a peedie bite to eat.'

Shona just wanted to fall face-first into bed, but she knew she'd probably wake in the small hours, hungry, thirsty and unable to get back to sleep. Freya was pushing her towards the kitchen and she suddenly found she didn't have the energy to resist.

'Thank you, Freya. I'm not sure I've much in,' she said, collapsing into a chair.

Freya studied the near-empty fridge, finally gathering up the bare makings of a mushroom omelette. She set a half-full bottle of chilled white wine on the table.

Shona leaned back and took two glasses from the dresser. 'Everything going okay with the guests?'

'All grand. You know, it's good that Becca doesn't want to come home, don't you think?'

'I suppose.' Shona filled the glasses. 'She doesn't want to leave her friends.'

'That's a positive sign, surely?'

Freya was right. It was a sign that Becca was finding some independence. Hadn't Shona been concerned about that ever since her student place in Glasgow was confirmed?

'I can't stop worrying about her.'

'You were never going to dae that anyway,' Freya said with a wry smile.

Shona smiled too. It was an inevitable part of parenting. *Cognitive dissonance*, the police psychologists called it. Being able to hold two opposing views at the same time. Wanting Becca to steer her own course, but also wanting her to remain dependent on her mother's guidance. There was a balance to be struck, Shona knew, but it was proving a painful process. Witnessing Sandra Dunlop's grief today hadn't made it any easier.

Freya put the omelette in front of her and she found she was ravenous, having eaten nothing but biscuits all day. If anything, Erin's death should serve as an unfortunate but timely warning about the dangers that drugs presented and make Becca more careful.

'Somebody else who can't stop worrying is Tommy,' Freya said quietly.

Shona took a moment to chew and swallow her mouthful of omelette, and it occurred to her that Freya might have been waiting for her to come home so that she could raise the investigation into Hayley's death with her.

'Tell him not to worry,' she said, knowing that was probably futile. 'I can't discuss specifics about the case… but we think Hayley might have been deliberately targeted. That doesn't go any further than you and him,' she emphasised. 'No inquiry by the RNLI or Triathlon Scotland, or anyone else, can begin until I find out what happened. And I will find out.'

'Targeted? What d'you mean?' Freya's frown deepened.

Shona had hoped to reassure Freya that Tommy was in the clear, but her words had had the opposite effect.

'I can't say any more, but it's not something Tommy, or any of the organisers, could have predicted.'

Freya nodded, apparently satisfied by Shona's assurances.

After a brief pause, Freya said, 'Is it right you're cooking with James?' She made it sound like Shona was indulging in Satanic practices.

'So much for Tommy keeping things quiet.' Shona took another mouthful and rolled her eyes, glad that the conversation was taking a new direction but apprehensive about what Freya might say next.

'I think he was in shock and had to tell someone. It'll go no further. How are you managing with the cooking?'

'Not that well,' Shona admitted.

'Oh, aye.' Freya inclined her head towards the fridge, signalling she could see that for herself. 'What are you trying next?'

'Pasta of some kind. James gets the ingredients delivered by some organic whatsit company.'

'Why don't we go through it beforehand? I can give you some pointers. It's no' cheating.'

'Freya, you're going to show me how to cook to impress a man that isn't even on the same continent and who isn't going to eat it?'

'Och no!' Freya flapped a tea towel at her. 'No' for his benefit. It's for yours.'

Shona thought for a moment, remembering some of the disasters she'd been faced with on previous Sunday nights. And she'd welcome the company.

'I can't argue with that. But I've always said this about you, Freya: you're an optimist.'

Chapter 11

Next morning, Shona and Murdo waited until Mari Watt had returned from dropping her daughters off at school.

Mari didn't seem perturbed when they introduced themselves and explained they were making enquiries into Hayley's death. When a squad car arrived and the two uniformed Specials got out, her face darkened.

'You've no right,' she said indignantly.

Shona presented the search warrant, and Mari stomped off down the corridor, leaving them to follow. She stopped by the kitchen island in the extension that overlooked a long back garden and glared at them.

The long, wavy dark hair that had been hidden under her swim cap lay across her shoulders. To Shona, it altered her appearance dramatically, turning the lean face she'd seen at the triathlon into fine-boned beauty. She wore running leggings and a thin hoodie, and there was a light sweep of make-up. Mari didn't offer them a coffee or even a seat, but stood silent and defiant, tapping her short nails on the marble surface, and staring the officers down.

To Shona, it showed that Mari Watt was nervous. The fact that she wasn't firing questions at them about why they were searching her house deepened Shona's suspicion even further. The hospital had responded cautiously to their enquiries, stating there was nothing of note on her personal records, but given the slew of medical malpractice and whistle-blower stories in the media lately, they might have had their own reasons for keeping quiet.

'Perhaps you'd like to sit down, and we'll explain why we're here,' Shona said.

Murdo returned from setting the two Specials to work upstairs and joined them, as Mari led the way around the corner of the L-shaped area to two sofas facing each other. There was a unit of open shelving full of trophies, framed certificates, and pictures of Mari with medals and in various victorious poses going back at least a decade.

'That's quite a collection,' Shona began, indicating the cabinet as she sat down.

Mari shrugged. 'That's my husband's doing. He likes to frame them. It's just something else to dust, isn't it?' She gave a self-deprecating smile.

Shona thought the woman took her triathlon success much more seriously than she was making out. This wasn't a few trophies in the downstairs loo, it was prime position. She was frequently runner-up in the league tables, behind Hayley. Perhaps she just got tired of feeling like second best.

'I'd like to go through your statement with you,' Shona began, and Murdo opened his notebook. Mari frowned, but there was no deviation from what she'd originally told them. She'd travelled to the event with her husband and children. She'd not seen much of Hayley before the race, except when the picture was taken.

Shona got out her phone and showed Mari the image. 'Why didn't you want to stand next to Hayley when this was taken?'

Mari stared at her. She looked as if she was about to ask why Shona thought that was the case, when it dawned on her. 'I thought I recognised you. The RNLI gear. You took the photo.'

At thirty-six, Mari Watt was *a handsome wummin*, as Murdo might term her. But she had a few years on Hayley, and maybe a few pounds around the hips. *Not that one, I look like a walrus...* Had that been Mari's comment?

Maybe she hadn't meant to kill her, just slow her down. Knock her off her game this one time so she could be the winner she so obviously was used to being.

Mari looked incredulous. 'That's why you're here? Your colleague's dead and I didn't want to stand next to her? That's why you're searching my house?' She shook her head, incredulous. 'I thought this was something to do with the hospital. Drugs going missing, or something.'

Shona and Murdo exchanged a glance.

'I'll tell you why I didn't want to stand next to Hayley. She was a bitch. I'm sorry, but she was. You know, it wasn't just her lack of fundraising for the club. She undermined everything I tried to do with her attitude.'

Jimmy, one of the Specials, came in from the kitchen and cleared his throat. Murdo got to his feet and went back around the corner to join him.

The single-word replies of previous exchanges were gone and the floodgates opened. 'If you can't get support from those you've supported… My husband and I helped her and Andy move into that house, and now she wouldn't even chip in for a fundraiser. It wasn't for the children's hospice, that would be bad enough. It was for the kids' diabetic charity. Have you ever seen a child die? D'you know what it does to a family? Hayley was only interested in what people, the club, could do for her. She…'

Shona felt a cold sensation creep up her spine. It wasn't enough that Hayley was dead, there was real hatred in Mari's face. Now the world had to know the woman's crimes, as she saw them, to justify her actions.

'Boss,' Murdo interrupted.

'Excuse me a moment,' Shona said, casting a strategic glance around the room. The only exits were back through the kitchen or via the patio doors, which appeared locked. She crossed to Murdo, reassured that he knew where the interview was heading and his eyes were clamped on Mari. He was a big man but could move fast if he needed to.

The other Special, Tom, had also come into the kitchen. Their faces were sombre. Jimmy held a shoebox-sized plastic container. Tom's hand rested on the cuffs at his belt.

Jimmy tipped the box towards Shona. Medical injector pens. Shit. Exactly what, in Professor Kitchen's opinion, caused the puncture wound in Hayley's thigh.

Shona returned to the sitting area, evidence in hand, her heart thumping. What happened next would dictate whether they got an immediate confession or the silent treatment. She was about to caution Mari, when the woman jumped to her feet, her beautiful face twisted with anger.

'Don't touch that. You've no right.' She took two steps towards Shona.

'Sit down,' Shona ordered. Murdo was at her shoulder, but his intervention wasn't needed. The woman stopped and seemed to crumple.

'You've no right to touch my daughters' medication.' She looked from Shona to Murdo and back. 'You know my girls are both diabetic, don't you?'

When she saw their blank faces, she lunged forward and snatched the box from Shona.

Shit. Shit. Shit. The children's diabetes charity. No wonder Mari was mad at Hayley's betrayal and apparent lack of support. Shona felt a wave of embarrassment mixed with anger that they'd come to this search so unprepared on such a crucial point.

'I'm sorry,' she said.

'I think you'd better go.' Mari hugged the box to her chest.

—

Outside, Shona sent the Specials back to the office. They were silent, unsure if they'd done anything wrong. They hadn't. The thorough search had only uncovered drugs associated with the Watt children's medication, and nothing else. As Shona and Murdo stood on the pavement a little way up from Mari's house, her sergeant was contrite.

'I should've got Hannah to give Kate a hand wi' the background check. Mibbaes she just forgot about the bairns,' Murdo said, shaking his head. 'Sorry, boss. How'd we miss somethin' like this?'

Kate was off her game, Shona knew, but this was such a basic mistake that it made her question her decision to let her DC continue to work. But the background checks hadn't been the only opportunity to understand Mari Watt's character and home life.

'How did I miss this, more like it!' Shona exclaimed. 'If I'd questioned that triathlon chair more thoroughly when he said they'd fallen out over a charity event, we'd have known the whole story.'

'Doesn't mean she didn't do it.' Murdo raised his eyebrows, and she had to admit that the holy trinity – *means, motive, opportunity* – did still apply to Mari Watt. But pursuing her without a firm lead was a high-risk strategy. Mari had no love for Hayley, and after this morning, probably none for Shona either. The Chief Super's words came back to her: *quickly and quietly*. Mari might talk to the press. What started out as a tribute interview about her former friend might quickly become a diatribe about her treatment by Police Scotland, and everything about the case would face increased media scrutiny.

'We didn't find any GHB,' Shona reminded Murdo. 'And Hayley would have been aware Mari was pissed at her, even if she thought it was unjustified. Kate was with Hayley right up until the race started. There was bruising. Hayley must have felt the injection. If she'd turned and seen Mari, behind her, she'd have said something.'

'Mibbaes.'

Shona folded her arms and leaned against the car. She still had a card to play with Mari Watt, but it was risky. After a moment's further consideration, she pushed herself off. 'I won't be long,' she said to Murdo and set off back towards the house. She felt bad about what had happened this morning and if she could defuse the woman's anger it would benefit the investigation, and keep things out of the media, whether or not Mari remained a suspect. She remembered Mari's triathlon statistics when she'd looked at the rankings and there was no evidence the woman had been using PEDs herself. Coming clean was a gamble, but she still had questions and perhaps Mari knew the answers.

'I've a couple more things I'd like to ask,' Shona said, when Mari answered the door. 'As a nurse, I hope your professional discretion will extend to this conversation.'

Mari still looked angry, but assessed her shrewdly, her curiosity piqued. She opened the door wider, allowing Shona to enter. Mari didn't invite her any further and they remained standing in the hallway. Shona revealed why they'd been searching for a medical injector pen. Mari's eyes widened at the news.

'Was Hayley using PEDs?' Shona said. 'If she was, where was she getting them? You mentioned drugs missing from the hospital.'

'She wasn't getting them from me,' Mari said flatly. 'Anyway, it's not PEDs, but usually morphine, methadone and temazepam that disappear from hospitals. Main issue is the record-keeping is poor.'

'Was anyone threatening Hayley? Did anyone else have reason to perhaps want revenge on her?'

Mari thought for a moment, then sighed. 'You're asking the wrong person. We were friends, then we weren't. If someone was threatening her, I wouldn't know.'

'Thank you,' Shona said, turning back to the door.

'You think Hayley was doping, then?'

'It's a line of inquiry,' Shona replied. 'But I'd be grateful if you didn't share that information at this stage.'

A look of triumph passed quickly across Mari's face. She hadn't been beaten by Hayley fair and square. Her rival was nothing more than a cheat. And in that moment, Shona realised, Mari Watt believed she had her victory.

Chapter 12

Murdo was heading back to The Secret Forest festival to talk to Clued-up, an organisation that anonymously tested any drug brought to them by festivalgoers. A warning had already gone out on the festival's app about Erin Dunlop's death, telling people not to take anything, but it was possible the testers had identified which drugs were circulating at the site.

Shona needed to be at the Royal Infirmary for Erin's postmortem. She hoped Ivan Jones worked as quickly as Slasher Sue. In the end, the PM took about twice as long, but an hour later she had findings that were just as unequivocal as the professor's. Cause of death was determined to be heatstroke combined with alcohol and MDMA – also known in pill form as ecstasy. Ivan added that most fatalities were from a combination of factors, not the drug itself, but this was likely a stronger than normal batch.

Shona called Ravi with the news. As FLO, he'd need to inform the family. Then she called Murdo.

'Ties in with what I've been told, boss,' he said.

In the background Shona could hear a thumping beat of music and the chatter of young voices. He was clearly still at the Portakabin that served as Clued-up's lab and office.

'Some o' the drugs brought in were low purity,' Murdo continued, 'but others contained the equivalent of three doses in one pill.'

Shona didn't want to lose momentum on the investigation into Hayley's death, but a fatally strong batch of MDMA circulating at the festival meant more young lives were at risk.

'Can we get some more community officers over there? Ramp up the message these drugs could be fatal.'

'Festival are fine about that. I've already had a word wi' Willie Logan.'

Shona recognised the name – Logan was Hayley and Andy's uniform sergeant.

Murdo lowered his voice. 'He was a bit frosty wi' me. I think he's cut-up about Hayley, and he's heard we're digging intae things that'll no' cast her in the best light. He might have words with you on Saturday.'

It was Wednesday, and Hayley's funeral would be in three days' time. 'Maybe we'll have some answers by then, Murdo.'

'Aye, I hope so,' Murdo replied heavily. 'The folk here have told kids if they're having drugs, to buy a couple and bring one tae them for testing.'

As a police officer, it irked Shona that charities like that even existed. As a mother, she regarded it with a mixture of horror and relief, and was sure most other parents felt the same. It was far from perfect, but realistically, their chances of confiscating every pill or powder on the site was zero. Clued-up, and similar organisations, had a track record of increasing engagement with drug safety at events through their regular messaging and app, and if it saved even a single young person's life, it was worth it.

'Thanks, Murdo. I'm leaving the hospital now. See you at the office.'

Back in the Audi, she sat, turning her phone over in her hand. She was tempted to head over to the festival herself. A visit from a detective inspector might underline how seriously they were taking the threat. It was absolutely not so she could check up on Becca.

The desire to hug her daughter, inhale her scent and feel those soft curls against her cheek was so overwhelming that she turned on the ignition and put the Audi in gear before she could stop herself. But then she remembered their last encounter. Becca certainly wouldn't welcome her mother's presence. She turned the key and the engine fell silent. Murdo would have done a good job hammering home the message. She mustn't let herself get distracted from where she could be most effective, no matter what she felt.

How big a drugs operation was she dealing with? She thought for a moment then dialled Force Intelligence and was put through to a weary-sounding Liverpudlian who identified himself as technical lead on organised criminal gangs and drugs. They weren't aware of any current activity on her patch, but festivals were a movable feast for gangs from large urban areas. They'd update her if they heard anything or linked Erin Dunlop's passing to other deaths, although none had been reported so far. 'You know how it is,' the guy had said before he hung up.

Shona mentally translated the conversation. Erin Dunlop was no more than one silly wee lassie who OD'd, and wasn't a priority. She was just another statistic that'd only become interesting as part of a bigger group. Shona fervently hoped that wouldn't be the case.

—

When Shona returned to Cornwall Mount, her staff kept their attention on their work, avoiding her glance. The room was stuffy with heat and expectation, a tension in the air like an approaching thunderstorm. Someone, probably Hannah, had brought a couple of portable table fans into the main room, but they did little more than stir the papers on desktops. Shona had no doubt that the embarrassing debacle at Mari Watt's home, likely relayed by the Specials who'd been present, would've gone round like wildfire.

Kate jumped up when she saw her boss arrive. Shona jerked her head towards her office, indicating she should follow her.

'I'm so sorry,' Kate said, gripping her notebook to her chest and hesitating on the threshold of Shona's open door as if she feared the magnitude of the bollocking she was about to receive.

'Of course, I knew her children are diabetic,' she hurried on. 'And I was absolutely sure it was in the briefing notes, I just…'

Shona pointed to the chair opposite her desk and Kate reluctantly sat down.

She'd been ready to tear a strip off her DC, but when she saw Kate's flustered appearance – the normally immaculate blonde hair escaping from its high ponytail – and look of horrified remorse for her mistake, Shona felt her anger begin to dispel.

'Look, we all make errors.' She thought guiltily of her own less-than-comprehensive interview of the triathlon club organiser. 'It's easy to miss something, especially when we're under pressure, and I appreciate you owning up to it.'

'You don't think her possession of injector pens is significant to the case, then?' Kate looked hopeful.

Shona thought it was significant, but with a valid explanation in place, unless they had more evidence – ideally from a witness who'd seen Mari Watt brandishing a medical injector at the triathlon – then there was little more they could do.

'Mari Watt will remain a person of interest until we can exclude her, but I think what's important now is that we move forward with both cases.'

Kate nodded and relaxed a little in her chair.

'Where are we with The Secret Forest?'

'We've been trawling social media around the festival and CCTV footage for drug activity,' Kate said. 'We're looking at Erin's camera card too. It's mostly bands or group shots with friends.'

'Okay, good. I want you to take the lead on the Erin Dunlop case. There's a credible threat from a fatally strong batch of MDMA at the festival. I need you to track down the dealers. It'll be mostly intelligence-based. You know the tech team best; get them working to their strengths.'

On any other occasion, Kate would have swelled with pride at being asked to spearhead such a significant investigation. It was the sort of job that looked great on a CV. Shona reasoned that Kate not only needed to regain her confidence, severely dented by Hayley's death and her recent slip-up, but she'd also benefit from time away from the public after her outburst at Sandra Dunlop's house.

However, Kate's expression told Shona that she didn't welcome the assignment.

'Any leads on dealers so far?' Shona asked, moving swiftly to nip any argument in the bud.

'Well, in her witness statement, one of Erin's friends, Christie Nicolson, mentions seeing her arguing with an unidentified man wearing an embroidered top and orange jeans,' Kate said, slowly.

'Good. What else?'

'Look…' Kate edged forward and dropped her notebook onto Shona's desk. 'Andy still thinks Kennedy is a credible suspect in Hayley's death.'

'You shouldn't be talking to him about the case,' Shona warned.

'But he's a cop, and I'm just keeping him informed of investigation progress.'

'That makes no difference,' Shona said, exasperated. 'Look, Kate, I decide the best operational deployment of my officers. You're telling me you're fit to work. I'm handing you an opportunity. Take it or take leave. Or I'll sign you off myself. What's it to be?'

Kate swept a strand of hair away from her face, her mouth settling into a firm line of displeasure.

'Update on the Erin Dunlop case by the end of the day. Clear?'

'Yes, boss,' Kate said. She picked up her notebook, and though she didn't slam Shona's door, she came perilously close.

Shona stared after her with equal parts frustration and empathy. She knew one reason she was tough on Kate was that, deep down, she thought the graduate entrant had side-stepped the hard graft that Shona herself had experienced coming up from beat cop. And Kate was too focused on promotion. You had to work on improving your weaknesses – family liaison, in Kate's case. She did value her DC's skills and knew that, if Kate could just get her attitude under control, there was no reason she wouldn't make it all the way to the top.

Shona jumped up from her chair and began pacing the room, in an attempt to shake off her irritation and marshal her thoughts, which were threatening to spiral off in multiple directions. Her first concern was Becca's safety at the festival, closely followed by the unravelling of the circumstances around Erin Dunlop's and Hayley Cameron's deaths, accomplishing the latter as the Chief Super had decreed – *quickly and quietly*. But there was also the peculiar phone call from the NCA about Delfont, and the persistent sense of dread it had set off in her mind – for herself and Thalia, but also for Tommy and Dan Ridley, whose only crime had been to help her when she'd asked. There was how Rob was faring in prison, and any number of things she'd forgotten to do at High Pines. And then there was James. He didn't really constitute a worry, more a bright beacon of light and warmth in an otherwise stormy sea of troubles, but the exact temperature of their relationship was something she was constantly monitoring.

She lifted her hair, piling it on top of her head. The faint breeze from the desk fan was cool on her neck. James said actors smiled even when they didn't feel like it, but it had the side effect of lightening your mood anyway. Shona didn't need a mirror to know all she was managing now was a rigid grin that would convince nobody. Back to the day job for her, then. She let her hair fall. Outside, she could see Kate with Vinny, who was scrolling through his phone, and Chloe, who was nodding sympathetically. The data analyst's glance towards the office and the apologetic half-smile when she caught Shona's eye told her that *Wee Shona* was indeed the topic of their conversation.

I'm not your mother, Shona had thought numerous times in the past when faced with delivering a boot up the backside to hapless, unprepared and underperforming young officers. Murdo represented a fatherly figure to staff, who all knew they could come to him for advice. So, what was she? *My warrior queen* was what James sometimes called her, teasingly. Her CID team was her 'work family' and perhaps she also had a role akin to a parent. A matriarch, perhaps. With Kate, she just wasn't managing it very well, but perhaps she could do better. After all, if Hayley Cameron had been able to confide her doubts about her abilities and performance to someone older and more experienced, then maybe she wouldn't have gone down the path of performance drugs to be better – a path that led, ultimately, to her death.

Chapter 13

When Murdo appeared in the office half an hour later, Shona told him about her decision to put Kate in charge of gathering intelligence for the Erin Dunlop case.

'Where's everyone else at?' Shona asked, her eyes on the line of administrative actions she was required to complete before she could start on the crimes they were supposed to be investigating. Detective Chief Superintendent Davies, her boss up at Kilmarnock HQ, seemed to run on paperwork like it was oxygen.

'I left Ravi up at the festival wi' a couple of the young community officers,' Murdo replied. 'See if they can find any witnesses from thon nearby tents, like you said. Lads and lassie might speak to them. I'm aboot thirty years too old for that job.' He sighed.

'I'm sure that's not true,' Shona said, as she hammered out yet another email to the building's maintenance team. When Murdo didn't say anything, she stopped typing and looked up. 'What?'

'D'you no' think you're pushing them all a wee bit hard?'

'Complaints?' Her brows knitted together.

'No, but I keep thinking, we wouldnae have missed the diabetes thing wi' Mari Watt if we were no' so stretched.'

Shona let her hands slide from the keyboard into her lap. Murdo was right, but what were the options? Four days on from Hayley's death and they had no one in custody, and no strong leads. With two investigations running, they needed more staff.

'I can ring aroon the Specials and Dumfries officers and civilian ops,' Murdo suggested. 'Put out a plea. But everywhere is cut to the bone as it is, an' plenty of folk are on holiday.'

'Did Dan Ridley get back to you on the Cameron family member you said was a bit of a player, or anything about Erin Dunlop's Carlisle drug connections?'

'I know he went to inform Erin's father. Want me to chase it up?'

'I'll speak to Dan myself. I want to make sure he's okay with us sending so much work his way.' There were protocols in place for cross-border policing and she'd emailed the Cumbrian CID boss, Lambert, receiving only a curt, one-line reply. It was clear that the DCI had little time for Dan, and even less for colleagues north of the border. She'd also messaged Dan a couple of times lately, and his replies had been shorter and less immediate than usual.

'Think we might be able to get him over?' Murdo said, hopefully. 'We could really do wi' more help.'

Dan had been seconded on a previous case, when a woman's body had been recovered from the Solway. Shona rated him highly as an officer, and a friend.

'I mean, both cases pertain tae drugs,' Murdo added, 'but we cannae really combine them, an' I'm no' sure that would lighten the workload anyways.'

Shona shook her head. 'No connections. Different markets and operating models. But Dan would be just what we need,' she agreed and hoped her Super would see it that way. Dumfries might have a lower crime rate than Scotland's central belt, but it was still a big patch to cover, and any major investigation would always stretch resources thin. Although both she and Dan had talked in the past about a permanent transfer to Dumfries, her Super had made it clear there was no funding available, but perhaps he'd okay a temporary arrangement. 'I'll give Dan a call in a minute, but first, let's grab a coffee. We need a proper chat.'

There wasn't time to go out, so they stood by the open windows in the shady stairwell with mugs of instant. Below, cars and pedestrians moved sluggishly in the heat. The grass on the verge was no more than a brown strip of dead vegetation.

They discussed strategies on neutralising the drugs threat at the festival and then turned to Hayley's death. Shona told Murdo that Kate had been talking to Andy Purdy and he was still convinced of the businessman Jack Kennedy's involvement in Hayley's death.

'Kate should know better.' Murdo frowned. 'And if Purdy thought Kennedy was a threat, why'd he no' do something earlier? Chap his door an' give him a friendly warning?'

'Marking his card would've been the natural, if not the sensible, reaction,' Shona agreed. She'd known plenty of cops do it. Sometimes it settled matters, other times it escalated them. 'If anything like that had happened, I think Kennedy would've made an official complaint out of pure devilment, and there was nothing in Andy's record when Ravi checked him out.' Murdo nodded in agreement. 'But injecting Hayley as revenge for an arrest...' Shona continued, 'Is that possible, d'you think? That's more like the action of someone she's busted for a drugs offence, for targeting girls in bars. Tit-for-tat. Or maybe just someone who wanted a cop's scalp.'

'Like a prank gone wrong?' Murdo said, considering.

'I mean, who'd have so little sense to think it wasn't risking her life?' Shona said.

'I can think o' plenty of candidates on that score.'

'Then find me some,' Shona replied, draining her mug of tepid coffee. 'Any rumours. Anyone's claiming it as their own work. And I want to know if it's part of a general increase in violence against officers.'

'I'll get uniform tae ask around. Might go some way tae building bridges with Willie Logan's lads and lasses. Maybe have another word with Hayley's beat partner, Joanne Mitchell too. She told Ravi she didn't know of any threats, but something might have come back to her.'

'How did Willie Logan find out that doping was a line of inquiry?'

Murdo shrugged. 'One o' the Specials mibbaes. You know uniform. Gossip's their favourite sport an' they're no' all as glaikit as they look at times. But my money's on Andy Purdy. You said he was pretty angry when you interviewed him, an' he'll be on the offensive if he thinks we're tarnishing Hayley's memory.'

Shona was considering this when her phone rang. Slasher Sue's number flashed up. 'I'd better take this,' she said, heading back up the stairs. When she entered the CID room, she tapped her screen.

'How was your session with Jones the Bones, then?' Sue said.

It seemed Ivan Jones's new nickname had been decided.

'It was fine,' Shona laughed, as she entered her sweltering office, then added, 'You were missed.'

Sue grunted, apparently satisfied.

'This a social call, or do you have something?' Shona felt her excitement mount, only for it to plummet again when Sue said she didn't have any more toxicology results yet.

'But I've looked at the Strava data,' Sue went on. 'Hayley was getting up during the night to use her static bike.'

'That's a thing with athletes, isn't it?' Shona said. She'd watched a movie with Becca about a Scottish cyclist who'd made two attempts at a world record on consecutive days, exercising every hour during the night to keep his muscles from seizing up.

'It can be,' conceded the professor. 'But it's also typical of someone doping with EPO. You need to circulate the increased number of red cells to prevent clotting. The drug's been implicated in the death of at least twenty cyclists through cardiac arrests. Thickened blood is harder to move.'

'Have you seen it in any deaths here?'

'It's so hard to detect, maybe I missed them. I can screen for an elevated red cell count but the data is complex – useless without an individual's baseline. The drug itself is very difficult to test for and there are no obvious side effects when using it. But there's something else.'

Shona pulled up her chair, opened her notebook and found her pen, ready for the complex data she had an inkling was coming her way. 'Go on.'

'I've been looking at Hayley's stress level stats from the watch.'

'Is that like blood pressure?'

'No. The Garmin uses heart-rate data to determine the interval between each heartbeat. The variable length of time in between each heartbeat is regulated by the body's autonomic nervous system. The less variability between beats equals higher stress. Increased variability means less stress.'

'So, it's not related directly to exercise?'

'If you were running, you'd have a higher, but variable, heart rate. However, if you were running from a bear, that heart rate would be just as high but with less variability. In evolutionary terms, it makes perfect sense. Hayley was experiencing regular but intermittent high levels of stress.'

'It goes with the job,' Shona said, dryly.

'This was even off duty.'

'Like I said, it goes with the job.' In Shona's experience, the stress never really went. It was why the burnout rate in response cops was so high. But then the conversation she'd just had with Murdo came back to her. 'Would such stress levels fit with Hayley being threatened?'

'The bear scenario is unlikely. But otherwise, yes, it would fit precisely.'

Chapter 14

Shona asked Hannah to prepare a summary of the timeline, highlighting any correlation between stress spikes and GPS locations, then she picked up her phone and dialled Dan Ridley's number.

He answered after a couple of rings. There was a pause before he spoke.

'Hi.'

'Dan. How are you?'

There was another awkward pause.

'Okay.'

Shona thought he sounded far from okay. Dan's usual warmth and enthusiasm were missing. Then it struck her. If she'd had a call from the National Crime Agency, then maybe he had too. Cumbria CID had been part of the initial investigation into Delfont's death, before it had been handed over to the Met, due to the London connections, and now the NCA. A seed of anxiety germinated in her gut. Might he have implicated her, accidentally or otherwise? Was his silence a guilty one? If they put him on the stand, asked him directly if he'd aided Thalia, with Shona's help, to leave the scene, he'd never perjure himself.

'What's the matter?' she said, before she could restrain the panic that was threatening to engulf her. 'Has something happened?'

'Not really. Just work stuff,' Dan said with a sigh.

She couldn't ask him straight out whether he'd heard from the NCA. It would seem like she didn't trust him. It risked bringing up horrifying memories that might have nothing to do with his malaise, and further widening the gulf that she felt had opened up between them.

'Well, just to cheer you up I've some more work stuff,' she replied, trying to sound upbeat.

'Yeah, I got Murdo's email and your messages. I'm sorry I haven't replied.'

To Shona, that sounded like more evidence he was distancing himself.

'It's fine,' she pressed on, updating him on the MDMA risk and Sandra Dunlop's view that her daughter's drugs issues stemmed from her stay in Carlisle. 'I'm going to ask Davies if we can get you on the CID team here for a month or so.'

She held her breath, worried his reaction would confirm her worst fears.

'That'd be so great.' Dan brightened.

'Oh,' Shona said, both taken aback and relieved by his enthusiasm. Maybe she'd been wrong about his reticence. He'd just been busy. His on-again, off-again relationship with Charlotte the jewellery designer was on one of its periodic downturns – could have been any number of reasons. 'Good.'

'I'll get a briefing document together on Finlay Cameron and associates,' Dan said. 'He's in Carlisle jail. Armed robbery and manslaughter. No record that his niece Hayley Cameron ever visited. And I'll see what I can dig up on Erin Dunlop's friends. There's no evidence we ever brought her in.'

'Thanks, Dan. That'd be a great help. See you soon.'

'Hope so.'

Shona stared at her phone, replaying their conversation, until her lock screen appeared – a black-and-white image of Becca on the beach, with High Pines in the background. She was overanalysing, she knew. But with Dan around the office, she might be able to gauge if her suspicions about the NCA were valid or not, without asking him outright. And, as she looked once more at the picture of Becca, who really didn't deserve to have her other parent in prison too, she fervently hoped they weren't.

—

It was nearly eight o'clock that night when Shona finally looked up from her desk. She'd cleared the backlog of actions and had a brief text exchange with Becca, which had calmed her and helped to clear her mind. Her priority in Hayley's case now was learning precisely what had passed between the woman and her sister Kimi when they'd met in the pub, so she'd sent Ravi to get any CCTV footage and talk to any possible witnesses.

The outer office was quiet, but a few dogged souls were still anchored to their computer screens. She shooed them home, aware of the volume of work they'd shifted but also how much there was to do. Burnout was a real issue on long investigations. She didn't want anyone going off sick now.

The sting had gone from the day, and a mellower light glowed behind the blinds. A desire to be by the sea, to feel the fresh evening breezes, took hold of her and she quickly closed all the documents open on her laptop and collected her bag and keys.

Back at High Pines, she changed into her running gear before setting off at a steady jog for Knockie Point. She hadn't spoken to James since dinner on Sunday evening. She found keeping busy relieved the loneliness and she didn't glance at her phone so much, hoping for a message.

She was missing Becca too, more than she'd admitted to Freya. It felt like she was fighting a war against her sense of aloneness on both fronts. There was no deep emotional connection to Rob any more, though she didn't feel it would be fair to divorce him while he was still in prison. She maintained what relationship they still had out of a sense of duty, and perhaps habit.

When she reached the small cove, she took out her phone and checked the signal. There was enough. A moment later,

James joined her FaceTime. When she saw him, her relief was instant, if quickly smothered by yearning.

'Guess where I am?' she said, panning her phone to show the white cockleshell beach and the smooth golden water, lit by the dipping evening sun. 'I wish you could feel this salt breeze and smell these wildflowers.' She angled the phone to show a froth of lilac petals. They'd probably escaped from a garden nearby and made themselves at home; she had no real idea what they were, but the scent was heavenly.

'Aw, darlin', you know how tae make a man homesick,' James exclaimed, leaning forward hungrily to catch every aspect of the bay. He wore shorts, patterned with neon palm trees, and a vivid red Hawaiian shirt, unbuttoned to reveal the smooth muscles of his chest and belly that contributed to his bankability and proved so alluring to his female fans. He sat beneath a fringed sunshade, next to a Californian blue swimming pool that shimmered in the midday heat. 'God, that's a lovely view.'

'I could say the same.'

'Ooh, cheeky wee minx.' He grinned with mock affront.

Shona grinned back. She could feel not only a stir of desire, but her burdens easing by the second, as they always seemed to when she talked to James. Perhaps she wasn't immune to a dose of Hollywood glamour, but it felt precious just to be in this beautiful place with James. 'Doesn't look like you're roughing it.'

'It's torture, I'm telling ye. I've only half an hour tae finish this mocktail before somebody brings me another.'

Next to him on the lounger lay a thick bundle of a script, a page folded over and filled with scribbled notations.

'You going back to work? Does that mean you're better?'

His dark, wavy hair had regrown and there was little evidence of the head wound he'd sustained, but the neurological damage affecting his co-ordination and balance, particularly on his left side, was taking longer to heal.

'Just havin' a mooch at what's around,' he said casually. 'Set insurance won't clear me for another couple of months, but ye know how long these projects take tae get off the ground. Still, gives me more time tae look at my wee darlin'. Here we are, beach tae ourselves.'

It was true, despite the glorious evening. Everyone must still be at dinner in the Royal Arms or putting kids to bed.

'It's how folk in fitness-obsessed California fit in affairs, ye know. Go out for a run. Come back sweaty an' straight in the shower.'

Despite the obvious and very appealing distraction that James provided, Shona found her thoughts drifting back to Hayley Cameron. Was that how she was sourcing her PEDs? Perhaps that's what the stress spikes corresponded to: a fear of getting caught. She lived with a cop, worked with cops all day. It would have been hard to hide anything, so she must have felt under extra pressure. And might whoever had been supplying her with drugs have a motive for killing her?

James must have noted her preoccupation, since he asked her if she was still worried about Becca. She'd already messaged him about the death at the festival and Becca's refusal to come home.

'Shall I have a word wi' her?' he said, concern written across his handsome face.

It was true that James and Becca got on well, and Shona knew he'd helped her with schoolwork, as well as asking for her ideas about High Pines.

'I don't want it to look like I'm recruiting allies to gang up on her,' she said, doubtfully.

'Remember what it was like to be that age? I was desperate to be independent, but terrified at the same time, and determined not to show it.'

'I was just the same,' she conceded.

'No' quite the same. I was this skinny wee runt wi' a big mouth and you were a goddess. No, not a goddess, a warrior princess.'

Shona laughed. 'And what am I now?' she said, already knowing the answer.

'I keep telling you. A warrior queen, obviously.'

'Don't feel much of a warrior queen at the minute.'

'Aye, but that's how you know you're the real thing.' He smiled and for some reason she couldn't quite pin down, she began to feel like maybe she could tackle what life was throwing at her. 'So, we've both got the house to ourselves, eh?' A mischievous grin spread across his face. 'We should make the most of it. I think you deserve a nice candle-lit bath. I'll join you.'

She was fairly sure where it would lead. The intimate aspects of a long-distance relationship had been the most challenging. In person it was often enough to move in a certain way, to guide a lover's hand – not that James needed any guidance – but translating that into actual words that didn't use nursery terms for body parts, or border on icky homemade porn, had been a difficult balance to strike. There had been some early awkward moments, but they'd ended in both of them bursting into giggles, and ultimately instead of destroying any sense of intimacy, it had helped to build it.

He sat up, bundled his script under his arm and leaned close to his phone.

'I've called a cab. Race ye home.'

Shona laughed, turned away from the beautiful view and sprinted up the cockle beach.

Chapter 15

Shona was in her office at seven the next morning. The current High Pines guests were proving gratifyingly self-contained, but that only seemed to exacerbate the sense of emptiness the house had taken on. She missed hearing her daughter's chatter, and even being ticked off for leaving a jam-covered knife in the sink – *Mum, dishwasher!*

Early as she was, she was surprised to see Murdo already hammering away on his keyboard, a large mug of tea at his elbow. Ravi soon joined them, carrying two lattes and a paper bag.

'You're a star, Ravi,' Shona said, as he placed the bag and coffee on her desk.

'Got you something else.' From the pocket of his pale linen blazer, he pulled out a memory stick. 'From the pub.' This was even more welcome. It might give them some idea of what had passed between Hayley and her sister during their encounter a fortnight before her death.

'D'you want to wait for Kate?' Ravi enquired as Murdo appeared at the door, drawn from his keyboard by the lure of pastries.

'She can't tell us what happened. She was in the toilets and only learned there'd been some sort of incident when she came out,' Shona said, taking a sip of coffee and gesturing them both to sit down.

'Those croissants?' Murdo said, although it came out as *cross-ants.*

'They're apricot croissants,' Ravi warned. Murdo's aversion to fruit was well known.

Murdo made a face, then shrugged, reaching into the bag.

'What would Joan say if she was here?' Shona asked with mock severity.

'Aye, well, she's no' here,' Murdo replied. 'What's that?' He took a bite and nodded towards the memory stick that Shona was slotting into her laptop.

'CCTV from Kirkpatrick Inn,' Shona replied, opening the file.

The quality was good and the angle, from above the bar, made Hayley easy to spot. A blue halterneck top showed off her toned shoulders. Her red-gold hair caught the light from the illuminated beer pumps and multicoloured bottles of spirits, as she chatted and laughed with friends. The group seemed to pulse outwards as Hayley hurriedly set down her drink and exited the frame, only to quickly reappear. She stepped backwards into shot, grasping a young woman by the upper arm, whose long, straight hair flew out in a golden sheet as she tried to escape. When the girl turned, they saw her face: a younger, softer, heavily made-up version of Hayley. This had to be Kimberley 'Kimi' Cameron.

There was no sound, but it was obvious that angry words were being exchanged, faces pressed close as Hayley shook her sister.

'Is she warning or threatening her?' Shona peered at the screen.

'Bar staff said it was over in a flash, so they didn't intervene,' Ravi replied. 'And none of her other friends heard what was actually said.'

'I'd say she's de-escalating the situation,' Murdo commented, approvingly.

Both Murdo and Ravi were adept at reading folk, Shona knew, but running the video several times failed to produce a consensus.

Kate had come into the outer office and was eyeing them with suspicion through the glass.

'Is it possible that Hayley had more contact with her family than she let on?' Shona said. The CCTV didn't look like a reunion of long-separated siblings, hostile or otherwise.

Murdo sighed, his face solemn. He was a protective and loyal sergeant to younger cops, but he was also pragmatic about individuals' struggles and failings. He'd absorbed the evidence of Hayley's doping without the shock and rancour displayed by Kate.

'You mean was she workin' fur the benefit o' her family?' he said. 'Was she a corrupt cop?'

'I know it's a bit of a leap on this evidence alone,' Shona conceded.

'Aye, well, Dumfries is a small toon. I think young Hayley worked hard tae distance herself fae the Camerons. Whether or no' she was successful is another matter.'

'There's something else,' Ravi said. 'That Android phone we recovered from Hayley and Andy's garage has been completely wiped.'

'You might do that if you intended to sell it,' Murdo said.

'Or to hide something,' Shona added, voicing what they were all thinking.

'Whoever owned it did a factory reset. There's only one number on it – an unlisted pay-as-you-go.'

'I want to know more about this family,' Shona said, sitting back and folding her arms. Maybe there wasn't a connection with Hayley's death, but if they had criminal leanings and were on her patch, she needed to have them in her sights. 'You said they were *an old family business*, Murdo. What did you mean by that, and is it worth me having a chat?'

'I doubt you'll get anything oot o' the father and brothers,' Murdo said. 'Clem's no' a big fella, but he's got a temper. A couple o' short stretches in his youth fur violent offences but managed to stay oot o' jail since. Officially, he has a garage an' runs a taxi company an' owns a few properties aroon Dumfries.'

'What about his sons?'

'All older than Hayley. There's the eldest, James Donoghue Cameron, generally known as JD, who's in his early thirties. Other two are Stevie and Ross, or Rosey, as he gets called. They're a close pack, wi' JD the brains, Stevie the brawn and Rosey happy to tag along in his brothers' wake. Officially, they buy and renovate hooses, run the taxis and help operate the commercial properties.'

'Unofficially?'

'It's likely they run girls and drugs, but nothin's ever stuck.'

'Then, we'll try talking to the sister. I'll go myself.'

'You'll need tae get past the aunt. She's Isobel Clark by rights but calls hersel' Belle Cameron. Stepped in tae raise the kids after her sister Kathleen died. I'll come with ye.'

'If you've history with them, the low-key option is Ravi.'

'No' sure if that's a compliment or not,' Ravi said, draining his coffee and getting to his feet.

Murdo looked doubtful.

'It's fine, Murdo,' Shona said. Ravi was handy when he needed to be, and she wasn't beyond taking down any threat, physical or otherwise, should it come to that. And despite the Cameron clan's reputation, she wasn't anticipating any trouble. 'It's just a courtesy visit to the family of the deceased, with a few questions thrown in. I'll just check these emails, then we'll go.'

A moment later, she wished she'd gone straight out. Detective Chief Superintendent Davies had vetoed her request to recruit Dan. If Shona thought she couldn't handle two cases, his email said, she should work on closing the most straightforward one and then redeploy her forces. He was talking to her as though she were a probationer. Not only was this piling on the pressure, it also scuppered her idea of quietly assessing if the NCA had approached Dan. Davies was lucky this hadn't been a face-to-face discussion or Shona might have punched him. Instead, in her frustration, she lobbed a heavy book across her office, sending her wastepaper bin flying. A few heads in the outer office looked up, but they were all wise enough to quickly drop back to their paperwork before she could spot them.

–

In the car, Shona asked Ravi how Erin's mother, Sandra Dunlop, was doing. As FLO, he was best placed to give an accurate assessment of how she and her partner were coping following Erin's death.

'She's a nice woman. I've sent a list of Erin's phone contacts to Dan. Is it right we might get him over as part of the team?'

'Been vetoed.' She let the irritation show in her tone, but not even Ravi would understand the full depth of her disappointment.

'Ah, so that was what the literary criticism was about.' When she looked puzzled, he continued, 'You hefting that book.' He grinned then his face became serious again. 'I'm pure scunnered we'll no' be seeing Dan the man.'

'Same, pal.'

They pulled up outside the address Murdo had given them. The detached property sat behind electric gates, and Shona's first impression was of a house transported from a more salubrious area and shoehorned onto a too-small plot. The pristine brick frontage was adorned with carriage lamps, leaded windows and hanging baskets, lush despite the heat. There was no garden, just a paved area crammed with SUVs and a top-of-the-range daffodil-yellow Mini with personalised plates, *KM1 XXX*.

Given their estrangement from Hayley, Shona wasn't obliged to make a family visit. Andy was noted on every document as her next of kin. But in addition to her unanswered questions, she didn't want their first meeting to be at the funeral on Saturday – assuming any of the family turned up. If she could defuse the possibility of an unpleasant scene later, then the trip to the Cameron household would be worth it for that reason alone.

It soon became clear that Murdo's prediction of a hostile reception was right. When they pressed the buzzer and introduced themselves, Hayley's father and three brothers came out of the house, heading for the SUVs. The boys were all taller than their wiry father. The two youngest were heavily muscled, but the oldest had the dead-eyed stare of a true predator.

Shona could see Ravi's jaw clenching under his smooth skin. Despite their size and numbers, she sensed the brothers weren't keen to take on an unknown quantity and after glaring at the two cops a beat longer than necessary, they drove off.

Belle stood on the doorstep, cigarette poised. She was immaculate, in heels, black linen dress and matching jacket. Her subtly dyed dark red hair fell to her shoulders in controlled curves and didn't appear to move much in the warm breeze.

She smiled at Shona in a *don't mind them* kind of way.

At her aunt's shoulder was Kimi. Shona caught a look of intense curiosity, quickly masked as she swept her golden hair carefully back from her face with long pink nails.

No offer of tea was forthcoming. In the lounge, the family dynamics were clear from the furniture. The father's leather armchair sat by the faux-flame gas fire, while the matching sofa, strewn with lad mags, was positioned opposite the TV. On the other side of the fireplace, set a little way back, was Belle's chair. There was no doubt who ultimately held the power – the men. But if Murdo's assessment was right, Belle was adroit at navigating the family dynamics, and Kimi was likely learning from her. Belle was the peacemaker, and sometimes peacemakers held the balance of power.

After Shona had expressed her condolences, she turned to Kimi. 'What happened between you and Hayley when you met in the pub?' Her tone was supportive but firm. She could sense the change in Belle's posture, could almost see her ears prick up.

Kimi seemed younger than her twenty-six years, like a teenager put on the spot over some misdemeanour. Her eyes roamed the room and when they finally came to rest on Shona, she gave her a shrug. 'Nothin'.'

'I've seen the CCTV. It was something,' Shona said, still smiling encouragingly.

Belle had crept forward to the edge of her seat. 'What's this?'

'We haven't spoken to all the witnesses in the bar,' Shona continued, leaving Belle's question for Kimi alone. She paused to let the implication of her last statement sink in. She credited Kimi with enough street smarts to join the dots. *This is a chance to get your story in first, and it'll be up to the polis to disprove it. As long as whatever you say sounds reasonable, you might just get away with it.*

Belle raised an enquiring eyebrow at her niece, and it was enough to prompt an answer.

'Cop in a bar doesnae want anyone else having fun,' Kimi said with a disdainful toss of her beautiful hair.

'So, she saw you with a controlled substance?'

Kimi scoffed. 'Ma sister's dead, not even buried, and you're trying to fit me up.'

Righteous indignation was surer ground for Kimi, and she was hitting her stride. Belle shot Kimi a severe look. This wasn't an issue of underage drinking, but she was still clearly treated as the baby of the family, although she was trusted enough to manage one of their nail bars.

'It must have been serious enough for Hayley to break away from her girls' night out and intervene,' Shona said quietly.

'She was sticking her nose in. It's what cops do, right? I wasnae talking to her.'

'If there was trouble, your brothers will have something to say about that.' Belle's words were half-consolation, half-warning, and Kimi took the hint.

'None of it was my fault.'

Shona turned to Belle. 'When was the last time you saw Hayley?'

The older woman made a show of slowly lighting her cigarette and then shrugged.

'Weeks? Months?' Shona prompted.

Nothing.

'Years?'

Belle gave a vague nod. 'We were never close.' Belle took another long draw then stubbed out the half-finished cigarette, signalling the end of the conversation.

There was a loud bang as the front door was thrust open, and a nightmare of a man burst into the lounge. Shona felt Ravi tense beside her, and her own first reaction – her beat cop muscle memory – would've had her reaching for baton and PAVA spray. But thanks to Dan's briefing document, she recognised the intruder. He seemed to swell at the sight of Shona and Ravi, his presence sucking the light and air from the room. In contrast, the scrawny lad at his back was a pale and imperfect photocopy, though enough resemblance lingered to make Shona think this must be one of his three sons.

'Uncle Fin,' Kimi said, startled.

Finlay Cameron had once been a trawlerman. Well over six foot tall and heavily built, his previous occupation and size didn't entirely account for his intimidating presence. There was malevolence etched in every line of his weather-beaten face.

'Fin, when did you—' Belle got to her feet, tidying her hair in a self-conscious flutter of her hands, jewellery rattling like tiny alarm bells.

Shona knew Belle had been about to say: *When did you get out?* but had swerved just in time.

'You should have said you were coming. You've just missed the boys. I'd have laid on a party.'

'Ah, I'm not one for fuss.' He stepped forward, dropping a heavy arm around Belle's shoulders and kissing her so roughly that Shona saw her put out a steadying hand.

He turned to Kimi. 'Not got a kiss for your Uncle Fin?'

Kimi tottered obediently forward on her high heels – knees together, coy, appeasing smile – but there was a pallor beneath her tanned skin, and her manicured hands curled into fists.

He grabbed her by the shoulders and planted a smacker on her cheek, then held her at arm's length and gave her ample figure a brazen appraisal.

'My, you've grown.' He let her go and as he stepped back, his son bobbed in with the speed of a boxer to land a kiss on the same spot.

'Hello, Cousin Kimi.'

She obviously felt on safer ground with him. Shona saw her give the young man a contemptuous look as she ran the back of her hand over her face, wiping away any marks of contact.

Finlay Cameron turned and stared at Shona. She stared back. Normal protocol would be to introduce herself, show her warrant card, and offer a hand and condolences for the loss of his niece, Hayley, a much-loved fellow officer, but it was like facing down a wolf.

'We'll not be keeping you,' Belle said, evenly, to Shona.

Fin leaned close to Shona. 'Aye, you'd better go.' He finally broke eye contact to give Ravi a contemptuous glance. 'And take your handbag with you.'

Once they were back at the Audi and out of sight of the house, Ravi stopped and leaned forward, hands on knees, and let out a relieved laugh.

'Jeezo, that guy's a pure bampot,' he said. 'That's one family you wouldnae want to be around at Christmas.'

'You okay?' Shona could feel her own heart rate descending with relief.

'Aye. I'd love to think we could do everyone a favour, arrest him for homophobic hate speech, bust the terms of his parole and bounce him straight back inside. But I'm not sure "handbag" would be enough to convince the fiscal.'

'Don't let him get to you.'

'I'm not. But if he's applying the term to me, he better be thinking Hermès or, at the very least, Gucci.' Ravi straightened up. 'And one thing's for sure. That Kimi knows more than she's saying.'

'Aye, she does,' Shona agreed. 'And I think Belle knows it too.'

Chapter 16

As Shona and Ravi got into the Audi, her phone rang. Detective Inspector Kenneth Dalrymple's name appeared. He was responsible for Galloway, to the west of Dumfries, and he and Shona kept in touch.

'Shona, I hear you're looking for a hand,' he said without preamble.

She didn't have time to worry if people thought she was losing her touch. Every DI had been there at some point. She outlined the issues.

'I can lend you my DC, Allan Peacock. He worked on that tractor trouble we all had last year.'

That 'tractor trouble' would be the international gang trafficking multimillion-pound agricultural machinery that they'd dealt with in a joint operation. With his tweed jackets and habitual downplaying, Shona felt like Dalrymple was a throwback to the 1950s. If he ever called her to say Galloway was experiencing *a little local difficulty*, she'd picture mass revolution and riot.

Shona only vaguely remembered Peacock's name from the case, however.

'Allan did his basic training with Andy Purdy and Hayley Cameron,' Dalrymple continued, 'and he's got a family connection to Dumfries – knows the area.'

Having moved Kate off the case, Shona didn't want another officer with emotional connections causing problems. 'Isn't he too involved?' Shona asked.

'Oh, I wouldn't say so. He's ambitious. Has an eye on promotion. I'll likely lose him to Glasgow or Edinburgh.'

It came with the territory, Shona knew. It was a miracle she'd hung on to Ravi and Kate this long, without them being transferred or promoted to another department. It was only a ninety-minute drive for Ravi to his hometown of Glasgow, but in many ways, it suited him not to be in his family's pocket, and his partner Martin was locally based. That might delay the inevitable where he was concerned. Kate's ties were with Edinburgh, and she'd made no secret it was her desired next step.

'Allan says he's not been in touch with either of them recently. He might be useful in interviews with family or friends. An outside pair of eyes.'

It was true that Peacock could hit the ground running. He knew the area and had met the key parties. He was close, but not too close. She couldn't get Dan, but maybe this was the next best thing.

'I can send him over tomorrow, if you like?'

'Thanks, Kenneth,' Shona said. 'I'd be very grateful.'

It wouldn't solve all of her staffing problems, but it was a start.

—

That evening, Shona had a disappointingly brief text exchange with James. His ex-wife, Samira, was bringing their eight-year-old twins Dove and Beau over to his house, and an afternoon at Los Angeles Zoo was planned. She couldn't help but feel a little jealous, but of what, precisely? Him seeing his ex-wife? That was a natural reaction, though he'd made it clear that while co-parenting well was a priority for both of them, they had no plans to reunite. Was she envious of the Hollywood glamour – an apparently charmed life in the endless sunshine? She knew this had its darker sides, with obsessive fans and high gun crime. James had spoken about finding a project to bring him back to

Scotland, but that might take years. She couldn't see where their relationship was going – she didn't feel it was fair to divorce Rob while he was in prison – but one thing she was clear on: with James, she felt like herself in a way she couldn't recall feeling for a long time. It was something she wanted to hold on to.

Taking her microwave dinner upstairs to the lounge, she ate with his book – *The Collected Works of Robert Burns* – next to her on the table. She took out her laptop and attempted to distract herself with work, reviewing case actions and making notes for tomorrow's briefing. She found the note about the wiped Android phone and its single contact. The number went straight to voicemail. She sent a text. *Call me. I'd like to talk to you about Hayley.*

When she closed her eyes that night, she felt James close. She pictured him lying by the swimming pool, reading, and imagined he was next to her, the light reflecting from the pages of his script, illuminating his face. His expression was intermittent clouds and sunshine as he made notes with a pencil in the corner of the page. If she reached out and brushed his warm skin, he'd turn to smile at her. She missed his masculine gentleness and imagined running the arches of her feet over his calf muscles, basking in this patch of sunlight for however long it lasted. She pictured this until the warmth of the imaginary sun and his presence eased her into sleep.

—

The CID office was buzzing with activity when Shona walked in. Her Charles Rennie Mackintosh mug sat at a table by the whiteboard. She scanned the room and was gratified to see a few extra faces she knew from around the station. Murdo had obviously been pulling in favours. Allan Peacock from Galloway CID was at the back, talking to Hannah, who was likely keeping an eye on him till he settled in. She only had vague memories of meeting him before. He moved with a coltishness that, added to his slight build and fresh complexion, made him appear younger than his years. If he'd been on her team permanently, she'd have sent him into schools and youth groups to warn about the dangers of drugs. Undercover, he'd likely be accepted as one of their own.

Shona called for everyone's attention, and people found places to sit or stand where they could.

'I'll keep this brief, but before we start, I want to thank you all for your hard work on these investigations – and welcome to DC Allan Peacock, who'll be joining us for a couple of weeks.'

He lifted a hand of acknowledgement to the group.

'Thank you, ma'am. I know you and your team's reputation, and I want to learn all I can.'

Shona saw Ravi raise a single eyebrow at Kate, half-impressed, half-ironic. As the equal ranking officers, he'd need to impress them if he was to fit in. But while Ravi saw newcomers as an opportunity to form alliances, Kate tended to view them as a threat. Shona was sure there'd be manoeuvring until the pecking order was established and she had an idea to speed up the process. When she'd discussed it with the Super and Murdo, both had given it the thumbs up.

'And due to the scope of both investigations,' Shona said, 'DC Ravi Sarwar will be temporary acting sergeant.'

There was a ripple of smiles and positive comments from everyone except Kate, who sat stony-faced. Ravi was the senior DC and to Shona it seemed ungracious of Kate not to congratulate him – it was another reason she'd been right to distance her from Hayley's case: the emotional toll was affecting her judgement.

'Right, settle down now, folks.' Shona opened her notebook, and the room quietened.

'In the case of Erin Dunlop, while the fiscal will likely decide her death was caused by drug misuse, we need to find out who supplied those drugs. Kate, where are we with that?'

Kate looked flustered, but eventually found her notes.

'Dan's cross-checking Erin's phone contacts with known dealers or drug lines in Carlisle. We've identified most of the people on her camera card as friends, no one known to us as involved in drugs. Still trying for an ID on the man that a witness saw Erin arguing with. We've half the CCTV still to review.'

'Okay, keep at it,' Shona said. 'Let's turn now to Hayley Cameron. She was using a performance-enhancing drug that may have contributed to her death.'

Shona saw Kate open her mouth to object.

'No, Kate,' she said, pointing her pen at her detective constable and addressing her directly. 'We've found no alternative explanation for the eight intramuscular injection points noted by Professor Kitchen.' She turned back to the room, ignoring Kate's sullen expression. 'But we also have the puncture wound, likely sustained on the day, and the presence of GHB in blood samples, which points to possible third-party involvement.'

Shona began ticking points off her fingers.

'Who was she sourcing the drugs from? We haven't recovered any, so where was she storing them? Was she being threatened by someone?'

Murdo leaned forward and Shona nodded for him to speak. 'There's no reports locally of spiking with GHB, either by injector pen or dropping it into lassies' drinks, an' general violence against officers doesnae seem to have increased recently.'

'Thanks, Murdo. This points to Hayley being specifically targeted. Why?'

Hannah raised a finger, indicating she had something to say.

'We've created the timeline you asked for.'

'Good. Professor Kitchen believes the Garmin data shows that Hayley was experiencing distinct episodes of stress, which may relate to her feeling threatened,' Shona explained for the rest of the team.

Hannah nodded to Vinny and Chloe, and the whiteboard came alive.

Instead of a conventional timeline, an interactive map appeared, complete with an avatar of Hayley, her cropped red-blonde hair and sports gear unmistakable. A horizontal bar across the top gave the date and time progression. Clicking on the drop pins brought up more data. There was a moment of respectful silence as they watched tiny Hayley running, cycling, swimming and going about her day-to-day business.

Once more, Shona was taken aback by the pace at which digital forensics was evolving. It seemed like every six months it became an entirely different creature. GPS from phones could lead to footage from dashcams, doorbell cams and CCTV, and arrests within hours. Younger officers seemed to take it in their stride, but Shona remembered the footslogging days of door-to-door, hunting for witnesses. From her perspective as a budget-conscious detective inspector, she was all for change. Murdo raised his eyebrows at her, impressed and perhaps in shared appreciation of progress.

'We've used the GPS to highlight where the elevated stress episodes occurred,' Hannah added. 'There doesn't seem to be an obvious link at this stage. I'll put this on the system.'

Shona noted the locations, all within the Dumfries area, but a mixture of urban and rural spots, with seemingly nothing in common.

'Right, what was she doing at these locations that caused her such anxiety or excitement? That's the focus of our inquiry now. We need to replicate these activities as close to the day and time they occurred. I want you running and on your bikes.' Normally, such a request would have been met with groans, but it was a measure of the team's commitment that no one treated this as an opportunity for a joke. 'You'll be reporting to Ravi. Everything you can get from these locations. Thank you.'

Chairs were pushed back, and there was a buzz of chatter.

Kate sat unmoving, staring at the table until data analyst Chloe tapped her arm and tried to show her something on a tablet screen. But Kate ignored her, got up and left the room without a word.

After a brief lunchtime walk and sandwich, Shona returned to her office. Half an hour later, she spotted Andy Purdy arrive in the CID room. He really shouldn't have been there. Shona stood up from her desk and tracked him as he crossed to where Kate sat. She gave him a brief hug and it was obvious from her expression that she'd been expecting him.

Murdo, on the phone in his corner spot, had seen it too. He frowned and also got to his feet, hoisting up his trousers with his free hand. Purdy was talking urgently to Kate, their heads close together. Murdo ended his call, but before he could reach them, Kate and Purdy were at Shona's door, the three of them entering together.

'Kennedy was stalking Hayley,' Kate said. 'Look.'

Andy held out his phone.

'Hello, Andy,' Shona said, noting that despite his clean jeans and collared shirt, he was unshaven and his eyes were bloodshot. 'It's best to call if you need a chat.'

She took the phone. There was a mixture of videos of the property developer Jack Kennedy: in the vicinity of Hayley's patrol car, others from what appeared to be a home security camera and even some from official ANPR.

Shona shot both Andy and Kate a furious look. 'If you've been mounting your own inquiries, not only will that get you suspended, but it could also jeopardise any future investigation.'

Both had the decency to look momentarily repentant.

'But he has been stalking her,' Kate insisted, 'and if we can match it to the stress—'

'Stop!' Shona held up her hand. 'Andy, I'm sorry. You need to go. DC Irving should know better than to involve you in any evidential matters.'

'She didn't,' Andy replied. 'I know this bastard did it.'

'All the same. It's Hayley's funeral tomorrow morning,' Shona said gently. 'Go home. Rest. You can leave this with me.' She gave them both a warning look. 'I know you're grieving so, for now, we'll say no more, but you both need to step back.'

Shona had to admit it did appear as if Kennedy had been turning up with suspicious frequency. She – not they – needed to talk to him, even if it was just to regain control of this line of inquiry. She couldn't do it today. The paperwork on the Erin Dunlop case was needed by the fiscal. She would visit Kennedy after the funeral tomorrow, before she picked up Becca from the festival. In the meantime, she prayed that Andy and Kate had the good sense to take a telling or both their careers, and potentially crucial case evidence, would go up in smoke.

–

That evening, Freya appeared in the kitchen at High Pines, carrying a full shopping bag, just as Shona was pouring her second glass of wine. She'd completely forgotten about their cooking session, but after profuse apologies, she poured Freya a glass and they set to work.

'You and James. Is it serious, then, d'you think?' said Freya, chopping an onion and not looking at her.

Shona let out a long breath. 'We both take it seriously.' She paused, trying to find the right words to describe their connection. 'I trust him.'

'Aye, well, sometimes it's best not to look too far ahead,' Freya said, then grinned. 'So, how do you manage being apart? I hear some folk these days swap sexy photos.'

Shona had seen how files, even deleted ones, could be extracted from devices and clouds, so she'd vetoed any such idea from the start. If you wouldn't print it on a T-shirt and walk down the street wearing it, don't send it into the digital world, a techy had once told her. Still, she had her memories, and they were rocket fuel where James was concerned.

'We manage,' Shona said, blushing, and giving Freya a cryptic smile. 'What about you and Tommy? Do you think you'll get married?'

'When you get to our age and are given a second chance, you treat it with care.'

Freya's first husband had ended up in jail, convicted of criminal activity on the North Sea oil rigs. It had taken Freya a long time to trust anybody again. Shona felt a pang of renewed guilt that she'd involved Tommy, however obliquely, in the aftermath of Thalia's killing of DCI Delfont by asking him to ferry them both across the Solway from Cumbria. It had been the drive to protect him and Dan Ridley, as much as Thalia, which overrode any qualms about not revealing what she knew to the authorities. She'd always thought that everyone deserved justice. Hayley Cameron and Erin Dunlop certainly did, whatever their poor decisions. But justice for Harry Delfont would mean prison for one of his victims, and to Shona that didn't seem like justice at all.

Chapter 17

Saturday morning arrived dry and bright. Shona was due to pick Becca up from The Secret Forest site at around one p.m. Prior to putting on her dark suit and white blouse for Hayley's funeral, she self-consciously removed the candles and her wine glass from the bathroom, and gathered up breakfast crockery from the bedroom, putting her plates and mugs in the dishwasher in case Becca scolded her. Wasn't it supposed to be the other way around between mothers and teenagers? Well, in a couple of months, she'd be able to make as much mess as she liked; there'd be no one to complain. Shona felt a sharp pang of sadness at the prospect.

At ten o'clock, she joined Murdo and Ravi at the back of the cemetery chapel for the civil funeral service. As she'd expected, there were press and TV cameras outside, but most remained at a respectful distance. As she'd entered, a journalist had approached her for a comment, but she'd referred them to the press release; it was a timely reminder that her actions were under scrutiny from not just her bosses, but the media too.

Kate was sitting towards the front with other members of the triathlon club, Mari Watt among them. The nurse caught Shona's eye and gave the barest nod of acknowledgement. No new evidence had emerged that pointed to her involvement in Hayley's death, but Shona still wasn't ready to eliminate her completely. She contrasted the woman's current respectful demeanour with the vitriol Mari had poured on Hayley in the interview at her house, and concluded that the woman had not only the knowledge and opportunity to have carried out the attack, but she was sleekit with it.

Hayley's coffin had been brought in, on the shoulders of her police colleagues, led by a piper. It lay on the bier at the front of the plain whitewashed interior, lit by a shaft of light from the nearest arched window, and was draped with the blue and silver Police Scotland flag. Her constable's hat and running shoes had been placed on top, alongside the floral tributes.

Given the uncertain circumstances of Hayley's death, there was a notable absence of top brass and, Shona thought, family.

Andy, at least, was present, wearing his uniform, but he presented a pitiful sight, alone in the front pew. When the unmistakable figure of Belle Cameron put a black-gloved hand of condolence on his shoulder, Shona realised that Kimi and Hayley's youngest brother, Ross *Rosey* Cameron, were in the row behind. Shona nudged Ravi and Murdo; she could tell by their furrowed brows that they'd seen them, too.

When the short service was complete, they followed the coffin as it was carried to the graveside. The cemetery sat on high ground near the river. Although they were bathed in warm sunshine, beyond the homes and churches of Dumfries itself, dark hills ranged away in all directions and a strong breeze was bringing clouds from the west. Among the granite headstones that punctuated the hillside stood more mourners, heads bowed, hands clasped in front of them – civilians and police officers alike.

Ravi left them, moving ahead to join Kate's group of friends.

'So, the Camerons. What's that all about, d'you think?' Shona said quietly to Murdo as they walked between the rows of uniformed officers standing to attention on either side of the path.

'Mibbaes they think Hayley wis deliberately targeted too, and they're wondering if it's a pop at the Cameron clan in general? It reminds folk how they had a polis in the family. We wondered oorselves if Hayley was doin' them a few favours, remember?'

Shona nodded. 'I do.'

Murdo pressed his lips together and nodded. 'Bad for business if folk think yer grassing to your nearest-and-dearest when there's a falling-oot among thieves. They'll be lookin' out for anybody that's come tae gloat. Havenae seen any likely candidates yet myself. Doesnae mean they're no' here.'

The Cameron trio had peeled away from the main party and were now standing among the gravestones at some distance from Andy Purdy, who was supported on one side by a tearful female constable, and on the other by a grim-looking man in his early fifties. Shona recognised him as Andy and Hayley's sergeant, Willie Logan.

Shona studied the family group closely, trying to unpick their motives. Belle's face was a perfect mask above a vintage Chanel two-piece. Hayley's fair-haired, thin-faced brother Rosey kept tugging at his jacket, as if ill at ease in his suit, and casting hostile glances at the other mourners, especially those in uniform. His actions combined to give the impression of the accused on his way to a date with the sheriff.

Kimi was most visibly upset. She tottered across the uneven grass on vertiginous heels, wearing a wide-brimmed boater-style hat with a short veil, dabbing repeatedly at her eyes.

Perhaps Murdo's assessment was right: the family were there to watch for anyone who'd come to gloat. But their actions could just as easily be interpreted as a show of their respectability as local business owners. Hayley's connection to the police was no threat to them as law-abiding folk. Or maybe it was genuine grief. Hayley's father and older brothers were notably absent, but perhaps these three members of the Cameron clan were attempting to bury the hatchet, along with Hayley herself. It was possible each had different motives, but what Shona wanted to know as she watched them was which, if any, of them might help her get to the truth behind Hayley's death.

The celebrant stood at the head of the grave and said a few words, most of which were snatched away by the strengthening wind. Shona caught a few as they flew past – *much-loved loyal friend, compassionate, ambitious, just, faithful*. Hayley was all those things, but it hadn't been enough to save her. It was impossible not to be moved by this collective grief, and Shona was struck by how many people Hayley must have helped in her short life, to draw such a crowd to her funeral.

The coffin was lowered, the final goodbyes said and the group by the grave began to move away. Some people came forward and shook Andy's hand. To Shona, he looked close to collapse, eyes wide, stunned by the finality of what he'd just witnessed.

The graveyard was almost empty, and she was moving towards him to offer her condolences, when he suddenly began pushing the remaining mourners aside, many of whom stepped back with shocked faces. Andy veered from the gravel path, stumbling among the grave plots, Willie Logan at his heels, face tight with concern. Andy began shouting, and it soon became clear to Shona that his target was a thirty-something man with slicked-back dark hair. The police officers nearest to him looked uncertain whether they should detain Andy's target or step in to prevent the looming confrontation.

'Christ,' Murdo exclaimed. 'It's thon property developer, Jack Kennedy.'

Shona could see Ravi gripping Kate by the arm as she tried to throw him off and join the pursuit.

Willie Logan caught up with Andy just as he finally lunged at Kennedy, who disappeared from view, going heavily down between two graves. Logan shouted to the nearest officers who, now clear in their duty, formed a buffer around Andy, who was lashing out with fists and feet at the prone figure.

'He did it! The bastard killed her!' he yelled.

Murdo and Shona were ten metres away, but remaining mourners were thinning – some craning their necks for a better view, but most making their way hurriedly back to the gate, confused and upset by this turn of events.

As Shona reached the scuffling group, faces turned expectantly towards her, and she realised she was the senior officer present. She was also aware that her stock was low with uniform, and this needed to be handled tactfully.

'Sergeant Logan, please take Constable Purdy to his car and see he's okay,' she said calmly, her use of ranks emphasising her authority. The wake was at a pub in town, a long enough journey for Andy to have hopefully calmed down by the time he got there.

Meanwhile, Murdo was hauling Jack Kennedy to his feet, leading him away.

'I know I can rely on you all,' Shona began, 'to remain respectful and not to speculate about this. It's been a very difficult time for PC Purdy, and he deserves our sympathy and support.'

There were murmurs of assent. Shona saw Sergeant Logan watching her carefully. Most of the officers seemed baffled by Andy Purdy's outburst, muttering it was all down to grief and a confused belief that this individual could somehow be responsible for his fiancée's drowning, but someone had supplied Andy with the ANPR images of Kennedy allegedly stalking Hayley. The last thing Shona wanted was a cop hit-squad dishing out their own justice.

'I know Hayley was a highly valued member of your team,' Shona went on. 'Understand that if there was any criminal involvement in her death, I will find it, and I hope you will extend courtesy and co-operation to my officers in pursuit of their duties. I and my team all offer you our condolences. Thank you all for your understanding and swift response. Today is about remembering and celebrating the unique individual Hayley was – we'll leave you in peace to do just that.'

There were further responses of *yes, ma'am* and *thank you, ma'am*, and Shona was relieved to see Andy being led away, his face in his hands, whatever fight he'd possessed gone out of him.

The graveyard was almost empty. Thank God the press and cameras had gone after the service, but she'd need to give the

Super the heads-up just in case reports of the incident leaked out. When Andy had gone after Kennedy, she'd caught sight of Belle Cameron watching events unfold, but now the family party had disappeared, and Shona wondered what they'd made of it.

Kennedy stood with Murdo in the shadows beneath a tree, dabbing the blood from a graze on his cheek with a handkerchief and pushing back his disordered hair.

'I've been wanting a word with you,' Shona began. She hadn't considered Kennedy would be at the funeral but this saved her a trip to his home address before she went to collect Becca at the festival. 'Mr Kennedy, did you kill Hayley Cameron?'

He looked at her, appalled. 'Of course I didn't.'

She studied his face for a moment. She wasn't sure she believed him, but you'd have to be a particular kind of idiot to turn up at a funeral crawling with cops if you'd done away with one of their number. So why was he here? She studied the shaken figure and his pale, anguished face. 'You look like you need a drink. Come on.'

—

The Kelpie was a traditional pub. Just after the eleven a.m. opening time on a Saturday, those inside were mostly locals whose minds were on their first drink and the likelihood of goals in that afternoon's friendly between Scotland and Finland. They paid no attention to three mourners from the nearby cemetery.

Shona took Kennedy to a table at the back, while Murdo ordered coffees for himself and Shona, and a whisky for the dishevelled businessman.

'D'you want to tell me what that was all about?' Shona said, when Murdo returned, and Kennedy had downed his drink. There wasn't much damage, beyond his pride and the graze on his face. She hoped he wasn't about to turn difficult and claim it as assault, which it clearly was. But in the face of twenty police officers who'd swear they saw him stumble, it would lead nowhere, except to the ticketing of his car every time he exceeded the speed limit by even a fraction.

Shona tried again. 'Why did you come to the funeral?'

'I loved her.'

Shona wasn't sure what sort of answer she'd been expecting, but delusional self-justification came in many forms, a romantic attachment among them.

'There's an allegation that you were stalking her,' Shona said, thinking of the videos Andy and Kate had collected. Perhaps his pursuit of Hayley hadn't been because of the unjustness of his arrest, but a strange, possibly even faux-romantic, fixation he'd developed in the course of it. Hayley could handle herself, but Kennedy was tall, broad-shouldered and looked like he worked out. He could easily be classed as a threat, and the rejection of his advances a potential motive.

Kennedy took out his phone and leaned his elbows on the table as he scrolled through the photos. He tilted the screen towards Shona and Murdo. The picture showed Hayley leaning over his shoulders from behind, arms around him as they both grinned at the camera.

'It began after she arrested me. Sounds like the start of a Hollywood movie, doesn't it?'

His accent was educated, his suit quality. He had dark blue eyes and a full lower lip that was just short of a pout. Kennedy was a handsome man. She could see why Hayley might have been attracted to him. He scrolled though a number of other pictures, and detailed how and when they'd met.

'We were discreet. I'm married. She was in a relationship. But the affection was genuine on both sides. I think so, anyway.'

He closed the image folder, then turned the screen once more towards Shona.

Call me. I'd like to talk to you about Hayley.

She recognised the text she'd sent to the sole number on the Android phone. Hayley must have wiped the device after every conversation. She was taking no chances. From the evidence he presented, it looked like an affair rather than stalking. But had Andy found out what was going on? Had he sent them after Kennedy on purpose, as revenge?

Shona glanced at Murdo, inviting him to ask any questions he had.

'Was anyone threatening her?' he said.

The businessman looked blank, then shook his head.

Shona thanked Jack Kennedy, adding that he should avoid the wake. He gave a wry smile and promised he would.

Once they were alone, she shared with Murdo her theory that Andy had deliberately misled them.

He swirled the remains of his coffee around the cup but didn't answer.

'It also gives Andy a powerful motive for killing Hayley,' she pressed.

'He was ten miles away, surrounded by cops an' the public an' probably the mayor, who'll aw vouch for him. Can't see how he's our man, even wi' that motive.'

They drove back into the centre of Dumfries and joined the others in The Vineyard wine bar, a more salubrious venue than the pub they'd just left. The wake was in full swing in the large upstairs room, the earlier incident at the cemetery apparently forgotten by most of the mourners. Andy Purdy stood by the bar, surrounded by his fellow uniformed officers. After they'd said hello, Murdo side-stepped the tapas on offer and helped himself to a plate of ham sandwiches. Shona joined Kate and Ravi at a table by the window.

When Shona relayed the conversation with Kennedy and described the photographs he'd shown them on his phone, Kate looked shocked, then shook her head.

'I had no idea.' There was the sting of betrayal in her tone.

'Perhaps she let Andy think Kennedy was stalking her to throw him off the scent,' Ravi said, and this time there was no reproachful glare from Kate.

Shona had to admit it was possible.

'What d'you want us to do now, boss?' Ravi went on.

The revelation of an affair had changed things, but it hadn't altered the basic facts of the case. Somebody had hated Hayley enough to kill her.

'Go home to your families and hug them tight. It's what I intend to do. I'll see you bright and early Monday morning. We'll start again with what we know. Then we'll get on with finding out who did this terrible thing to one of our own.'

Chapter 18

There wasn't time to go home and change out of her dark suit, so Shona drove straight to the pick-up point at The Secret Forest. They'd need to take a formal statement from Jack Kennedy, but as Ravi had been thorough with the businessman's alibi and obtained timestamped photos from the golf tournament he'd attended, showing him on the first tee just as Hayley had entered the water, she had no grounds to consider him a suspect.

Kennedy's revelation had been hard on Kate. Shona had no doubt that she and Hayley had been close, but the number of key things her best friend had chosen to hide from her was mounting. Kate had to be asking herself how well she really knew Hayley, and Shona understood from her own past experiences – her husband Rob chief among them – that was a lonely and dispiriting place to be. Kate had already mentioned she was thinking of giving up triathlons, worried that she'd experience flashbacks each time she swam. Shona had urged her once more to consider therapy. You had to work through it. She knew from the lifeboat that traumatic events could take root and didn't necessarily fade with time as people hoped they would. It was clearly already affecting her behaviour, and things could get worse for Kate, particularly if she had no one to talk to, so Shona made a mental note to raise the issue again if her DC didn't act on her advice soon.

Shona checked her messages. Becca hadn't replied to her text announcing her arrival. Irritated, but not surprised, she got out of the car, donning her sunglasses. There was a line of other parents waiting for their offspring. The lucky ones had bagged spots under the trees. The rest, including Shona, looked set to participate in the customary penance of being broiled alive for their sin of wishing, just this once, to collect their kids at the pre-arranged time.

A steady stream of the more organised festivalgoers were coming out of the gate, which was flanked by painted signs reminding them to hand sort their rubbish and that any leftover food was being sent to a local anaerobic digester to be broken down into biogas and biofertiliser. Becca had been keen to take the carbon-neutral shuttle bus to Dumfries train station with her friends, but Shona pointed out she'd have to drive further to pick her up, negating any environmental benefit. Was Becca more worried about her eco-credentials suffering if her new friends saw her mum arrive in an ageing petrol Audi? Or was she concerned they'd remember she was a cop, and therefore clearly part of the patriarchal capitalist system? Either way, Shona wished now she'd agreed to meet Becca at the train station. She could have been sitting in a cafe with a panini and an iced coffee.

Other overheated parents were also looking at their phone screens and probably calculating if they could idle their engines to get the air conditioning going, without being instantly publicly shamed and banished from the carpark.

Shona took a breath. At least it wasn't raining, and she didn't have anywhere pressing she needed to be, a rare moment of stillness in her carousel of job and High Pines.

Opening her phone, she began scrolling through her messages. There'd been no more calls from the NCA, and she felt a twinge of guilt over Dan. She'd not delivered on her promise to bring him on board and had begun to wonder if her true motivation had purely been a subliminal desire to flush out the truth about whether or not he'd talked to them. If he had been approached, would he now think she was punishing him for a perceived betrayal? The situation was threatening to drive a wedge between them, as she'd always known it might, but it wasn't a conversation she could have with him on the phone. Her finger hovered over his WhatsApp as she considered the kind of cryptically worded message she and Thalia occasionally used, but she couldn't frame a question that was both specific enough for Dan to understand and obscure enough to hide its true meaning from anyone else, should an investigation proceed.

To distract herself, she sent James a text, just to say she hoped he'd enjoyed the day at the zoo. He replied instantly with a heart emoji, though it must have been around five a.m. there, and sent a picture of him with the twins, feeding a camel. She sent a heart in return. Both local and long-distance relationships required a lot of the same things to work, but she'd realised early that when there's an entire continent, an ocean and several time zones between you, any delay in replying seemed to gain an unwarranted significance.

James regularly sent surprise packages of flowers and clothes, but the gift that she kept returning to was a photograph. She pulled it up now on her phone and it still had the same power – an instant dopamine hit – that it had had when she'd first seen it a few months before. It had begun as separate school pictures of them both – Shona in her Goth era, curls replaced with straightened jet-black hair and heavy eye make-up; James, a skinny version of his famously muscled physique, wearing a brown leather jacket. He'd had the images digitally combined so they were standing together beneath a beautiful apple tree, which he said represented the time it had taken for their love to blossom, and how it would keep on growing in the future. It was so realistic that when Shona had first seen it, she'd racked her brains for the moment when it had been taken, knowing all the while that it had never actually happened. It didn't make it any less real, he'd said. Now it had become an implanted memory which she found both alluring and unsettling. She'd no wish to rewrite the past, to downgrade the love and happiness she'd shared with Rob. In truth, she'd largely forgotten James in the intervening years, or at least consigned him to a teenage crush. But now their love seemed to be growing of its own accord, its existence creeping both backwards and forwards through time.

Shona took a swig from her water bottle and studied the young people coming out of the gate. They all appeared to be dressed alike, in crumpled and muddy clothes, with braided hair, hats and sunglasses, and she scrutinised their features looking for her daughter, but without success.

She returned to her phone and chatted with James, who soon signed off with a flurry of kisses. He'd always been clear about his expectations. This wasn't a fling. He wanted her to share his life, but understood she had to make that decision for herself. For Shona, it was less clear. She had no doubt that she loved him and had never felt so connected to anyone, not even Rob in the good days. She and James had whole conversations without speaking a word. But what she wanted had always been subsumed by what was good for Becca, Rob, High Pines, her job. She'd always been the one keeping all the plates spinning. Putting her own desires first was going to take some practice.

When Shona checked the time, she was surprised to see that forty minutes had passed. Her texts and voicemail messages to Becca were still unanswered, she noted with irritation. Twenty minutes later, her irritation had morphed into a creeping sense of unease. Checking the other cars, she saw that most of the parents who had arrived at the same time as her had now gone. She'd been watching the gate and thought she'd seen Becca's friends board the bus fifteen minutes before, but was sure her daughter wasn't among them.

Suddenly, the unease blossomed into full-blown alarm. Becca had been answering messages regularly, so why wasn't she now? A vision of Erin Dunlop, unmissed by friends and dead in her tent, morphed into one of her daughter in the same position. Chucking the empty water bottle through the open window onto the passenger seat, she grabbed her bag and locked the Audi.

The bulked-up gate marshal in his black T-shirt and hi-vis must have seen her pacing the carpark for the last hour, but still shook his head when she approached.

'Sorry. Can't let you in without a pass.'

She'd been hesitant to look like an overbearing parent, to storm onto the site, but as she pulled out her police ID, she wondered why on earth she'd worried about that when her daughter's life could be at stake.

'I'm Detective Inspector Shona Oliver,' she said, watching the customary sea-change occur on the security guard's face. 'I need to access the campsite.'

He could have checked with security control, found her an escort, but this late in a week of twelve-hour shifts, he'd obviously taken one look at the determination on Shona's face and decided the easiest course of action was to step aside.

There would be an explanation, Shona told herself as she followed the signs for *The Sleep Zone*. Maybe Becca had forgotten their arrangement and jumped on the shuttle bus after all. That didn't explain why she wasn't texting from Dumfries train station – *Mum where ARE YOU??!!*

Ahead, the multicoloured assortment of tents sat among the trees like a fairy-tale encampment, but the greenish light filtering through the leaves gave the place a sickly look. Beyond, Shona could just see the small loch, with its central island and the blackened remains of Glaistig, the green lady, burned at the festival's end and no longer on hand to keep even a cursory eye on wayward children.

She stumbled through the tents until she found the empty space where Erin Dunlop's blue tent had been, now removed by the authorities. Becca has said hers was the red one nearby. It was empty. She cursed her low-heeled court shoes, which might be appropriate for funerals but were less useful among tree roots. Looking up, she saw Becca's friend – the blonde girl – Christie, and a bleary-eyed young man she didn't recognise, near another cluster of tents, and realised in the disorientating uniformity of the camp that she was in the wrong spot.

Shona hurried over. Christie must have remembered her from their previous encounter because her expression became wary.

'Christie, isn't it?' Shona said, her breathing ragged with exertion.

The girl nodded uncertainly.

'I'm just here to collect Becca. Where is she?' she demanded.

'Becca?' The girl stared back blankly. Shona resisted the urge to shake her. Literally, what was wrong with the lass? They'd recently witnessed the death of one of their friends, and if that wasn't a sufficiently bonding experience to fix the names of your companions in your mind, then it bloody well should be.

'Oh,' she said, as if she'd suddenly recalled who Becca was. 'No. Sorry. Haven't seen her today.'

'Okay.' Shona forced a bright smile. The area was practically empty. Christie and the lad looked like they'd just woken up and were awkwardly saying their goodbyes after a short-lived romance. 'Any ideas where she might be?'

The boy scrubbed through his messy dark hair, plunged his hands into his jeans pockets and looked blank. Christie shook her head.

Shona began pulling open the neighbouring tents, all of which were empty, save for discarded sleeping bags, bottles and clothes. She was about to set off back towards the main stage area when she suddenly remembered she had the security control's number in her phone contacts and stabbed at the screen. It rang for a long time then went to a messaging service.

'What's wrong with everyone?' she muttered. 'It's not a crime against nature to answer your bloody phone.' Her mind began to speed through possible scenarios. She was lying dead elsewhere... Or she'd been found alive, but taken to hospital without ID? Is that why nobody had contacted her?

She hurried back towards the gate, reasoning she'd meet a marshal with a walkie-talkie soon. But when that failed, she diverted through the crowd towards an area of stallholders –

holistic sound therapy, *basket weaving* – and stopped dead in her tracks.

'Becca!' she yelled with such anger that festivalgoers moved away, forming a wide arc around her as if she were a particularly hazardous boulder in a torrent.

Becca jumped as if she'd been on the receiving end of an electric cattle-prod. The stallholder she'd been helping pack up – a woman in her sixties with long, white hair and a purple kaftan – stared at Shona in alarm.

'Why didn't you reply to my texts? Where were you? Why weren't you in the carpark at one o'clock?'

'Three o'clock. You're picking me up at three o'clock,' Becca yelled back.

'That's not the sort of detail I get wrong, Rebecca.'

'Well, obviously, it is, and,' she added with a dramatic flourish, 'my phone is off to save charge, if that's all right with you.'

'No, it is not all right with me. You cannot be out of contact.'

'I'm an adult, for fuck's sake. I could get married or join the army.'

That neither was likely wasn't enough to diffuse Shona's anger. 'Do not swear at me, lady,' she said in a voice that made even experienced members of her CID team quake in their boots. But instead of looking contrite, Becca's expression darkened.

Shona saw a flash of Rob in their daughter's defiant posture, and the thought that Becca had inherited more than his height and square shoulders made her gut contract. Risk-taker, gambling addict, felon. She'd make damn sure her daughter would not become any of those.

'This what it's going to be like when I'm in Glasgow?' Becca's face was hard with fury. 'You turning up to check on me every minute? *Becca, the polis are at the door,*' she mimicked an imaginary flatmate. '*Oh, wait, it's your mammy!* Give me some credit. Yeah, I've made mistakes, and I'm sure you have too, but I learned from them.' Becca hoisted a canvas tote bag. 'You know this is your case. It's about Erin, not me.'

She turned and stomped off towards the parking area.

Shona stared at the bag now looped over Becca's shoulder. One handle came loose and she saw it was filled with crafts that her daughter had made – something tie-dyed, a dreamcatcher, a wooden animal.

She fought the desire to take refuge in the past. Her daughter was still a child she needed to protect. But even as she thought it, she knew it wasn't the whole truth.

'I'm so sorry,' Shona said to the stallholder.

'No problem, hen,' the woman replied with a sympathetic smile. 'Lassies, eh? I've got five of them at home. Why d'you think I do the festivals.'

But as Shona set off after her daughter, she knew Becca was right. The case had spooked her more than she cared to admit, even to James or Freya. And with everything else on her plate it was possible she'd been mistaken about the pick-up time. She was so lucky. Erin's mother would give anything to be in her shoes right now. Her daughter was coming home with her. That was all that mattered, and for that she was profoundly grateful.

When she reached the parking area, Becca was leaning on the car, her back to her mother. Shona activated the locks from a distance. Once her rucksack was stowed in the boot, Becca got in the passenger seat and folded her arms.

'I'm sorry. I love you,' Shona said, when she settled behind the wheel. The words had never been more heartfelt.

After a moment, Becca reached out and squeezed her mother's hand.

'I know. I love you too.'

Chapter 19

On Monday morning, Shona headed into Dumfries, but not to the CID office in Cornwall Mount. She'd spent Saturday evening on a walk along the shore with Becca, then dropped into the Royal Arms for dinner. It had been a surprisingly successful evening, given their argument earlier in the day.

On Sunday, she'd made it to lifeboat training in the morning, then cooked and ate with James in the evening. There was enough for Becca, but she rarely joined them, tactfully making her excuses and heading straight for the TV in the upstairs lounge. When the box of ingredients had arrived, and it wasn't far off what Freya had predicted, thanks to her coaching the result had been surprisingly good. The delivery always saved Shona time shopping, but it would be nice once in a while to do what normal couples did: wander the aisles with James, holding hands and picking ingredients, then driving home together.

James thought she looked pale and tired, and told her she should take time for herself. 'What, like a manicure?' she'd asked, remembering how she'd once seen him with painted toenails. 'Aye, if you like,' he'd replied, and it was then that the idea had come to her.

She called Murdo to tell him she had thought of a way to discover what had passed between Hayley and her sister Kimi during the altercation in the pub, a fortnight before her death. He listened to her plan, but didn't sound convinced, especially as it meant she would be going alone.

Diamond Nails was just off the high street. The business was registered in Kimi Cameron's name, as her own enterprise.

Shona suspected the family used it to clean dirty money – not an uncommon practice, especially in cash businesses – but she had no proof to back that up.

Shona had chosen her outfit with care, one very different from her usual trouser suit. If she looked like a lady who lunched, not a cop, she might not alert the other girls in the nail bar, or whoever else might be watching. She'd finally settled on a blue Jasper Conran printed silk wrap dress lurking at the back of her wardrobe. She'd last worn the outfit for a London wedding five years before and was relieved to find it still fitted. With penny loafers, a pale blue pashmina and a clutch bag, her look struck the right balance between smart and casual. She sent a snap of herself to James, to show him what he was missing, and he replied with a sizzling heart. Perhaps the picture would serve a second purpose, she thought with dark humour, of helping to identify her body if her visit to the nail bar went badly wrong.

As she sat in the Audi a little way up the street from the shop, she wondered again what she could do to persuade Kimi Cameron to talk. What could she offer the woman in exchange? To decide that, she needed to know what Kimi wanted.

'Regular of Kimi's, are you?' The pale-skinned lass with the blonde bob behind the counter eyed her doubtfully when she asked for the owner by name, glancing at the state of her nails.

'I know,' Shona replied, pulling an embarrassed face. 'Stable-block renovations, what can you do?'

House alterations would imply she couldn't afford to employ a decorator, but everyone knew that truly rich folk would do anything for their horses.

Kimi looked through the beaded curtain from the back office. Shona casually took off her sunglasses and saw that the young woman recognised her. But Kimi said nothing to the receptionist. It was Monday morning, quiet. Not an unusual time for a busy lady to indulge in a little personal maintenance.

Shona took out a wad of cash. 'I'm happy to wait. Maybe hang around all morning.' She laughed, as if this was an amusing idea for someone with a whirlwind life such as hers. But her words also contained a veiled threat — a cop sitting in your reception for hours could maybe see more than was healthy.

Kimi took the hint and swayed forward on her high-heeled mules, smoothing the short skirt of her white uniform, and directing Shona to a nail station at the far end of the room. When they were seated opposite each other, Kimi took Shona's hands in her own, assessing the short and slightly roughened nails.

'Keeping it natural today, are we?'

Shona saw the receptionist smirk, but her smile disappeared when Kimi sent her to make coffee for them both. Shona said she'd have oat milk, calculating correctly that would require a trip to the shop up the road.

'I wanted to make sure you were okay after Saturday,' Shona began in a low, pleasant voice. 'The funeral can't have been easy.'

Kimi arched a sceptical eyebrow as she brought out the file and got to work.

'Your sister had a brilliant life ahead of her.'

Kimi's fingers tightened their grip.

'Well, maybe you wouldn't consider it brilliant,' Shona went on. 'But she was in control of her own life. Free to make decisions, earn a good wage. She was respected and listened to by people around her. Cared for by her colleagues, who'd lay down their lives for her if it came to it.'

She wanted Kimi to compare her own existence in the hothouse environment of the Cameron compound, treading a careful path between her overbearing father, three semi-feral brothers and the looming threat posed by her newly released Uncle Fin. And then there were Uncle Fin's three sons. Shona had learned from Dan Ridley's briefing document that they were a match for Kimi's own brothers. The eldest cousin, Gavin — or *Geezer* — had form for ABH; the middle one, Shaun Cameron, known as *Stab* or *Stab-Happy*, had knifed a guy in bar brawl; and the youngest, whom Shona had seen that day with Uncle Fin, was Mark, known as Mad Markie or *M&M*, and he was on his way to outdoing his older siblings. Viewed a certain way, Kimi was a pawn between two evenly balanced sides of the chessboard, and little pieces like her didn't generally fare well. Belle had carved out her position as a queen and might defend her niece, but Kimi was vulnerable, whatever way you looked at it.

When Kimi said nothing, Shona switched to a direct approach.

'Was anyone threatening Hayley?'

'How'd you expect me to know that?' Kimi replied, her full lips closing into a hard line.

'There's not much between you in age,' Shona tried again. 'You must have happy memories of growing up together?'

Kimi had finished filing one hand and moved on to the other. Shona felt she was fast running out of ideas and fingers.

'Long time since we were kids,' Kimi said heavily, as if she was eighty-six instead of twenty-six.

'How did Hayley get on with the rest of the family?'

'No contact.'

'And how did Hayley feel about that?'

Another shrug.

'So, what about when you saw her recently? The argument in the pub.'

Kimi gave her a glance that made it clear she knew they'd reached the principal reason for the visit. She sighed and seemed to make up her mind.

'Dinnae suppose it matters now. Some lads at the pub were giving us aggro. She told them tae piss off. I told her tae mind her own business.'

'Boyfriend?' Shona asked. Kimi just gave her a look of derisive scorn.

'Boyfriend? You met ma brothers? Naebody's gonna hang around, wi' them breathin' doon their necks.'

Kimi filed harder, catching the quick, and Shona gave an involuntary start.

'Sorry,' Kimi said. She set down the file and shook a bottle of clear varnish plucked from a rack of startling colours beside her.

'There was something else, wasn't there?' Shona pressed.

Kimi drew the brush across every nail on Shona's right hand before she answered.

'Hayley wanted me tae come and live with her an' Andy.' She snorted as if the idea was ridiculous. 'Live wi' two cops. That'd be ma life gone.'

It was unclear whether this meant her brothers would react violently to an apparent betrayal, or if Kimi viewed it as a case of out-of-the-frying-pan-into-the-fire when it came to others imposing their restrictive views on what she could and couldn't do.

'I suppose you'd have had to give up this place?' Shona suggested. Being nominally her own boss in the nail salon might be the life raft she clung on to.

Kimi shrugged, her expression non-committal. 'Might have been okay wi' just us two.'

She thought of Hayley and Andy's box-sized starter home with Kimi and her full wardrobe and shoe collection in the spare room. It wouldn't have been a happy existence for any of them, but maybe Hayley rationalised it as a safer environment than the Cameron household for her little sister. It was no surprise Kimi was tearful at the funeral. Not only had her only sister died, but any dream of a different life, however unappealing it might have initially seemed, had died with her.

'Don't you like Andy?'

'He's just like a' the rest.'

The rest? Did she mean her brothers? Uncle Fin? Kimi had witnessed Andy Purdy's attack on Jack Kennedy at the cemetery, so maybe this wasn't such an unexpected appraisal.

'How do you mean? Was Andy violent towards Hayley?' His alibi was solid, as Murdo had pointed out, but Shona was still interested in the dynamics of the relationship. Was it Andy's violence that had sent Hayley into Jack Kennedy's arms?

'D'you think Andy killed her?' Kimi's face was impassive, but there was something of her aunt, Belle Cameron, in the calculating way she was assessing the implications of Shona's question.

'We've no evidence to suggest that's the case,' Shona parried, leaving room for Kimi to enlighten her if she knew otherwise.

But the young woman just shrugged. 'I just meant, *men*. You know.' She rolled her eyes in contempt but below her expression Shona saw a glimpse of fear and wondered what daily dangers Kimi was forced to navigate just to maintain her own safety. Whatever they were, it was evident she wasn't about to confide in a cop.

The nails were finished by the time the receptionist returned, apologetic and breathless, with the coffees in tall glass cups.

Shona paid her bill, adding a handsome tip, which included her contact details folded between the notes.

'S'all right,' Kimi said, pocketing the cash and indicating a sofa by the shop window. 'Nae hurry. Sit there an' finish yer coffee.' Then she bustled about, setting things unnecessarily straight in the nail bar with a nervous energy that made Shona think she was weighing up a decision in her mind. Finally, she checked her appointments with the receptionist, waved her vape and announced she was popping outside, catching Shona's eye as she did so.

After a full minute, Shona got up and returned her coffee cup to the receptionist.

'Better go. Thank you so much for fitting me in.'

'Nae problem. Mind yer nice manicure on they horses, now,' the receptionist replied. 'We can do great nail art wi' wee ponies on them if you fancy, next time.'

'Lovely.' Shona smiled, replacing her sunglasses to hide her amusement at what Murdo might say if she returned to the office suitably attired: *D'you ken you've cuddies on yer nails, boss?*

Kimi was standing in front of the estate agents' window next-door, out of view of her own premises. Her back to the street, she was scrolling through her phone. Shona stopped next to her as if browsing the houses on offer. A steady stream of traffic was loud enough to mask their conversation from anyone standing nearby.

'Whatever's going on, Kimi, I can help you,' she said, eyes fixed on a four-bed church conversion for sale in Thornhill.

'Hayley used tae say the same thing,' she replied, her lips hardly moving, voice barely above a whisper.

'Hi,' said a male voice at Shona's elbow.

At first glance, she thought she'd been cornered by a student keen for her to sign up to some good cause or other – a charity mugger, or 'chugger', as she believed they were termed. Then she recognised DC Allan Peacock, looking at her in his best eager-beaver mode.

Kimi flashed him a smile, tossing her sheet of glossy hair back. Peacock stared at her like an animal caught in the head-lights.

When she turned back to Shona, the beautiful face was blank and cold.

'Sorry, DI Oliver, there's nothing I can tell you.'

-

Shona spent the journey back to the office admonishing Detective Constable Allan Peacock in precise detail as to why a junior officer should never, ever interrupt a senior one in the process of interviewing a potential witness. When she dismissed him in the carpark at Cornwall Mount, he shot up the stairs like his tail was on fire. Shona went to the loos and changed into the spare dark trouser suit and shell-pink blouse she kept hanging in a suit carrier in her office.

'What was that all about, Murdo?' she said, quizzing him about Peacock's arrival at the nail bar.

'I wis never happy aboot you going there alone,' he said stubbornly. 'Ravi will back me up.'

Ravi made a *don't drag me into this* face, unwilling to take sides between his sergeant and his inspector. 'Doubt Uncle Fin comes in tae have his nails done, but you never know.'

When Shona had told Peacock he'd cut off a potential witness, he'd looked stricken.

'To be fair, he's a grafter,' Murdo said. 'He plotted a walking route an' has visited six of thon pins on the map.'

Hayley's shift log had recently been added to the map. Her beat partner, Joanne Mitchell, was on leave and not contactable by phone, Sergeant Logan had told them, but nothing had stuck in his memory as an out-of-the-ordinary job, so the locations all needed checking.

'Peacock's also been giving Kate a hand wi' drugs intelligence on the dealers in Stranraer,' Ravi added. 'Wee suck-up, if you ask me.'

Shona gave him a censorious look. She began to feel she'd been too optimistic about getting Kimi to open up, even before any hope had been dashed by Peacock's untimely arrival. There never was much hope, if she was honest. She updated Murdo and Ravi on what Kimi had told her.

'Makes sense,' Murdo agreed. 'Hayley would likely step in if lads were hassling some lassies, even if it wasnae her wee sister.'

'And she didn't know if Hayley had been threatened?' Ravi said.

'She said not,' Shona replied. 'But I think there's still plenty Kimi Cameron isn't telling us.'

Kimi might have been too scared to ever leave and live with Hayley, but she might also have calculated she'd be better off – in terms of money and power – at home. She thought of the coquettish way Kimi had tottered, smiling, towards Uncle Fin, the age-old tactic of appeasing violent men by pandering to their ego. She was playing a dangerous game there. As the youngest – the indulged baby of the family – perhaps she expected that everyone ultimately would dance to her tune. She was clever, but was she clever enough, Shona wondered, to recognise the jungle she was walking through or that other people were smarter still than her?

Chapter 20

In the hazy heat of the afternoon, two separate briefings would have been better, but the truth was that Shona just didn't have enough folk to do that, or indeed the time. The intelligence team were working across both cases, with Ravi managing the Hayley Cameron investigation and Kate the Erin Dunlop death. Murdo, as usual, was keeping the whole show on the road. Shona didn't want to drag anyone away from their desk, so she went to the whiteboard and banged the metal mug that held the pens on the nearby tabletop.

'Listen up, folks.' When everyone was looking her way, she began. 'I won't keep you long, and thank you for all your efforts so far. Erin Dunlop: updates, please. Kate?'

Shona had already called Dan about the contact list in Erin's phone. She'd wanted to break the news of Allan Peacock's arrival herself, but he'd already heard it from Kate. He was initially chilly with her, but she'd emphasised that she'd done her best to get him over and that his input was vital. It had occurred to her that maybe it was a blessing that she hadn't brought him into the team. It would give the NCA less to chew on if they hadn't yet picked up their previous association. Dan had seemed mollified by her assurances and, yes, there were a couple of names from the Carlisle contacts they'd warned for possession. He'd follow it up.

'Uniform have pulled in a couple of known dealers on our patch,' Kate began. 'Word is that the festival suppliers were an outside team.'

It tallied with what Force Intelligence had told Shona about festivals being a movable feast for gangs. The good news was that they'd likely travelled elsewhere and there'd be no more deaths on her patch. The bad news was that they had little chance of catching up with them and their fatally strong batch of MDMA.

So, tie the case up and hand over what you've gathered to Force Intelligence. Let them deal with it. The echo of Detective Chief Superintendent Davies's words was seductive in her ear. It would make sense but felt like a betrayal to Sandra Dunlop, who deserved answers as to why her daughter died and the knowledge that someone would be held responsible.

'I'm not convinced there's no local angle to this,' Shona said. 'Drug supply is a business like any other. The Secret Forest is new, small-scale. It's not Leeds or Glastonbury. Chances are it's not on the big OCGs' radar yet. Get Jimmy and Thomas out there, talking to users. Find out what they're being offered and warn them. Ask if there's any new county-lines operations doing three-for-two deals or the like.'

She turned to her acting sergeant. 'Ravi? What about Hayley?'

'We've checked the timings with the shift workers Hayley sometimes trained with, and none of the high-stress incidents correspond to when she was with them – only when she was out on her tod. Still checking those locations, but Vinny's got something.'

The interactive whiteboard behind her sprang into life, making Shona jump. She had no idea how he was doing that. Sometimes, she wondered if the CID operation was slowly becoming a digital matrix of Vinny's creation. One day she'd open her office door and come face to face with an AI avatar of herself sitting at her desk. She'd be fine with that, as long as digital-Shona took over all the boring jobs – budget meeting, overtime returns – she was welcome to those.

On the screen, an American website for training supplements appeared, complete with its own branded merchandise which, to Shona's dismay, included a range of lethal-looking tactical hunting knives. She couldn't imagine they had a legitimate place in any gym kitbag.

'What am I looking at?'

'This was in her laptop's wiped history,' Vinny said, and proceeded to scroll through a list of PEDs, including some names Shona knew from her chat with Slasher Sue – erythropoietin, or EPO, and somatropin, also known as human growth hormone. The drugs weren't cheap – ranging from fifty quid for a small bottle of pills into the thousands for bundles of training supplements.

'Hayley's bank details confirm purchases from the website,' Chloe said. 'The packages probably arrived disguised as protein builders or something similar,' she added, as if that would somehow mitigate things, and side-eyed Kate, who was sitting just up from her. 'There were also regular cash withdrawals from her account that could have been drug purchases.'

They didn't need to wait for the tox results to confirm it. There was no way around it: Hayley was doping.

'I'm not being funny, boss,' Kate began, her tone laden with indignation. 'But isn't this a waste of time?'

Shona frowned. Anyone who began a sentence with *I'm not being funny but...* was far from amusing. They were perilously close to being a cheeky wee besom.

'I mean, what about the GHB in Hayley's system? That didn't come from this website. You are still looking for who killed her, aren't you?'

Shona was about to remind Kate that GHB could also be used as a performance enhancer, and Erin Dunlop's case was her principal area of interest, but that wasn't the real issue. Showing any level of disrespect in front of the team was out of order.

'DC Irving, have I given you any indication that the focus of the investigation has changed?'

'No, ma'am...' Kate stuttered. 'It's just... Why are we still concentrating on this, when her killer's out there?'

Shona hadn't wanted to do this in front of the team, but Kate had crossed a line. Now this wasn't just about an officer struggling with the psychological and emotional impact of a case, this was a direct, and very public, challenge to Shona's authority and leadership. She took a step closer, deliberately lowering her voice so that Kate was forced to strain forward to hear.

'I know you're ambitious and it's to your credit. I know that you think you can do my job better, and maybe one day you'll be a DI and SIO, I don't doubt it. But this backchat won't get you far.'

They eyeballed each other, Shona willing Kate to take a telling before she was forced to suspend her, which was in nobody's interest. Kate's jaw was a hard line, her stare unblinking. Shona stood with her shoulders back, hands clasped before her. Something about Kate's personality had told Shona this day would come – a lack of respect, a lack of judgement had always been on the cards. From the corner of her eye, she saw Murdo frown, and perhaps her DC saw it too. Kate's resolution faltered as she realised no one was going to back her up. There was an awkward silence that seemed to stretch, until finally, Kate looked away.

'Yes, ma'am. Sorry, ma'am,' Kate mumbled.

Shona acknowledged this with a nod, then turned to her support staff. Vinny was unmoved, but Chloe was biting her lower lip and looked as if she couldn't wait to get out of the room.

'Thank you, Vinny, Chloe. Good work.' She lifted her notebook and checked her list of outstanding actions. 'Ravi, let's get that statement from Jack Kennedy. Without being indelicate, if he was engaged in clandestine hook-ups with Hayley, then he should be able to cross a few more places off our stress map. Anything else?'

'Any o' thon web purchase fae this country?' Murdo said, taking his cue from Shona and proceeding as if nothing had happened.

'There's a pattern of web payments we haven't allocated yet,' Chloe offered. 'But also, the cash withdrawals.'

It was possible Hayley hadn't been sourcing everything by post from abroad. When Slasher Sue's tox results dropped, Shona wanted to be ready.

Shona nodded. 'Keep looking for suppliers. Since possession of some PEDs for personal use isn't illegal, but manufacture and supply in the UK is, it gives someone a potential motive to silence Hayley.'

Ravi raised his pen, indicating that he had something to add. Shona nodded for him to go ahead.

'The triathlon club chair thought she was talking to someone at another club about going pro. Could be somethin' for us?'

'Good point. Ask the club members we've interviewed if they know. Any names come up as potential coaches, run a check, and make a tactful approach. Were they concerned about their conversation with Hayley? Did they discuss performance enhancers? But don't make it sound like we're asking them if they dope their athletes.'

'We still haven't found where she was storing these drugs, boss,' Ravi added, making a note.

'Where've we not searched? Could that be one of our stress locations?'

'Aye, hiding your stash is bound to up the heart rate,' Ravi replied.

'Any likely candidates? Allan, you've been doing the rounds. Lock-ups? Storage facilities? Anything like that? Could even be somewhere she visited regularly when she was on shift.'

Peacock was sitting on a desk at the back, looking as if he'd prefer to keep a low profile; Shona thought he'd likely remembered the tongue-lashing she'd given him after he interrupted her and Kimi. Well, if it kept him on his toes, fine. 'Nothing yet, boss.'

'Well, keep at it. These stress peaks can't all be collaring criminals and coffee stops.'

'Why coffee stops?' Peacock said, puzzled, before he could stop himself.

'Have you seen the price of a double macchiato these days, pal?' Ravi said, in a move calculated, successfully in this case, to lighten the mood. There were tentative smiles and nods around the room.

Shona smiled too. 'Remember your days on the beat? I meant it's usually just when you've got your coffee that a code zero, officer down, comes in and your stress rates go through the roof. But in Hayley's case, that's not the whole story, is it? We need to know what else she had to fear.'

Shona made a point of catching Kate's eye. She'd asked for trouble, and she'd got it. But Shona wanted her to know there was still a way back for her, if she could learn from the experience. Loyalty to your friend was one thing, but Kate needed to show loyalty to her team and her boss. If she wasn't prepared to do that, she might as well pack her bags.

Chapter 21

Jack Kennedy wasn't on site at the St Aiden's Park development on the outskirts of Dumfries, but Shona and Ravi were directed to his two-room office above a jeweller in the town centre. The address corresponded to a stress location on the digital timeline map, visited on three occasions by Hayley in the two weeks before her death. It had been checked by Jimmy, one of the Specials, but there was no record of the jeweller calling the police, and he'd thought perhaps Hayley had been window shopping for a ring, with or without fiancé Andy. Could that be counted as a stressful experience? Perhaps Hayley was having doubts about her engagement. It now looked as if she'd had a different relationship goal in mind but, aware of her own complicated situation, she tried not to judge.

The stairs were narrow, but thickly carpeted. Kennedy answered the buzzer himself, leading them through an outer office containing two desks, into a well-furnished and surprisingly modern space, with a roof extension and large windows. He was pulling on his grey suit jacket, giving the impression he was on his way out, but when Shona made it clear this wasn't a social call, he gestured them to a teal-coloured sofa and took a seat opposite. He looked tired and there was a bruise on his cheek, a legacy of the clash with Andy Purdy two days before.

'I need a formal statement about your relationship with Hayley,' Shona said. 'We don't believe her death was accidental.'

He looked shocked at that and sat back on the sofa, his arms spread along the back as if he needed holding up.

'Will my wife have to know about this?' he said.

'I'm not planning to interview her at this stage.'

That his concern was all for himself, not for the unexplained death of his lover, told Shona a great deal about Kennedy's character.

'Did Hayley ever talk about being threatened?'

'Threatened? Who by?'

'That's what we're trying to find out. Did you know she was using performance-enhancing drugs?'

The shock was quickly replaced by an awkwardness. 'I saw the puncture marks on her stomach and thigh. My wife had breast cancer and some of her treatment…' He tailed off as he tried to judge Shona's reaction, but she kept her face carefully neutral. 'I asked Hayley if she was ill,' he continued. 'She said she wasn't. Then I worried she was an addict of some kind, and I really can't be involved in anything illegal.'

The whiff of pure self-interest was pungent, but at least Kennedy had been more observant than Andy Purdy.

'So, what did you say?' Shona prompted.

'I kept asking her and she finally admitted the injections were to help her get over an injury that would affect her triathlon rankings. She couldn't afford to slip down. She was pretty clear it was nothing illegal.'

'Did she ask you to keep the medication here for her?'

It was a guess, but a straight question might get them the straight answer they needed, especially if Kennedy was keen to co-operate. Ravi, who'd been typing on his tablet next to her, looked up.

'She did,' Kennedy replied. 'But I refused.' He looked uncertain as to whether that made him a better person or not in their eyes. 'I did see where she kept the syringes.'

'Where?'

'She went into the bathroom here…' He indicated a door off the corridor. 'And I saw two pre-filled, in a tin.'

Although EPO came in pill form, it was much more effective when injected and had to be taken at fixed times, so it seemed likely this was what Kennedy had witnessed. It also provided a potential explanation for the stress spike in Hayley's biodata recorded on her watch. A fear of being caught.

'The tin had a piper on it,' Kennedy said.

Shona had been hoping for an address, a location.

'A piper?' Ravi said. 'Like bagpipes? In Highland dress?'

'That's it,' Kennedy said, with enthusiasm now the focus of their questions was no longer on him. He made a shape with his hands. 'About the size of a mobile phone.'

Shona looked at Ravi. He'd been in charge of the search at Hayley and Andy's house. She knew he must be sifting his memory for any such item. A moment later, he met her eye and shook his head.

Shona thought of the logistics of conducting an affair with a full-time job and a partner at home.

'When and where did you see each other?'

He seemed thrown by this change of tack. 'When we could. Roughly twice a week. Here. Hotels sometimes. A couple of times we met up in the forest, when she was out training.'

She thought about what James had said about Californians conducting affairs under the guise of park runs. He'd been right, although, due to the weather, such folk in Scotland were obviously hardier souls.

'The day you saw the syringes in the tin,' Shona said. 'When was that?'

He blew out a long breath and shook his head. 'A few weeks ago?'

'What was Hayley wearing that day?'

'It was around lunchtime, so her uniform.' He grabbed his lapels, moving them up and down in a way that suggested Hayley had been wearing her hi-vis tactical vest.

'She didn't have a bag with her?'

Kennedy shook his head.

The contents of Hayley's locker at Loreburn police office had been returned to Andy, so Ravi should have found the tin at home. She wasn't sure what she'd been hoping for, perhaps a gym kitbag hidden away somewhere. They'd already checked the Elite Health Spa, where triathlon club members had reduced-rate memberships, but none of her possessions had been stored there.

'And she never mentioned being threatened, or said anything that made you think she felt unsafe?'

Shona expected him to shake his head immediately, given that she'd already asked him this, but instead he leaned his elbows on his knees, pulling his fingers down across his lips as he considered.

'Sometimes, she talked about the difficulty of living in the same town as her family.'

'Her family threatened her?' Shona said. It was the first time she'd heard any mention of Hayley's own view of the situation. Kimi hadn't offered any, beyond them not having contact.

'Hayley said she needed to make a move. I was sad that she'd be going elsewhere. I liked what we had, but I always thought she wanted more out of life.'

'Did she ever talk about her sister?' If Hayley was planning to move away, perhaps that had been the reason she'd asked her sister to come and live with her – although Kimi hadn't made that clear, which meant she was either holding back or hadn't been aware.

'Not that I remember.'

'Okay,' Shona said, disappointed. A witness to Hayley injecting herself was the final corroboration they needed on the doping, and at least they had a description of the container some of the drugs had been stored in. But they were still no nearer to finding out who might have spiked her with the fatal dose of GHB.

Shona was beginning to get a strong sense that Hayley's life was compartmentalised. She had close relationships – Andy, Kate, Kimi, Jack Kennedy, her triathlon friends – but she didn't necessarily share things that pertained to one connection with any of the others. And that was making the pieces of this puzzle harder and harder to put together.

Chapter 22

The sun shone on the early-morning calm of Kirkness estuary. A cloudless sky seemed to reach down, painting the surface a matching blue. On the far bank, the woodlands were mere indigo smudges, their brilliant greens still caught in the shadow of the previous night. Shona was on the deck behind the kitchen at High Pines, in her pyjamas, drinking coffee and FaceTiming James. Murdo's name flashed up on the screen, and she checked the time. It was 6:30 a.m.

'I need to take a call,' she said, blowing James a kiss. Murdo wouldn't ring at this hour unless it was urgent. James blew a kiss in return, and the poolside palm trees and blue velvet Californian evening disappeared.

'Boss.' Murdo sounded tense. 'It's Ravi. He's okay. So's Martin. But someone torched their hoose this morning.'

Shona leaped to her feet, tipping coffee over her white cotton pyjamas. 'Torched?'

'Aye. Petrol through the letterbox.'

She ran through the kitchen, dumping her mug in the sink, and headed for the stairs. 'Where are they now?'

'In wi' one o' their neighbours.'

'I'm on my way.'

'Take your time, boss. The boys are fine. Fire Investigation are here.'

—

When Shona arrived at the street near the river, she was relieved to see Ravi's home still standing. She had no difficulty in picking out the three-storey townhouse he shared with Martin. A fire tender was parked outside, and a black comma of soot extended upwards from the front door. Someone had spray-painted homophobic graffiti across the red sandstone – *beware of homos, burn gays* – with a couple of swastikas for good measure.

She'd seen such things often enough in her time with the City of London Police, but the idea it was happening here in Dumfries – taking root like some poisonous vine – made her sick with anger. There'd been hate crimes here before, of course. Mostly shouted abuse and the odd assault, although Ravi would say it was still under-reported. However, this felt like another level, more vicious. This was attempted murder.

When she showed her police ID, a fire officer directed her to a house two doors up. Murdo let her in and led her through to the basement kitchen.

Ravi was pacing the tiles. Martin sat at the table, his fine-blonde hair wet and a towel around his shoulders. Two red streaks ran down his cheeks on either side of his nose, where someone had previously clamped an oxygen mask. They'd obviously been able to shower, but a thick tang of smoke lingered in the room. Both were wearing Partick Thistle football hoodies, patently not their own.

'Shona.' Martin's smile was as welcoming as ever. He had the ability to make you feel your visit was the highlight of his day, a skill he put to good use at the addiction services centre where he worked.

She put her hand on his shoulder. She wanted to hug them with relief but didn't think it appropriate, as the SIO on the case, and anyway, she wasn't sure she'd get near Ravi, who was bristling with anger.

'I think you should both go to hospital to get checked,' she said firmly. From her casualty care on the lifeboat, she knew that side effects from smoke inhalation could take twenty-four hours to show and any irritation to the lungs needed prompt treatment, but they waved away her concerns.

She was about to ask them what had happened, when a small, thin woman of about seventy, with impossibly orange hair, came into the kitchen.

'Josie, this is my boss, DI Oliver,' Ravi offered.

'Oh, hello,' Josie said in a sing-song welcome. 'It's very nice to meet you. Ravi's told me all about you.' She had a loaf of frozen sliced bread in her hands. 'I was just about to make toast. How's your Becca? Finished her exams?'

It was obvious there was a whole social circle of Becca's that Shona wasn't party to. Martin had helped Becca with her maths Higher and she'd often spent an evening at their place.

'Yes, she's finished,' Shona said. 'Thank you.'

'Such a clever girl. She looks like you,' Josie declared, giving her the once-over. 'So d'you think you'll catch the wee bastards who did this, then? If I get to them first, I'll wring their bloody necks. Sit down, will you.' She turned away, attending to the toast.

Shona pulled out a heavy kitchen chair and looked enquiringly at Ravi.

'Fire alarm woke us around five a.m.,' he began. 'Could smell it from the top landing. Smoke and petrol. I shouted to Martin an' he called it in. Got the fire extinguisher from the kitchen. Didnae know if it would work.'

'It's for electricals,' Martin added. 'I mean, who has a chip pan these days?'

'It helped,' Ravi went on. 'But some o' the petrol had gone through the floorboards to the basement, so we went out the French windows at the back. Fire crews were here quick.'

'Literally just had the basement drywalled, too,' Martin added. 'One minute you're planning a new office, next you're climbing through your neighbour's hedge at five a.m. Lucky you didn't think we were burglars, Josie.'

'The yellow pyjamas were a dead giveaway, son,' Josie assured him. 'Here, I hope that's okay.' She put a plate in front of him, loaded with two thick slices. 'I've no' done it too dark.

You'll no' want to be reminded of earlier, since you were almost toast yourself.' She patted him indulgently on the shoulder, and Shona got the impression there was a hierarchy of favourites in Josie's world, with Martin at the top. Murdo looked on enviously from the other end of the table.

'You didn't see anyone?' Shona asked Ravi.

He shook his head but pulled out his phone. 'We've a camera doorbell at the front, wi' motion sensors. The fire has proper goosed it, but just before, we got this.'

He showed Shona a video of two young-looking male figures in dark jeans and hoodies, with scarves across their faces, arriving on a motorbike. The pillion passenger had a small rucksack and was clutching what looked like a square petrol can. They came up the shallow steps towards the front door. The one who'd been driving peered at the bell, then spray-painted over the lens and the picture went black. Despite how close he came to the camera, the scarf disguised his features.

'So.' Shona raised her eyebrows. 'Who d'you think they are?'

Ravi and Martin exchanged a glance.

'Got to be someone from Martin's work,' Ravi began. Martin shook his head, but his partner went on. 'You get so much hassle every day, pal. I'm no' jokin'. I don't know why you don't just change your job description from addict rehab to addict punchbag.'

'You've been assaulted?' Shona said, remembering an incident in the past, when she was pretty sure Ravi had retaliated and taken the law into his own hands.

'It was nothing.' Martin waved it away.

'Tell her about the notes. An' the texts. Death threats.'

'Everyone gets stuff like that. We have a zero-tolerance policy but not all clients read the paperwork. And I always get an apology. Eventually.'

'It's one of your clients,' Ravi said. 'So, get your thinkin' cap on, buddy. I want some names.'

'That would be really helpful,' Shona said.

Eventually, Martin sighed and nodded.

'Well, whoever it was, they'd nae sense if they thought they'd get away wi' it,' Murdo said. 'This close tae the centre, we've cameras everywhere. Thank you, Josie, that's very kind.' He took the proffered plate with three slices on it, and Josie pushed the butter and jam towards him, smiling. Perhaps Martin had competition. 'Soon as I finish this, I'll knock the neighbours up, those that arenae up already, an' get any security footage they have afore they go tae work.'

'Listen…' Shona began. 'Why don't you two come and stay at High Pines. There's room and we've good security.'

'Thanks, boss, but Josie's offered.'

'My boys are in Dubai,' Josie said, but didn't elaborate, handing Ravi and Shona their toast.

'And we could do with being close,' Ravi added. 'To sort the house out.'

'My lovely house,' Martin said, with a dramatic sigh.

'Never mind your lovely house. It could have been your lovely funeral.'

'Only long-stemmed lilies on the coffin, please.'

Ravi pointed a finger at his partner. 'Don't even joke.'

'Will the graffiti come off?' Shona couldn't imagine what it would be like living there with all that hate visible on the outside, never mind the fire damage inside.

'I thought it would be impossible with sandstone,' Martin replied. 'But the fire crew are hosing it down and I've a number for specialists who can steam-clean it, apparently. They do all the tenements in Glasgow, you know. With the gangs, it's a thriving business. And chemical-free, so it won't harm wildlife.'

Ravi shook his head at Martin in disbelief.

'It's fine, honestly, Ravi,' Shona said. 'Don't come into the office today. We'll manage.'

'You are kidding me? One – that's them winning.' Ravi ticked off the points on his long fingers. 'Two – if I stay here, I'm gonna strangle this wee bampot.' He gave Martin a soft and affectionate pat on the cheek, and his partner beamed back. 'Once I've got the place secure, I'm coming in. An' Josie will be Martin's bodyguard till I get back.'

'Them wee bastards'll no' get past me.' She indicated a silver baseball bat that sat in the corner of the kitchen, which Shona assumed belonged to one of her sons. 'I was designated hitter for the Edinburgh Diamonds. Can still swing a bat.'

'I've seen her in the park,' Martin confided. 'She'd put your windows out at a hundred metres.'

Murdo, who in addition to rugby had, in his youth, played for Langholm Cricket Club – a Scottish sporting rarity – looked impressed.

'I'll be sending regular patrols,' Shona said to Josie. 'I don't want you getting in any bother.'

'It's them that'll be in bother if they come back.'

'I don't doubt it, Josie, but let's not put it to the test.'

Shona thought it unlikely that anyone would be back, but she wasn't taking any chances. It was a cowardly act, but one that could have cost Ravi and Martin their lives. They'd find whoever did this, Shona vowed, if she had to drag in every one of Martin's clients, past and present, and shake them until the truth dropped out.

Later that afternoon, Ravi – as good as his word – turned up in the CID office, looking remarkably fresh and smoke-free in linen trousers and a T-shirt, but minus the Partick Thistle hoodie. Everyone gathered around him to express their sympathy and support, and even Kate asked after Martin. The fire damage was confined to the hall floor and basement ceiling. The upstairs doors had been shut, but it would still take a few days to air the house out and the hall would probably need repainting. Since the graffiti was classed as criminal damage, insurance would cover it.

Despite Murdo's assertion about the culprits appearing on city centre CCTV, it seemed they'd been careful. Video from neighbours hadn't yielded much more than the doorbell cam, but eventually footage was recovered. They'd been able to grab the licence plate and see that the bike was stolen. It was later found burned out on an industrial estate on the outskirts of Dumfries. A number of cars had been tracked leaving the area at around 5:30 a.m.; one, with false plates, had disappeared into the small country roads that ran along either side of the border. The control room was doing its best to pick up any ANPR sightings in either Scotland or England but without luck, and it was possible the plates had been swapped again.

'Let's drop in on Andy Purdy,' Shona said to Ravi after she'd updated him in her office. 'I want to check how he is after Saturday and see if there's anything else he wants to tell us in light of what Kennedy said about the PEDs.' She also wanted to know if he did send them after the businessman because of the affair, and whether he might have plans to exact any other retribution that might land him in trouble. He had a clean service record, but grief could make people act in unpredictable ways, and perhaps with Hayley gone, he felt he had nothing left to lose.

'We need to ask him about that tin, too,' Ravi said. 'I'll just grab my jacket.'

'Not your hoodie?' Shona grinned.

'They belong to Josie's lads.' Ravi lowered his voice. 'Martin made me do a selfie of us, an' he's threatening to have it framed. I mean, Partick Thistle. My family are all Queen's Park fans. Oldest football club in Scotland,' he said, proudly. 'Putting us in Thistle tops is just making us a target for abuse all over again.'

Shona smiled. 'I'm glad to hear he wasn't too spooked by what happened.'

Ravi got to his feet. He took two steps towards the door, then paused.

'You know, folk don't take Martin seriously. He camps it up for comic effect, but underneath he's much tougher than me. I just lock folk up. He actually has a go at fixing them, an' that's a much harder job.'

Chapter 23

As Shona and Ravi approached Andy Purdy's house, they saw Allan Peacock driving away, his youthful face deeply serious. Glancing in their direction, he acknowledged them with a smile and wave. Shona hoped the company of his old friend from training had lifted Andy's spirits.

The bereaved constable had made no significant changes to his way of living since Shona's previous visit and she wondered how long it would be until the half-drawn curtains, dirty crockery and duvet on the sofa became a permanent fixture. While the widescreen TV showed a paused image of an animated Xbox assassin leaping from a burning building, Andy himself shifted about the twilit room with the sluggishness of a deep-sea diver. The game controller lay on the coffee table before him, but he made no move to switch it off.

'Okay, pal,' Ravi said. He reached over, hit the power button, and the figure on the screen disappeared.

'How are you, Andy?' Shona began.

The length of time he spent considering the question seemed at odds with the shortness of the answer. 'Fine.'

'I wanted to see how you were and also tell you that we've talked to Jack Kennedy, and we're satisfied he's not connected with Hayley's death.' *And so should you be*, was the message. She steeled herself for an outburst, but Andy merely raised his eyebrows as if acknowledging a mundane piece of news.

'When did you first realise the nature of his relationship with Hayley?'

'Thought he was stalking her. Makes me an idiot, doesn't it?'

It wasn't what Shona had asked.

'What made you think that? Did you see them together? Did Hayley tell you he was stalking her?'

When Andy said nothing, Ravi added, 'Best just tell us, pal. You're not in any bother for banjoing Kennedy. Most of us would have done the same, and he's no' making a thing of it.'

'I was in the station when they brought him in that first time,' Andy said quietly. 'He was flirting wi' her. Imagine, you're supposed to be a respectable businessman hauled in for a breach of the peace and you're so arrogant, you're hitting on the arresting officer.' He paused and shook his head. 'Hayley just laughed. Said it happened all the time.'

'Maybe he thought she'd let him off if he could charm her.' Shona recognised the scenario. 'When did you realise they'd met again?'

He buried his face in his hands and Shona had to strain to hear his words. 'That's the worst of it. He's no' the stalker. I am.'

Ravi and Shona exchanged a look. Had he been following Kennedy from the start?

'I knew the PIN on her phone, so I checked where she'd been. I followed her up on one of her forest runs. I saw Kennedy's car.' He looked up at them, his face a mask of pain. 'I really thought he was stalking her, until I saw them together. And I did think he might have done something to her to stop his wife finding out. When she died, I wasn't thinking straight. He didn't have anything to do with her drowning, did he?'

'No,' Shona said. 'And it would have saved us a lot of time if you'd just been honest with us.'

He nodded slowly. 'I'm sorry. I thought of fronting Kennedy. Warning him off. But I didn't get the chance. Maybe I just didn't have the guts.'

He was close to tears now. Shona didn't want him to give way completely, so she changed tack.

'Hayley had an injury that was affecting her triathlon performance, is that right?'

'She damaged her shoulder a while back,' he said, sniffing. 'But it didn't stop her training.'

'Perhaps it should have?' Shona said, eyeing Andy carefully. This tallied with Kennedy's statement that Hayley's drug use was to overcome an injury. If Andy knew anything, this was the time to reveal it, but he just looked at her, his face blank.

He shrugged. 'You'd need to ask her coach.'

'Who's that?' Shona frowned. There'd been no mention of a coach and Kate was clear that Hayley had managed her own training. They'd both used the same apps and nutritional guides on the internet, and before the revelation of doping, Kate had taken this as indication of Hayley's superior talent and application to her sport, though she likely thought differently now.

'The guy who runs the triathlon club,' Andy prompted.

'Gordon Anderson?' Shona thought again of the trim manager of the Elite Health Spa. Nothing about him had rung alarm bells. Might Hayley have told Andy that she was *out with her coach* as cover for her affair with Kennedy? Either Andy was mistaken or Anderson had lied to them.

'Andy,' Ravi said, notebook open on his knee, 'can you remember if there was a wee tin wi' a piper on it among Hayley's belongings, when you got them back from her locker?'

He shook his head. 'No. Don't think so. Sorry.'

'You saw Hayley that morning, before the triathlon?' She was covering old ground, already in his statement, but it was possible he'd remembered some new detail.

'Yeah, we had breakfast. I made some protein shakes. Left at the same time.'

'How did she seem? Happy? Anxious? Worried?'

'She was fine.'

'What was her demeanour in general?'

'Fine.'

'Were you and Hayley planning to move away after you got married?' Shona asked, moving the conversation on to a hopefully more fruitful vein.

'We'd talked about it. Maybe Glasgow.'

'What will you do now?'

He shrugged. 'Don't know. She wanted to make CID. Not sure it's my thing,' he said with a stunning moment of self-knowledge.

'What about Hayley's relationship with her sister, Kimi Cameron?'

'Didn't have one,' Andy replied. 'Hayley didn't see her family.'

'Okay, Andy, thank you for your time. One last thing… Now you've had a chance to think about things, has anyone come to mind who might have targeted Hayley?' She thought of what Ravi's partner, Martin, had experienced, an escalating pattern of abusive texts and death threats before someone made a physical attempt on his life. This was a common scenario but so far, they'd failed to find anything that indicated it had been the case with Hayley.

Andy just shook his head. This time, tears fell freely. 'No. No. Why would anyone want to kill her? She was amazing.'

-

In the car, Shona sat considering what they'd just heard. Ravi, next to her in the passenger seat, was unusually subdued. Perhaps it had been a mistake to bring him to an interview with the victim's bereaved partner after his experience this morning, when he'd narrowly avoided filling that role himself.

'What d'you make of that?' she said.

Ravi was quiet for a moment longer. 'No' sure. Grief makes you do weird things. But I just know, if it was Martin, I'd be moving heaven and earth to find out who was responsible and put them away. I wouldnae be at home on my Xbox.'

Shona agreed. 'Maybe the doctor gave him something?'

'Benzos, you mean?' Ravi rocked his head from side to side, considering. 'Aye, maybe. Martin says it's one of the ways people get hooked. A few weeks on the stuff is enough. But it's more like he's given up. Wouldnae be surprised if he goes on long-term sick and leaves the force. If he could get through this, it'd make him a better cop, or maybe a more compassionate one, an' that's never a bad thing.'

He turned to face her, hooking his arm on the back of her seat.

'That thing about Hayley's injury and this *coach* of hers. I spoke wi' Gordon Anderson last night. He doesnae know who Hayley might have approached as a future coach but was certain she didn't have one at the moment. He's a qualified personal trainer for the health club, but he mostly manages the place.'

'Sue says it's generally the coaches who have the knowledge and access to PEDs. If he's a qualified personal trainer it puts him in the frame. He was with Hayley right before the race. Might even have told her it was one of her regular jabs?'

'Why through the wetsuit?' Ravi countered. 'There were nae other punctures. Why this time an' no' others?'

'Good point,' Shona conceded. 'Was she paying him?'

'Can't say for the cash withdrawals from Hayley's account, but there's no suspicious card payments to Elite Health Spa or Gordon Anderson direct, just her regular monthly membership.'

'If he was running a sport-doping operation, putting cash through the books would effectively launder it,' Shona considered.

'Aye. But the spa's part of a chain, and there'd be a risk an auditor would pick up on it. And I think he does the triathlon club purely for fun. Although you've got to be no' right in the heid to think any o' that palaver is fun. He also didn't know Hayley had an injury, which he would've if he'd been coaching her, even unofficially.'

In some ways, Anderson was the perfect fit for a suspect. Like Mari Watt, he had the opportunity and perhaps the means, but what was missing in his case was a motive. She remembered his downcast expression as he detailed how much of a loss Hayley's death was to his club – developmentally, financially – not to mention the bad publicity.

Shona told Ravi her thought that the *coaching* was a cover for the affair, and he agreed that was also possible.

'So, Andy is either mistaken or lying,' Shona said. 'There's something not quite right.'

'Aye, but no motive and a cast-iron alibi – probably the benzos, like you said.'

'What about the idea that Hayley wanted Kimi to come and live with her,' Shona mused. 'She doesn't seem to have shared that with Andy.'

'It'd be natural for the older sister to want to protect the wee one.'

'Think so?' Shona, an only child herself, and mother of an only child, found it difficult to unpick the motivation.

'Oh, aye, cannae escape it, even when you're grown-up.'

As the youngest of five siblings, Ravi probably knew what he was talking about. 'My oldest sister, Mina, is definitely the boss. We all try an' gang up on her at times, but it never works. But see, if you were in trouble, it'd be Mina that pulled you out o' the shit.'

'D'you think that's what Hayley was trying to do for Kimi?' Shona had been hoping the woman would get in touch, but she hadn't.

'Mibbaes,' Ravi said.

She nodded as she pulled on her seat belt and prepared to start the car. If that was true, it told her a lot about the relationship between the sisters, but what it didn't shed any light on was how the elder of the two had ended up dead in the Solway Firth.

'Who's the other person you spend time with when you're a response cop?'

'Your partner,' Ravi said. 'First person Murdo and I thought of, but she didnae have anything to say when we talked to her. She's gone off on leave an' Sergeant Logan says she's not contactable.'

'Isn't that a bit odd? You said yourself, if something happened to your partner, you'd want to find out who was responsible. Wouldn't that also apply to your work partner?'

'Depends if it was Kate.' He grinned, then his expression turned serious. 'But, aye, I'd be chapping at your door, wanting answers. You think Joanne Mitchell is ghosting us?'

'Maybe. Murdo says Willie Logan is solid, but I don't think he's keen to have us rifling around in his operation, especially with drugs of any kind involved.'

Shona thought of her Super's directive to conclude the case *quickly and quietly* and keep it out of the media. She imagined Sergeant Willie Logan backed that idea 100 per cent, but it didn't mean that Shona wasn't going to make her investigation a thorough one.

'Want me to find the elusive PC Mitchell, then?' Ravi said.

'I do. Now we know a bit more, it's time for another chat.'

Chapter 24

When Shona got home, she lowered the car window and enjoyed the pleasant breeze while she fired off a quick email. Updating Detective Chief Superintendent Davies would reassure him that she was progressing the inquiry into Hayley's death while keeping it under the radar. The apparent accidental drowning of a police constable during a charity fundraiser was tragic, but beyond the initial story, and brief, respectful reports of the funeral, which thankfully hadn't mentioned the rammy afterwards, not particularly newsworthy.

Halfway across the parking area, her phone rang.

'Why did you reinterview Andy Purdy?' Davies demanded.

'To ask him what he knew about the drugs Hayley Cameron was using.'

'You're telling me yet another police officer is involved? Is this the message we want to send the public? Our beat cops are going out high as kites?'

That was a nonsensical response, and she would have told him so, but a thought about a different kind of misdemeanour in public office surfaced in her mind. If he knew the NCA were sniffing around, he'd take her off the case, and how would she explain that to Murdo? He'd be shocked at her decision not to turn Thalia in for Delfont's murder. His good opinion of her mattered more than any awards or promotions ever could.

'I'm not sure Purdy is telling us the whole story,' she said carefully.

'Is he a suspect?'

'No.' She couldn't honestly say he was, but wanted to dig a bit deeper. Something was *off* with Hayley's partner, though she couldn't put her finger on what.

'If he's not a suspect then Purdy isn't where you should be looking,' Davies snapped. 'I don't want you going near him again. We'll end up with his federation rep shouting harassment of a bereaved officer, and that *will* go public.'

'No, sir.' It took all her restraint not to argue. She couldn't risk it. If she ever found herself forced into a corner by the NCA, she wanted to be sure Davies would help her out of it.

—

She was hardly in the back door before Becca was bombarding her with questions about the attack on Ravi and Martin. She was close to them both, had been texting Martin, but it was obvious to Shona that she remained unconvinced by his jovial downplaying of the event.

'So, who have you got for it?' she demanded.

'Have I missed a memo? What is this – give-your-mother-a-grilling day?' Shona replied, still irked by her call from Davies. She pulled a bottle of chilled white out of the fridge. 'We haven't arrested anyone yet.'

Ravi had removed anyone from Martin's list who didn't fit the approximate height and build of the lads on the brief images captured by the doorbell cam. They'd been left with eight possible suspects, at which point Shona put her foot down over Ravi's further involvement, handing the whole thing over to Murdo. He'd drawn up an early-morning arrest strategy and impressed upon their acting sergeant not to jump the gun and go knocking on any doors that evening.

'You need to stop them, Mum.'

'We will. Murdo is on it. You can trust him, even if you don't trust me,' Shona said firmly. She took her daughter by the shoulders, turned her around and pointed her to the freezer.

'Now food and film.' They were due to have a virtual movie night with James, and Shona was aware she was already late.

Becca shook off her mother's hands, and Shona couldn't help but feel her daughter held her responsible for what had happened, as though she'd failed somehow in not preventing the attack. Their relationship since her return from the festival had been marked by peaks and troughs. A few things at High Pines hadn't been done while Becca was away – not all the recycling had been sorted and an email query from the organic veg-box supplier had gone unanswered. They were unimportant and easily fixed in Shona's mind and she felt unjustly criticised. Was her continuing involvement with James behind it? Becca liked James, placing the blame for Rob's imprisonment and the breakdown of her parents' marriage squarely on her father's shoulders. Shona has stopped short of telling her about Rob's affair with his PA, but she might have worked it out. What did Becca mean when she said at the festival, *I've made mistakes, so have you, but I've learned from them*? Perhaps she'd just hit the stage where she looked at her parents' life choices in general and condemned them. Shona could remember doing the same, but having been abandoned to her grandmother's care by a junkie mother and a vanished father, she felt she was entitled to that opinion.

Becca put two pasta bakes in the oven and set up the TV, while Shona answered the Zoom call from James on the laptop. They'd taken it in turns to pick the movies, his choices betraying his greater knowledge and interest, and ranging from *Les Amants du Pont-Neuf*, a French love story about two home-less people sleeping under the famous Paris bridge, to the more stylish superhero movies. Shona's choice of *Truly, Madly, Deeply* earned a gasp of appreciation from James. They avoided crime dramas at Shona's insistence, and James's own films at his, both citing them as being too close to work.

On this occasion, Becca and James's eight-year-old twins were joining them. They had their mother, Samira's, dark colouring, but James's blue eyes. Beau in particular favoured his father, and Shona was sometimes struck by a facial expression that she recalled James having in his younger days, when they were at school together.

Becca doted on Dove and Beau, who also seemed to enjoy her company, and they were soon smiling, waving and generally face-pulling at each other as Shona went to collect the plates of pasta from the kitchen. When she returned, Becca had popped down to the bathroom and Shona overheard Beau asking his father about *Aunty Shona*. She stopped just out of camera range.

'Is she your girlfriend?'

'She's my oldest friend. We went tae school thegether,' James replied.

'I thought Mom was your best friend?'

'She is. But you're pals wi' Lucas *and* Jackson, aren't you?'

'I don't think it works the same with girls, Dad,' Beau said seriously.

'It absolutely does, son,' James replied, but Shona saw Beau shaking his head as he walked away.

In the end, they settled for *Back to the Future*. They'd all seen it before, but it was a guaranteed crowd-pleaser. They muted the Zoom call, to avoid the dialogue bouncing around, but Shona and James texted comments to each other, appreciating their children's enjoyment as much as the relaxing aspect of time away from her work and his rehab.

When it was over, they found themselves alone while everyone had gone for refills of Coke – *Decaf for you two or your mammy's gonna kill me*, she heard James shout to the kids.

'Listen, there's something I want tae ask you,' James began. 'Will you and Becca come tae New York afore the end of summer? That'll be halfway for both o' us.'

'What about High Pines?'

'Close it for two weeks. I'll send you the tickets.'

Shona felt an immediate burst of elation at the prospect of a fortnight with James in New York, followed by a swift nosedive at the impracticality of the plan.

'But I have my job, and we can't shut High Pines at the busiest time. We need the revenue.'

'Wouldn't it be good for Becca tae have a break? And you? I mean, when did you last have a holiday, eh?'

The sound of the twins bickering floated across the Atlantic and Shona could hear Becca coming back up the stairs.

'Think about it, darlin'. I'd so love tae be with you again.'

'I'd so love that too.' She grinned, and for a second all the practicalities faded into the background. She leaned towards the screen and blew him a kiss, as a bubble of joy filled her chest. He mimed catching it and sending it back, and soon they were giggling together like the teenagers they once were.

Chapter 25

Shona's first stop to get the inside track on office politics in uniform had previously been the Two Kirsties: a pair of tough and experienced beat cops who were around Shona's age and who'd worked with her on past cases. But she was hampered on this occasion by the fact that the formidable PC Kirsten O'Carroll was on an extended trip to New Zealand, while her partner PC Christine Jamieson had taken a stint training new recruits at the Police Scotland College in East Kilbride. So, on Wednesday morning, when she walked into an interview room at Cornwall Mount to meet Hayley's partner, she'd no idea what to expect.

Joanne Mitchell was twenty-four, six inches shorter than Hayley, and had straight, dark hair that was pulled back into a tight bun. On the table in front of her was a coffee which she was slowly turning in circles, but not drinking. She had sharp, serious features and an intense gaze. Shona thought she must rarely smile, even off duty. In a good cop, bad cop scenario, there was no doubt which role would naturally fall to her. She wore black uniform shirt, trousers and tactical vest, which on her looked more akin to a carapace than utility garment. It was like being regarded by a large predatory insect, which, all in all, made her the perfect responder.

'It's nice to finally meet you,' Shona said, as she and Ravi sat down.

'I wasn't aware you were looking for me, ma'am.'

Shona frowned. It was never good to start off with a lie. 'Did Sergeant Logan tell you to make yourself scarce after you'd given your statement?'

The young woman didn't blush and her expression remained neutral, but the two quick blinks told Shona she'd hit the mark.

'Should my federation rep be present, ma'am?'

'You're not in any trouble, PC Mitchell.' Shona smiled. 'We just want a chat about Hayley, if that's okay. Can I call you Joanne?'

The officer looked as if she'd prefer to remain on official terms, but in the end she consented. It was going to be another warm day outside, but the atmosphere in the room was decidedly chilly. Shona checked her phone for updates from Murdo's raids on Martin's potential persecutor, then turned her screen face down on the table.

'We won't be recording this, but is it okay if Sergeant Sarwar takes notes?'

Again, there was scrutiny and delay before she agreed. It was shaping up to be a long morning. But there was something in Joanne's cautious assessment of her situation that made Shona think she might just have something interesting to say.

'I've read your statement,' Shona began. The four brief paragraphs had been heavy on fact but light on depth and colour, as she'd expect from someone who probably dealt with at least a dozen incidents every day. 'But we need some more details. Can you tell me how Hayley was feeling in the weeks before her death?'

Joanne looked taken aback. She'd provided the date and time she last saw Hayley. Reported there were no notable incidents on their recent shifts and that Hayley had mentioned nothing significant. She regarded them both closely, weighing them up, and Shona felt once more how effective this young woman might be at unsettling suspects. Joanne sat back and folded her arms, and Shona thought they'd get nothing.

'I'm sure you're as keen as we are to find out what happened to your partner.' Shona caught a flicker of something in the young woman's face. 'We think there was third-party involvement in her death.'

A moment later, the young officer looked pointedly at Ravi's notebook.

Shona gave Ravi the nod and he closed it.

Joanne pulled her chair forward and leaned her elbows on the table. 'Hayley was a solid cop. You'll hear nothing bad about her from me.' She spoke with a maturity that belied her twenty-four years, and Shona saw the same ambition and gritty ability that she'd observed in Hayley. No wonder they'd been such an effective pairing. She thought of the Two Kirsties, revered equally for their abilities to defuse situations and for coming down hard when necessary, and how Hayley and Joanne might have been their successors, if only things had worked out differently.

'I heard you were looking at performance-enhancing drugs,' Joanne began, 'and whether they had a role in her death. I'm sure Hayley was investigating something off the books.'

'What makes you think that?' Shona said cautiously, but she could already feel her stomach tightening at the prospect of a new lead.

'She would disappear off sometimes, when we were in the town centre at lunchtimes. She never went far.'

Shona felt her excitement plummet. Beside her, Ravi slumped in his chair. Joanne looked from one to the other and back, and must have seen the disappointment register in their faces.

'I'm not talking about Jack Kennedy. I mean other times.'

'You knew about Kennedy?' Shona said, taken aback.

'It wasn't common knowledge, but it wasn't a secret either. Although Andy Purdy was probably the last to know.' There was contempt in her voice that betrayed her low opinion of Hayley's partner. 'Always thought she could do better than either of them.'

That no one from uniform had seen fit to mention this during the investigation was an indication to Shona how quickly they'd closed ranks around one of their own. Perhaps they'd done it to protect Purdy or not to sully the memory of Hayley. They might even have been aware of Kennedy's rock-solid alibi before CID were. It put the uniform sergeant Willie Logan's scrutiny of her at the funeral in a new light. He was working out what she knew.

'So, if she wasn't seeing Kennedy, then who? Do you think Hayley's disappearances were connected with PEDs?' Shona said, interest rekindled.

'There was never anything specific, but a few things she let slip made me think it was drugs. And I think she was borrowing surveillance kit on the quiet. It's usually the guys who do that, if they think their wife or girlfriend is playing away.'

Shona raised her eyebrows but didn't comment on the ethicality of the practice.

'I don't know what she was doing with it, and never saw any material she gathered,' Joanne emphasised.

'We've corroborated evidence she was using PEDs herself.' Since information from her investigation was already circulating, she saw no reason to keep this from Joanne.

'That's not illegal.'

'You think she was going after the distributers?'

Joanne stared hard at Shona. 'She thought the reason she wasn't in CID already was that folk didn't trust her, 'cos she was a Cameron.' A flush of colour came to her pale cheeks. 'If she brought in high-value intelligence on a big operation it'd be her passport out of uniform. Think of it, DI Oliver, she was in the best position to do it. An up-and-coming triathlete with a track record. She could talk to folk others wouldn't get close to.'

Shona could feel pieces of the puzzle dropping into place. Hayley was using PEDs, but she was also mounting her own undercover operation, and this is what had gotten her killed. Perhaps the idea had come to her when she injured her shoulder. She'd only admitted to Kennedy part of what she was doing because he'd noticed the injection sites, and he was unlikely to reveal how he'd seen them to anyone. She'd kept it from Andy and Kate because they'd have warned her off or told her sergeant, Willie Logan. With a move to CID, she could get a transfer to Glasgow or Edinburgh, or London even, and take Kimi and Andy with her. The distance and her elevated detective status might even protect them all from pushback from the Camerons.

Suddenly, it was as if the chill in the room had broken into a golden dawn.

'For the record, I never considered Hayley's background a bar to her being in CID.' Shona didn't want to add that her own upbringing on one of the worst, crime-ridden estates in Glasgow had been what was popularly termed, *disadvantaged*. 'I'd already approached her about joining my team.'

Is it something you'd be interested in? It was almost the last thing she'd said to Hayley. She pictured the tall athlete in her slick wetsuit, and Hayley's reply came back to her. *It's my aim.* Shona had taken it to mean she wasn't quite ready, or didn't think she was experienced enough yet, but Hayley could have meant that she was already working on something that would help her achieve her goal.

'Who was Hayley investigating? Did they threaten her?'

Joanne sat back, visibly deflated. 'I don't know, but she was definitely edgier in the weeks before the triathlon. I've been racking my brains, but I've got nothing. Whatever she knew, as far as I could tell, she kept it to herself.'

Shona, to her surprise, found she wasn't downhearted. They had what they'd been lacking since the start: a clear motive.

'It's all right, Joanne. You did the right thing for Hayley by telling me. You can leave the rest to us now.'

—

When Shona got back upstairs, she called Kate into her office and updated her in private on her belief that Hayley had been mounting a covert operation, which had made her a target. It wasn't an apology – Shona had nothing to apologise for – but there was no doubt their working relationship had suffered, and it was time to reset it and move on. Kate slumped her shoulders, heaving stifled sobs, and her head dropped into her hands. But when she looked up at Shona once more, her face was radiant. It was as if her friend Hayley – the clever, resourceful, determined woman she knew – had been restored to her.

'We'll need to review everything we have,' Shona said. 'Key question is who was supplying her and what made them think it was necessary to kill her? Maybe they knew from the start she was a cop and thought the fact she was a user herself meant she wouldn't talk. Or perhaps they found out, panicked, jabbed her and thought it would be passed off as an accident.'

If it hadn't been for Slasher Sue's sharp eyes, perhaps it would have been, and a taint would have hung over the organisers – including Tommy's and the RNLI's role – for a long time to come, even if they had been officially exonerated.

'She was investigating something dangerous.' Kate was nodding, rubbing her eyes with a tissue. 'I knew there had to be a reason she didn't tell me. She was protecting Andy and me, but we could have helped her.'

'Her strategy was risky, but I think she had your best interests at heart when she made that decision,' Shona said gently. 'I don't want any corners cut, but tie up all the loose ends you can on Erin Dunlop's death.' It wasn't ideal and she could see her hopes of providing Sandra Dunlop with some answers fading into the distance. 'Don't punish yourself, Kate, for what happened,' Shona said, knowing she was the worst at taking her own advice. 'The best way you can help Hayley now is by finding her killer.'

—

Shona sent Ravi out with one of the Specials to knock off the last unchecked pins on the stress map, so they'd have all the possible data ready for a case review later that day. Since Murdo was downstairs, interviewing the suspects in the arson attack, it provided the added bonus of getting Ravi out of the building while the eight were whittled down to the likely culprits, assuming they hadn't all been in it together.

On Vinny's desk, there was a pile of bagged phones and computers. Chloe was currently going through all their social media in a bid to place any of them at, or in the vicinity of, Ravi and Martin's house, at the time of the incident. Digital forensics had come on leaps and bounds, but criminals were always looking at ways to evade it, sometimes successfully, sometimes not. She hoped it would be the latter on this occasion.

Shona had just finished combing through the list of uncompleted actions and reprioritising them across all three cases – Erin Dunlop, Hayley, and the arson and attempted murder of Ravi and Martin – when her phone rang. No caller ID.

'It's Dave Hennessey, from the NCA.'

She'd almost convinced herself she'd never hear that voice again.

'Inspector Hennessey. How are you?' Even to herself, the enthusiasm of her greeting sounded fake. 'What can I do for you?' Her uneasiness was threatening to spiral into panic.

'I'd like to meet face to face, if that's possible,' he said.

She was gripped by twin desires to delay that possibility for as long as she could, and also get it over with quickly. Not asking him the reason for the meeting would be a clear admission that she knew he was coming for her, and why.

'Is there activity I should be aware of on my patch? It's a long way to travel for a chat,' she replied, keeping her voice even.

'Oh, not so far,' he replied, giving no indication where he was.

The nearest official NCA office was in Warrington, as Manchester had enough OCG activity to keep them busy. But there were under-the-radar bases in Scotland and the thought that he might be sitting in his car around the corner, already watching her, made her heartbeat climb another notch.

'Is there an issue I can help you with?' she pressed. 'It'd be useful to know of anything that may potentially impact on how I deploy my resources.'

She was grasping at straws, but if there was an operation underway against an organised crime group, perhaps even related to the festival, that would be an infinitely more welcome reason for his visit.

'We'd certainly be keen to work with you,' Hennessey said, and it crossed Shona's mind that there was a third possibility: they were aiming to recruit her. She'd tried to blow the whistle on Delfont's activities. It hadn't worked and it had landed her in a whole lot of shit she was still trying to free herself of. But she had tried, and perhaps that was the indication they needed to consider offering her secondment and a promotion. Whether or not she wanted it was a bigger question. With Rob in prison in London, Becca off to Glasgow and James in America, she felt her ties with the Solway loosening, but was that a good thing or not? It was too big and complex a question to find an easy, or immediate, answer.

'Fine,' she said, keeping her tone light. 'Let me know when to expect you.'

She was still mulling over Hennessey's call when Hannah tapped the glass by her open door. Her expression told Shona she was not going to like what she had to say and the pulling together of her cardigan before she spoke was a key tell that the news was of the worst kind.

'Boss, control have had a call. Volunteers clearing up at that Secret Forest festival have found the body of a male. Apparently, they were packing up tents and he was inside. Been there a few days by the sound of it.'

The phrase: *just when you think you're out of the woods* had never felt more appropriate.

'Thank you, Hannah.' Shona pushed herself up on the arms of her chair, scanning the outside office for who to take. Murdo had his hands full, Ravi was out, Kate was busy.

'Allan's just back from his break,' Hannah suggested.

Lingering irritation from the incident with Kimi, or lingering guilt over not getting Dan seconded from Cumbria – and her mixed motivations around that whole episode – was likely behind her aversion to taking Peacock. She was becoming like one of those old detectives who would only work with certain team members because *they knew her ways*. His DI, Kenny Dalrymple, rated him and she'd been very grateful when he'd arrived, so what was the problem? *Just get over yourself, woman*, her inner cop told her.

'He never stops talking about you, you know,' Hannah said shrewdly. 'How much he's learning. How great the team is here. And he's a grafter. Filled the stress map in practically single-handed. Borrowed a mountain bike and been out running. He's been looking in on Andy Purdy, too. I've told him everyone gets a beasting from Wee Shona before they're accepted into the pack.'

'That's perilously close to insubordination, Ms Crawford.'

'Aye, well, you can't sack me. I'm the only one who knows where the good biscuits are hidden.'

Shona pulled her jacket from the back of the chair. 'Right, Allan it is,' she said, trying not to sound like he was the last available partner at a school dance. 'Send him in.'

Chapter 26

The tent stood in the most secluded part of the woodland. The afternoon was cool and overcast, the trees lowering the temperature further. Given the hot weather over the last few days, Shona thought it was surprising no one had found him earlier by the smell alone, and a miracle no animals had got to him. But when she saw the state of the body, the idea that he'd lain there since the festival finished five days previously seemed to fit. This was the last area to be cleared, although the rectangular blue tent, with its two sleeping compartments and central living area, was now unlikely to be among those repurposed for a future festival.

The familiar figure of Jones the Bones – as Shona now thought of the Welsh pathologist – arrived a few minutes later. After pleasantries and the usual macabre humour – *If only you'd called me sooner, DI Oliver, I could have offered you a two-for-one deal* – Ivan Jones confirmed that rigor had passed, and his initial assessment of larval infestation of the body would place time of death somewhere around the previous weekend. He could give her a more precise answer after the post-mortem.

'I guess it's too early to give me a cause of death?'

'You're thinking of Erin Dunlop, and whether this is linked to the extra-strong batch of MDMA?'

'Mind-reading also one of your skills, Doctor?'

'Your SOCOs should certainly be considering it,' he said, returning her smile. 'No obvious marks of violence on the body, stab or gunshot wounds. No sign of a ligature around his neck, though I can't rule out strangulation at this stage. I think he died in this position, on his back. It might be natural causes. He's aged twenty to thirty, and young men do die of heart attacks, but I'd want to rule out drugs and alcohol at an early stage. Will you be joining me tomorrow morning for the necessary proceedings?'

Shona thought of the work piling up on her other cases. She was desperate to advance inquiries into Hayley's covert activities. Kimi was top of her list. The custody clock was ticking on the eight folk that Murdo had pulled in over the arson attack. If this death was connected to Erin Dunlop's, she wanted confirmation from Kate that paperwork and any existing lines of inquiry were as complete as possible before they began further investigations.

Ivan Jones must have been watching her face as he waited for an answer. 'I could sing you a song while we go about the post-mortem, if that would persuade you. I've a very fine voice, so my mother says.'

Shona smiled, aware her reluctance must have been visible to him. 'I'm sorry, Ivan. I was just juggling priorities in my head.'

'Slasher Sue won't let you down, you know,' he said, his expression serious. 'She'll get to the bottom of what happened to Hayley Cameron, if she has to go over to the toxicology lab and fill the test tubes herself.'

'I know,' Shona said. 'To be honest, we've had witness confirmation of the victim's use of PEDs, and we think that's what made her a target, though we still need Sue's conclusion on the precise cause of death.' She considered Ivan and the first impression she'd had that he might also have been a sportsman. 'Where would you go for those kinds of drugs, beyond US websites?'

'It's almost always the coaches,' he said firmly. 'They have the contacts and the most to gain.'

'That's what Sue said.'

'It's because they also control all the biomedical monitoring, so they can cover things up. Who was her coach?'

'Didn't have one,' Shona replied.

He looked thoughtful. 'There's research that says around 50 per cent of serious amateurs are using PEDs. You can buy pretty much everything you need from websites, while chat rooms will give you guidance on dosage. It's risky but less so than buying recreational drugs off a dealer, as this fellow here probably found out.' He nodded to the tent and its unfortunate occupant.

He was right about Hayley. There was no indication in her emails or phone contacts that she had found a coach to take her on, and Shona had already discounted Anderson, despite what Andy Purdy had said. All they had from other triathlon club members was the general opinion that she was aiming to turn professional and therefore looking for one. The wiped history on her laptop pointed to online purchases. But if she was gathering evidence on a supply chain, where was it?

'So, DI Oliver, do we have a date for tomorrow?' Ivan beamed at her.

Allan Peacock was approaching through the trees, notebook in hand, his stride purposeful.

'Would you be offended if I nominated a substitute?' Shona said.

'I'd be heartbroken, but there's always another time.'

'This is DC Allan Peacock.' Shona beckoned him over. 'He's helping us out for a few weeks and keen to gain as much experience as possible. I'm sure he'd be glad to attend the post-mortem tomorrow in my stead.'

She expected Allan to look reluctant, but he smiled and offered his hand to Ivan Jones, then turned to Shona. 'Thank you, boss.'

DC Allan Peacock was proving a revelation in more ways than one. After they'd said goodbye to the pathologist, he updated her on their victim. No ID or phone had yet been recovered, but he'd already contacted Hannah with a description of the victim and asked her to check missing person reports. He'd also tasked a uniform officer to get a statement from the volunteer who'd found the body and asked the site office for a guest list for this section of the camp, as well as a list of anyone who hadn't signed out when the festival finished.

'That might be problematic,' Allan warned, dipping his head to read from his notebook. 'Not everyone signed out. Security were a bit lax on the last day.'

Shona remembered how the guard had waved her through when she'd come to collect Becca. She'd flashed her badge, but he'd barely glanced at it.

'Staff did a sweep of the camp that evening, before the night crew came on, but their focus was securing plant and materials to prevent theft. I know Kate checked the list of festival crew on the Erin Dunlop case. No red flags. Site security all have up-to-date licences.' He paused and looked up at her.

Shona had to admit she was impressed. A faint recollection came back to her of the tractor-smuggling case. Something he'd done must have been significant enough to make her remember him.

'Good,' she said. 'And thank you for taking on the PM tomorrow.'

'It's a pleasure, boss. Well, not a pleasure as such.' He smiled. 'But I am keen to learn everything I can. I volunteered for this job because I know your reputation. And because I wanted to help Hayley and Andy.'

They moved a little way into the trees to allow the SOCOs to remove the body. He had a fluent and easy charm, with just the right amount of humility, which probably played well with senior officers and witnesses alike.

'How well did you know Hayley and Andy?' Shona asked.

'Not well,' he admitted, smiling as if caught out in a white lie. 'We trained together, but there were thirty of us in the group. I knew Andy better. Hayley was a couple of years older. She seemed so confident. It's shocking what someone did to her. Are there any new leads?'

'Some evidence came to us this morning that she was investigating a supplier of sports doping drugs.'

'That makes sense.'

'D'you think?' Shona said. Here was a chance for another perspective from someone who knew Hayley. He might not have seen her recently, but the intensity of training together meant individuals' strengths and weaknesses were often laid bare, as instructors pushed recruits to their limits and sometimes beyond.

'Hayley was ambitious, resourceful,' Allan replied. 'If she saw an opportunity, I think she'd grab it.'

It chimed with Shona's own assessment. Add to that the motivation of removing her sister from a toxic situation, and making a better life for her and Andy, and she could see how Hayley would have taken that path.

'I think we've done all we can here,' Shona said. She'd become accustomed to the smell, but the removal of the body had intensified it and she wasn't keen to linger. 'Let's get back to the office and see if you can ID our victim. Well done, Allan. I mean it.'

'Thank you, boss. I'll stay if that's all right? I want to make sure I get those lists from the organisers. I'll get a lift back with uniform.'

'That would be fine.' Shona smiled her approval. Hannah would gloat at her revised opinion of Peacock but if it meant the work got done quicker, then she could put up with that.

—

When she returned to Cornwall Mount, Shona saw an unexpected visitor sitting in the corner, by Murdo's empty desk.

'Dan!' she exclaimed. Although she was pleased to see him, his sudden appearance had wrong-footed her, as she struggled to understand why he might be there. Had he also been summoned to a meeting with the NCA and come to deliver bad news in person?

There was no outward sign he was troubled or unhappy to see her, but there was something different about him that she couldn't put her finger on. Of course, he was no longer the gauche young detective she'd first met when he'd temporarily taken charge of a case involving a young woman's body recovered from the Solway Firth by the Kirkness lifeboat crew and brought in at Silloth, on the Cumbrian shore. That had been nearly three years ago. He was in his early thirties, the tight cropped blonde hair the same, but there was more muscle around his shoulders, and she thought maturity had brought him a quiet confidence.

'What brings you here?'

'I really just came to see how Ravi was,' he replied. 'Such an awful thing to happen.'

'It was, but he's okay. And Murdo's rounding up the culprits, we hope.'

There was nothing immediately concerning in his tone and expression. He couldn't have known she'd be out and she didn't believe he was actively avoiding her.

'Come into my office so we can have a proper chat,' she said.

He picked up his mug and followed her.

When she'd filled her own cup, they sat opposite each other at Shona's desk and something of their old easiness returned.

'How's Becca?' Dan said.

'Driving me mad, so no change there.' Shona smiled.

Questions about the NCA crowded her consciousness, but somehow she couldn't bring herself to ask him straight out if he'd been approached. Dan was smart, he'd know what was at stake. Surely, he'd tell her if anyone had been in contact? She was pushing aside possibilities she lacked the courage to face, she knew that, but nothing was certain yet. *Dinnae invite the Devil tae dine at yer table*, as her gran used to say.

'So, have you brought me anything nice from south of the border?'

'I might have,' he said cautiously, putting his empty mug down on the desk. 'I've been checking out Erin Dunlop's clubbing contacts and I heard a rumour about girls being spiked with GHB in clubs a while back.'

Shona nodded. 'Slasher Sue told me about reports in Nottingham and Sheffield.'

'Well, this wasn't reported to us, but apparently, a sixteen-year-old girl ended up in hospital. She refused to talk to the cops, as she shouldn't have been in the club in the first place. I'm trying to track her down.'

'One of Erin's friends?'

'No. Might be something or nothing.' He shrugged. 'Erin had two known dealers in her contacts. One's inside, the other's dead, so I doubt they were supplying at your festival.'

'I've just come from there,' Shona said and told him about the second body.

'Another MDMA death?'

'Too early to say.'

'Boss.' Vinny had tapped her door and come in, a tablet held against his chest. 'I have something.'

He turned the screen to show her. There were two pictures side by side. The first was a crime-scene shot from earlier, showing the body of the man at the festival. Next to it was a group picture of some girls. With a start, Shona recognised Becca. Dan was also frowning at the scene.

'You're gonna have to give me a clue, Vin,' Shona said. The shot was from days ago at the festival but her fingers still itched to grab her phone and check her daughter was okay.

'This is from Erin Dunlop's camera card,' he said, pointing to the group shot. 'This man...' He indicated a background figure, half-turned away, wearing an orange T-shirt with brown piping and embroidered, hippy-style jeans. 'The clothes are the same as our new victim was wearing.'

Suddenly, Shona saw it. This wasn't about some danger to Becca, imagined or real, though she could imagine plenty, both as a cop and a mother. This was about their unknown dead man in the blue tent. 'Brilliant, Vin. This might get us an ID.'

'You've already got one,' Dan said, peering at the image. 'That's Billy Gillespie. He's a thug. A dealer.' He turned to

Shona. 'You know, it's funny, you asking about Finlay Cameron the other day. Billy used to work for him. Pretty sure he still does.'

'I've just remembered there's a reason I keep you around, DC Ridley,' Shona said with a grin.

—

It was only when she got into the Audi to head home – sitting with the engine off for a moment to let a wave of tiredness pass – that she realised she hadn't contacted James since their movie the night before. She checked her phone and saw a number of unanswered messages – one pressing her to set a date for the New York trip, followed by: *Distracted by work or have you gone off me?* She composed a reply – *Who is this please??* – but then deleted it, thinking the humour might fall flat. Checking the time, she saw it was noon in LA. She dialled his number and when she told him she'd been dealing with another death at the festival, he apologised profusely.

'I'm sorry,' he said. 'When I dinnae hear from you, my mind just filled the blanks wi' negative thoughts.'

'Same,' she conceded, stopping short of telling him she'd been tempted to google paparazzi pictures of him out and about in Hollywood to check who he was seeing, equally terrified that one day she might spot him with another woman, or that she herself might be plastered across the internet.

'Got a cure for it, though,' he said. 'Forget the New York trip. Move to LA.'

'What?' she spluttered, sure she'd misheard him.

'I mean it, darlin'. You could take on a security consultancy role for movie sets, do what you did for me.'

She was wide awake now. 'What about Becca? What about High Pines?'

'Rent the house oot. There's universities here. I'm sure archaeology is a thing in the US too.' There was determination in his voice. 'I mean it, love. I'm lookin' at jobs that'll bring me back to Scotland, but it might be years afore I can get a project green-lit. But you could come here. Think about it. What's tae stop ye?'

He was right. What was to stop her? But his offer felt spur of the moment, and she could think of plenty of reasons to reject it. It was too soon. They were still working out who they were to each other. He was asking her to turn her back on the life she'd built for herself. But how could it be too soon when they'd known each other since they were kids? And what exactly would she be turning her back on – struggling to keep High Pines afloat? Holding back a revolving door of criminality with a shrinking budget and bosses more concerned with image than justice? And now this business with the NCA, which could finally rob her of her liberty and dignity, and blight her daughter's future.

Here was a chance to reset their lives in a new country. A fresh start. After everything she'd endured, didn't she deserve the chance of a happy ending with the man she loved? She did. But even as she told herself this, she knew the answer was not that simple.

'I'll think about it. I will,' she said eventually.

It might not be the answer he wanted to hear but, right now, it was the only one she had.

Chapter 27

After a sleepless night, Shona arrived early at her office. The two deaths at the festival, Ravi and Martin, Hayley Cameron's investigation into sports doping, and James's suggestion she pack in her job and move to LA to be with him had all chased each other around her mind every time she'd closed her eyes. She felt like wave after wave of questions was piling up on top of her, leaving her gasping for air. She popped two paracetamols from the blister pack in her desk drawer and took a gulp of water from her refillable bottle. Over dinner, she'd asked Becca about the group photo from Erin's card that showed the dead drug dealer Billy Gillespie in the background. Did she know him? Becca had hit the roof, and they'd only narrowly avoided a repeat of the don't-you-trust-me argument. When her daughter had calmed down, she'd admitted to having seen him in Erin's company, but hadn't spoken to him herself. On top of everything else, Shona had missed a text from Kimi Cameron. *Cancellation tomorrow, contact me for an appointment.* She'd texted a reply and called, but only reached her voicemail.

Murdo was making his way to his desk when he rerouted to her open office door.

'Tell me you went home last night,' he said.

As she swallowed the last mouthful of water, Shona held out her arms to indicate the yellow linen short-sleeved top she had on with her blue suit. When he looked blank, she said, 'Fine detective you are. This wasn't what I was wearing yesterday.'

'Aye, well – you always look smart, boss.'

'Nice recovery. But tell me you haven't been here all night?'

He sighed, sitting down opposite her and draping his suit jacket across his knees. 'Cannae put any of oor suspects close to Ravi and Martin's place at the time o' the attack. Had to bail them. But we've enough from social media an' the texts they sent Martin to do two o' them for hate crimes.'

'Charge them,' Shona said. 'See if uniform will give us a hand with that and get them before the sheriff this morning. Who else are we looking at?'

'It's possible it's somebody Martin doesnae even know,' Murdo replied glumly. 'Thon vehicles we tracked are bothering me a bit. It's the planning involved. Lift a bike fae somewhere then torch it afterwards is one thing. Cars wi' false plates, driving out tae the borderland, then doubling back somewhere is no' the kinda joined-up thinkin' any o' these guys we lifted possess.'

Shona nodded. 'Did you see Dan when he was here yesterday?'

'Aye. Nothing tae say our firestarters turned up on his side of the border. There's a guy he kens who collates graffiti fae all o'er the place, so he's gonna look at it.'

Shona recounted what Dan had told her about the historic GHB attack in the Carlisle nightclub, and the identity of the second victim at the festival and his connection to Finlay Cameron.

'He's checking Billy Gillespie's home address in Carlisle,' she added, 'but he's sure it's him. I've sent Allan Peacock to the PM this morning. Kate's confirmed with Erin Dunlop's friend, Christie Nicolson, that Gillespie's the man she saw Erin arguing with and Becca said she saw him hanging around.'

Christie had mixed up the description of Gillespie's clothes, saying *embroidered top and orange jeans,* instead of the other way around. Vinny was furious, not believing anyone could make a mistake like that, but then he and Chloe had been searching CCTV for days, so perhaps he was right to feel aggrieved.

At the mention of Finlay Cameron, Murdo's expression had darkened. 'I'm no' happy about him hanging around.'

Shona crossed her arms and leaned her elbows on the desk. 'I've an idea about that.' She gave him a conspiratorial smile. 'The terms of his parole say he must reside overnight at an address in Carlisle. If he is here, maybe we should pay a wee call and remind him of that fact.'

'No' a bad idea,' Murdo said. 'What's your strategy for the visit?'

'We visit the Camerons. Officially, to update the family on our inquiries around Hayley's death. Then, we leave a patrol car outside the address to make sure Uncle Fin is gone by tonight.' Shona's face became serious. 'I need to check on Kimi too. She sent me a text, but I can't raise her. I want to ask what she knows about Hayley's investigation of the PEDs suppliers. We still haven't found the tin with the syringes in it that Kennedy saw, and if Hayley was gathering evidence, where is it?'

Murdo nodded. 'Aye, I've been thinkin' about that. Hayley was a canny lass. There'd be audio and video files. Documents. A record o' meetings.'

'Right. They weren't at her and Andy's home, or in her locker at Loreburn. She didn't leave them at the health club or with Kennedy, though to be fair I wouldnae trust him to hold my chips, never mind confidential information.' The businessman's overwhelming self-interest would mean he'd have dumped anything he thought might lead to trouble, legal or otherwise. Murdo's expression said he agreed with that assessment. 'So maybe,' Shona continued, 'Kimi was the one she trusted.'

'Or she might no' have wanted tae involve her wee sister because she knew it was dangerous.'

'Equally possible,' Shona conceded. 'Either way, we have to ask her.'

'We do. But this time, I'm coming with you, and we go through Dan's briefing document thegether first. Don't want things getting' oot o' hand.'

'You'll get no argument from me on that score.'

An hour later, as Shona drove them to the Camerons' house, Allan Peacock called with the post-mortem findings. It was Jones the Bones's opinion that Billy Gillespie had died in a similar way to Erin Dunlop, from a drug overdose. Toxicology would confirm it.

'Okay, thanks, Allan,' Shona said on the hands-free. 'Have a word with Sergeant Sarwar when you get back. See what he's got for you.' She was surprised how quickly she'd become used to Ravi's change of rank, temporary though it was. Would he be happy to go back to being plain detective constable after this? She wasn't sure. He might not even want to remain in Dumfries, given what had happened.

When they drew up to the Camerons' house, it looked as if the family were home. Kimi's Mini and a clutch of SUVs were behind the electric gates. Shona pressed the buzzer, Belle answered and the gate opened. But when Murdo and Shona reached the doorstep, it wasn't the aunt who stood there, but Clem Cameron, flanked by his sons.

'Clem.' Murdo nodded; the other man just stared back. After a long moment, he turned his gaze on Shona. 'Didn't expect to see you back so soon, Inspector.'

His accent was more cultured than she'd expected, a closer fit to the wealthy property owner than to his criminal roots. He had on black jeans, T-shirt and a leather jacket. From the back he could pass for someone twenty years younger. His lined face gave him the vibe of an old rock star, without the warmth or charm. The two oldest boys, JD and Stevie, were beefy bookends on either side of him. Shona caught a glimpse of the fair hair and shark-like eyes of Rosey, who was hovering in the background, but there was no sign of Kimi.

Shona heard the gate behind them swing shut.

'I'd like to update you on the inquiries into your daughter's death, Mr Cameron. May we come in?' she said.

'No, Inspector. You may not. And there's nothing you can say that I'd be interested in hearing.'

'Not interested in who killed your own flesh and blood?'

'In her line of work, I'm sure she made enemies.' Clem Cameron's tone was offhand but there was a tightening of his expression.

'Mr Cameron, did you supply Hayley with performance-enhancing drugs?' She didn't think it was the case, given their estrangement, but she wanted to goad him to see how he'd react.

He spread his hands in a convincing show of mystified outrage. 'Why would you think that?'

'I hear your family has a reputation for sourcing difficult-to-obtain items.'

He pointed a pistol-like finger at her. 'You must be thinking of my great-grandfather, the first Clement. A whisky connoisseur and a hero of the common people during less enlightened times.'

'I'd like to speak to Kimi.'

'She's not here,' Clem said. 'Gone shopping.'

'What about your brother, Finlay? Is he around?' Shona said casually. 'And please don't say you're not your brother's keeper, when I know he's been enjoying your hospitality. Things too hot in Carlisle? Or maybe you have a job for him here, while he finds his feet.'

Clem frowned and the eldest son, JD, seemed to pick up on his father's irritation. Flexing his fists, he took a step towards Shona. She kept her eyes fixed on Clem, ignoring the eclipsing bulk of his eldest son.

Murdo took a corresponding step forward and held up his hand, palm towards JD. 'Far enough, son.'

In the space left by JD at Clem's shoulder, Belle materialised out of the gloom of the doorway like a particularly well-coiffured apparition, the Camerons' own dark lady.

'James,' she said, her tone carrying a warning note probably familiar to JD since childhood.

For a moment they all stood like gaming pieces locked in position by the corresponding gravity of the others, until Clem broke the spell.

'I know you're busy,' he said evenly. 'So please don't bother updating us again.'

The gate behind them swung pointedly open and Murdo touched Shona's arm.

'Goodbye, then,' Shona said calmly, her eyes meeting each of the Camerons in turn. She nodded to Belle, who acknowledged her with a tilt of the head and a cool smile.

'Good luck wi' yer arson case, Inspector,' Clem called after her as she walked back to the gate. 'Nothin' worse than folk arsin' around.'

Shona heard him snigger at his own feeble joke, and the boys joined in. But she didn't feel like laughing. It was as if someone had dropped ice down her back. She steeled herself to keep walking. Of all the cases he could have picked, why the attack on Ravi and Martin? Clem Cameron had made a big mistake in mocking her. A reckoning was coming.

—

Back at the office, she dumped her bag under her desk and called Ravi to join her. She'd been silent on the drive back, not trusting herself to speak before she was sure. Murdo had given her sideways glances from the passenger seat and probably thought she was pissed off at not apprehending Finlay Cameron.

'Boss?' Ravi said and stopped halfway through her door. His shirtsleeves were rolled back, showing his muscled forearms, and the silver bangles and woven bands he often wore. He had a bundle of papers cradled in the crook of one arm, mobile phone balanced on top, and he was obviously in the middle of something.

Shona beckoned him in, her eyes on the screen of her laptop. A moment later, Dan Ridley appeared on the video call.

'Where's Murdo?' She craned her neck, searching the office. 'He needs to see this.'

Murdo was making his way across the office, carrying two mugs, a half-full packet of custard creams sticking out of his jacket pocket.

'Went to Billy Gillespie's address this morning,' Dan said. 'No one's seen him for two weeks, which would fit with the festival timings. I'm chasing up his friends.'

'Thanks, Dan,' Shona replied. 'Right, I'm just going to share this file.'

Ravi and Murdo leaned in as she moved the cursor about the screen until she found the right button. The video clip captured by the incinerated doorbell cam appeared.

Ravi sighed and straightened up. 'Don't need to watch it. I'm seeing this in my sleep.'

Dan, visible in a box at the corner of the screen, frowned. Shona froze the image as the first attacker approached the camera and sprayed it with paint.

'What did Clem Cameron say as we were walking away, Murdo?' Shona looked at her sergeant.

'Some crack about us solving our cases.'

'Our arson case, Murdo. *Nothin' worse than folk arsin' around.*'

Murdo peered at the screen again. 'That's no' any of the Cameron boys, too small. Suppose they could've put someone up tae it.'

'Ravi, d'you remember when we talked to Belle and Kimi, and Uncle Fin arrived?'

'No' likely to forget that in a hurry.'

'What did he say to you?'

'Well, it was to you, actually, but some homophobic jibe about handbags.'

Shona tapped the screen with her finger. 'Remember who was with him? Watch this guy. You too, Dan.'

Ravi put down his papers and leaned closer, studying the screen. His forehead creased with effort as he tried to see what Shona saw.

'See the way he bounces on his toes. That high-stepping gait.' Shona looked at her acting sergeant. 'What if Martin wasn't the target? What if it was you? Remember Kimi's cousin who tried to snog her and she was having none of it? That's a good match for our firebug. Mad Markie Cameron.'

They ran the clip twice more, until Ravi began to nod in recognition.

'Dan, what d'you think? You've seen him around.'

'Right height and build,' he confirmed. 'Might explain why he and Uncle Fin aren't hanging about in Dumfries.'

'Wee bastard,' Ravi hissed.

'Dan,' Shona said. 'Do you think your half of the Cameron clan has the capability to plan and execute something like this?'

'I'd say 100 per cent,' Dan confirmed. 'Got the right mix of cunning and grubby violence. Question is, what can we do to prove it?'

'Can you locate Uncle Fin and Mad Markie? I want eyes on them all the time.'

'Sure,' Dan said. 'Why'd he do it, though? Fin's on parole. He's taken a big risk.'

'You mean beyond being a raving, bigoted psychopath?' Ravi said.

'Oh, I think he's that all right,' Shona agreed. 'But did you see Clem's face, Murdo, when I asked him about giving Fin a job?'

'Aye, he wasnae happy. JD thought so too. He was ready tae take a pop at you and me.'

'He might have, if Belle hadn't stepped in,' Shona said and Murdo nodded in agreement. 'Think about it. Fin's come out after four years. Times have changed. You said yourself, Dan, they're not the force they were in Carlisle. What if Finlay Cameron fancies a bit of what his brother's got? He spots an opportunity at The Secret Forest festival, puts one of his old dealers in there. Festivals are a movable feast for drugs operations is what Force Intelligence told me, not really on anyone's patch.

He needs to show Clem he's someone to be reckoned with, so he sets loose Mad Markie for a little light arson and attempted murder. Let me have a slice of your cake, or you'll get some of the same.'

'No wonder Clem looked worried,' Murdo said. 'That's a grand bit more than havin' tae hide the family silver when yer cousins arrive.'

'So, me and Martin were just a convenient target for a show of strength against his brother?' Ravi said. 'If I hadn't been there when the psycho turned up at the Camerons' place, none of this would've happened? Kinda makes it worse.'

'At least it wasn't one of Martin's clients,' Shona offered.

'Aye, not this time. So, what do we do now?'

'Firstly,' Shona replied, 'you and Martin are coming to High Pines. It'll be safer for you two, and your friend Josie, if Uncle Fin fancies having another pop. No argument. Then we review everything we know about Erin Dunlop's and Billy Gillespie's deaths, and the arson and attempted murder, and see how we can tie them to Fin Cameron.'

'Something tells me it's not going to be easy,' Dan said.

'It won't be,' Shona replied. 'But it'll be a damn sight easier now we're looking in the right direction.'

Chapter 28

Shona crossed to where Kate was sat with Vinny and Chloe, signing off on the last of the digital forensics from the festival.

'Don't pack that away just yet,' she said, and saw their faces fall. 'Kate, I need you to do something for me.'

Her detective constable followed her into her office and closed the door. Shona updated her on developments from earlier that morning – the potential connection between the attacks on Ravi and Martin and the festival deaths, and the looming threat of a turf war breaking out between the two sides of the Cameron clan.

'What about the investigation into Hayley's death?'

'I'm pausing that until we have the final toxicology results,' Shona said.

'But if the PEDs suppliers killed her, they'll already be covering their tracks.'

'I'm aware of that.' Shona was more than a little annoyed that Kate seemed to have forgotten the very public marking of her card when it came to questioning your boss, and what had happened to Ravi and his partner, especially as they might still be at risk. 'I also need you to do a welfare check on Kimi Cameron. We didn't see her at the house this morning. Her father said she was out shopping, but her car was in the drive.'

'Maybe she got a taxi. Her dad owns a firm. And she might have, if she was planning a Prosecco lunch.'

It was possible. Shona couldn't see Kimi walking far in those heels. 'I still want you to go to the nail bar. I can't send the Specials. Don't raise any suspicions.'

She'd have liked to have gone herself, but she and Murdo needed to set out a new strategy, and the receptionist at the nail bar might recognise her.

'D'you think she's at risk?'

'Would I be sending you otherwise?' Shona's irritation was growing by the minute. It was like Kate knew just how to push her buttons. 'Look, Hayley thought she was at risk. She tried to get her sister to leave. Do this for her.'

It was a low blow, but Kate couldn't deny the truth of the statement. And if it provided her with the motivation to get the job done and get back here, so Shona could allocate the next round of tasks, then frankly it was justified in her book.

Kate looked mutinous but went off to get her jacket as Shona's phone buzzed.

'It's Dave Hennessey. I'm downstairs,' the caller said when she answered.

It took a second for her to connect the name to an identity. Dave Hennessey, National Crime Agency. A knot of anxiety gripped her stomach. She'd be justified in sending him away – he hadn't called in advance. James's offer to move to California popped up like a particularly seductive jack-in-the-box. Oh, come on, she asked herself, is that really you? Big sunglasses and hand luggage only, jinking onto the first available flight to LA. She weighed up putting him off against just getting whatever he wanted over with. Murdo was already laying out lines of inquiry and they could go through them when she got back.

'Your timing's not great, Inspector. I can only give you twenty minutes,' she warned.

'That's fine. Probably best if I don't come up to your office.'

Shona agreed. Murdo had the uncanny ability of spotting the designation of any enforcement officer he encountered, from excise officials to military cops.

'Take a left from the front entrance and go over the bridge. There's a cafe about two hundred yards along St Mary's Street. I'll be right behind you.'

Dave Hennessey was not what she'd been expecting. He had shoulder-length, light brown hair and a scrappy beard, and wore gold rings in both ears. A faded khaki jacket and loose jeans hung on his thin frame, and his blue eyes had a slight prominence that gave the impression you were being permanently scrutinised. Shona was willing to admit the sensation was probably elevated in her case by the knowledge that he certainly was examining her and making his assessment. She just wasn't sure why.

It quickly became clear that he wasn't there to inform her about a covert operation on her patch or to recruit her, not in the conventional sense anyway.

'When Detective Chief Superintendent Delfont went to the Lake District property, he'd been celebrating his return to duties after his suspension. But it's my belief he wouldn't have got comfy in his office chair.' The accent was indeterminate. Not Scottish. She thought south somewhere, maybe Essex.

'Why was that?' Shona said, in a neutral tone.

'New allegations of corruption,' he said. 'We want your help digging into past cases.'

At least he wasn't asking her about Delfont's death. She should have been relieved, but it felt like a trap. Where was this going? She'd have thought any further allegations of corruption would have been quietly swept under the nearest rug.

'Of course I'll co-operate.'

'As you know, we believe Delfont was the victim of an OCG hit. A falling-out of thieves, if you like. So, you had suspicions about his criminal connections when you worked on his team?'

Shona narrowed her eyes at him. 'You know I did.'

'And you shared your misgivings?'

'Yes, and look where it got me.' Shona continued to stare at him. 'You'll have read the file submitted to the CPS. You know what he did to me and why. I've given a statement about incidents involving the corruption of witnesses and obtaining false confessions. It shows a clear motive as to why my husband and I were targeted.'

Hennessey regarded her across the table, deliberately letting the silence stretch, hoping she'd fill it. Basic interview technique. He couldn't expect her to fall for it. But as the seconds ticked by, she couldn't stop the questions popping into her head. Had he talked to Dan or Thalia? Once he'd gone, she wouldn't get another chance to find out where the investigation was going. She decided to risk it.

'Can I ask,' she smiled, 'are they questioning any of the other women Delfont targeted?' The case had been dropped by the CPS. One of the victims pulled out, another had a breakdown. And the third had a husband in jail, claiming Delfont had framed him. She didn't say it out loud, but she could see by his face he knew.

'There's been more than a whiff of brimstone around Delfont for years,' Hennessey said. 'Makes you wonder how he got away with it. Some people might say it was a different time, the chain of command was everything. If you complained, you were frozen out, unable to do your job. People saw you as a traitor.' He paused. 'I'm sorry if this is a difficult conversation for you.'

He was apologetic but she wasn't fooled, and he hadn't answered her question.

'I'm still not clear how I can help you?' The minutes were ticking by, she'd have to go soon. She wouldn't be sorry. Despite Hennessey's unthreatening demeanour, the drift of the conversation wasn't what she'd expected, and each new question filled her with trepidation. This wasn't just about Delfont's murder, something else was at stake here.

Hennessey leaned his elbows on the table, laced his fingers together and gave her a self-deprecating, almost apologetic, smile.

'You see, Shona, many of the cases we're looking at involve you.'

'I was his DI. And it's a matter of record that I reported my suspicions.' A lump of fear had come into her throat, but swallowing it dry would be conspicuous, a non-verbal admission of guilt. She lifted her coffee cup with both hands to disguise their shaking and took a mouthful.

He pressed his lips together and shook his head. 'It must have been so difficult. Who did you report it to?' he said, voice soft and sympathetic.

'Superintendent Tom Hughes.'

'He's dead.'

'And Chief Superintendent Simon Parker.'

'He's retired.'

'But you can still interview him.'

'Stroke, I'm afraid.'

She couldn't be the only serving officer left who knew that Delfont was corrupt, could she? The purpose of Hennessey's visit was clear to her now. He was looking up the chain of command to see how far the rot stretched. Shona didn't know the full extent of it, but the phrase 'one bad apple' was rarely an accurate one.

'Are you planning other arrests?' She racked her brains for who might be in their sights.

'We're just trying to build a picture. How is your husband's case? I hear he's planning an appeal.'

Was Hennessey offering her some sort of deal? Help getting Rob out of prison in return for dishing the dirt on her previous superiors? If he was, this would be the moment to tell him what she and Thalia had uncovered about Delfont's past, his criminal connections, how he'd recruited those he arrested with threats and manipulations, in order to build a web of influence and corruption. But if they'd found all that, so could the NCA. If she were to reveal that together they had actively pursued Delfont, it risked shining a very different light on his murder, and that was the last thing she wanted.

Rob was guilty of arrogance, professional negligence and infidelity, but he wasn't a money launderer. The chance to wipe the slate clean, for her own reputation and future as much as his, was a seductive one.

'My husband's barrister is open to any new evidence that might provide grounds for an appeal.' She drained her coffee cup and smiled, but Hennessey just studied her coolly and made no corresponding offer. She scrutinised him for a moment longer. 'I'm sorry. I have to get back. We've quite a substantial workload at the moment.'

'Yes, so I hear.' Hennessey rolled out his sympathetic face once more. 'I'm sorry about your colleague. Is it right that it might be murder? Must be very difficult to investigate a case when it's one of your own.'

'Isn't that what you do?' she said before she could stop herself, needled by the inference that, as a woman, any emotional engagement would get in the way of her doing a good job. 'We all knew Hayley Cameron, but if anything, that just makes everyone on the team more committed to finding her killer.'

She got up and looped her bag over her shoulder. If he wanted her to dish the dirt on previous colleagues, it had to be by the book. Why should she be scared of him? He had nothing.

'And next time you want a chat, I'd appreciate it if you'd inform Detective Chief Superintendent Davies, so we can discuss the parameters of any interview before we start.'

She would help if she could, but she didn't want the good cops thrown out with the bad. She said goodbye to Hennessey and stepped out into the street.

When she'd first joined the police as a probationer, she'd been so shocked at the casual culture of misogyny and violence in the name of justice that she'd almost packed it in. It had been hard to maintain any respect for some of her colleagues, but she knew that to let it show would mean banishment and could even get her killed.

Disloyalty was a greater sin than corruption. When she called for backup, it wouldn't come. Every day they'd faced rapists, murderers, paedophiles, terrorists – the worst of society. She'd been kicked, punched, spat at, and sometimes it had been hard to control the pain, fear and anger, not to retaliate or launch a pre-emptive strike.

After one particularly violent incident when she'd seen a fellow officer assault and humiliate a handcuffed, mentally disturbed woman, booting her out of the back seat of the car when they'd arrived at the station, she'd gone to her sergeant.

He'd nodded and said he'd speak to the officer concerned.

'But it's a mistake to think you're any better than he is,' he'd said, shocking her into silence. 'You just haven't been pushed that far. But when you are, you'll have a choice. Either hit back or step up. Uphold the values you swore to uphold. And you'll have to make that choice not once, but thousands of times in your career.'

Shona had been vain enough to think she was different, right up until she'd dragged Thalia away from Delfont's dead body. Had she done the right thing, protecting Thalia from the consequences of her actions? Sometimes the difficult thing was the right thing. Was that what Hayley Cameron had concluded? She could have used the PEDs, recovered from her injury and walked away. But she hadn't, and it was a decision that had set her on a collision course with her killer.

On the short walk back to Cornwall Mount, she reviewed what had just happened. She'd met Hennessey, seeking reassurance that Thalia – and by association Dan, Tommy and herself – was not in the frame for Delfont's killing. She certainly hadn't achieved that. And what had Hennessey wanted? She'd told him nothing he didn't already know. It had been a waste of time for both of them, but she couldn't shake the feeling that whatever trap Hennessey had laid, she'd somehow stepped right into it, and she hadn't seen the last of the NCA.

An hour later, Shona and Murdo had their strategy in place. Their key priorities were linking Finlay Cameron or his son to the attack on Ravi and Martin's house, and also establishing their connection to Billy Gillespie and the festival drug operation. The CCTV from The Secret Forest had previously been scanned for drug activity, but now they had an ID for Billy Gillespie, Vinny and Chloe were busy logging sightings of him and contacts he'd made. Shona went over to their workstations and made sure they knew she appreciated their efforts.

Dan had confirmed that Finlay and his sons were resident at the same address – the one on Fin's parole file – and had been clocked there at lunchtime. He'd also supplied them with all the information Carlisle CID had on Mad Markie Cameron, including known associates and phone numbers, and vehicles registered in his name. Hannah, at the neighbouring desk, was running the data through their systems.

An iPad showing the Billy Gillespie crime scene photos was sitting on top of a pile of papers, next to Hannah's terminal. As Shona perched on the end of the desk and began swiping through the images, something struck her. The festival tickets were expensive but, in keeping with their eco principles, you got a discount if two or more people were sharing the pitches. Judging by the state of Becca's and her friends' tents, they'd crammed in as many of their mates as they could. She examined the interior of Gillespie's tent, with its twin bays and central living space.

'Hannah,' she said, 'have we traced whoever was sharing with Billy Gillespie?'

No spare clothing or identifying paperwork had been found at Gillespie's tent to suggest anyone else had been living there. The SOCOs had said DNA was unlikely to provide any leads, as the repurposed tents and the high-traffic nature of the site would yield vast numbers of profiles. Also, if they weren't looking for a third party in connection with the victim's death, any processing would have a low priority and take months, even years. It was significant, however, that given this was likely an unintentional overdose, no drugs had been recovered. Nothing. Not even an empty blister pack to give a clue as to what he'd taken.

To Shona, that said that someone had cleaned up before they'd cleared out.

'Allan gave us a name and DOB supplied by the festival office. Liam Gallagher,' Hannah said. 'Couldn't trace anyone with that name and birthday. Likely false, given it's also the name of one of the Gallagher brothers, from Oasis. Maybe he's a fan.'

'Okay, thanks, Hannah.' Shona looked around the office for Allan Peacock but he was nowhere to be seen.

Shona took out her phone and texted Dan – *Billy Gillespie, known associates??*

On it, came the immediate reply.

'You know this vehicle we ANPR-ed after the fire at Ravi's,' Hannah said, sitting back from her computer and tapping her chin with a pencil. 'The one with the false plates.'

'Aye. We lost it in the camera-free wee roads of the border badlands,' Shona replied.

'The plates were genuine, cloned from a Renault Clio, but our target car was a grey Nissan Juke.'

It had proved impossible to track such a common vehicle either on the side roads, the main A74(M) or the M6.

'There's a grey Nissan Juke on the list Dan Ridley gave us,' Hannah said. 'Registered to Shaun Cameron.'

'That's Stab-Happy Shaun. Markie Cameron's brother.'

'Stab-Happy? I'm guessing he didnae get that nickname doing cross-stitch.'

'Stitches were involved,' Shona said dryly.

'Well, I've searched the cameras for that vehicle, including the one at the end of their road, and unless he was tucked up in his bed, which is what his lawyer will say, that car can't be placed anywhere else at that time.'

'So, it's either in a garage or making cross-border trips under a false flag?'

'That's my thinking,' Hannah confirmed.

'Any idea on the driver?'

'Vinny's about to start cell siting those phone numbers. Give us an hour or two and we might have something for you.'

Chapter 29

Shona had sent Ravi to take Martin over to High Pines and get him settled. The guest suites were full, so Shona had asked Becca to sort out their third, rarely used, bedroom upstairs. It faced the back of the house, away from sea views, and was currently stacked with boxes relating to Rob's trial. Clearing it would be quite a job. She'd half-expected her daughter to protest and if it had been anyone other than Ravi and Martin, she might have. 'Just dump everything in my room,' Shona suggested.

'Don't worry, I was going to anyway,' Becca had replied.

There was a satisfying hum of productivity from the main office, which might have something to do with the cooler weather. By the time she got the air conditioning fixed, it would be time to start complaining about the lack of heating.

Her phone rang. She could hear it in Dan Ridley's voice as soon as she picked up: excitement, with just a touch of pride. Her heart leaped.

'I've just picked up Billy Gillespie's camping partner,' he said. 'Denied he'd been there but I phoned the festival office and they sent me a photocopy of his registration. Used his own driving licence. Can you believe it?'

'This'll be our mysterious Liam Gallagher,' Shona said. 'Well done, we struck out here.'

'No, no. His name's Harry Taylor. He's known as Cody, though. I think that's a reference to codeine, but who knows? Anyway, when I told him we were investigating his mate Billy's death, I thought he'd go no comment, but the first thing he said was, "I didn't kill him." He's got three phones at his place and plenty of gear. There's a ton of videos on his handset of him, Billy and Mad Markie partying and doing the gangsta stuff, you know? Filming themselves rapping and waving money about. It's a start.'

'It's more than a start. You're putting us to shame here.' It wasn't like Hannah to make a mistake like that, mixing up a name she'd been given to trace, but they were all under pressure and the main thing was they had their guy. 'Will he give the Camerons up as his suppliers, d'you think?'

Dan made a noise that conveyed uncertainty. 'Not sure. I think Uncle Fin still has friends inside. Cody might think it's safer just keeping his mouth shut and taking the fall. If I ping you a headshot of him, can you send me any CCTV frames from the festival, so I can ramp up the pressure? I'll be interviewing him in an hour or so.'

'Sure.'

Through the glass partition, Shona saw Kate come in and stop to talk to Ravi, who'd also just returned. At least those two seemed to have made up. She suddenly felt a stab of guilt at how dismissive she'd been of Kate's earlier concerns over the investigations into Hayley's death being placed on the back burner. She didn't want the trail of the PED's suppliers going cold either.

'Dan, did you ever find that lassie who'd been spiked with GHB in the club?'

He sighed. 'Sorry, boss. Meant to update you. Dead end, I'm afraid. It was over a year ago, and she couldn't remember much about what happened. Her mates got her to hospital. They thought it was a young guy she'd been dancing with, and a couple of them were so pissed off at what had happened that they went back to question the doormen, gave them a hard time.'

'Impressive. They sound like potential recruits for Cumbria Police.'

'Wish we had more like that on the force. But that was as far as they got. Doormen fobbed them off. Said they couldn't do anything about it because he was connected, a celebrity. Even gave them a name for the guy – Alan Partridge. Only later did they realise the doormen were taking the piss. Bastards. No chance of witnesses or CCTV now.'

'Okay, thanks anyway.' It had been a long shot from the start. 'I'll go and have a chat with the troops now. See if we've got enough to arrest Mad Markie Cameron for the arson, connect him to the dealing and hopefully catch Uncle Fin in the net too. All going well, I'll be buying you breakfast tomorrow.'

'Sounds good, boss, talk to you later.'

Their relationship had regained some of its former ease and Shona was in two minds about whether she should even mention the NCA's investigation of Delfont. In one sense, it did concern Dan – should Hennessey ever chap him up, she wanted him forewarned. On the other hand, if she could avoid dredging up that awful night, she would. Dan must still wish she'd never involved him in the first place, and so did she.

As she ended the call, Kate tapped her door, then stuck her head around it.

'No joy with Kimi, boss. I called the nail bar, asking for an appointment, but they said she didn't have any spaces today. Walked past it twice, and she's definitely not in there. In between, I did a round of a couple of shops and a few pubs where I thought she might go for lunch. Have you tried calling her again?'

'I have. Voicemail. I'm getting a wee bit concerned. I mean what young woman doesn't keep checking her phone these days? She's got my contact details. We need to talk to her about Hayley's investigation. But it has to be at the nail bar. We can't go back to the house. Even if the father and brothers aren't home, we'll not get past Belle.' Although she thought Kimi was in a vulnerable situation, she had no real reason to think she was facing an immediate threat. 'Let's give her some more time to make contact.'

'I could stake out the nail bar,' Kate offered.

'I need you here.'

Kate opened her mouth to argue, but Shona shook her head.

'The Carlisle arrests take priority. We'll talk about this tomorrow.'

After a further rebellious look, Kate eventually nodded and left the office.

Once she'd gone, Shona had to admit she was more concerned about Kimi, and the lack of progress in finding Hayley's killer, than she'd let on. She was considering who she might call to push matters along – forensics, Slasher Sue – when Hannah came bustling into her office. For once, she wasn't gathering together the two lapels of her cardigan, nor folding her arms in frustration; instead, she was wearing the broadest smile Shona had seen in days. She felt her heart lift in anticipation.

'I'm gonna like what you have to tell me, aren't I?' Shona said.

'You're no' a detective inspector for nothing, are you? Come and see what Vinny's found.'

Vinny's central screen showed a map of the Borders area. A route was delineated by a neon green trail beginning in Carlisle, reaching Dumfries, and then returning. As Shona looked closer, she saw the line was broken in the centre of the town, near the bend in the river, close to where Ravi and Martin lived.

As usual, it was Chloe who acted as tour guide.

'This shows the route taken by the phone number assigned to Mark Cameron on the night of the arson attack at Ravi's place.'

'You can place him there?' Shona wanted to punch the air. 'But why is the line broken?'

Vinny obligingly zoomed in at dizzying speed and came to rest at the industrial estate where the burned-out motorbike was found. The phone-tracking loop began and ended at the junction of the access road and the main road.

'He switched his phone off when he was on the motorbike?' Shona said and Vinny nodded. 'But will that be enough if they're not bang outside the house at the time recorded on the doorbell cam?'

'The length of the journey by bike is a close match for the time the phone was switched off.'

'Will it be enough for a jury?' Shona wondered out loud.

'A key factor is prior user behaviour,' Chloe said. 'Is the user in the habit of switching their phone off regularly? If they're not, did they do it at this key moment in an attempt to alter their digital footprint and evade forensic technique?'

'Can we argue that here?'

'Oh, yes,' Chloe said confidently.

'So, when did Mark Cameron last switch his phone off?' Shona said.

'He hasn't switched it off for two years.'

A slow smile spread across Shona's face. 'That's good enough for me.'

—

Shona and Murdo put their heads together and an hour later they'd come up with a plan. She checked the wall clock, half-stood up behind her desk and did a headcount of the outer office. It looked like everyone was there.

Ravi saw her looking and she made a *round-them-up* motion with her hand, then pointed to the conference room, finally displaying five fingers, meaning: *five minutes*.

He signalled: *Coffee?* A thumbs up from Shona concluded their office semaphore.

She ran through the key points once more with Murdo, who as usual headed off a few logistical snags resulting from the cross-border nature of the operation. Their warrant cards and powers of arrest were valid in England, but as soon as they brought their suspects back over the border, the twenty-four-hour custody clock would default to the Scottish twelve-hour rule, although Shona could authorise extensions.

Dan was investigating if there were any further offences on which they could hold Mad Markie, his two brothers and Uncle Fin in England. If he found something, this meant he could rearrest them, if necessary, extending the time they had to charge or release them.

The conference room was full, with some staff standing against the wall beyond the central table, and a couple even perched on the window ledge. Word had got round that a breakthrough had been made and, since the arson and attempted murder concerned one of their own officers, everyone from civilian staff to Specials wanted to be in at the finale. Ravi was given special deference and a good seat near the head of the table, and the detective constables, Kate, and Allan Peacock, sat close by.

As Shona and Murdo arrived, the room hushed. She took a moment to scan the eager faces, making eye contact with as many as possible before she began.

'Since we may be making arrests tomorrow in both the drug inquiry and the arson and attempted murder of Sergeant Sarwar and his partner, I want to say a word about the investigation into Hayley Cameron's death.'

A shimmer of alertness seemed to run around the room.

'We are not deprioritising the investigation, but I believe we've gone as far as we can until we get Professor Kitchen's final report – which will hopefully be soon. All the Garmin stress-map locations have been identified and checked, is that correct, Hannah?'

Hannah nodded.

'So, we can track her movements fully for the two-week period before her death, when a witness tells us she was actively investigating her PEDs supplier, and that is where we'll concentrate the next phase of the investigation.'

Kate was looking increasingly agitated, wriggling in her seat, crossing and recrossing her legs, as if she could only just contain her frustration. Shona was aware that emphasising there were still unexplored lines of inquiry reinforced Kate's view that the boss was letting things slide. Years ago, as a young cop, she would've rolled her eyes too at the snail's pace at which older, so-called more experienced, officers seemed to pursue an investigation. Shona stared at the detective constable until she sat still, the message clear; Kate had already been issued with her final warning. Any outburst now would result in suspension.

Shona returned to the laying out of the objectives for both the arson and the festival drugs cases. First, apprehending Mark Cameron, his electronic devices, and vehicles, thereby linking him to the attack on Ravi and Martin's house. The second was to show Cameron's connection to Billy Gillespie, the dead dealer at the festival, and advance the hypothesis that the Carlisle Camerons were expanding their drug business north. Linking Uncle Fin to the arson attack or the drugs at this stage would be helpful, so they were also bringing him in and seizing his phone.

'If you haven't met Finlay Cameron yet, you're in for a treat. Anything we can find on this guy that contravenes his bail conditions and gets him back inside is an automatic gold star.' Shona opened it up to the room. 'Questions?'

'What about the second man on the motorbike?' Allan asked.

'We've no leads on his identity, but Dan Ridley is profiling known associates of Mark Cameron, so hopefully we'll get him too.'

There were a few more questions – mostly about the practicalities, which Murdo chipped in answers for.

When everyone was happy, Shona said, 'Finish up and get yourselves home. It'll be a very early start tomorrow morning. Be at your best.'

She watched as Peacock went up to Ravi and shook his hand, and Kate briefly laid a reassuring arm around his shoulder. If there was one thing she was proud of, it was that the dynamics of her team, thought they might flex and bend, always returned to their mutually supportive state, even when new folk were added. Ravi came over as the others left.

'Sorry we won't have you with us on the arrest,' Shona said. They'd already discussed it. Legally, the defence might raise it as an issue, but she also didn't want to put Ravi through a potentially ugly confrontation. 'I need you to hold the fort here for me, and maybe have a wee review of the Secret Forest drugs material. Anything, anything at all that we've missed that might give us a stronger connection to the Camerons than Billy Gillespie's tent mate, Harry Taylor, sharing a love of rap and making home videos with Mad Markie.'

'Aye, fine.' Ravi sighed.

'With any luck, this time tomorrow we'll be charging Mad Markie.'

'Aye,' Murdo agreed. 'Top job fae Vinny. Maybe we'll no' be needing Dan's graffiti handwriting expert after all. Did a' thon paint come off yer walls?'

Ravi nodded. 'Martin sorted it, though I doubt he'll want to go home soon. Sounds like he's well settled in at your place,' he said to Shona. 'Cooking wi' Becca tonight, apparently, and we're not to be late. It's like some crackpot America sitcom. The gay couple, his boss and her madcap daughter all living in a lighthouse-shaped B&B by the sea. I'm gonna call it *Tales of the Solway* and sell it to your pal, James McGowan. You could be the next Mrs Madrigal.'

It was further proof to Shona that James had been accepted as part of her life by her friends and colleagues, although the sensitive nature of the circumstances meant they didn't question her about the details or future plans. What would Murdo and Ravi say if they knew she was thinking of leaving them all behind? She'd made a conscious decision not to let the NCA spook her, but her subconscious was still shouting at her to run. She loved what she'd built at Dumfries CID, but nothing lasted forever. Murdo might shock her and opt to retire. Ravi, having had a taste of being a sergeant, might move for promotion. She couldn't let others' plans sway her decision.

'Well, hopefully, we won't be late back to High Pines tonight.' Shona grinned. 'And Solway's Mrs Madrigal? I suppose it's always nice to have career options.'

She'd broached the subject of a move to LA in the broadest terms with Becca, who surprisingly had not totally blown the idea out of the water. A new life. But that's what she'd hoped when she'd come to the Solway. That move had taught her that it took more than geography to truly escape your old problems and start anew.

'Right, Murdo. Away home. Let's see what tomorrow brings us.'

Chapter 30

Shona left for Carlisle at three a.m. She crept softly through the house, trying not to wake the others, but found Ravi in the kitchen, nursing a herbal tea.

'Good luck, be careful. Hope they both resist,' he said. 'Then you can Taser the bastards from me.'

An unseasonal gale had blown up from the south. It stormed across the Solway, reaching into the sheltered Kirkness haven like a cat into a mouse hole, pawing at the yachts and small boats, and sending them rocking nervously on their anchors. As Shona turned the Audi inland, heavy drops of rain pursued her and shattered on the rear window. In the darkness and driving squall, if felt as if she'd already travelled a long way since the congenial supper and warm bed of the night before. Neither Ravi nor Martin had asked Shona about James, but both had toasted him as an absent friend, and she imagined Becca had probably filled them in on the details.

In a lay-by on the outskirts of Dumfries, Shona stopped to pick up Murdo. The all-day burger van was already serving its first customers. His vehicle would be safe there, they'd save a bit on mileage and she'd get a cup of tea into the bargain. He was standing angled away from the driving rain, his jacket hood up. Two cups were balanced on top of each other, and he held damp paper bags containing bacon rolls in the other hand.

'Got one for you, boss,' he said once he'd wrestled open the passenger door and got inside. But Shona found she had no appetite and Murdo didn't seem too disappointed about finishing both rolls himself. She'd had a big helping of vegan spaghetti carbonara last night, cooked by Martin and Becca, but despite her faith in Murdo's and Dan's organisational abilities, she found she was nervous enough to pass on breakfast. There was so much riding on these arrests, with two major cases encompassing two overdose deaths, a drug operation and further counts of attempted murder and arson all linked together. It was a pity, given the family connection to Hayley, that they couldn't attribute her death to any of the Camerons. They really had nothing to gain by killing her, beyond seeing her as a source of shame within their criminal fraternity.

They crossed the border and dropped down onto the flatlands of Solway Moss. Ahead, between swipes of wiper blades, Shona could just make out the deeper darkness of the Lakeland Fells. The rain easing off turned out to be just the storm drawing breath. Brake lights came on as the traffic slowed once more, and the hammering on the windscreen was an incessant drumroll of noise. Shona and Murdo would have had to raise their voices to speak, but neither of them had much to say; the moments before an arrest were times of reflection, double-checking and silent prayer.

Shona drew up on the Raffles estate, just round the corner from their target address. The rendezvous point was a secluded area between two rows of garages. A group of vehicles had already arrived, including Kate's car, with Allan Peacock in the passenger seat. There were also two custody wagons, Dan's car and a blacked-out panel van with its back doors open. Inside sat the firearms team, and Murdo went over to talk to them. Given the Camerons' track record, Dan wasn't taking any chances, and he'd requested a unit from Penrith.

Shona got out of the car, opened the Audi's boot and was pulling her stab vest on over her black Police Scotland fleece when Dan came over.

'We'll clear the building, you make the arrest,' Dan said, which she thought was generous of him. 'Once we've got Mad Markie and Uncle Fin, I'll call the parole service. If we can get

Finlay Cameron for as much as aggravated littering, we'll have him back inside by teatime.'

'Oh, I'll have him for much more than that,' Shona said, grimly, adjusting the Velcro straps and closing the boot.

'I hope so,' Dan said in a low voice. ' 'Cos, frankly, you don't want him on your patch and I don't want him on mine, so Carlisle jail is the popular choice for both of us. Who's your exhibits officer?'

'Allan Peacock will take charge of any drugs or weapons.'

'And Kate?'

'She'll be taking Markie in,' Shona replied. 'Any sign of movement at the house this morning? Do we know who's in there?'

Intelligence had said the house was occupied by Finlay and his sons – Markie, Stab and the eldest, Gavin 'Geezer' Cameron.

'I've a couple of spotters down the road from the house. It's all quiet. Two SUVs out front. No sign of your grey Nissan Juke, but we think one of these garages is theirs.' He pressed his lips together, his face serious in the dim glow of the streetlamps. 'Got to assume Fin and the three lads are in the house. They're all dangerous bastards.' He pointed to her vest. 'You might need that if Stab-Happy Shaun is at home. Here.'

He held out a radio with an earpiece.

She pulled a hair tie from around her wrist and gathered her curls into it. Though she'd only been standing outside for a few minutes, the cold and the building adrenaline were combining to make her hands shake. She took the radio from Dan and, under the appearance of checking where the rest of her team were, turned away to disguise the tremor as she fitted her earpiece.

Murdo and Kate had their kit on, too. Allan was clutching a sheaf of evidence bags and talking to a female Cumbrian officer holding a clipboard.

The first of the armed officers stepped out of the van.

The charcoal tones of the night were giving way to the grey of early morning.

Dan checked his watch.

'Ready?'

Shona nodded.

'Let's get on with it, then.'

The house in the next street was ex-local authority, and maintenance obviously hadn't been at the top of the Camerons' to-do list. A sofa sat in the scrubby front garden next to a line of battered wheelie bins. Even in the pre-dawn light, Shona could see that the paintwork around the window frames was peeling. The front door had been patched just below the lock, where someone had previously tried to kick it in. Half the garden fence had been removed and concrete put down. A pair of incongruously clean and polished SUVs sat in the makeshift drive, but no grey Nissan Juke. The place certainly wasn't a match for the Dumfries Camerons' cushy set-up. No wonder Uncle Fin wanted a bite of what they'd got.

The rain was coming down again, heavier than ever. The air felt thickened by it, and to Shona their progress suddenly seemed impossibly slow. The armed unit led the way, keeping tight to the neighbour's overgrown hedge, the torches on their rifles sweeping ahead like searchlights. The chatter Shona had heard in her earpiece had dropped to nothing as the black caterpillar of marksmen reached the Camerons' front fence and slipped soundlessly through, using the vehicles as cover.

Go! Go! Go!

The silence splintered as the battering ram met cheap wood.

Door breach!

A series of overlapping shouts rang in Shona's ear.

Police, make yourself known. Police, show me your hands. Police, get on the floor.

There was the briefest moment of hush, then the screaming started.

It was only a few minutes but to Shona it seemed like an hour. Murdo and Kate were either side of her, shuffling from foot to foot – as impatient as she was to know what was happening. After far too long, a series of shouts came over the radio – *Clear!* – until Dan, who'd gone in behind the firearms team, called to Shona that she could enter the building.

He met her at the front door, his face grim. Behind him, in the hall, two young women in fluffy bathrobes and slippers were arguing with Cumbrian officers as they and their children were herded towards the kitchen at the back of the house.

'Markie isn't here,' Dan said. 'Neither are his brothers.'

'Shit. What about Finlay Cameron?'

Dan tipped his head towards the front room. 'You better come in.'

Shona pushed back her sodden hair, stepped dripping onto the hall carpet and removed her radio earpiece.

For the briefest moment, she wondered if Uncle Fin was dead, but that small surge of elation was quickly followed by indignation that, if so, he would escape justice and a long prison sentence. But when she walked into the lounge, she found him very much alive.

Finlay Cameron sat in the armchair by the fireplace, fully dressed and waiting. His cuffed wrists rested serenely in his lap. He turned his furrowed face towards Shona, the dark eyes pits of malicious glee.

'Good morning, DI Oliver.'

The room was lit by the harsh overhead light, the curtains open. Moments earlier the house had been asleep, but Finlay Cameron hadn't. He'd been sitting here in the dark, like an ogre in a cave.

The two large sofas that were pressed up against the walls seemed to shout their emptiness.

She took in Finlay Cameron's freshly pressed shirt and suit trousers, the polished shoes.

How did he know? How did the bastard know they were coming?

The garage lock had been forced. There was no Nissan Juke. Not so much as an aspirin was found in the house.

Finlay Cameron was put in the back of a custody wagon and sent to Dumfries, but without the car or Markie, he must have known they had nothing.

Shona and Dan stood in the empty garage. The rain had thankfully cleared but the promise of sunshine later didn't lighten Shona's mood. Dan looked apologetic but she told him it wasn't his fault.

'Phone the probation service anyway,' she said. 'Tell them Uncle Fin's been lifted by us on conspiracy to murder. That ought to get his card marked.'

'I've put out an all-points on Markie, Stab and Geezer. I've got uniform doing the rounds. And I've notified the ports. Just hope they haven't skipped to Ireland, or the Isle of Man.'

'That a possibility?'

'Heysham ferry is only an hour and a bit away. They've an aunt in Douglas.'

'I'm almost hoping they have legged it. Makes it look like they've got something to run from. When we catch them, I can get the sheriff to remand them as flight risks. The charges are serious enough. Might give us time to dig up enough to nail them all.' Shona sighed. 'Thanks for all this, Dan,' she said, knowing he'd have called in a few favours to put the operation together at such short notice.

'Well, that breakfast you promised me is on hold for next time.' He smiled. 'I hear you've got Ravi and Martin staying with you. What's that like?'

'Absolute madhouse.' She smiled back. 'But Becca's thrilled.'

'And how's things, generally?' His voice was low.

The others all stood at a distance; Murdo was pointing to the main road, and Shona thought he'd be telling Kate and Allan of a shortcut he knew to get them back quicker.

Their eyes met and her resolve not to mention the NCA evaporated.

'Listen, Dan,' she lowered her voice even though the level of activity outside would defeat any potential eavesdropper. 'I'm so sorry I involved you in what happened.' Even alone, she didn't want to utter Thalia's or Delfont's names for fear of resurrecting some malicious spirit that would wreak vengeance on them both for their part in that night's fateful events six months before.

'Don't be,' he said firmly. 'I'm glad I could help you when you needed it. You did the right thing for your friend. And I know if the tables were turned, you'd do the same for me.'

She saw the simple truth in that statement and wondered why she'd ever thought their friendship was in danger. 'I've missed you, *charva*.' She grinned, using the Cumbrian dialect for 'lad'.

'Get away with ya, *lasso*.' He smiled back.

'There's something else,' she said, then outlined the calls and meeting with Hennessey. She thought his demeanour would change at this threat, but he just shook his head.

'Only four people know what happened, and two of them are in this garage.' The other two were Thalia and Tommy. 'None of us have anything to gain by talking to the NCA, have we?'

He was right. She hadn't been thinking clearly about any of it. The relief was so complete that she felt her shoulders drop and a wave of tension flow out of her. She put her hand on Dan's arm to steady herself. 'I've been so worried.'

He squeezed her elbow. 'Don't be. And you can always talk to me, about anything, remember that.'

'Same.' She nodded and they both smiled.

Outside, Shona saw Murdo watching them and took a self-conscious step back.

She held up her phone. 'I'd better talk to Ravi. I'll update you later on what Uncle Fin has to say.'

They said goodbye and he moved off to talk to the firearms team, who were packing up their gear.

'How did Uncle Fin know we were coming?' Ravi exclaimed, echoing Shona's own major concern.

'Lot of folk in the briefing,' Shona said. Despite the information about the Hayley Cameron inquiry reaching uniform, she'd never considered a leak from her team would be a problem. But from the moment she'd seen Finlay Cameron sat calmly in his armchair, wearing a grin of satisfaction, she'd been racking her brains as to who among her staff might have a Carlisle connection.

'Can't see it,' Ravi said, following her line of thought. 'What about Dan's team?'

'Dan was careful. The only people who knew who the targets were, and the address, was the firearms team, and they came up from Penrith. Local guys were only told it was the Camerons about twenty minutes before.'

'Okay, so you seem to be saying it's somebody here.'

'Something we need to consider. Whoever it was gave them enough notice that Markie was off on his toes. Oh, I'm sorry, Ravi, I wasn't thinking.'

Only then did she realise that Ravi was not the person to be exploring this with because, if someone on the team had interfered on the arrest of two criminals who'd perpetrated an attack on him and his partner, it would be a personal betrayal on the highest level.

'Look, leave it with me,' she said. 'We're heading back. I'll talk it through with Murdo. Between him and Hannah, if someone's aunt's cousin once dated Geezer Cameron, they'll know,' she said, attempting to lighten the mood. 'In the meantime, can you tell the custody sergeant at Loreburn to expect a delivery?'

'Okay, boss. By the way, what's Liam Gallagher got to do wi' The Secret Forest festival?'

'He's a glitch in the matrix,' Shona said.

'That his new band?'

Shona laughed and the release of tension felt good after the morning's events.

'Hannah somehow got the wrong name for Billy Gillespie's tent mate, Harry Taylor. I think she's a closet Oasis fan.'

'Naw,' Ravi said. 'Black Sabbath all the way.'

'I can see it,' she agreed, smiling to herself and picturing her cardiganed, middle-aged data analyst letting loose at a heavy-metal gig. 'Listen, we'll be back in an hour. See you then.'

Murdo was by the Audi, waiting, his hands deep in the pockets of his sodden rain jacket. His face reflected what Shona felt. That someone had betrayed them to the Camerons was bad enough, but now Uncle Fin and his boys were going to get away with arson, attempted murder, and all the rest. Unless Murdo and Shona stopped them.

Chapter 31

Kate and Allan must have stopped for coffee, because Shona and Murdo were first to arrive at Cornwall Mount.

On the journey back from Carlisle, they'd pulled apart both the cases and their team members. Nothing other than a leak could explain how the Camerons knew in advance that they were being targeted, and Shona was determined to go through the office with fire and sword until she unearthed the culprit.

She yanked open the entrance door from the carpark, Murdo behind her like a disgruntled bull, and nearly ran slap-bang into Ravi.

'Boss,' he said. His face was pale and rigid with anger, and he seemed to have been waiting for her.

Just then, Kate and Allan pulled up behind Shona's car.

Ravi's expression underwent a swift transformation, his usual affable self reappearing with such speed that it stopped Shona in her tracks.

'Kate. Allan, pal. Bad luck,' he said in a consoling tone, stepping aside to let them pass. 'Hannah's got the kettle on. See you in a minute.'

Kate and Allan Peacock looked at Shona for confirmation, and she told them to go on ahead.

Ravi let the door fall shut, then beckoned them close to the wall, glancing up at the stairwell window, checking that they couldn't be seen or overhead.

Shona raised her eyebrows at Ravi, inviting an explanation, but he put his hands on his hips, hanging his head for a moment. When he looked up, the fury was back.

'It's him. The sleekit, wee bastard. The only reason I didnae rip the fucker's head off just now is that I want to do it in court, so we can take Finlay Cameron and his bampot sons down too.'

Shona stared at him. She felt Murdo stock-still at her shoulder.

'What d'you mean, it's him?' she said. She followed the direction of Ravi's previous glance. 'Our leak is Allan Peacock?'

Had Ravi grasped at the idea that Allan was the traitor because he felt – as she did in that moment – that it was more palatable than suspecting a colleague: one of the Specials Ravi had encouraged, or a member of the civilian staff who had been working with him for months or even years.

'Liam Gallagher.' Ravi's voice was little more than a whisper.

'Yeah,' Shona said, struggling to follow his line of thinking. 'Hannah got the name wrong. They're under pressure. It happens.'

'Hannah doesnae make mistakes like that.'

'Aye, that's true,' Murdo agreed.

Shona, on reflection, had to admit it was so rare an occurrence as to be statistically unrecordable.

'No one used the name Liam Gallagher to camp at The Secret Forest,' Ravi went on. 'So how come Allan gave Hannah a printout showing a photocopy of a driving licence? Who did he talk to?'

'He went over to the festival office on his own,' Shona said.

'No reason you should have been there,' Murdo agreed.

'When I'd finished at the crime scene,' Shona went on, 'he said he'd get a lift back from uniform.'

'Giving him time to pick up the fake driving licence,' Ravi finished.

'But how did he plan that in advance? He couldn't have known I'd take him with me.'

'Billy Gillespie's tent mate, Harry Taylor, knew his pal was dead long before we did,' Ravi said. 'There'd have been time to concoct a strategy to block any link back to the Camerons.

I mean, he's convincing. I didnae want to believe it mysel'. He could charm the teeth outta yer heid that one, I'll give him that.'

Shona tried not to flinch at the unintentional sting in Ravi's words. Peacock had been the willing worker in awe of her team and leadership, and she'd fallen for it.

'We'd check the driving licence he gave us with the DVLA,' Shona said slowly, 'find out it was a fake, and think we'd hit a dead end.'

'An' if Dan hadnae been in the office thon day,' Murdo added, 'an' saw Vinny match the clothes on our victim in the tent with pictures from Erin's camera, an' recognised it was Billy Gillespie intae the bargain, it woulda been a dead end.'

'We'd have run DNA and probably got Gillespie's ID eventually,' Shona said, 'but it would have slowed us up.'

'And Peacock did it,' Ravi said, 'for the same reason he warned the Camerons we were coming this morning. So they could cover their tracks.' The anger was radiating from him in waves. 'We need to arrest him now.' He turned and put his hand on the door, ready to pull it open.

'Wait,' Shona said, concentrating hard as she tried to interpret this new vista, foggy and indistinct, that was opening up before her. 'What's Peacock doing here at Dumfries CID?'

Ravi stopped and exchanged a glance with Murdo.

'He volunteered tae help us out after Erin Dunlop died.' Murdo frowned. 'We had two cases running. If he's tied up wi' Finlay Cameron, it makes sense he'd want the inside track on the festival investigation, head off any trouble for them.'

'He volunteered for Hayley's case,' Shona said. 'Because he'd trained with her and Andy Purdy.'

'Might have said that as a cover,' Murdo replied. 'A wee bit of misdirection.'

Ravi nodded in agreement, but Shona was shaking her head.

'We can't arrest him until we're sure what he's up to.' She glanced at her watch. They'd need to go upstairs soon or the others would wonder what was keeping them, and she didn't want Allan Peacock alerted to the fact he was under suspicion.

'We've got to arrest him now,' Ravi exploded, struggling to keep his voice down. 'How d'you know it wasnae him that gave Mad Markie mine an' Martin's address? We could've been killed. You cannae leave him running around loose inside a CID operation.'

'Then we'll have to contain him,' Shona said, holding up her hand to placate Ravi. 'And when we do arrest him, we make sure it'll stick.'

A plan was beginning to take shape. Her big mistake when she'd reported DCI Harry Delfont for corruption was not having all the evidence nailed down. She'd believed an impartial investigation would follow and fill in the blanks. She wasn't about to make that mistake again. This time there would be an investigation, and she knew just the cops for the job: her own.

'Him bringing us a dodgy driving licence isn't enough,' she said. 'I want you both to dig up everything you can on Allan Peacock. Murdo, find something to keep him busy for the next twenty-four hours, and in the office, where we can see him.' Shona looped her bag over her shoulder, took a step towards the door, then stopped. 'What if he did come because of Hayley? If Peacock *is* connected to Uncle Fin, he'd likely be in touch with the Dumfries Camerons. Maybe they wanted to know what was going on with Hayley's death, in case it was a pop against them by a rival outfit like we first thought?'

'That scenario only works if she's part o' the family,' Murdo reminded her. 'We havenae found anything to say she was working for them.'

Shona bit the smooth flesh on the inside of her lip, aware that both men's eyes were on her, looking for answers that she was still searching for herself.

'Hannah said Peacock had been to most of the locations on the map Vinny and Chloe put together,' she said. 'Checked them all out *practically single-handed*, were her actual words.'

'Aye, that's right,' Ravi confirmed.

'If Hayley wasn't working for the Camerons, then what if she was working against them?' She watched Ravi and Murdo sift through the probabilities, weighing snippets of evidence against each other as she'd done moments before. 'Hayley's partner Joanne told us she thought Hayley was investigating something that would get her into CID and put an end to wagging tongues about her criminal relatives. We've found no evidence she was getting performance-enhancing drugs anywhere but online, so maybe it wasn't suppliers of PEDs but her family she was investigating?'

Ravi rubbed his hand across his chin. 'The elevated stress points are mostly locations in town, with a couple in the forest, but they don't match when she was meeting Kennedy. Some were when she was on duty, but most weren't.'

'But they could correspond to her evidence-gathering,' Shona said, 'which might explain Peacock's enthusiasm for visiting them.'

'Tracking her to see whit she had,' Murdo agreed, nodding, his face serious. 'If that's the case, thon's a dangerous game Hayley was playing, wi' no backup. Nae wonder her stress levels were through the roof.'

Shona could feel her excitement mounting. This could be the breakthrough they needed, but it would mean nothing unless they could prove it. In the meantime, they had Finlay Cameron upstairs, with damn all against him, and the clock was ticking.

'What'll we do aboot Uncle Fin,' Murdo said, as if he could read her mind.

'We stick to procedure,' Shona said. 'Interview him over the death of Billy Gillespie and the whereabouts of his sons. He'll likely go no comment. If Peacock has briefed him, he'll understand what we've got is thin where he's concerned, but Dan's going over the house in Carlisle again and looking for the boys, so I might be able to extend his detention for another twelve hours on that basis.'

'So, we're treating the Cameron family as prime suspects in Hayley's death?' Murdo asked.

'They've got to be,' Shona said emphatically. 'I hate to trot out the old means, motive, opportunity... but who else could be behind this? I mean, Murdo, you said the Camerons have always escaped arrest. Hayley might have been onto something we've missed.'

'Should we tell Dan about Peacock?' Ravi said quietly.

Shona considered for a moment, rubbing her eyes. 'No, let's keep it to ourselves till we know how far this goes. If Finlay Cameron has one of ours in his pocket, he could have friends in Carlisle nick too.'

'Isn't that reason to warn him?' Ravi said.

'After this morning, he already knows we've a leak. He'll go careful.'

'And Kate?' Murdo said. 'How's she gonna react?'

'That's why we don't tell her yet,' Shona replied. 'I want to be sure.'

Ravi's expression said he already was.

'We need to bring Hannah in on this,' Murdo said, and Shona immediately saw the practicality of the statement. Most of the data processing was done, but they needed a guide to its highways and byways.

She nodded her agreement, then let out an exasperated sigh. 'Why would Peacock do this? He's got an exemplary service record, a glowing reference from DI Kenny Dalrymple. Why would he risk his career?'

'Usual reasons,' Ravi said flatly. 'Money. Or he might be being blackmailed. Either way, he's made his choice.' He grabbed the handle and pulled the door open. 'I've no sympathy for him.' He stepped aside to allow Shona and Murdo to pass.

If what they suspected was true, Shona had little sympathy for him either. But she couldn't help reflecting that, as in her own case, the reason someone crossed the line between upholding the law and transgressing it wasn't always as simple as people thought. Helping her friend Thalia escape, and Allan Peacock's actions, which risked putting his friends and colleagues in danger, weren't comparable as far as she was concerned, but the law viewed it differently. She supposed that what it came down to was loyalty. Now she needed to find out where Allan Peacock's truly lay.

Chapter 32

Ravi went ahead, Murdo entered the CID office a minute later, and Shona brought up the rear, muttering loudly about pool cars and parking arrangements, giving the impression that this was what had been behind their delay.

'Murdo! My office,' she barked at her sergeant, who'd only just taken his seat. 'The rest of you…' She swept an accusing finger around the CID room in a convincing display of frustration and displeasure at the morning's events. 'Anything, anything at all, we can nail Finlay Cameron with, I want to hear about it now!'

She gave Murdo an apologetic smile as he came into her office and sat down. He shrugged his shoulders and replied with a good-natured grin, as if this was normal service – which to some extent it was – before his expression became serious again.

'Have you thought of something to keep Peacock occupied?' Shona said.

'I'll get him going through thon street dealers we rounded up when we were lookin' at who was supplying at the festival. I'll tell him we're reviewing their info for links to Finlay Cameron. That'll catch his interest if he's their man, an' keep him busy.'

'Good.' Shona nodded her approval. She checked the time on the wall clock. 'Thoughts on interviewing Finlay Cameron?'

Murdo pursed his lips. 'This isnae his first poker game, an' he kens our hand is empty. Could threaten him wi' recall tae prison, but he'll have considered that an' have his response ready.'

'He likes to grandstand. Maybe I could goad him into saying something?' Shona suggested, aware of just what a dangerous move that might be in the confined space of an interview room, and how many uniform cops it would take to bring Uncle Fin to his knees. 'Given his views on gay people, I'd take Ravi in with me if there wasn't a conflict of interest, but Ravi might punch the bastard, and I wouldn't blame him.'

Murdo shook his head. 'Goading him willnae work. He'll no' bite. Too much to lose.'

'So have we, if he gets out,' Shona replied.

She saw Ravi walking out of the CID room, pulling on his jacket, phone clamped to his ear. She raised herself up from her chair, peering over Murdo's shoulder through the glass partition until she located Allan Peacock, in deep discussion with Kate at her desk. What was he up to? Had she made the right decision in not arresting, or at least suspending, him as soon as Ravi told her his suspicion? If he caused further harm, she'd have to defend that decision, possibly in disciplinary proceedings. Suddenly, she knew there was no going back now.

'Let's give Uncle Fin our best shot,' she said, gathering her papers and notebook together. 'Then I want you back on Allan Peacock. Shut him down, Murdo. Fast as you can.'

—

It was as Murdo had predicted. Finlay Cameron sat in his chair in the interview room, arms folded, a grin playing on his face each time he responded to her questions. *No comment.* Did he know where his sons were? Had he conspired with Mark Cameron in the arson and attempted murder of DS Sarwar and Martin Scott? Did he know Billy Gillespie? Was he, Finlay Cameron, concerned in the supply of drugs at The Secret Forest festival? *No comment.* The malevolent amusement never left his face.

Back in her office, as she replayed the interview in her mind, it was his barely contained jubilant demeanour that more than anything convinced Shona they were on the right track.

If he hadn't been so smug, if he'd feigned bemused concern for the accusations against himself and his son, or protested his innocence, laying out his understanding of his precarious position in regard to prison recall and brandishing it as a justification that she'd got it all wrong, then maybe she'd have questioned the direction they were pursuing.

He knew she had nothing. But what Finlay Cameron didn't know was that she knew how and why he knew. This, she hoped, would be her winning card.

The day dragged on. Everyone was at their desks, checking and rechecking evidence, alibis, CCTV and witness statements, doing their utmost to find something to place Finlay Cameron at the festival, near Ravi's house, or any other locations associated with Erin Dunlop, Billy Gillespie or his tent mate and fellow dealer, Harry 'Cody' Taylor. Shona kept a close eye on Allan Peacock, as throughout the slow hours of the afternoon he moved from desk to kettle to refill his coffee cup. At one point, he left the office, and she saw Murdo get up and follow him, only for them both to return a minute or two later, probably from the bathroom as a result of all the coffee. The rest of her attention was divided between Hannah and Murdo, interrogating their body language each time they crossed the room to consult, their heads close together, for any sign of progress.

The custody clock crept closer to six p.m. and what Shona now realised was inevitable: the moment when she'd have to release Finlay Cameron and see that ugly grin on his ugly face widen in triumph. His solicitor, who'd taken extensive notes of the one-sided interview – her questions, his non-answers – had already warned her against trying to extend custody for a further twelve hours. Maybe Cameron's confidence wasn't misplaced. He, and Allan Peacock, had covered their tracks so well that there was no hope of finding anything.

To distract herself from this sobering thought, she opened her laptop and pulled up the interactive graphic of Hayley's final weeks. The pins showed the stress locations that Peacock had visited. What did they have in common? Six were houses in the centre of Dumfries. One was a warehouse; the other three were rural, on the 7stanes mountain biking trails near Dalbeattie and in the Forest of Ae, north of Dumfries. Shona leaned her elbows on her desk and cradled her chin in her hands.

If Hayley had been investigating Cameron criminality, this combination of locations – viewed selectively – pointed to a familiar business model: a drug distribution network. Warehouse for storage, domestic properties for dealers to work from, quiet forest trail carparks, with no CCTV, for taking deliveries.

Shona searched for the reports added by Peacock after his visits to each address. The documents were extensive, listing the history of each property and current owners, the accessibility of the forest locations and average visitor numbers. Nearest ANPR was noted. Business tax returns, outstanding traffic offence penalties related to the addresses, criminal records of previous tenants, and on and on. It looked like a thorough job but amounted to nothing. All the properties were conveniently empty. No witness statements, no recovered additional CCTV from doorbell cams or neighbours' surveillance systems.

Shona tried to refocus her thoughts on the original traveller of these routes. Hayley was smart. She'd used her Garmin to track her training and other activities. She would have been aware she was leaving a digital footprint. But was it more than that? Was she leaving a breadcrumb trail because she knew her life was in danger?

Shona sat back and threw her pen onto the desk. She was sure that, at the end of a maze of paperwork, the Camerons were the true landlords. But there was another possibility. If Shona was looking for the evidence Hayley was presumed to have gathered, then so was Peacock, and as he'd tracked her last routes, had he found it? That might also explain Finlay Cameron's confidence.

She got up, determined to rid herself of the thoughts that were circling around her head without revealing their significance or otherwise. She made yet another tour of encouragement around the office, willing her staff onwards. Back in her office, she texted Becca that she'd be late home and immediately got a thumbs-up reply. When she messaged James, there was no response. It was early morning in LA and he might be at the gym, and she tried not to read anything into it. She'd have to give him an answer soon.

Just as she was steeling herself to face Finlay Cameron and his solicitor again, Ravi came back into the office. He crossed at a nonchalant pace to where Murdo sat. As he reached the sergeant's desk, he turned and sent Shona a quick look that made the fine hairs on her arms stand up. He'd found something.

She got up from her desk and, in an unhurried fashion at odds with her thumping heart, drew the vertical blinds on the windows that separated her office from the main room. Whatever Ravi was about to tell her, she didn't want Peacock getting wind of it. A moment later, Ravi and Murdo arrived at her door, and she ushered them in.

'What have you got?' She looked from Murdo to Ravi and back, as she paced the small room, unable to sit down. She could see it was something, but there was an absence of triumph in either of their faces, just a grim determination leavened with something like disgust.

'I did a bit of digging,' Ravi began. 'Somethin' you said, boss, about families. Clem Cameron is from Carlisle, came up here when he got married. What about the rest o' the family? Siblings?'

'There's another brother?' Shona stopped pacing, not sure she wanted to hear news like that. She looked at Murdo, but he just shook his head; his local knowledge had, for once, reached its limits.

'Not a brother. A sister,' Ravi said. 'Laura Cameron. Divorced after a short marriage to a small-time crook who disappeared. She died ten years ago. Lived over at Annan. That's where I've been. She'd no convictions. Worked in a bakery. Kept herself to herself, according to the neighbours.'

'What was the name of the crook she married?' she said, unease creeping over her.

'David Peacock.' Ravi gave them a moment to absorb this before confirming what they'd already worked out. 'One son. Allan Alexander.'

'So that makes him…' Murdo began.

'Finlay and Clem's nephew,' Ravi finished.

'Shit. How was this never picked up?' Shona said.

Ravi shrugged. 'Who knows. Never in trouble with the police as a teenager, kept his head down. Neighbours were pretty disapproving of how Peacock treated his mum. They knew him as Alex, and he wasn't around much for Laura's final years because, get this, he was living with a girlfriend in Carlisle.'

'And I think we know who else he was hangin' oot wi' south of the border,' Murdo said, jaw tight with disapproval.

'Didn't Hayley know he was her cousin?' Shona said. 'They trained together, for God's sake. I asked him about her and all he said was that she was a couple of years older and that he knew Andy better. Is that credible, d'you think?' She turned to Murdo.

'Hayley left home at eighteen,' he said. 'Peacock's no' an uncommon name aroon here. Hayley might never have met her aunt or her wee cousin, if Laura Cameron was keeping away from her folks.'

Shona thought of Kimi and how Hayley had tried to get her away. Perhaps any Cameron woman who was lucky enough to get out made damn sure she stayed away.

'Maybe she did know who he was,' Ravi said. 'I mean, she was a straight cop so would have assumed he was too. Any reminder they were both connected to the Camerons was something she'd not want brought up. Nowhere for that relationship to go, a dead end.'

She stared at Ravi. Dead end.

And then it hit her. It hit like a storm wave, knocking her off her feet. She took a step back and put her hand out, steadying herself against the desk. The anger in her sergeants' faces turned to concern. Murdo grabbed her elbow. She felt the rough edge of the filing cabinet graze her palm.

Dead end.

What was it Dan had said about the girl who'd been jabbed with GHB in the Carlisle nightclub? He'd hit a dead end. No CCTV or witnesses, and the doormen had told her mates that the guy they were looking for was a celebrity. Being hooked up with the Camerons might make you that. Untouchable. They'd said his name was Alan Partridge.

'Oh my God,' Shona said. 'Not Alan Partridge. Allan Peacock.'

The others looked at her blankly, but with growing concern.

She thought back to the moments before the triathlon race, how the different groupings had lined up. Her fellow lifeboat crew member, Callum, went first in the men's race. Then Hayley and Kate in the women's, followed by the youth group. They were bunched together on the shore, identifiable only by their numbers.

Anyone in that group could have walked up behind Hayley, jabbed her and disappeared into the crowd of indistinguishable wetsuited figures in swim hats and goggles. Hayley would have felt it, but when she turned around, there would have been no clue as to what had just happened.

When Allan Peacock had first arrived, she'd thought how much younger he looked than his age. She remembered the lad at the triathlon she'd handed the number to after it had fallen from a bike. His swim hat had been blank, but somehow she'd thought the bike was his. He could have been anyone. He could have been Allan Peacock.

'I know how he did it,' she said. 'I know how he killed Hayley.'

Chapter 33

Shona told Murdo and Ravi how she believed Peacock had walked calmly up behind Hayley and jabbed her with GHB moments before she entered the water. She shared their doubts about how anyone could have accomplished this in front of hundreds of witnesses before walking away, but at the same time she was convinced she was right.

'Get Hannah in here,' she said. 'There's got to be something that places Allan Peacock in Kirkness before or after the race.'

When Murdo beckoned the data analyst into the office, Hannah began, 'I'm still trying—'

But Shona held up her hand to stop her and quickly explained that the focus of the investigation was now on Hayley's murder. Hannah nodded, her face emotionless. She paused only long enough to tug up the sleeves of her cardigan and confirm the immediate priorities of her search, and then she was gone.

'What about Kate?' Murdo said. 'She needs tae be in on this now.'

Shona agreed and gave Ravi the nod. 'Keep it low-key. I don't want Peacock spooked. I'll be calling Dan in Carlisle in a minute to update him. Murdo, go check with Hannah if she needs anything from their data guys.'

They both left, and Shona paused to reflect that this might be the toughest thing she'd ever had to say to a detective constable – that the man she'd just driven to Carlisle with, whose back she'd watched during a house raid, was the man Shona believed to be responsible for the death of her best friend. A moment later, Ravi was back, ushering his colleague into the chair beside Shona's desk.

'I'm sorry, Kate,' Shona said when she'd finished. Her DC stared at her, blank and uncomprehending.

'Why? Why did he do it?' Shock was turning to anger.

'We need to draw up an arrest and interview strategy,' Shona said. 'Until Hannah finds something, all we can prove is that he's Clem and Finlay's nephew, and he fed us a dodgy driving licence. It isn't enough. Murdo will be back in a minute. Get some coffees and we'll crack on.'

She stopped looking from Kate to Ravi, aware that they'd both had quite a day already, and that there might be further shocks to come. 'You guys up for this?'

'You kidding, boss,' Ravi said.

'I'm up for this.' Kate jumped to her feet, her face dark with fury. Before Shona could stop her, she'd reached the door and was heading back into the main CID office.

But Ravi went quickly after her. 'Never mind the kettle. Get yer coat. We need the good stuff. Americano for you, boss?' he called over his shoulder as he hurried after Kate.

Shona followed them out into the main office in time to see Kate bypass the kettle, and head straight for where Allan Peacock was sitting, on the far side of the room.

'Kate!' Shona snapped as Ravi increased his speed. Murdo had left Hannah's desk, seen Kate's destination and was moving to head her off.

Peacock's attention was focused entirely on his screen until he heard Shona's shout. He looked up, and a rapid series of expressions crossed his face as he saw Kate bearing down on him – curiosity, incomprehension, alarm.

He jumped to his feet, but he wasn't quick enough. Kate seemed to accelerate and in two strides she was there. She drew back her right arm and let fly a punch that sent Peacock backwards over his chair. He landed heavily and she moved to follow up with the left. Ravi caught her wrist just in time, the momentum spinning her around. He held her tight in a protective embrace as he attempted to drag her away.

'You bastard!' Kate screamed at Peacock.

Everyone was staring at the unfolding scene. Murdo had reached Peacock and was pulling him to his feet.

'You two,' Shona shouted at the Specials, Jimmy and Tom. 'Help Sergeant O'Halloran take him to interview room one.' They could delay Peacock's arrest no longer. 'Murdo, you know what to do.'

Fifteen minutes later, as Shona was writing furiously on her pad, Murdo arrived to tell her it was done. Allan Peacock was in an interview room downstairs, and had been formally arrested and cuffed. A charge of perverting the course of justice would do for now. Vinny had his phone.

'Did he say anything?'

Murdo shook his head. 'He knows how this works. He'll probably go nae comment like his uncle.'

'I've extended Finlay Cameron's detention on the grounds of new information. His solicitor's losing the rag downstairs, but the Super's backed it, though he's also made it clear we'll not be pals if we don't wrap this up fast. We need to convince Peacock it's in his interest to talk to us.'

Ravi returned, exhibiting an impressive display of calm. But Shona knew from the way he smoothed his hair back that he'd been deeply unsettled by what had happened.

'Is Kate all right?' Shona said.

Ravi nodded. 'I called Hayley's beat partner Joanne. Figured she'd be the best person, in the circumstances. She's taken Kate over to Loreburn to get her out of the way.'

'Thanks, Ravi. Good work,' Shona said, indicating he should take the seat next to Murdo. She'd need to deal with Kate later, but for now there were other priorities. 'My money was on you banjoing Finlay Cameron, never saw that coming.'

'Me neither. But I tell you what, that's some right Kate's got on her,' he said with an admiring grin. 'Will she face disciplinary action over it, though?' His smile faltered.

'She lamped a fellow officer in the middle o' CID room, in front o' a dozen witnesses. Cannae see how she'll avoid it,' Murdo said, grimly.

'Murdo's right,' Shona said. 'But what we can pin on Peacock will influence any proceedings, so let's concentrate on that.'

She opened her notebook and picked up her pen, signalling they should start.

'Allan Peacock volunteered for this investigation – that shows intention,' Shona began. 'Went to DI Kenny Dalrymple. Must have thought all his Christmases had come at once when he heard we needed help.'

'And he arse-licks his way around the team, making himself useful and butterin' us all up,' Ravi said with disgust.

'I've asked Dan to show an image of Allan Peacock to the girl in Carlisle who was jabbed with GHB. See if she can pick him out in a digital line-up.' She consulted the bullet points she'd just jotted down, then something that wasn't on her pad occurred to her. 'Murdo, did you send Peacock after me to the nail bar?'

His brow furrowed as he searched his memory. 'I mind I wasnae happy aboot you going in there on yer tod,' he conceded. 'But no, I didnae send him.'

She remembered Kimi's face when Peacock had come up to them. It wasn't just the automatic flirt response of any pretty young woman to an attractive man; she'd recognised him and deployed the same simpering smile she'd used to appease Uncle Fin. *Sorry, DI Oliver, there's nothing I can tell you.* He'd intervened to prevent Kimi talking. It was a warning that the Cameron clan were watching her.

'Okay,' Shona began, 'so Hayley was investigating something. What if Kimi was helping her? She must have seen stuff at home. I'm sure she recognised Peacock at the nail bar. Maybe she even told Hayley about him and other things besides?'

She paused as they all considered this. 'Ravi, remember Belle's horror when Uncle Fin turned up at the house?'

'Aye, I remember.'

'I think that was genuine fear, not just 'cos we were there, or she wasn't expecting him. The Carlisle dealers would already be at The Secret Forest,' Shona went on. 'Uncle Fin wasn't taking no for an answer. With another few mouths to feed in the shape of him and his sons, the whole of the Camerons' business would've been reorganising, expanding. Maybe that's what Hayley got hold of.'

'The argument in the pub.' Ravi nodded slowly. 'With new alligators climbing into the pool, she wanted Kimi to finally leave.'

'We really need tae talk to that lassie,' Murdo said.

Shona pulled up Kimi's number and called. She shook her head at the others. 'Voicemail.' What if she was right, and Allan Peacock was behind her disappearance as well? If he'd killed her too, she'd never forgive herself.

Hannah tapped her door and came in. 'Sorry to disturb you, boss, but we've got him.' Her relish was visible. Allan Peacock had crossed the wrong person with his false driving licence dupe. 'One of the no-shows remembers selling his triathlon entry for cash to a man matching Peacock's description. We think we've got him on the yacht club CCTV, leaving the event just after the women's race started.'

'Yes!' Shona slapped her desk. 'Well done, Hannah.' But then a new anxiety flooded in. 'Is there anything so far to link him to the Camerons?'

'Oh, aye.' A broad smile of satisfaction flooded her face. 'Our Mr Peacock has been a very silly boy.' Then her expression became serious again. 'I'm sorry, Ravi, I know this must be hard to hear. Vinny's cracked Peacock's phone. It's all there. He's our second arsonist. He was the other lad on the bike. His device travelled an identical route to Mark Cameron's. They switched them off together.'

Ravi's face was impassive. Shona put her hand briefly on his. At least they knew the worst now and that the person responsible would likely go to jail for a very long time.

She checked her watch. 'Right, let's put this to him. Let's see how he feels when we arrest him for Hayley's murder.'

Chapter 34

Allan Peacock sat in the interview suite in his shirtsleeves. A bruise was flowering on his left cheek where Kate had hit him, but he'd waved away any suggestion of further medical checks. His solicitor requested the cuffs be removed for the interview. Shona reluctantly agreed, giving Murdo the nod.

Peacock had been in rooms like this before, but she wanted to make sure that this time he understood which side of the table he was on. Perhaps it worked, or Peacock swiftly calculated he could limit the damage by appearing to co-operate. When faced with the evidence of his presence at the triathlon, he crumbled, but steadfastly denied he was in league with the Camerons or had tipped them off that morning.

'I never meant to kill Hayley,' he said. 'Just discredit her as a police officer and an athlete.'

'Why was that, then, Allan?' Shona said, trying not to sound sceptical.

'I was jealous, I suppose,' he replied, turning baleful eyes up to her. 'It was a stupid thing to do. We'd argued. She taunted me that she was physically superior to me because she was a triathlete, that she was a better police officer. It was a moment of madness. I never meant to kill her,' he repeated. 'I should have known you'd catch me. You and your team's reputation are so good.'

Flattery was obviously the most frequently deployed weapon in his arsenal of charm, and she winced at how effective it had previously been. He was already rehearsing his defence. She could see him in the witness box. A man who looked young for his age, of previous good character. He'd try to turn the jury so they'd believe that somehow he was the victim. Men who killed women often gave that a go, sometimes successfully. *She made me do it* still had currency with a surprising number of otherwise decent men and women. The attempted murder of Ravi and Martin in the arson attack would be harder to deny.

'What about when you poured petrol through Sergeant Sarwar's letterbox and set fire to it?' She saw him catch himself. He'd been about to protest it wasn't him, he'd just driven the bike. 'Had he offended you in some way?' Shona went on. 'The graffiti indicates a straightforward hate crime. You're an experienced police officer, what would you say?'

She needed to show that his actions weren't those of someone backed into a corner and forced to act defensively They were malicious, premeditated and at the behest of an organised crime group.

His expression hardened just enough to tell Shona he knew what she was trying to do. 'Just because my phone was there doesn't mean I was.'

'Where's Kimi Cameron?' Shona said. His expression was so smug that she wanted to reach across the table and give him a matching set of bruises on the other cheek.

'Don't know what you're talking about, Inspector,' he said, coldly.

After that, as if realising he couldn't gain the upper hand in this interview, he retreated, as Murdo had predicted, into *no comment*. Since he was a police officer, she didn't want him later claiming he'd been unfairly shamed by being processed by colleagues, so she arranged for him to be transferred to Kilmarnock to be fingerprinted and photographed. He could appear before the sheriff there and be remanded out of the area. Murdo would go with him to make sure he was safely handed over.

Shona went back up to her office. Peacock's arrest had been met with a mixture of outrage and bewilderment by the rest of the officers and the civilian staff. With feelings running high, and a limit to what more they could do that evening, Shona sent everyone home. Then she called Peacock's DI, Kenneth Dalrymple, and broke the news. He took it in his usual composed manner, but the pauses between his replies were long enough to tell Shona that he was having trouble marshalling his anger and disgust. All the cases Peacock had worked on would need to be reviewed and past convictions might be deemed unsafe as a result. Shona didn't envy him that.

Call over, she picked up her jacket and set off for Loreburn police office.

Kate was sitting with Joanne Mitchell in the family interview room, with its colourful cushions and a toy box in the corner. The beat cop had removed her tactical vest and was now dressed in her short-sleeved uniform top and trousers. But somehow, she still managed to look intimidating, and Shona wondered if she resented that CID hadn't apprehended her partner's killer sooner.

'Has he gone yet?' Kate said.

Shona shared the sense that their building was contaminated as long as Peacock remained there. 'Won't be long.'

'Will I be charged over what I did?' Kate said, her face defiant. 'Will I lose my job?'

'I don't know, Kate.' Shona sighed, her tone made blunt by the exasperation she felt over her DC's actions. 'What on earth possessed you? You understand the whole case could be undermined by what you did?'

Neither Allan Peacock nor his solicitor had said anything at the interview, but there was every chance they'd use Kate's actions to bolster his defence, highlight the unconventional manner of his arrest, perhaps even argue that the charges should be dismissed on procedural irregularities.

'I just couldn't bear it,' Kate said, her face a picture of misery. 'His lies. The pain he's caused. Sitting there, watching us…' She put her hand to her mouth, stifling a sob. 'My best friend,' Kate whispered. 'My beautiful, funny, amazing Hayley, and he killed her. For what?'

'What did he say at the interview?' Joanne asked, quietly.

Shona didn't think it would help either Kate or Joanne if she recounted what had happened in detail. 'He denied a connection to the Camerons. Claimed he wanted to discredit Hayley over some personal slight. It's bullshit. We'll nail him with the toxicology, the CCTV from the yacht club and the witness he bought the entry off. That's just for starters. Once we start kicking over stones, who knows what'll crawl out.' Shona leaned forward and took Kate's trembling hands between her own warm palms. 'It's best you take a few days off. I don't want to formally suspend you over what's happened.' She saw Kate bridle at the notion she was being removed from the case, but the protest was short-lived. Given the circumstances, there was no way around it, and Kate had to know that.

'Listen,' Shona continued, hoping to soften the blow. 'D'you want to inform Andy of what's happened? I'd rather he didn't hear it from the media. I can send Ravi, if you'd rather?'

'No, I'll do it. I'd like to. D'you want me to drive past the nail bar on the way? I won't stop. Just see if anyone's there. I'll text you.'

'I'll come too,' Joanne said. 'I haven't got my car and you can drop me off home before you go to Andy's.'

'Okay,' Shona conceded, reassured that Joanne would be both a steadying influence and backup should anything untoward happen. 'Just a fly-by.'

'Don't worry, boss,' Kate said, wiping her eyes and sounding calmer now that she had a purpose to focus on. 'I think if something had happened to Kimi we'd have heard by now. You don't survive in families like that without learning how to look after yourself. She's probably gone off on holiday and is sunning herself on a beach somewhere.'

'I hope you're right.'

After Kate had left with Joanne, with renewed assurances they wouldn't go into the nail bar, Shona was left alone in the empty silence of the room. She knew she should feel jubilation, but all she could see was Hayley's body in the bottom of the lifeboat and think of the waste, the devastation her death had brought to all those who loved her, including her sister.

The girl appeared to have vanished. She had no grounds to institute a search at the Camerons' home. Kimi was over eighteen and not a vulnerable individual, although Shona would strongly argue about that.

She rested her elbows on her knees, scrubbing her fingers through her hair. She'd sent Ravi to High Pines to give Martin the good news that one of the culprits for the fire was in custody and to tell Becca she'd be back shortly.

She checked her watch. *Shit*. Finlay Cameron was still in the cells, but without testimony from Peacock, they had nothing on him. He'd have to be sent home once the custody extension ran out. Since his brother owned a taxi company, they could shoulder that expense, she wasn't dispatching a squad car. As if summoned by her thoughts, Dan's name appeared on her phone screen.

'D'you want the good news or the bad news?'

'I'd like two lots of good news, if I have a choice,' Shona said.

'Can't confirm yet it was Allan Peacock who jabbed the girl in the club. Showed her the photograph and she hasn't ruled him out, so I'm going to request an in-person line-up.'

'Okay,' Shona said. It would strengthen their case if they could prove he'd previously used this MO to attack women, but a public appeal might bring other victims forward, whose testimony would do that job. 'Is that the good news or the bad news?'

'Oh, that's the bad news,' Dan said brightly. 'The good news is I've spoken to Finlay Cameron's probation officer. She says they'll recall him on the grounds that…' He paused and she could hear the pages of his notebook being turned. 'That they have reason to believe he is actively thinking about re-offending and that there is no requirement to wait for the outcome of a police investigation or criminal proceedings.'

Her spirits rose at this unexpected positive news.

'I'll be up to get him tonight,' Dan continued. 'Just chain him to a lamp post and warn the local wildlife to stay away till I get there. If he's back in jail, we've breathing space to track down his boys.'

Shona updated him on Allan Peacock's refusal to implicate the rest of the Camerons.

'D'you think he'll change his mind?'

'Who knows. If he's sitting in segregation he might have second thoughts.' An email alert appeared on her phone. 'Dan, I've got to go. I'll see you in a bit.'

She said goodbye to Dan, then clicked on Sue's email.

It contained the full toxicology results. Useful, but not essential now they had their man. Shona felt a certain wariness about reading it, as if Hayley's reputation and image would be further tarnished by the extent of her PEDs use, which she now felt was in keeping with her driven character. If more than 50 per cent of amateur athletes were reported to have used them at one point, Hayley seemed likely to have done too. Maybe it didn't feel like cheating any more.

As she finished reading, Slasher Sue's name flashed up on her phone. 'Hi, Sue, I've just seen your report land. I was about to call you,' Shona said. 'We've got our man.'

'That's very heartening to hear. Very well done, Team Shona. I'll look forward to the whole story on Monday. I don't want to keep you on a Friday night. There's something I just want you to be aware of. Can you scroll to page thirty-five and read the conclusion?'

Shona read the paragraph three times, and it still didn't seem to make sense.

'Ketamine? Orally administered? Is ketamine a performance-enhancing drug?'

'Possibly, but not in this quantity. And it's an anaesthetic. You might use it to relax, help you sleep but not right before a race. There was a lack of stomach contents due to the vomiting during drowning, but it was still present in gastric swabs.'

'So how would it have got into her system?'

'Well, I doubt she swallowed it wrapped up in a Rizla paper, known colloquially as a K-bombing. It's not in her water bottle, we tested that.'

'What about her beaker? I saw her with a protein shake?'

'Nothing like that among the items we received. Anyway, it might have been given to her in a sports gel. They're simple enough items to tamper with and are strongly flavoured, so she wouldn't have noticed. The foil wrapper could easily have been discarded. The timing is tricky, but my conclusion is that the ketamine would have caused the confusion and respiratory failure that led to her drowning, even as the GHB was making its way into her system. Both are present, but it was the ketamine that killed her.'

'Not the GHB?' Shona felt as if she'd hit a sinkhole and was spiralling down into new and murky depths.

'No.'

'The ket was administered before the GHB?'

'Yes. The results are clear.'

'How is that possible?'

'Establishing the chain of events falls squarely under your job description, ma dear.'

'Okay, Sue. Thank you.'

'Call me if you want to talk further,' Sue offered, clearly sensing that her findings had confused, rather than clarified, matters.

The sun had gone behind a bank of western clouds. Twilight deepened in the empty room, shadows altering its contours and geography until darkness seemed to lurk in every corner. Shona sat as the gloom settled around her.

Peacock had the track record of a nightclub predator. It was possible he'd slipped the ketamine into her drink, as he might have put GHB into any number of girls' glasses. But why risk it? He'd perfected his method with the injector pen, and a triathlon in daylight was a very different set-up. Hayley would have noticed someone near her kit or fiddling with her drinks.

An alternative explanation nagged at her mind until she was forced to acknowledge it. Despite Peacock's confession, with all its self-justification that he hadn't meant to kill her, only one other conclusion made sense.

There was another killer, and this one had definitely wanted her dead.

—

Shona called Murdo and updated him on the professor's report. He was silent when she told him her conclusion. There was nothing else they could do tonight. They should sleep on it, he'd said, and she'd found no sensible argument against this suggestion.

As she drove home through the summer night, the edges of high clouds still daubed with the tints of the sunset, her exhausted mind and body sought the comfort of James once more. She was aware she'd neglected him over the last few days, and that she was putting off the decision about a move to LA. She justified this to herself by considering she hadn't had time to think properly and also because she somehow didn't want the grime of her cases to enter their world. He'd have listened in a way Rob never did, and it was that, as much as security concerns, that had stopped her from mentioning things to her husband. Rob knew everyone in the village, and half of Dumfries and Galloway, having grown up here. His family still ran the principal auctioneers' business in the area, dealing with everything from land sales to art valuations. It hadn't been fair to burden him with secrets and suspicions about those he might meet or be tempted to gossip about in the pub. She didn't want to think of him now. Neither she, nor Becca had visited for a while. Rob's barrister had told him there were currently no grounds for an appeal, in her opinion, and during their last phone call, in his disappointment and frustration, he'd lashed out at Shona, with James's involvement in the business once more a flashpoint.

Before she'd left Loreburn police office, she'd sent James a text of apology, but again there was no immediate reply. Rest. Regroup. Allan Peacock was right about one thing: she had a damn good team and the answers were there in the evidence they'd already amassed. They just had to find them.

As she pulled into the parking area at High Pines, she rolled down her window, sitting for a moment and listening to the sounds of the summer night – the last twittering of the birds, Friday night conversations and laughter drifting up from the Royal Arms, the murmur of the sea in the estuary. The air had grown chilly. She pulled on her suit jacket and began a final scroll through the emails on her phone, anxious to draw a line under the eventful day and not carry its burdens into the house. An address with an NCA suffix caught her eye. That Dave Hennessey was back didn't surprise her. The contents of the message did, and she felt a familiar foreboding.

She was invited to attend an interview at Kilmarnock police office on Monday at ten a.m., pertaining to her knowledge of DCI Harry Delfont's connections with organised crime. They could have done that here, in Dumfries, but they were making a point. Her boss, Detective Chief Superintendent Clive Davies had been copied in. Her inbox contained a further email from him. He appreciated she had three fatalities to tie up, one of them the murder of a cop. He'd not quite got the *quickly and quietly* he'd hoped for, but containment to one rogue officer and the chance to take down an OCG had consoled him. He would back her all the way; bringing in a new SIO *at this stage* would delay things. But his message was clear: she needed to get these NCA guys off their backs pronto or face the consequences.

Chapter 35

The next morning, Shona woke to a thick mist that had rolled up the estuary, cloaking High Pines in an impenetrable cloud, obscuring the sun. She knew she should go down and make herself a coffee, but it felt like a huge effort.

Ravi and Martin had insisted on leaving early that morning for their house by the river. Shona tried to warn them against it, but neither of them thought Mad Markie would show his face in the town. They'd decided they'd rather be on the spot for the repairs. Or rather, Martin would. Ravi, in contrast, was bracing himself for major renovations and told Shona he doubted a pitchfork-carrying, fire-bearing mob would shift Martin again. He'd adapted and moved on. Shona admired Martin's resourcefulness and found herself agreeing with Ravi's earlier assessment that his partner was much tougher than he appeared, but she'd got Josie's phone number off Becca and told their baseball-bat-wielding neighbour to call at the first sign of trouble.

High Pines would feel emptier, and she knew part of the reason she wanted them to stay was for moral support. In her mind, she scrolled forward to the time when Becca would also be gone. Could she carry on living here alone? How long could she *rattle aroon in an o'er big hoose*, as Murdo might term it. Her low mood was inspired, she knew, in part by last night's double whammy of the forthcoming NCA interview and the prospect of a second killer, heralded by the professor's toxicology report. Now she'd thought about it more, it was unlikely that any progress could be made in understanding its implications until after the weekend. None of the other forensic experts would be available. They had one person in custody, and a manhunt underway for Markie Cameron and his brothers. Perhaps that was all that was possible, and she'd just have to be patient.

She checked her phone. Murdo and Ravi had agreed that although patience was the order of the day, they'd go into the office this afternoon for a couple of hours and sort through any uncompleted actions, ready for Monday. Shona knew she'd probably join them. There'd been no reply from James. Sleep had eluded her and she struggled with the time-difference maths. Early here was late there, right? Perhaps he thought she was busy. She'd said as much in her apologetic text.

Shona got out of bed, and after a moment's thought, pulled on his hoodie, which hung in the wardrobe. A trace of his scent still clung to the fabric and it was like being wrapped in his arms, a small consolation for the distance between them, but a consolation still. She'd decided sometime in the early hours that if it could be made to work for Becca and High Pines, she'd do it. She'd move to LA. Leaving the lifeboat would be her only regret, but they must have something similar in California and who knew when a chance like this would come again. She'd be mad to turn it down. She loved James and she was pretty sure he loved her. Decision made.

Becca was in the kitchen, buttering toast. She looked despondent; Shona thought she was already missing Ravi and Martin.

'You all right, darling?' Shona said, reaching up to plant a kiss on her daughter's mass of jumbled hair. 'Missing those two reprobates already?' She smiled, attempting to lighten the mood.

Becca sat down and chewed thoughtfully on her toast while Shona poured her coffee and then joined her.

'It was awful what happened to them,' Becca said after a minute.

'Yes, but we got one of the arsonists and we'll get the other,' Shona assured her.

'Maybe I'll defer university for a year.'

Shona stared at her. Where had this come from? 'Why? Don't you want to do the course? Is this about what James said about studying in the US? I'm sure we could make it work.'

Becca shook her head. 'It's not just that. I was talking to Martin. He said something about Ravi and I realised I thought the same. Every day you go out the door, I wonder if you'll come back. I've lived with your being a police officer and on the lifeboat for so long. I worry you'll get attacked or hurt, or just be in the wrong place at the wrong time. I worry that some lowlife you've put away will see you crossing the street and think it funny just to give you a scare, but his foot will stay on the accelerator and, and…' She gave her mother a fierce, meaningful look. 'Now I'm worried that something really bad will happen when I go away to university, wherever that is. I worry you'll take more risks without me at home. I worry you'll be lonely and get sad. I mean, even if James was around, he'd need to go away for work…' She threw down her toast as choking sobs overcame her.

Shona jumped and drew her daughter into a fierce hug. 'I worry about you too.' Concern about Becca's safety in LA had made her cautious about the move from the start. 'And I know there's no point in me telling you not to worry about me. But I don't want you not to live your life because of it. And this idea about moving to LA, we'll only go if you want to.'

'I know.' Becca sniffed. 'James sent me links to US archaeology courses, and told me not to worry about the fees, but he's not pressuring me or anything,' she said, seeing her mother's concerned expression. 'They all look brilliant, and I really like James. I guess the thought of leaving High Pines is beginning to feel real.'

'Is that what you want to do?'

'I don't know. Maybe? Do you?'

Shona's earlier certainty was wavering. 'I don't know. Maybe?' she said, and they both laughed through their tears.

'There's always going to be changes in your life, darling. But hey, the sun is shining. Let's just go out and enjoy it this morning.'

Becca smiled and wiped her eyes. 'God, Mum. James's touchy-feely Californian ways are really rubbing off on you.'

'Aye, for sure.' Shona grinned. 'Cannae guarantee there's no' a deep-fried Mars bar on the horizon, though,' she said in an exaggerated Glasgow accent. 'Come on, let's have breakfast and get outside. A walk will do us both good.'

Shona ran upstairs to dress. When she took off the hoody, it was like she was pushing James away, and she felt the pain like a hard lump in her chest. Her heart had made the decision to go, but her head was telling her it wasn't going to be as simple as she thought. The pull of LA and the push of the NCA were tearing her apart.

—

They were just on their way out when Shona picked up her phone and saw a shout had come in on the RNLI crew app. She hadn't opted to be on call, and her pager wasn't switched on, but the alert still sent her pulse racing. When she'd seen the mist this morning, she'd known there was a good chance they'd be called out.

'You want to go to the lifeboat station, don't you?' said Becca knowingly, but without rancour.

'I'm not going on the shout, but we can maybe help them wash down the boat afterwards.'

'Okay.' Becca shrugged. 'Since we're *going with the flow, dude.*'

The shout, it soon transpired, was from a holidaymaker whose dog had chased a gull over a cliff and got stuck at the bottom. The owner, a middle-aged man, had climbed down but then found he couldn't get back up, and the tide was coming in. His wife had called the coastguard. Both the dog and his owner appeared uninjured. A rope team was standing by, but it was decided that Kevin the cockapoo and his 'dad' could best be recovered by the lifeboat. Tommy had gone out on the water with Sophie and Callum.

Freya was waiting by the boat hall door with the rest of the shore crew.

'Shouldn't be long,' she smiled. 'Seem to spend half ma time waiting, and the other half running aroon like a mad thing. Tea?'

It had been on the local news this morning that they'd arrested someone in connection with Hayley's murder, and Shona thought Freya's brightness was partly down to the likelihood that any investigation into the triathlon would exonerate both Tommy and the organisers in general.

'Tea would be great.' Shona smiled.

As she cradled her cup and searched the lifting fog for the returning lifeboat, she reflected on her conversation with Becca that morning. Her decision would affect those around her too, yet she'd told no one. It was time to confide in Freya about James's offer.

'What'll you do out there?' Freya frowned, but didn't seem as shocked as Shona had thought she would be. 'Can't see you being a lady of leisure. You'd be bored stiff.'

'He thinks there'd be work for me,' Shona said. 'There's a number of options beyond straight film-set security.' She'd been googling the possibilities. 'A former colleague of mine from the Police Intellectual Property Crime Unit at the City of London Police works there as a private anti-piracy consultant, preventing theft or illegal distribution of movies. It's big business.'

'So, what's stopping you?' Freya asked, astutely.

'I don't know,' she said, chewing her lip. Close as they were, she couldn't mention the NCA investigation and the horrifying thought that she'd end up in prison if she stayed.

'Aye, well,' Freya said, eyeing her shrewdly and patting her arm in a show of support. 'There is nothing tae be done to hurry it along. It'll just have to work itself out. I'm sure you'll make the best decision for you and the lass.'

Freya was probably right, she usually was, and Shona felt a chink of light, the possibility that there were resolutions to all her problems, if she could just find them. Allan Peacock and the Camerons, however, were a more immediate concern. And that was a situation where she didn't have the option to see how the cards would fall.

On Monday, they'd have to review Hayley's murder, the arson, and probably Erin Dunlop's and Billy Gillespie's deaths. She'd tried to remain upbeat when she'd told Murdo about Slasher Sue's revelation on Hayley's cause of death, but she was far from sure they'd manage to uncover sufficient evidence when everything they knew about the Camerons and Peacock said they were astute at covering their tracks. The review would be tough. It was too easy when you'd been looking at evidence for weeks to go off down the wrong track, see patterns that weren't there, and reach dead ends. There'd been a few of them on these cases so far. They couldn't afford any more.

She'd called Kate but it had gone to voicemail, and she didn't want to pester her, even though she hadn't updated Shona on whether she'd spotted Kimi last night on her way to see Andy. No doubt she had other things on her mind, like salvaging her career. Shona would take a drive past the nail bar later.

Shona was upstairs, washing her mug, when the orange blob of the *Margaret Wilson* came into sight in the estuary. As it approached the shore, it became clear they'd decided against trying to land the man and dog near the cliffs and had brought them back to the lifeboat station for medical checks. Shona refilled the kettle and flicked the switch, as she was sure tea would be appreciated by the owner, if not the dog, and then went back downstairs.

As the tractor was backed down the slipway, and the D-class lifeboat recovered, Sophie – the agricultural student and newest crew member – hopped out with Kevin the cockapoo under her arm, like a stray lamb. To Becca's delight, she waved her over to help hold the dog while she checked him for injuries.

'We've bred our own sheepdogs for years and they often get into scrapes,' Sophie said, as she ran her hands over the dog's limbs and flanks. 'Although, unlike this wee fella, they're generally smart enough to get themselves out again.' The dog submitted to Sophie's attention, unperturbed by the immersion suit and helmet, glancing up at her with something like awe, and only breaking away from his tail-wagging admiration to lick Becca's face.

Once the boat was washed down, Shona joined Tommy.

'Must be nice, hanging aroon drinking tea while others do the work,' he said with mock disapproval.

They were sat upstairs in the crew room. The casualty's wife had arrived in her car to collect husband and dog. Sophie had pronounced Kevin uninjured – his biscuit consumption and jigging about confirmed it.

'Did you get your shortbread, then?' Tommy said.

'Just tea. It's not a crime, is it?' Shona grinned.

'No, I mean your thank you.'

When Shona looked puzzled, he continued.

'Lassie came in to say thank you. Brought you a wee tin of shortbread. I think she was the sister of thon colleague of yours who drowned at the triathlon. Had on the same kinda kit, wi' a baseball cap and trainers. Blonde. Bonny wee thing, right enough.'

Shona stared at him, her heart thumping in her chest. 'When did she come in?' Baseball cap and trainers didn't sound like Kimi, but who else could it have been?

'Couple of days ago. What's the matter, you've gone as white as a sheet, lassie.'

'The tin.' Shona got to her feet, pushing back the chair. 'Has it got a piper on it?'

'Mibbaes. Aye. I mean, it's a wee tin, right enough, more like a personal thing. No' enough shortbread for the whole station, but…'

'Tommy,' Shona said with forced patience. 'Have you got it?' She was suddenly gripped by an irrational fear that it had been taken away by someone or swept into a bin.

'Aye, aye, haud yer horses. It's here somewhere. I forgot you must be starving, what wi' eating yer ain cooking. Wait...' He pulled out a drawer. 'I mind it rattled a bit, so I put it away safe, thinking maybe it's a donation. Coins, you ken.'

Shona was beginning to think she'd be forced to push Tommy aside and systematically search the whole station, when he turned around and held out his hand.

It was just as Jack Kennedy had described. About the size of a mobile phone, and on the lid a piper in full Highland dress.

Shona went to the medical kit and pulled out a pair of surgical gloves.

'Okay,' she said to an astonished Tommy. 'You can give that to me.'

Chapter 36

Shona's first instinct was to call Murdo and the team, followed shortly by forensics, and drag them from their weekend comforts, but first she had to be sure. This was the missing piece of the puzzle; she could feel it. But it could still be a coincidence. Any blonde girl might have dropped off a thank you; they got them every week or so. Perhaps it was just a coin donation she could feel shifting within the tin. People turned up with jam jars of five-pence pieces and occasionally children brought their piggy banks to donate, but somehow she didn't think this was the case here.

Tommy was watching her from across the table. Outside, she could hear the rest of the crew chatting and laughing, Becca and Sophie with them.

Shona took a deep breath and eased off the lid.

It was tight, the red paint worn away with repeated use.

Inside, she found what she'd been half-expecting. Two syringes, their tips safely capped, packed around with tissue paper. They were labelled with an EPO brand name, and both still contained what appeared to be the liquid form of the drug.

Shona sat back and rested her hands on the table, palms up. It confirmed what Kennedy had said. Kimi had brought it to the lifeboat station because it was a safer option than a police station. She'd wanted Shona to know the truth about her sister, but they'd already reached this conclusion by another route and now it felt like an anticlimax, a reminder that the PEDs, while part of Hayley's life, were not the reason she'd died after all.

She'd bag them as evidence, but it was not the breakthrough she'd hoped for only minutes ago.

She carefully laid the syringes back on the tissue paper, but they wouldn't sit flat enough to replace the lid. Shona removed them and frowned, pulling out the paper that was more tightly packed than she'd realised. It came out in one go, like a cake out of a mould, and as it did so, something plastic clattered onto the tabletop. She picked it up. It was a tiny replica energy bar on a key chain. Shona had seen them given out as freebies at sports events, the triathlon included. As she turned it in her hand, it came apart.

'Well, that's a clever wee thing,' Tommy said.

Not a toy or a fridge magnet, but a more useful promotional item.

A thumb drive.

Now Shona understood Kimi's reluctance to come to the police office or even contact her. She knew who Allan Peacock was and she knew that he'd find out if she reached out to Shona through official channels. But the lifeboat station was a safe place. Here was where people had tried desperately to save her sister's life and where, in her last moments on earth, she'd been cared for by them until all hope had gone. If this memory stick contained what Shona hoped it did, this spot might also be the starting point from which Hayley would get justice. To Kimi, it must have felt like a good place to begin.

Shona dialled Murdo's number and told him what she suspected: here was the surveillance material and other evidence Hayley had compiled on the Camerons. He should call Ravi and Kate, and get over to High Pines with a secure laptop. Forensics could have it afterwards; she wanted a shot at opening any files now.

Thirty minutes later, Murdo drew up at the back gate, with Ravi close behind him.

'It's like Hotel California this house,' Ravi said when he came into the kitchen. 'I'm starting tae think I'll never leave.'

Shona was about to remind him that she'd wanted him to stay all along, but given the reason for their meeting, even a light-hearted reply didn't seem appropriate.

'No Kate,' Murdo said. 'Isnae answering her phone. She said something about maybe going up tae Edinburgh and her folks. Probably no' a bad thing.'

They booted up the laptop with the thumb drive in place and the internet connection disabled. Just in case opening the files triggered a remote-access delete.

Becca made everyone coffee, then tactfully went up to her room.

Five minutes later, they'd opened the files and scanned most of their contents.

'Jeezo,' Murdo said. 'It's a' there. Whit a waste. She'd have flown in CID. Always said it.' He shook his head in regret.

There was a kind of family-tree drawing of the command structure: her father Clem at the top, the three brothers his lieutenants, leading down to the grassroots dealers. And there it was in black and white: Uncle Fin's stake, complete with the proposed areas of expansion. Shona had no doubt Kimi had been the origin of some of this and may even have hung around the house, actively gathering material for her sister.

But it wasn't these files that drew Shona's eye. There was a spreadsheet named *AP*, and a Notepad document with the same initials. It detailed how much Andy Purdy owed Hayley's family. Most were records of gambling debts, a few were loans. The dates stretched right back to his police training – Shona suspected his association with Allan Peacock had started about the same time. Perhaps Peacock had tempted him into debt, as a way of recruiting or blackmailing him into doing favours for the Camerons. Or perhaps Purdy had mistakenly thought Hayley's family would go easy on him, given the connection. It must have been a doubly satisfying revenge by Clem on his daughter – her partner, and a cop, in his pocket. It certainly explained why Shona had the feeling Andy was hiding something.

'When d'you think Hayley found out?' Ravi asked quietly after he'd read the notes over her shoulder.

'From the diary entries,' Shona replied, 'I'd say about six months ago, but the debts go back six years.'

When Hayley had first discovered he owed money to the Camerons, she appeared to be horrified, although she still thought he was a victim. There were notes detailing how she'd told him he had to report what they'd done to him, but he was afraid of losing his job. Shona, who'd dealt with Rob's gambling, understood that Andy was probably unable to control his addiction. Unless he sought help, he wouldn't stop, and the Camerons' hold over them both would have tightened. Perhaps this expansion of their operation, prompted by pressure from Uncle Fin, had ramped up demands on Andy Purdy that weren't just about money, but also about inside information on police operations or making evidence disappear.

Kimi must have known too. *He's just like a' the rest*. Shona had taken it to mean that Purdy was like men in general, but now it seemed like she'd been comparing him to her family members – corrupt, tainted, criminal. No wonder she didn't want to move in.

'Want us to pick him up?' Murdo asked.

'Yes, I do,' Shona said. As they'd been reading the files, Shona had gone over in her mind the last time she'd spoken to Hayley, in the transition area just before the triathlon. When she'd asked about Andy, Hayley had raised her sports beaker to toast her partner. *He's with me in spirit*, she'd said as she'd drained her protein shake.

'Oh, God,' she said, momentarily burying her face in her hands. When she looked up at Ravi and Murdo, she saw they'd worked it out too.

Shona had no doubt now that it was Purdy who'd spiked Hayley's shake. When she'd drunk the fatal dose of ketamine, probably taken from the drug-confiscation locker at work, he'd been ten miles away, surrounded by other cops. The perfect alibi.

What she wasn't sure about was why.

'We should all go,' she said. 'Kate's told him Peacock's in custody for Hayley's murder, but pleading it was an accident. He'll think he's in the clear. A condolence visit from a senior officer and colleagues won't be unexpected. Once we're in, we'll take him.'

Chapter 37

The curtains at Andy Purdy's house were half-drawn as usual; the front lawn unmown and mostly dead. The house had the air of a property long-abandoned, although it had only been two weeks since Hayley's death and, on her first visit, Shona hadn't thought it seemed unkempt. There were a few cars parked on the neighbouring drives. Mid-afternoon on a Saturday in summer, most folk were off shopping or taking the kids out.

Shona had put on her dark suit and white blouse. Murdo and Ravi were in their regular work clothes. They looked an appropriately sombre party for a condolence call as they approached the front door. Murdo knocked. Shona was watching the curtains for any movement but saw none. Andy's car was in front of the garage, but Ravi had his eyes on the street, in case their target had gone to the shops, or visited a neighbour, and walking back, chose to avoid his visitors.

When they'd knocked for the third time without an answer, Ravi suggested he try the rear, in case Andy was in the garden. A few minutes later, he returned.

'Back door's locked. Curtains are shut. Maybe, he's…' Ravi stopped, a frown forming behind his sunglasses, so Shona initially couldn't tell what had caused it. She followed the rough direction of his gaze and saw what had caught his interest. 'Is that Kate's car?' he said.

Parked halfway down the street on the opposite side was a vehicle the same make and colour as Kate's Mini. Ravi crossed to the edge of the pavement, walked around the vehicle and made his way back to where Murdo and Shona stood.

'It's hers,' he said quietly.

Shona gave Murdo the nod.

He began banging the side of his closed fist against the door. 'Kate? Andy? Open up.' He kept up the rhythmic thumping, pausing only to open the letterbox and call through it. He shook his head at Shona.

Shona checked the time: two p.m. Kate hadn't texted her about the nail bar. No one on the team had spoken to her since early yesterday evening. She scrolled through her contacts until she found Joanne Mitchell's number.

'Joanne, just a quick call. Have you talked to Kate today?'

'No ma'am. We drove past the nail bar last night. All quiet. She dropped me off and said she was heading to Andy Purdy's. Is there anything wrong?'

'No, no,' Shona said calmly, though her heart was beginning to thump. 'Just some admin stuff. Thanks, Joanne.' She ended the call.

'Think she's inside?' Murdo murmured, eyes fixed on the house. 'Both cars are still here but someone could have picked him up...'

'...and taken Kate with them as a hostage,' Shona finished. They were both thinking of the Camerons, north and south of the border. Mad Markie, Stab — any of Hayley's cousins and brothers. She hoped it was the latter, rating Kate's chances of survival higher with one of Clem's boys rather than Finlay's.

Ravi had walked backwards up the garden path, eyes on the upstairs bedroom windows, phone clamped to his ear while calling for uniform backup. The irony that it was likely to be someone from Andy's shift wasn't lost on Shona; she hoped the sergeant, Willie Logan, wouldn't see fit to delay assisting them on the basis of misplaced loyalty, as he had likely done over Hayley's affair with Kennedy. Purdy was popular with colleagues.

'Boss,' Ravi hissed to Shona, covering the phone's mic with his hand, 'I saw movement behind the curtains. There's someone upstairs.'

Shona assessed the front door, which looked like it was already shaking under Murdo's pounding.

'Break it in,' Shona said. Threat to life. Crime in progress. Whatever. She wasn't waiting any longer. Kate might be lying inside, injured.

Murdo lifted his foot and struck the door just below the lock. Ravi joined him. On the second contact, the door sprang open. None of them were wearing protective gear, never mind body-worn video. She didn't believe Andy had a firearm, but even the most regular household offered an array of makeshift weapons.

They heard a clatter from the upstairs landing.

Ravi was about to push past her, but she put out a hand to stop him. She'd lost colleagues in London this way. She fished in her bag for her car keys and threw them to him.

'Get my vest. It's still in the boot.'

Murdo was bristling, his fists balled. 'Purdy! Get yersel' doon here,' he yelled in a voice that would make most constables scurry to obey the order. When there was no sound, he called, 'Kate? Are you okay?' Again, silence. 'There's a dog on its way, Purdy. I'm sendin' it in fur ye. Last chance.'

Shona strained her ears for any clue to where Andy or Kate was located. Front or back bedroom? The bathroom? The loft?

'We need to make sure he doesn't dreep down from a bedroom window. Go round the back, Murdo. Contain him but don't approach if he's armed.' There were fields behind the estate and she didn't want a full-scale manhunt across open country on her hands. Murdo didn't look happy to leave her, but he didn't argue either, heading off around the side of the house.

Ravi returned with the vest. It was too small for him, but Shona thought he was about to sling it on over his head without attempting to do up the Velcro side straps.

'Give it here,' Shona said, dumping her handbag by the open front door.

Ravi looked like he might rebel at that, gripping the heavy vest just out of her reach. She gave him a look of warning, then stepped forward and took it from his unresisting hand.

'I'm coming in with you,' he said, realising what she intended to do.

She wanted to order him to stay back, wait for backup, but she knew it would be useless. 'Just keep behind me, for God's sake,' she warned, and he nodded.

'Andy! I'm coming inside!' she called in a calm and clear voice. 'I know you think you're in trouble, but I'm here to help you. You need to make yourself known. Do it now, Andy.' She pushed the front door tight against the wall to her right. Ahead were the stairs; to the left, the living room. Through the partially open door she saw the TV was off; the sofa and chair were grey shapes in the semi-darkness.

'Don't come any closer or I'll kill her!'

The panicked voice wasn't coming from upstairs but from the gloom of the living room.

'It's okay, Andy,' Shona said, struggling to remember what she'd learned on a one-day negotiators course five years ago. Police Scotland had specialists but there wasn't time to call one. 'I'm going to stay here so you can tell me what you need.'

The door obscured most of the room from view, but she judged Andy must be behind it, by the armchair. They were like priest and penitent in a confessional, and she only hoped Andy would feel remorse for his sins and release Kate quickly.

Ravi tapped her arm and mimed checking upstairs, in case Andy was bluffing and Kate was the source of the noise they'd heard. Shona shook her head. She didn't want Ravi out of her sight. But he nodded again, vigorously, and put his finger to his lips, *I'll be quiet*. It was true Kate could be lying gagged and tied up or injured. Or there could be a second assailant, one of the Camerons. She only had a split second to make the decision. *Be careful*, she mouthed. He nodded and began advancing up the stairs.

Shona's eyes were adjusting to the dark of the front room and she saw that the shape she'd first imagined was the low coffee table was in fact two suitcases, lying open as if someone had been disturbed while hurriedly stuffing items inside.

She still didn't understand Andy's motive and for the briefest moment she wondered if he and Kate were lovers, had conspired to kill Hayley, and were now running off together, only to have Shona arrive before they could escape. She remembered them in each other's arms as Hayley was loaded into the ambulance. How Kate always sprang to Andy's defence. How they both tried to push the idea of Kennedy as stalker and killer. But no. Impossible. Kate was a loyal and conscientious officer. Peacock's treachery was making her see phantoms and shadows everywhere.

She quickly leaned back, glancing up the stairs. The upstairs landing looked different, and she realised why. The picture, *Sleep Eat Swim Ride Run Repeat*, was no longer there. She could just see the edge of the frame, which was now lying on the top step. That'd been the noise they heard. Shit. Kate wasn't up there. Purdy had her.

'Andy, I just need to know Kate's okay. Can I speak to her, please?' Shona inched forward, until she was close to the door. Listening hard, all she could make out was ragged breathing, but whose it was, she couldn't tell.

'No! Get your men out of my fucking house.'

'It's all right, Andy. It's just me. You can talk to me.' Now what? Emotion and empathy followed by open questions, the negotiation trainer had said. 'You sound upset. What would you like to happen next?'

'You're going to let me walk out of here.'

'Yes, I am, Andy. I'm going to get you both somewhere safe.'

Saving folk was what she did. It's what James had told his son when he'd asked what Aunty Shona's job was. Ravi was safe because she'd guided her team to identify the arsonists, and she would save Kate too.

'You're lying, I can hear it in your voice, bitch.' His pitch was climbing, panic overtaking him.

As a beat cop, he'd be handy in a fight. Too risky for both her and Kate. She wasn't going in. But why hadn't she heard even a muffled sob from Kate? She had to assume he had a knife to her throat. Scanning the confined space of the lobby, she searched for anything she could utilise as a weapon. A row of hooks held coats and one of Hayley's cycling helmets. She eased the helmet down as quietly as she could and clutched it in her left hand, closest to the gap in the door.

'Andy, I'm not lying.' It was harder and harder to keep her tone even. No sounds of any approaching sirens reached her. Where was backup? 'I know what the Camerons did to you. I've seen Hayley's notes, and how much she loved you and wanted to help you.'

'Hayley was a lying bitch, just like you. She told me she'd stand by me if I went to you lot, and all the time she was fucking Kennedy behind my back.'

His voice had grown louder and a split second later she knew why.

The living room door crashed into Shona even as she braced her arms up for the impact. She stumbled but kept her feet. The door was yanked open again and Andy charged screaming at her out of the gloom. She felt a thud, like a punch, as the blade deflected off her stab vest and she swung the helmet. The knife tip met its hard shell and skittered across it until the blade slid through a gap and embedded in the foam lining. Purdy's left shoulder was still caught by the swinging door and when he tried to twist the knife free, Shona didn't hesitate but barrelled into the gap, knowing her only hope in this tight space was to bring him down. She hooked his leg with her own, the momentum took him backwards and she felt the sting on her forehead as it connected with his nose.

They hit the ground hard in the darkened room, the breath jarred out of her.

Andy let go of the knife, still embedded in the cycling helmet, and grabbed her hair. The body armour lent her some weight, but he was more than twice her size and would easily throw her off.

'Stay down! Stay down!' she gasped, desperately, ramming a knee into his crotch but only connecting with the flesh of his thigh. She shoved the heel of her hand under his chin, forcing his head back as he swung a punch at her face but hit her shoulder. He drew back his fist for another try but before it came, an arm reached from behind her and a perfect left hook connected with Andy Purdy's jaw.

Shona rolled to her side as Ravi pinned the stunned Purdy to the floor. Blood had begun to ooze from her nose and forehead, but she fumbled for a set of handcuffs from a loop at the back of her vest. Ravi turned Andy Purdy face down and slapped them on. She scrambled to her feet as the first response car screeched to a halt outside. Murdo came running through the front door.

'Where's Kate?' Ravi said as he and Murdo restrained a still struggling Purdy.

'Calm yersel' doon,' Murdo barked at his captive. 'Where's our Kate?'

Shona hauled back the curtain, flooding the untidy and unaired room with light.

And that's when she saw her.

Kate's blonde ponytail was a bright streak across the dark carpet. She lay partially behind the armchair, with her face turned away from Shona, as if she'd been heading for the kitchen to make tea. Ravi had seen her too. He let out a gulping sob and rushed forward. A pool of blood had dried around her and even before they turned her over, Shona knew Purdy had been bluffing. She'd been dead for some time.

Murdo had dragged Andy Purdy to his feet, his hands at his throat.

'Get him out of here!' yelled Shona. 'Now, Murdo. Out!'

Two squad cars were on the drive, their lights sweeping the room with flashes of blue like the stuttering frames of an old movie. Their occupants stood at the battered front door, their faces frozen with incomprehension.

'I am arresting you…' Murdo began through gritted teeth, his face inches from Andy's. When he finished, he pushed Andy Purdy towards his colleagues.

Then he was next to Ravi and Shona, head bowed, a hand on each of their shoulders as they kneeled by their fallen colleague. Shona pulled Ravi towards her, and he allowed himself to be held as they both wept.

Chapter 38

Early on Sunday morning, Shona slipped out of High Pines and made her way into the CID office at Cornwall Mount. Allan Peacock was now in a remand cell at HMP Kilmarnock but had accepted her request for a video call, which she didn't want to do at home. She dreaded the sight of Kate's empty desk. Better she dealt with that now, while the office was unstaffed. Tomorrow, others would be looking to her for explanations. They'd blame her for not seeing the danger and, ultimately, sending Kate to her death. Why wouldn't they? She blamed herself.

But when she reached the top of the stairs, head thumping, grimacing at the aching in her legs and back from yesterday's encounter with Andy Purdy, she saw the office wasn't empty. Enough light seeped around the edges of the closed blinds to reveal Ravi sitting alone at his desk, staring into the empty space opposite, once occupied by Kate. Pain radiated from his slumped shoulders and she could tell he'd been crying.

'We'll move everything around,' she said quietly, joining him. It would be cruel to remind him every day of the loss. 'Perhaps it's time for a change of layout anyway.'

'No, don't,' he said. 'I don't want tae forget. I want to see her every single day. Not just how she died, but who she was. She stopped me getting too cocky, y' know. Brought me down to earth.' He flashed her a knowing grin, tinged with sadness. 'I need to remember. One day it might save my life.' Perhaps, he was recalling the fire, his own lucky escape, and how their positions might have been reversed, and Kate would be sitting here now, mourning him.

Shona nodded, realising how selfish she'd been to suggest it. Of course people would want to be reminded of her.

'Is it okay if I pack up her stuff?' Ravi said.

'Hannah will do that.' There was a plant – a ponytail palm – the others had given her for her birthday, a phone charging cable that looked like a bead necklace so no one would 'borrow' it, and her mug with *Katherine the Great* on it. Taken together, they seemed meagre mementos for such a bright talent.

'I'd like to do it,' Ravi said. 'I'm on my way up to Edinburgh to see Kate's parents. I want to take something of her with me. Might help them see she was loved.'

They'd already been informed of their daughter's death and as Kate's senior officer, she'd be going to see them herself in the next few days, but she was deeply touched at Ravi's thoughtfulness.

'Martin's insisting on driving me,' he added. 'You know…' He made a fluttering motion with his hand to indicate his partner wasn't taking no for an answer. 'I'm sorry about your bashed heid,' he said, pointing to her injured forehead, where it had connected with Andy Purdy's nose during their struggle.

Shona self-consciously touched the bruise. 'You should see the other guy, as they say.' Becca had given her a severe talking-to when she got home last night, blood from her nose splattered on her white shirt, her eyes bloodshot – *Look at the state of you, Mum, and you've got the cheek to lecture me about personal safety!*

'Aye, well, boss, shouldnae have left you on your own. But on the bright side, it's all roon the place you headbutted a beat cop twice your size who was comin' at you with a chib, so get all those budget requests and maintenance jobs in now. Nobody'll want to take you on for a while.'

Shona smiled, appreciating the humour as a salve for both their pain.

After Ravi had gone, Shona opened her laptop and tried not to flinch when she saw Allan Peacock's face appear in an interview room at the prison. As a remand prisoner, he was in his own clothes – blue formal shirt, open at the collar – and for a second it felt like this was an innocent catch-up call about a case. His solicitor wasn't sitting in. Peacock had guessed she'd come back to him with a revised offer – a plea bargain deal, which he wouldn't want to risk getting back to the Camerons, if his lawyer had links with them, but he still wanted to see what it was.

'Good morning, Detective Inspector Oliver,' he said, charming smile at full volume and making a show of peering at the screen, where Shona's injuries were all too visible. 'Are you okay?'

'I'm fine, thank you, Mr Peacock,' she replied. She wouldn't address him as a police officer; he'd lost that right. 'This interview is to ask if you've anything to add to your statement.'

They'd got plenty to piece together the Camerons' network and plans, and Andy Purdy's history, from Hayley's evidence, but a live witness who could be cross-examined in court would raise their chances of convictions. Lists of arrests were already being drawn up on both sides of the border – Clem and his boys, Uncle Fin and his. She wanted to catch as many in the net as possible, though it was possible Belle Cameron might slip through.

'Exactly what should I be adding?' he said, teasingly. Despite the charges he faced, his position – a foot in each camp, the Camerons' and Police Scotland's – had given him a false perception of power, believing he could manipulate both sides to his advantage.

'You won't have heard…' Shona began. 'We arrested Andy Purdy last night for Hayley Cameron's murder. He administered a dangerous substance to her via a sports drink she took with her to the triathlon. Did you know of each other's plans?'

'What?' His expression of bewilderment said they hadn't.

She relished the look on his face as realisation dawned. He'd confessed unnecessarily. If he hadn't tried to justify his action in jabbing her with GHB as a *moment of madness*, it was unlikely that he'd have faced any charges concerning her death, and Andy Purdy would have carried the whole can.

'It was material recovered from Hayley herself that led us to him. There's plenty more besides. You get a mention. Is there anything else you'd like to tell us, Allan, about your association with the Camerons and their drug distribution?'

But he was looking at her with undisguised hatred, as if she'd tricked him into confessing to Hayley's murder, which might be his revised defence in court, but they both knew where the truth lay. A moment later, he jabbed the keyboard and ended the call.

Shona slammed shut her laptop lid, wishing she could squash Peacock like the parasite he was. She hadn't the witness she wanted, either against the Camerons or Andy Purdy, but she didn't doubt that he was plotting how he could turn this new twist to his advantage.

Murdo arrived and came straight into her office, his face creased with grief and tiredness. He studied her injured forehead and clicked his tongue in displeasure.

'If the circumstances were different, I'd tell you to give me some credit for not getting stabbed,' Shona said. Had Kate been wearing a vest, would she still be here? It was unfair to even consider the idea, but Murdo knew what was going through her mind. He'd have asked himself the same question.

'She couldnae have known what she was walking intae, and neither could you.'

'How could I let it happen, Murdo? How?'

'We all think that, but nae o' us has a crystal ball.'

She could tell him that the Super had told her not to pursue Purdy as a suspect, but Murdo would know that wasn't the whole story. It was her own decision to obey the chain of command because she feared what the NCA would do to her – that had been the deciding factor. She'd have to live with that fact forever. Detective Chief Superintendent Davies had tactfully not brought up her previously considering Purdy as a suspect, for his own discomfort as much as hers, but he had been successful at postponing tomorrow's NCA interview.

Having brought down the Camerons – a major, cross-border OCG – and handed Hayley's intelligence on networks to the NCA on a plate had also helped to hold them at bay. But she knew that they suspected she'd done so not by solid police work, but by some nefarious means, so instead of clearing her of the taint of corruption, it had only increased their suspicions. They'd made it clear that they'd be back for a chat in the near future.

That realisation was lightened only by the fact they'd caught the people responsible for Erin Dunlop's death and brought at least some resolution for her mother Sandra.

Murdo checked his watch. 'Want tae get this over with?'

Andy Purdy was downstairs in an interview room. The apprehension of a murderer should be an occasion for celebration, for rounds of drinks in the pub, but not this time.

'Right,' Shona said, standing up with difficulty. 'Let's see what he has to say for himself.'

Purdy leaned his elbows on the table and stared at Shona. His face was puffy, and there was an ugly cut on the bridge of his nose, which, she thought with satisfaction, she must have inflicted when she'd taken him down. He held his cuffed wrists out to Murdo, expecting them to be undone, but the sergeant glowered at him and shook his head.

'I deem you tae be a violent individual. The restraints will remain.'

Andy turned to the ruddy-faced solicitor in tweeds who sat on his left, but the man looked disinclined to challenge the forbidding Murdo on the point. Instead, he took a sheet of paper from his folder and read a prepared statement.

'My client wishes to say that in the matter of DC Kate Irving's death, he acted in self-defence. We will be seeking a psychiatric assessment, as my client believes he is suffering from PTSD due to his work as a response officer. He strongly denies he was involved in the death of his fiancée, PC Hayley Cameron. My client denies assaulting officers who forced entry to his home. He will not be responding to further questions.'

Shona asked them anyway, advancing her belief that when Kate arrived to tell him about Peacock's arrest, he thought she was on to him, panicked and killed her.

'And did you string Hayley along, agreeing you would come to us, but when she grew insistent and you found out she was having an affair, decided to kill her?'

Without body-worn video, there was nothing to corroborate what Purdy had said to her yesterday, but it was a strong motive.

She was faced with the possibility that Purdy might not be held fully accountable for what he'd done, due to his mental state. In her own mind, she had no doubts. He'd deceived Hayley and he'd deceived Kate, both sharp police officers, and they'd paid with their lives.

'Our pathologist has reported that ketamine was the murder weapon, as it had been administered before other drugs. This alone – combined with the knowledge that the victim was about to enter the water – would have been sufficient to cause her fatal harm. You told us in the initial statement after Hayley's death statement you made a protein shake for her that morning. Will we uncover traces of ketamine in your kitchen?'

Shona had no doubt they would. The previous search of the property had focused on PEDs and although Andy might be forensically aware, the house was hardly clinically clean. A drug dog would find what they needed. The sports beaker had failed to turn up, despite Slasher Sue instigating a search. Shona had sent uniform to collect Hayley's possessions from the race area immediately after her death. Either it had fallen from her bag or, more likely, Andy had been able to tamper with the evidence chain before it reached forensics.

'My client is invoking his right to remain silent, Inspector. So, unless there are any further charges you'd like to discuss, this interview should terminate.'

It was clear she'd get no more out of him.

Outside, in the corridor, he was led away by officers from Kilmarnock, following the trail of iniquity blazed by Allan Peacock of being remanded out of the area. Shona turned to Murdo.

'How long d'you think he'll get?'

'If the fiscal sticks wi' murder, it'll be life. Both him and Peacock might plea culpable homicide, though. It'll be down tae the jury.'

The sentence scale for culpable homicide in Scotland ranged from life imprisonment right through to a non-custodial sentence. Evidence of previous good character, risk of further harm to the public, acceptance of guilt, and remorse, as well as the fact that they were serving police officers, would all be factors in sentencing.

As Shona made her way upstairs, she hoped both Purdy and Peacock would never see the free light of day again.

-

Murdo left soon afterwards, and she had the sense he wanted to be home with his wife Joan to gather strength for a difficult week ahead, when they'd be arresting the Camerons and their wider network.

Before Shona left too, she called Dan with the news about the likely charges and he told her he'd had some news of his own: he'd been offered a job with the Metropolitan Police.

'Will you go?' Shona said. A confused mix of pride at his new job, regret at his departure and worry for what it would mean for their friendship bubbled up inside her. 'You should go.'

'I'll take that as a vote of confidence,' he replied.

'Oh, you'll always have that,' Shona assured him.

'Thank you. That means a lot to me.'

The irony that, with Kate's death, there would finally be a vacancy for a detective constable on her team wasn't lost on her. It was what Dan had longed for, but it suddenly felt like he'd outgrown those dreams.

'You're not getting rid of me,' he said. 'I'm a proud Cumbrian, and there'll always be a little bit of Kirkness that feels like home. I'm sure you'll be there to welcome me with a plate of Freya's scones.'

She knew he meant that the nightmare of Delfont and the NCA would soon fade, and she wouldn't end up in jail for helping Thalia. She hadn't told him of James's offer – a new job, a new life was on the horizon for her too – and she wouldn't say it now. This was his moment and she didn't want to overshadow it.

'I'm sure I will, Dan. We'll see each other soon,' she said, trying to inject the words with certainty, but they sounded hollow even to her.

Chapter 39

The evening had started out fine. Shona had gone to help Tommy sort out some kit on the concrete apron outside the boat hall, an apology for missing training that morning, but also a brief respite from thoughts of tomorrow's return to the CID office. Ultimately, she'd solved both cases, but she'd lost something too. The place would never be the same for her. She'd built her team at Dumfries from scratch when she'd arrived from London three years ago, with the dream of a new start, and Kate's death had broken that apart.

When, after half an hour's work, there was a crack of thunder and the clouds rolled in, bringing with them rain, they retreated inside and Shona found being at the lifeboat station, in the place where Hayley had died, was less of a distraction than she'd hoped.

Earlier, as she'd washed up, Shona had received a text from a withheld number.

Thank you for what you did for Hayley and for me. Don't worry, we had a new life planned and a bit put away. It's just a pity she didn't get to enjoy it. Now I live for us both.

Perhaps Kate had been right: Kimi was sunning herself on some beach somewhere, partly curtesy of those cash withdrawals from Hayley's account, which had likely gone into the sisters' 'escape fund'. After all that had been lost, it felt good to know Kimi was safe and well. Perhaps she'd followed in the footsteps of her aunt Laura and would be one of the Cameron women who made it out.

As they stood watching the downpour, Tommy handed her a cup of tea.

'So, when are you going?' he said.

Her mind had been so taken up with Kimi, Hayley and Kate that she looked at him, puzzled.

'To LA,' Tommy clarified. 'When are you leaving for LA?'

'I'm not,' she said.

It was only when Tommy had asked her that the final realisation had come to her. Despite everything that had happened, her connection to this place and the people around her was just too strong. She loved James, but she'd been tempted to consider a move not because she saw a life for them together, but by an easy way out – from the difficulties of her job, from the work at High Pines, but mostly from her fear of the NCA inquiry. She wouldn't run from her responsibilities. She'd stay because she needed to help herself and her team recover from the trauma of losing one of their own. She'd stay because Becca had already chosen a path – university in Glasgow, not California, and what she needed now was stability, a place to come home to until she forged her own way. She'd stay because even if she went, the decisions she made on the fateful night of Delfont's death would follow her, even to the sunshine of California and James's bed.

She'd tell him tonight. It would likely be their last ever evening of cooking and eating together. Her heart was breaking but it was the only way. There was another crack of thunder and the cloudburst began to beat like an infinite number of steel rods onto the grey surface of the firth. She let the rain fall on her face to hide her tears.

'Aye, I can see how you'd miss this,' Tommy said, indicating the rain, not making any judgement but giving her time to compose herself.

A family scurried along the seafront.

'Come in, come in, afore you're drookit!' he called, and they ran, laughing, into the boat hall – a mother, father and two young children – shaking the rain from their jackets. The smallest boy carried a bucket filled with cockle shells and begged to be allowed outside again. Eventually, his mother relented, and he jumped in the newly formed puddles with glee. Shona took the opportunity to wipe away her tears and joined in their amusement.

'I've got a wee bit of news mysel',' Tommy said, quietly, his expression serious once more.

Shona felt a chill as a thought struck her. 'You're not ill?'

'No, no, nothing like that,' Tommy blustered. But Shona wasn't convinced. He was one of that generation of men, like Murdo, who'd claim they were fine even with a limb hanging off.

Was he moving away? He'd asked when *she* was going, so it must be on his mind.

'You and Freya are retiring to Orkney?'

'Whit? Are ye mad? One heathen Orcadian is enough to deal wi', without being surrounded by them. That bang on yer heid has made you daft.'

'So what?' said Shona, genuinely at a loss.

'They're giving me an award. An MBE,' he said sheepishly. 'For services tae the community and maritime safety.'

'You're kidding!' Shona laughed with relief and genuine joy. 'That's amazing.' She set her cup on the ground and hugged him.

'Aye, watch oot there,' he cried, his tea slopping over the rim.

After all her worries that the events around Hayley's death would damage Tommy's and the station's reputation, she was thrilled to find he was being rewarded for his hard work and dedication.

'Is Freya pleased?'

'She's buying a hat. We're off tae Holyroodhouse. Can I trust you to mind the place when I'm away?' he said, indicating the lifeboat station.

'Course you can,' she said, patting his arm.

As Shona looked out across the firth, searching for any patch of light that would signal the end to the squall, an incomplete rainbow, fractured and shimmering, appeared over the grey sea.

There was a local word for that. Something in old Scots. She looked at Tommy enquiringly and he seemed to know what she was searching for.

'A watergaw,' he said. 'A part rainbow.'

Shona smiled. She was cold and wet and miserable. But it would blow over.

'D'you know, Tommy, I think you're right. I really would miss this.'

Acknowledgements

Bringing a book into the world is a collaborative process and so warm thanks are due to the wonderful team at Canelo, including Executive Publisher Louise Cullen and Assistant Editor Alicia Pountney, whose insight and knowledge helped smooth the process.

Thank you also to my brilliant development editor Russel D McLean, for taking it to the max once more, copy editor Daniela Nava, proofreader Jan Adkins and the sales and marketing team who help ensure the book finds the right readers. A special thank you to my super-agent, Anne Williams at KHLA for her continued support and her early perceptive and pertinent comments on the manuscript.

I'm indebted to the RNLI station at Kippford who were once again generous in offering details about their life-saving and inspiring work.

Thank you to Christine Cooke for invaluable tips on nail art and all-round cheerleading.

A special thank you to my home team – Mickey, Leo, Sam, student social worker Thomas, and events manager extraordinaire, Chloe – who provided me with fascinating and diverse insights into issues surrounding addiction, sports doping, fitness training and music festival culture. You can find out more about the work of drug testing charities by following The Loop – loop_uk – on social media.

My wonderful former Crime Writing MA cohort at the University of East Anglia continue to be a huge source of support, providing a steady stream of sympathy, humour and the occasional kick up the backside that all writers require from time to time. Thank you all.

My pal Charles Simpson has been on this writing journey with me from the beginning and continues to reveal new and surprising areas of knowledge, helping me fill the gaps in my own. Thank you once more for your inspiration.

CANELOCRIME

Do you love crime fiction and are always on the lookout for brilliant authors?

Canelo Crime is home to some of the most exciting novels around. Thousands of readers are already enjoying our compulsive stories. Are you ready to find your new favourite writer?

Find out more and sign up to our newsletter at canelocrime.com